THE UNHOLY HOUR

EAGLE BROTHERHOOD SERIES

KAT LE VEQUE

OLIVERHEBERBOOKS

Copyright 2003, 2014 by Kathryn Le Veque

This title was previously published as Resurrection

Cover design by Kim Killion

Published by Oliver-Heber Books

0 9 8 7 6 5 4 3 2 1

AUTHOR'S NOTE

They call themselves the Eagle Brotherhood.

We've all got 'that' group of friends. People we've bonded with that just 'get' you and you get them. Whether you bond over common interests, or a job, of even just mutual friends, we've all found that connection at one time or another.

Same with the Eagle Brotherhood.

It started with five Americans. They were young, brilliant, idealistic, and met during a semester abroad. When I first wrote this series, many years ago, it was originally called the American Heroes series. It was supposed to be about guys who knew each other as young men, but who went on to live their own lives and have their own adventures. Ordinary guys in extraordinary circumstances was how I described it. There were only five in the beginning, but somewhere along the line, we added two Brits as 'honorary' members. There are actually more books slated to be written, but I just haven't gotten around to it yet. One of the Eagle Brotherhood — Nash Aury — even has a sequel mostly written to his book, so this is really a series that has a lot of growth potential. And why not? It centers around men who are honorable, chivalric, and end up facing some really stressful and, in a few cases, dangerous situations. Some explainable, some not. That's the fun of it.

But it all had to start somewhere.

Each Eagle Brotherhood book starts out with the same *"How it began"* preface so you, as the reader, knows where these guys connect because they don't appear in each other's stories. It's a rather interesting connection, but one that opens up the hero of each tale — and eventually the heroine — to one heck of a story. These guys are connected to me as much as to each other.

They really are a true brotherhood.

I hope you enjoy the stories in this series because they were a labor of love to write. You don't have to read them in any particular order:

The Burning Hour
The Sunset Hour
The Secret Hour
The Unholy Hour
The Devil's Hour
The Killing Hour
The Ancient Hour

Happy reading,

AQUILA FRATRUM

Seven men.
Each with a story to tell.
Welcome to the world of the Eagle Brotherhood.

Years ago, five Americans on a semester abroad met at the home of their sponsor in Yorkshire, England. They were taking the same course at the University of York, including the son of their host. But it wasn't the course in International Law that bonded them. It was an incident from that time, something that happened on a dark and stormy night in an alley behind a bar in York called *The Calcaria*.

It is something that changed their perspectives forever.

These days, the men who once called themselves the *Aquila Fratrum* or the Eagle Brotherhood — a name based on the Americans who were military-based at that time — have gone forth in their lives. They are men in normal, everyday professions who succeed in extraordinary things. Their paths aren't smooth, and they aren't perfect, but they understand more than most that life is never about the smooth or the perfect. It is about the imperfect and the difficult. It's even about the unexplainable.

And, above all else, light overcomes the darkness.

Aquila Fratrum.

Ordinary men who have lived extraordinary circumstances.

And the women who love them.

HOW IT BEGAN
MORE THEN TWENTY YEARS AGO, THE CALCARIA, YORK

MICK MCCONNELL, PROPRIETOR

"Beck." A big man with a crown of auburn hair spoke with a drunken slur to his words. "Beck. *Seavington!*"

The blond Californian on the other side of the table, who had been half-lidded as he watched a group of women across the darkened room of the pub, jerked at the sound of his name as if he'd just been slapped.

"What?" he said, looking at the man with the auburn hair. "Christ, Phipps. Can't you just leave me alone for a minute?"

Archer Phipps struggled not to laugh. "Why?"

"Because you're breaking my powers of concentration, you ass."

That broke the table out in snorts of laughter. The man seated next to Beck, big and blond and with a mega-watt smile, put a hand on Beck's shoulder.

"What in the hell are you concentrating on?" he said, leaning over to see what Beck might be seeing. When he spied it, he gestured. "Over there?"

Beck full-on pointed to the women across the pub. "There."

"Those?"

"*Those.*"

"Well... what are you trying to do by staring at them? Just go talk to them."

Beck scowled at the man. "Because I'm trying to lure them with the power of suggestion, Trevor," he said. Then, he looked around the table and pointed. "It works. Colt over there has a laser stare. He doesn't even have to say anything — women know what he's thinking just by the expression on his face. Isn't that right, Sheridan?"

Colt Sheridan, clean-cut and square-jawed, waved an annoyed hand at the man he'd spent nearly every day with for the past six months. "Some of us don't have to be obvious," he said. "Look at Nash. All he has to do is give them one of those sexy, down-home expressions and they're falling all over themselves. I don't have anything on him."

Across the table, Nash Aury, the quiet and diplomatic sort with a Louisiana drawl, laughed softly. "It's all in the face," he said, gesturing to the big dimples in each cheek. "I don't have anything y'all don't have, but we don't have anything that Serreaux has, so maybe we should just give it up and let him take the lead."

The group looked over at Ethan Serreaux, a man with a French parents even though he was born in America. Dark-eyed and dark-haired, he looked like he'd just come off the pages of a men's magazine. When he saw that the entire table of semi-drunks was looking at him, he smiled lasciviously.

"*Belle fille,*" he said in his best Maurice Chevalier impression. "*Asseyez-vous sur mes genoux et dites-moi à quel point vous me voulez.*"

Everyone burst out laughing except for Beck, who slowly banged his forehead on the table. "You sound like Pepe Le Pew," he said. "Shut *up!*"

More laughter, most especially from Archer and the last man of their group, a giant of a figure who wasn't part of their academic group. Fox Henredon was in the process of obtaining his Ph.D. in Archaeology with an emphasis in Egyptology from Oxford. In fact, he'd come back a few months ago from a dig near Aswan and when he visited his best friend from grade school, Archer, he'd come across the Americans temporarily housed in Archer's pad. He'd gotten on so well with them that they'd made him an honorary member of their group. But not just the group — of their secret society, as well.

Aquila Fratrum.

The Eagle Brotherhood.

The whole secret group was really meant as a joke, but the basis of it — the honor, the patriotism — they took seriously. Three out of the five Americans had come from Annapolis and all five of them were majoring in International Law, hence the purpose of the semester abroad course. Archer was taking the same course, and he'd been the host house, and given that they were all within a few years of each other age-wise, they'd all bonded over common likes, common dislikes, and a passion for adventure.

It was a guy gang like no other.

But tonight, they were drinking to the group that would soon be separating. The course at the University of York was finished and the Americans would soon be heading back to their native lands, but promises of reciprocal visits had abound all evening. Nash, in particular, had invited everyone to New Orleans for the holidays because his family, having made their money in sugar, had a massive house that could accommodate everyone. Beck, Cord, and Colt had already committed to it, but Ethan had family obligations he needed to get out of. Archer was trying to figure out how to break the news to his parents, who were possessive of his time, while Fox was on the verge of committing. He'd never been to New Orleans and a street named after liquor intrigued him. As the Brotherhood planned their next gathering, Beck stood up from the table.

"I need to find the loo," he said, looking around. "Where is it? Back behind the bar?"

The problem was that he was drunker than the rest of them and probably not in great shape to find anything, so Cord stood up next to him.

"Back in the corner," he said. "Come on, little brother."

He had Beck by the neck, pulling him back behind the bar where there was a dark corridor that led to bathrooms and the kitchen. The term 'little brother' was essentially referring to Beck's age because he happened to be the youngest out of their group. But he was also the toughest. Beck Seavington could out-fight anybody, Fox included, and Fox had participated in underground fight clubs during his earlier college days. He'd won money at it, too.

But Beck's fists were quite lethal.

The Navy wanted him that way.

Cord went with Beck so he wouldn't get into any trouble. Cord was an enormous man, having played football, and the rumor was that he was being scouted by the NFL. He wasn't a fighter by nature, but no one was going to test of man of that size. He'd just push the scrapper, Beck, in front of him, anyway, and let the career Navy man do the damage.

Every group had a scrapper.

It smelled like stale booze and bleach back here and the door to the men's room was locked. Beck rattled it but it remained fixed. With a heavy sigh, he looked at Cord.

"I can't wait," he muttered.

Cord tipped his head in the direction of the door to the alley out back, which was next to the kitchen door.

"Outside?" he said.

Beck nodded, which nearly threw him off balance, and charged through the back door. Cord followed him and they ended up in the dirty, damp alley behind the bar. It smelled worse out here, like garbage and animals. There were crates against the wall, broken down cardboard boxes, and little else. There were two ends to the alley, but they were standing closer to the end that dumped out onto the street where *The Calcaria* was located. Beck was looking for a discreet place to relieve himself when the back door smacked back on its hinges again, spilling forth the rest of their group.

"I think we're done with this place," Archer said, rubbing his eyes because the alcohol was messing with his vision. "There's another pub down the way called Valhalla. Let's go there."

Beck had found a spot behind some crates. "Are the women more proactive there?" he asked. "I mean, will they actually come up and talk to you? I don't think my mind control is working."

Archer grinned. "Do you seriously want a woman that approaches you?" he said. "The wooing of a woman is an art, Beck. You don't want some nervy woman up in your grill, do you?"

The others snorted in agreement. Ethan and Nash were by the back door, leaning back against the wall, as Colt went to stand next to Beck. Fox went to stand with Cord, maybe as a lookout since they really shouldn't be pissing in an alley, when three men suddenly appeared from what was a small walkway between buildings. It was dark, so no one really noticed, until one of the men walked up behind Colt and put a knife to the man's back.

Then, everything changed.

The drunken, happy mood was gone.

"Easy, big man," the man said. He was short, with a dirty

jacket, but the knife he'd produced was quite large. "If you want to keep your kidney, you'll relax, mate."

Everyone froze — Ethan, Nash, Archer, Fox, Cord, Beck, and most of all, Colt. But his features never changed expression, even as he felt the prick of cold steel against his right kidney.

"If you're looking for money, you're too late," he said steadily. "We're coming out of the bar, not going into it. We've spent our money."

The man in the dirty jacket grunted as his friends also produced big knives. "Somehow, I doubt it," he said. "We were watching you inside. I think you're from money, so you've got more where that came from, Yank. I think all of you have more."

With that, his friends began to move. One of them was heading for Ethan while the other one was heading for Archer. The group, as a whole, instinctively started to back away from the men approaching, but Fox refused to budge. At seven inches over six feet, he had that luxury of being stubborn.

"You blokes really think you're going to rob guys who are twice your size?" he said incredulously. "You're either incredibly stupid or way too overconfident."

"I'll go with stupid," Cord muttered.

Fox quickly agreed with him. "Stupid, for sure," he said. "There are seven of us and three of you. You may be able to take out a couple of us, but there are five of us left who will break your fucking necks. Are you ready for that?"

That brought some pause to the man's companions, but the man in the dirty jacket poked Colt enough to draw blood.

"Give me your fucking money!" he hissed. "Another word and I'll cut a hole in this man big enough to stick my hand through!"

Colt didn't even flinch when the man jabbed him. He kept his right hand up while his left once reached into his pocket for his wallet. But as he was doing that, and the other two men with knives were advancing on Ethan and Archer, no one happened to be watching Cord.

And that would be their fatal mistake.

"*Quaere ferro scopum tuum*," Cord suddenly mumbled. "*Oboedite mihi!*"

Inexplicably, the man holding the knife to Colt's back jerked. He jolted. His hand flew up and the big blade he'd been forcing on Colt flew up and into his own throat, straight back through so that the tip came out of the back of his neck. It went through him like a bullet. As he staggered back and fell to the ground, his friends were momentarily startled and that gave Cord the opportunity to turn against them.

"*In molles venter it ferrum*," he growled, lifting a big fist as if to punch the men straight in the face. "*Utrumque vestrum!*"

The men screamed as the hands holding the knives came up and plunged the blades into their bellies as if they had a mind of their own. They went down as Ethan, Nash, Archer, Fox, Beck and Colt made haste to back up, away from what was evidently going on. No one knew what was happening and it was best to get clear considering knives were slashing all over the place.

At least, everyone but Cord backed up. He pointed a finger at the men who had just stabbed themselves in the belly.

"*Ferro ad carnem, ferrum ad os*," he said in a low tone. "*Collum secari debet.*"

The men with knives in their bellies suddenly withdrew those knives and stabbed themselves in the neck, three or four times, until they could stab no more. They simply lay there and bled as Cord turned to his stunned group of friends.

"We need to get out of here," he said quietly. "Before the cops come. *Quickly.*"

No one moved. They stood there, eyes wide at what they'd just seen. Colt, who was the closest to Cord, grabbed him by the arm.

"What in the hell just happened?" he asked in awe. "What did you do?"

Cord looked back at the men bleeding out on the alley floor. "I protected us," he said simply. "We really need to go."

"Protected us *how*?" Fox was at Cord's side, his handsome face seriously. "What did we just see, Cord? Hypnosis of some kind?"

Cord scratched his head. "No," he said reluctantly, looking at the curious group. "Can we just get out of here, please?"

"Not until you explain," Fox said.

He was serious. No one was moving, not really. Exasperated, Cord sighed heavily. "Fine," he said. "I did it to save Colt's life. That guy was going to kill him."

Colt, who had blood running down the right side of his torso, stepped forward. "He probably was," he said. "Nobody is disputing that. But *what* did you do?"

Cord looked at his friend. "It's not something I really talk about," he said hesitantly. "I haven't... I haven't done that stuff since I was younger, but you all know I'm descended from Abigail Williams. When we all talked about our families and stuff, I told you guys that I was descended from one of the chief accusers of the Salem Witch Trails."

"You did," Colt said as his gaze moved to the men on the ground. "But what does that have to do with it? And done *what* stuff?"

Cord was clearly reluctant. "My dad likes to call us Casters," he said. "Abigail Williams was an accomplished witch and that trait is passed down in my family, like red hair or freckles. Only it's some kind of power we can summon. What you saw was a spell. I turned their knives against them."

"You're a witch?" Colt repeated in shock. "Seriously, Cord? Like — magic?"

Cord didn't answer. He just started walking, very quickly,

and the others instinctively followed. They came to a walkway that led out onto the street and, nearly running, they headed up towards the main road.

"Yeah, like magic," Cord finally said as they came to the main avenue. "You saw it. I can't explain it more than that, but I wouldn't have done it if I thought we could have gotten out of that without Sheridan missing a kidney. Just... do yourself a favor. Forget you ever saw it."

"Wait," Ethan said as they began to walk, very quickly, towards the area with the car park. "We can't just leave. No matter what happened, or how it happened, we have to call the police."

"And tell them what?" Cord said. "That we got attacked and that I used a spell to turn the weapons against the guys who attacked us? They would think we were nuts."

As Ethan shook his head in disagreement, Archer grabbed him by the arm and pulled him along. "They would want to know who stabbed those guys," he said. "They'd take our fingerprints and find out that none of our fingerprints were on the weapons. How in the hell are we going to explain that?"

Ethan wasn't sure, but he didn't like running from a crime scene. "Guys, we can't leave," he said, trying to drag his feet. "We were witnesses to what happened. We have to..."

Cord suddenly came to a halt and grabbed Ethan by the shirt. "What do you think is going to happen?" he hissed. "Ethan, I don't want to run any more than you do, but I'm the one who killed those guys. That's the bottom line. And I'm not doing time for it and I'm not going to show the York Police how I turned those weapons against them, so forget it. We're not calling anyone. We're getting out of here and you are giving me your word that you'll never repeat what you saw. I need you to swear that to me."

Ethan could see how upset Cord was and he put up his

hands in a gesture of surrender. "I swear that I'll never repeat it," he said. "Don't worry about that. But if anyone else saw us..."

"Who is going to see us?" Cord said, letting go of his shirt. "No one saw us. We're going to fly home tomorrow, anyway, and we'll be out of here. Done."

Ethan nodded, but he wasn't happy about it. Even if he wasn't happy, at least he understood. The entire group began walking again, very quickly, with the car park in sight. Beyond that, freedom.

Freedom from something they hoped wouldn't come back to haunt them.

Cord most of all.

"You... you really *did* that?" Beck finally said. He was still astonished by what he'd witnessed. "How in the hell did you learn how to cast spells?"

Cord school his head. "I told you," he said. "It's in my blood. But I don't like talking about it, so let's just drop it... okay?"

"But we saw it."

They had reached the car park by now and Cord came to an abrupt halt, facing the group. He was normally a congenial guy, but the event had him spooked.

"I know you guys saw it," he said. "But you need to swear that you will never repeat it. You will never tell anyone. Because if you do, I'm going to be in a shitload of trouble. How in the hell am I going to explain to anyone that I used witchcraft to kill some criminals?"

"But it was in self-defense," Ethan stressed. "No one is going to convict you, or any of us for that matter."

Cord's frustration bled through. "But we would have to explain *how* it happened," he said. "Don't you get it? One question would lead to another, questions you don't want to answer. Trust me."

Nash, who had been silent for the most part, put a hand on

Cord's shoulder. "Cord, where I'm from, voodoo and witchcraft are part of the culture," he said quietly. "I've seen things I can't explain, so I believe what you're saying. I know what I saw. You have a gift, but it's a gift people don't understand. We've all witnessed something tonight that was... well, pretty damn amazing."

Cord registered some relief as he realized he had the support of Nash. The guy wasn't going to hound him. After a moment, he looked at the rest of the group. "You know, we've joked about calling ourselves the Eagle Brotherhood, but I think we really *are* a brotherhood now," he said. "We've experienced something that could have cost us our lives. It was small, but it happened. You saw something you shouldn't have seen because I did something I shouldn't have done. But to protect you guys... I'd do it again. I hope you know that."

"I feel like I owe my life to you," Colt said, reaching out to shake Cord's hand. "You were brave to do what you did, Cord, knowing... well, knowing that it wasn't something for all to see. But you did it and I'm grateful. I'll take an oath of silence on the Eagle Brotherhood if that's what it'll take. To protect you because you saved my life, I'll do anything. And if you ever need me, no matter where I am, I'll come. That's a promise."

More hands began shooting out, covering Colt and Cord's hands. It was a vow, a promise, not to discuss the event that bonded them more than a school or allied nations could. It was a bond that went deeper now because they harbored a secret. More than that, they had crossed into the realm of a brotherhood that would protect or kill for one another.

The true test of a brotherhood.

It was an oath that would take to their graves.

Wherever life would take them.

PROLOGUE
YEAR OF OUR LORD 1307, FRIDAY, OCTOBER 13TH, CASTLE DOMME, FRANCE

THE FIGHTING WAS FIERCE, even at dawn. The castle on the mountaintop had been under siege for three days; three long days of bloodshed had weakened them considerably, but still, they fought.

Clouds the color of blood feathered across the sky like the brush strokes of a macabre painting. The knights called a sky like this *le démon vole*; demon wings. It was as if the entire sky and earth were covered with demons, all determined to bring about the feast of Armageddon. With all of the men on the mountain, engaged in mortal combat, to some it was as if the end of times had, indeed, arrived.

The gate of the castle had long burned away, reduced to ashes by flaming arrows. The portcullis remained, scorched but still intact, a barrier between the inhabitants and the outside world. It would take more than flames to destroy the old iron grate.

The besiegers, however, had managed to get a foothold by extending ladders to the battlements and propelling themselves over the side. It would only be a matter of time before someone got to the chains that still held the portcullis in place. Once the grate was lifted, the skirmish would soon end.

The rocky, circular courtyard was littered with the dead, the dying, and the remaining able-bodied men. One knight was in charge, directing the combat on the walls from below. He was a big man with chiseled features and his weary brown eyes watched as man after man fell, mostly his own, men he had fought and lived with for the better part of his adult life. He knew the tides were turning against them and further knew there was no way to stop it.

Two knights abruptly appeared at his side, battle-weary, one sporting a large bloody gash across his neck. These were his lieutenants, a pair of seasoned Teutonic knights worth their fighting weight in gold.

"Sie haben für uns geschickt, mein Herr?" *You sent for us, my lord?*

The commander cast them a long look. They were shocked to see such defeat in his eyes, a realization that did nothing to ease their apprehension. But he did not speak to them in their language; he spoke to them in the language of the Templars. All Templars understood it, regardless of their country of origin.

"En effet," he replied. "Je vous exige pour une mission, une tâche la plus importante." *Indeed. I require you for a mission, a most important task.*

The men nodded, eager to please their grand master but fearful of what would be asked of them. When the portcullis suddenly shuddered as the enemy attempted to lift it, the knight in charge stiffened with trepidation.

"The Holy of Holies," he hissed to his men. "It is yours. Protect it with your life and take it to La Rochelle. We will all meet there when this is over, God willing."

The portcullis trembled again, the great iron teeth gnashing against the rocky soil of the mountain. The commander shoved one of the knights, urging him to move when the man could not seem to move on his own. The knight and his companion fled to the keep, a squat building three stories tall and several feet thick, built entirely of stone. Until today, it had been their sanctuary. Now they were determined that it not be their tomb.

The retractable wooden steps leading to the second floor were raised to prevent the enemy from breaching the keep. It took several painful minutes before it could be lowered. The men fled up the steps and into the keep, dark and cool and foreboding.

Once inside, there was a large room to the right, used for the chapel. Gloomy and dirty, it had a table at the far end upon which two fat tapers sat, burning low. A red cloth was thrown over the wood with a worn holy book resting atop it. This room had been one of such comfort, but they found no comfort at the moment.

The knights stumbled forward, weak with exhaustion and fear, falling to their knees as they reached the table. What they sought was not on top of it; it was underneath it.

A heavy iron chest, approximately the length, breadth and width of a man's arm sat huddled against the stone floor. The knights, in the midst of their rush, paused a moment to gaze at it. At least a thousand years old, the chest had seen far more of the world of men and misery than they could ever fathom. There was much mystery attached to it. But the sound of the screams outside shook them from their thoughts of reverence and one of the men made a grab for the box.

"We must be gone." There was panic in his voice.

The chest was heavy. He struggled with it all the way to the door. When the two reached the entrance, they were faced with a bailey crowded with fighting and dying men. The portcullis was up and the enemy was pouring through like blood through a gaping wound.

What they had feared for three days had come to pass. The screaming and sounds of battle were familiar to them, both horribly unsettling and strangely exciting. The men looked at each other, drawing courage from one another in knowing what must be done. Theirs was perhaps the most vital mission of all.

"Get behind me," the knight with the free hands instructed. He unsheathed his sword, the hilt emblazoned with the seal of the Knights Templar, two knights astride one overworked charger. His brow was heavy with sweat, with apprehension, of what he must do. "No matter what the cost, one of us leaves this place with the chest. Understand?"

The knight holding the chest silently agreed. He was the most vulnerable, unable to defend himself should he have to. He stayed close to his companion as they moved into the fray.

Dust and flying metal were everywhere. The knight with the chest labored with the weighty bundle, ducking behind the man in the lead. He could feel the blows that his companion was receiving, hard enough to unbalance him. It took him a moment to realize that it wasn't only French knights in the skirmish, but many English as well.

He saw at least four knights bearing the banner of the Earl of Savernake. Savernake had been on the First Crusade, allied with their leader, de Payens, when the order of the Templars had been founded. Through politics and greed, the Anglais had turned their backs on their former brothers in arms just as the French had. This battle wasn't about accusations of Heresy; it reeked of avarice. They all wanted what the Templars had, bad enough to kill for it.

But they would not get it. There was a great deal of hate bred in time, bitterness multiplied over the decades. The day of the Templars had finally come to a bloody end. As the two knights approached the jilted portcullis, the knight carrying the load felt an overwhelming pain to his back. He stumbled, realizing he'd been gored. It took a few seconds for him to realize the wound was fatal. He fell dead onto his face, sending the chest onto the ground.

His companion followed him in death shortly thereafter. The English knights who had ensured their seamless passage to Heaven kicked the bodies aside, making haste for the chest. The largest of the knights knelt down, righted the box, and threw the ancient bolt.

He and his two associates peered inside. Though the battle raged, none of the three, for the moment, noticed. Bodies fell all around them, bloody and maimed, but they had no perception. They only saw what was in front of them.

"Is that it, de Serreaux?" one asked eagerly. "Have we found it?"

The big knight, still on his knees, nodded slowly. "It must be," he muttered. "See how they struggled to protect it?"

"They died for it."

The large knight didn't give a second thought to those he had just killed.

"I have heard tale of this miracle from my father and his father before him," he said, "but I never believed we would actually find it." He ran his hand over the edge of the iron box reverently. "God has led us to it, of that I am sure."

One of the two knights still standing lifted his visor. His green eyes blazed as he, too, knelt into the dust next to Captain Etienne de Serreaux. It only seemed appropriate. Removing a mailed glove, he gingerly touched the fabric, so old that it had retained none of its original splendor. It was coarse, the original color faded into an unrecognizable hue. He drew his fingers back from it as if it burned to touch it.

"Enfin, c'est arrière où il appartient," he whispered.

De Serreaux heard the softly uttered words; he wasn't beyond the awe the others were feeling, but he was more adept at hiding it. The chest and its contents were his and in his possession he fully intended they should remain.

He had what he'd come for.

ONE

"LA VESTAGLIA DI LUCIUS?"

"That's what they call it."

"But what does that mean?"

"The Lucius Robe."

"I've never heard of it."

With the phone trapped between her shoulder and ear, Cydney Hetherington was making a feeble attempt to work and talk to her fifteen-year-old daughter at the same time. It was the usual call at the usual time, the very moment Olivia walked in the door after school let out.

Cydney was distracted from the conversation when someone walked into her office, which wasn't so much a private office as it was a large desk in a cubicle situated in a corner of the old museum library.

Being a nonprofit institution, the Western Pacific Museum of Art and Antiquities was busting at the seams and tended to place personnel wherever a spot could be found – like putting the Director of Operations in the library. It could have been worse; the Controller was in a former janitor's closet and an administrative assistant had a section of the copy room.

At least Cydney didn't have to live with the smell of old pine cleaner, but the caveat with setting up shop in the library was that docents, scholars, and any number of other people constantly wandered in and out. This particular person was the curator's assistant and handed Cydney some papers, no doubt meant to increase her workload to an insane level. Cydney took the stack and tried to find a place for it on her cluttered desk.

"Look it up on the Internet," she told her daughter. "It's the robe that Christ is supposed to have worn during his trial before Pilate."

Olivia's voice was tense with excitement. "Like the Shroud?"

"Sort of; only this one was in a private collection for hundreds of years before finally being donated to the Bristol Museum of Antiquities back in the nineteen-fifties. We managed to get it on loan, swapping it for some items from our Egyptian collection." She pitched forward in her chair, anxious to get off the phone and get on with her work. "They're having a big Egyptian exhibit and we're having a big opening with relics from the Holy Land. I'll tell you more about it when I get home."

But Olivia wouldn't be brushed off so easily. "I know about the opening already. I love the name of the exhibit– Resurrection. It sounds so mysterious."

Cydney nodded patiently. "Pretty cool, I agree. You should see the artsy-looking set we built for it. Anyway, I'll tell you more when I get home."

"But...!"

"When I get home, Olivia Grace. I've got to get back to work or they'll fire me and we won't *have* a home. Get it?"

"I get it. See you later."

She hung the receiver up with a smile on her lips, knowing that Olivia was already on the Internet furiously looking up everything she possibly could on The Lucius Robe. Her daughter was an educational militant, voraciously filling her head with knowledge of things that interested her like relics and Egyptians and anything to do with that fictional place called Middle Earth. The Lucius Robe was another of those fascinating things she wanted to know about. For Cydney, however, Biblical relics weren't her thing – a wing renovation and museum security for the new exhibit opening were.

The door opened again and the head of security strolled in, distracting Cydney from her thoughts. Stu Longe was one of the most decent people that she had ever known, an ex-Marine in his mid-thirties, devoutly Catholic, with buzzed blond hair and big blue eyes. Stu had made it his mission in life to find the right girl, a virgin and a Catholic, to have a gaggle of kids with. So far, he hadn't had much luck and at his advanced years of thirty-five, he was still single.

"Hey," he plopped his big body down in her guest chair. "What's going on, Cyd?"

Cydney glanced at him from her computer screen. "Not much. What's happening in your world?"

"Any luck on hiring more people for the exhibit opening?"

As the Director of Operations for the Western Pacific Museum of Art and Antiquities, security management fell under Cydney's jurisdiction. The museum wasn't big enough to warrant a full-fledged security department, which was odd considering the priceless status of their collection, but since they'd never had any real security trouble the Board would never approve additional funds.

Cydney repeatedly told them that it would only take one incident for there to be a real security issue, but the old boys on the Board wouldn't hear of it. Never let it be said they took advice from a woman, and a beautiful young one at that.

"I've got four of them for you, part-time, starting Thursday," she said. "I put their resumes in your In-box."

"I haven't looked," he grunted. "I've been up in the gallery."

"Did you see the case for the robe? They finished it this morning."

He nodded. "Pretty space-age stuff."

Cydney was proud to agree. "Hermetically sealed, temperature controlled, and virtually vandal-proof."

"That'll give us one less thing to worry about." He sat back in the chair, crossing his big arms. "Have you seen the thing?"

"The Robe?"

"Yeah."

Cydney was typing and talking at the same time. She stopped filling out the purchase order to buy parts for the antiquated HVAC system.

"They brought it in a crate that's big enough to put a car in," she told him. "Did you see that thing?"

Stu snorted. "I sure did. And all of that private security that came with it; I swear, some of those guys thought they were James Bond. I don't think they liked it when I told them that their services were no longer required."

Cydney joined his laughter. "Unbelievable," she agreed. "But, then again, we are talking about the most controversial relic since Noah's Ark, so I guess it's fitting. As for the robe...," she shrugged, "I saw the curator open the crate. All I saw was the corner of something that looked like acrylic casing and that was from a distance. My job is to make sure the exhibit and the display case are ready."

Stu nodded his head faintly, thinking of his own job. "I just wish they'd let us hire special security for this."

"We were lucky to get the special case."

He let out his irritation, something that had been building for months.

"I've got twenty-two people, three-quarters of which are retirees who couldn't do much if the situation got critical," he said. "I'd hate to have them try; someone might fall down and break a hip with all of the excitement. With the crowds we're expected to have, I'm really dreading this opening."

"I explained that to Mr. Hemeshuk," Cydney said patiently. "He thinks that allotting money for the special viewing case was enough of a security measure."

"It's sure as hell not."

"I know," she agreed. "Look; the guy wasn't made the Museum Director because he was qualified for the job. I think it was part of the dowry when he married the Chairman of the Board's daughter."

Stu pursed his lips in disgust. "Milt Hemeshuk, former sports agent, makes good by marrying into money."

"Don't sound so bitter."

It was a lighthearted comment and he smiled. "Better him than me, I guess." He got up out of the chair. "Well, I think I'll wander down to the vault and see if I can catch a glimpse of this thing."

"Like I said, the last I saw, they were opening the crate. That was about an hour ago."

"Want to come?"

It was the best offer she'd had all day. "Okay, twist my arm."

The basement level of the museum, where the business offices were located, was a dank place. Stu held the door leading into the hallway open for Cydney, admiring the rear view as she passed by.

It had become habit for him to check people out, purely from a security standpoint, but he seemed to check her out more than most. Cydney was of average height, about five feet five inches, with nice legs, a slender waist and larger than average breasts that he spent a lot of time attempting to figure out if they were fake or not. She had dark blond hair with a hint of red in it, cut into one of the long layered styles that could be really sexy with a toss of her head.

As nice as that package was, it was her face he really liked – big hazel eyes and a beautiful smile complete with a big dimple in her left cheek. And she was a lot of fun, too. They'd gone out with fellow employees after work and she was hysterical when she had a couple of drinks in her. Guys around the museum called her drop-dead gorgeous and Stu couldn't disagree. Too bad she wasn't Catholic, or a virgin, as he'd regretted far too many times since he'd known her.

Cydney's heels made a clicking noise on the old concrete hallway as they made their way down to the massive art vault. It had a fire suppression system that, when activated, sealed the only door and evacuated all of the air from the room in less than twenty seconds to smother the fire. It was state-of-the-art, nearly the only system that was updated in the old building that housed the museum.

Built in the nineteen-twenties, the three story stone and concrete structure had once been a school before the patron of the Museum, philanthropist Walter Ridenour Frank, purchased the building to house his private collection. In fifty years, it had grown into a world-class institution.

The door to the vault was open. It was enormous, like a bank vault door. Cydney went inside, followed by Stu. It smelled like chemicals inside and, as was usual when inside the vault, Cydney let out a sneeze. Several feet away, surrounded by the museum preparators who tended the artwork up in the galleries and kept the vault in order, sat the enormous open shipping container.

The curator was a trim woman with brown eyes and brown curly hair. Hearing the footsteps, she looked up from the crate. "Hey there," she greeted. "You've come at the right time."

Cydney came to a halt a few feet away. "How's that?"

As Stu moved in for a closer look, Anne-Michelle Thompson, known as Am, took a moment to stand away from the crate. She removed a glove and scratched the itch on her arm she'd been feeling for the better part of an hour.

"We're going to remove the casing and move it up into the exhibit," she gestured at the forklift in the corner.

"So you've inspected the exhibit case?"

"I have. We're good to go."

"And the rest of the exhibit?"

"You've done a beautiful job. Everything looks great, down to the last detail."

Cydney was relieved; part of her job was also setting up the exhibits, from having the cases built to hanging banners and arranging security. Anne-Michelle was hard to please, but the women had worked well together over the years and Cydney knew what she expected.

"Thanks," she replied. "With the exhibit opening in two days, I'll feel better having some time to make sure our main relic settles in nicely before everything goes on display."

Before Anne-Michelle could reply, a male voice suddenly interrupted.

"This is the biggest show we've ever had," he announced.

They turned around to see Milt Hemeshuk entering the vault, butting in to the conversation uninvited. Milt had to make sure he had the loudest voice and was heard above all else. He'd only been with the museum for two years and, so far, hadn't shown much aptitude for running a multi-million dollar organization. He was just a fast-talking man with a big mouth who had married well.

But in spite of that, Milt was lean and attractive, with gray hair and blue eyes. Every time Cydney saw him, she couldn't get over the story Stu had told her about Milt standing in the men's bathroom, spitting into the urinal and relieving himself at the same time. He would just stand there and let spittle drip out of his mouth, watching it go down the drain with his urine. Stu wouldn't go into the restroom now when Milt was using the facilities because it freaked him out.

"I would say this is certainly the most important relic we've ever had," Cydney agreed, trying not to linger on Stu's story.

Milt was a fast-talker, as if he were always making that big deal. He clapped his hands together eagerly.

"This relic will bring them in from all over the world," he declared. "More people will equal more revenue, and Lord knows that won't hurt us a bit. We'll route them through the gift shop on their way out. Brilliant!"

Cydney nodded her head; it was always wise to concur with the boss. "We've managed to pull together quite a collection even without the robe," she reminded him, as if he really cared. "Coins with Pilate's name on them, ankle bones with first century spikes through them. Something for everyone."

"But the robe is the le morceau lourd," Milt insisted. "I'm very excited for the grand opening on Thursday evening. There will be a lot of benefactors and the potential for a lot of donations. This has all got to go off without a hitch, Cydney."

She took it as a direct threat to her job, which it was. But he moved away from her before she could defend herself. She and Stu exchanged impatient glances.

"Good thing his wife had him take French lessons," Stu said under his breath. "That'll be really important when the French ambassador attends the opening. What the hell did he say, anyway?"

Cydney eyed the boss, hoping he didn't notice they were mumbling about him. "I think he meant to say the best piece, or something like it. He said 'the heavy piece'."

Stu closed his eyes. "What an idiot."

A couple of the preparators moved in with crowbars to disengage the fasteners on one side of the crate. One of the men, a skinny young kid with a Ph.D. in Art History, was having trouble and Stu took the crowbar from him, using his strength to pop open the side. When the other fastener let go, the entire side collapsed against the floor.

The crowd held their breath as the forklift, with another preparator on board, lurched forward. Anne-Michelle and the army of employees steadied the acrylic case as the prongs of the lift wedged beneath it and began to elevate. Cydney, Stu and Milt stood back as the case cleared the crate and the forklift began to grind towards the vault door.

"I'm hoping they measured the door to make sure that case fits through it," Cydney muttered to Stu.

Stu looked as if the thought hadn't occurred to him. "I would think they did that before anything else. At least, I hope so. That case has got to be nine feet tall."

"The doorway is nine feet six inches wide. Not much room for error."

For the first time, they all received a clear look at the acrylic case that contained the robe. It was covered with a fine sheet of opaque wrapping, a very fine bubble wrap to prevent any scratches to the acrylic. No one had seen the actual robe yet, simply the dark outline through the protective cover. Anne-Michelle and a couple of the preparators moved forward, quickly removing the bubble wrap. When it came off completely, everyone strained to get a look.

Mounted on a felt-covered mannequin torso, the garment was far less spectacular than anyone had thought. Great care had been taken to ensure that no part of the fabric moved, as the sleeves were carefully secured against the frame with heavy stainless steel pins and the front of the robe was laid open so that the interior could be seen.

It looked like a simple housecoat that had perhaps been a shade of blue or purple at one time. It was difficult to tell. The lining, however, was of an unbleached linen or cotton, upon which the deterioration of the centuries was evident. But there was no doubt, the closer one looked, that there were many brownish-colored stains across the inside of the robe in the area that would have, theoretically, lain against someone's back. Anne-Michelle was in awe as her professional eye moved across the fabric.

"I've studied up on this," she said. "It's really a fascinating story."

"Do tell," Cydney knew something about it, but she wanted to hear what Anne-Michelle knew, being the expert.

The curator didn't need further prodding. "Legend says that a knight from the Fourth Crusade brought it back in an old iron chest, having purchased it from gypsies somewhere in his travels through Europe. His family kept it in that chest for nine hundred years until it was donated to the Bristol Museum of Antiquities. It was the museum staff that took it out of the chest and mounted it without so much as making any attempt to study, repair or otherwise conserve it. They just plopped it on the form and sealed it. What you basically see is a two thousand-year-old garment that's hardly been touched."

"Then why do they call it The Lucius Robe?" Milt sounded like a fifth grader asking the teacher a question.

Anne-Michelle replied patiently. "Because history tells us that after Jesus Christ had been beaten and tortured, the Romans threw a robe on his body and a crown of thorns on his head and called him the king of the Jews. When they were finished ridiculing him, a Roman centurion named Lucius Petronius Sulla pulled the robe off and exchanged it for the cross that Christ would eventually be crucified on. Some scholars believe that Lucius was really a closet Christian because he secretly kept the robe."

"So how did it end up with gypsies in France?" Milt wanted to know.

Anne-Michelle continued. "There are a few theories on that, but the most popular belief is that when Lucius was sent back to Rome, he didn't want to take the chest with him, so he buried it beneath the Temple Mount in the hopes of retrieving it someday. He never returned, but on his deathbed, he confessed everything to his servant, who was a Christian, and the servant spread the word throughout the Christian community about Lucius' treasure. Pilgrims dug around the Temple Mount for hundreds of years looking for the chest, but it wasn't until the Crusades came that it was found by the Knights Templar." She tore her gaze away from the robe and looked at her captive audience. "They had apparently heard the legend, too, and made a concerted effort to locate it. That's how it found its way to Europe and was either bought or stolen by the Earl of Savernake. It was his descendants who donated it to the museum."

There was a heavy silence as the group digested the story. Stu, the consummate Catholic, crossed himself and moved in to get a better look.

"So Lucius told his servant that this robe belonged to Christ, and that it was stained with his blood?" he asked.

"Lucius was an eyewitness to the trial and crucifixion," Anne-Michelle confirmed. "I'd love to get this thing out of the cover and get a closer look at it. There has never been any scientific study done on it like they have on the Shroud. No one really knew for sure if it existed until fifty years ago and the museum has always denied requests to study it."

"But it's in our possession now," Cydney said. "Why can't we arrange to have it studied?"

Anne-Michelle smiled ironically. "I thought of that, too. But it's explicitly in our loan agreement with the antiquity museum that we can't allow any study, scientific or otherwise, on this piece. We'd be in violation."

"Not if they didn't know."

Anne-Michelle shook her head. "I'd love to, Cyd. But we can't jeopardize the museum like that. The legal ramifications alone would be unfathomable and it would ruin our reputation with every other institution around the world."

Cydney gave up on her suggestions, moving up beside Stu to get a better look. It was just old, crumbling material that could quite possibly be the most amazing relic in history. She gazed at the sleeves, the stains, her focus running along the neckline and the seam between the body and the arms. It was fairly simple in lines and design. Then, something strange caught her eye. She looked closer. Her heart began to pound.

"Am?"

"Yes?"

"Take a look at this."

The curator looked closely at the area Cydney was indicating. After several long moments, her expression went slack. She looked at Cydney as if trying to find some confirmation of what they were both seeing.

"Are you serious?" she breathed. "Do you know what that looks like?"

Cydney cocked an eyebrow at her, quite calmly. "Didn't they beat up Christ pretty good during his trial?"

"So the Bible tells us."

"Smacked him around a bit, landed a few good blows to the face?"

"I'm sure they did."

"Hard enough to...?"

Stu would not be ignored from the conversation. "What are you two looking at?"

Anne-Michelle was incapable of talking at the moment. She just stood there, staring at a speck of something none of the rest of them could see. Cydney put her finger on the acrylic.

"What does that look like to you, Stu?"

He peered closely. Then his mouth popped open. "My God... that looks like...."

———

"... a *tooth*?"

Cydney was still having a hard time with the concept. Olivia was nearly jumping up and down with mere thought of it.

"That's what it looked like," Cydney replied. "When I left work, Am was on the phone to England trying to talk to the director of the museum it came from. She was trying to get the guy out of bed."

"But a tooth?" Olivia repeated. "Mom, can you imagine if it's true? What if that's Jesus' tooth?"

Cydney shrugged, toying with her macaroni and cheese. It was dinnertime at the Hetherington household and The Lucius Robe was the hot topic of conversation.

"I don't know," she replied honestly. "I don't have an answer. Maybe there is no answer. I mean, it's not like we can prove it's really Jesus' tooth."

Olivia fell silent, unusual for the teenager. A sophomore in high school, she was taking all college prep classes, including Calculus. Olivia had been brilliant from a young age and even at fifteen had the makings of an eccentric genius. Cydney worried about her sometimes because she seemed detached from kids her own age. Fifteen going on fifty was an understatement.

"I read about the robe today after I talked to you," Olivia

said after a moment. "It's like the Veil of Veronica or the Spear of Longinus. It's the holy relic to end all holy relics."

"It's pretty powerful, I'll give you that."

"But a tooth?" she was back to the subject at hand. "I learned in my chemistry class that maternal DNA is the same from generation to generation and that teeth are one of the best places to find DNA. All you'd have to do is find someone in Jerusalem who can tell you who Mary's family was. There's got to be scholars like that who can tell you about her lineage."

"And?"

"And...," Olivia responded like her mother was an idiot. "Get a sample from some relative. The mother of Jesus did exist, right?"

Cydney looked at her daughter, more logical and excited about the possibilities than Cydney was at the moment. Olivia would make a great scientist someday. But the truth was that Cydney just didn't know what to think. She finally sighed and set her fork down.

"Look; I'm only Operations, not scientific endeavors. I don't know the first thing about DNA sampling. If you've got any bright ideas, then you'd better email them to me at work so I can pass them along to Am. She's the authority on this." Finished with her dinner, Cydney stood up from the table and collected her plate. "One more thing, Liv – you need to keep this to your-self. I don't want you talking about this to anyone. I'm not sure what kind of consequences this could lead to, but I don't need you involved in anything. Understand?"

Olivia made a face; she looked much like her mother did when she was annoyed. "Who am I going to tell?" she wanted to know. "The kids in my marching band? My math teacher?"

"A teacher who could pick up the phone and call the local paper," Cydney snapped gently. "That would open a whole can of worms and I'd be in trouble for it."

Olivia's expression suggested how ridiculous she thought her mother was, but the absence of any argument meant that she understood.

It was a peaceful evening in their little house in the city of Arcadia, California, about fifteen miles from the museum. Cydney and her husband had bought the two-bedroom bungalow several years ago before the real estate market went crazy. They had a nice little yard and Olivia had a fat orange cat she had named Agent Orange.

All in all, it was a nice life, perfect except for the fact that Brad Hetherington's shadow still lingered everywhere. Even though it had been eight years since his death, Cydney still saw him in every room, nearly every night. She felt him all the time.

Not like a ghost, but more like a memory. Sometimes, she looked at the front door and remembered the rainy night that the cops had come to tell her about the accident. She'd painted the door and changed the hardware to alter the appearance and the memories associated with it, but it was still the same door. She could do nothing to change the fact, much as she'd tried.

Brad had been changing a flat tire on the side of the freeway, they had told her. The bobtail truck never saw him until it was too late. The rain had been heavy and the roads slick. The truck swerved, but it still hit him. The truck had flipped onto its side and slid into the center divider. The driver and his passenger weren't hurt, but Brad was beyond help. The cops thought it might make her feel better to know that he'd never felt any pain. He'd died instantly.

It hadn't made her feel better to know that. In fact, it took a good three years before the pain wasn't a constant daily companion, like a migraine that never went away. These days, it was easier to look at the faucet Brad had tried to install but ended up just messing up the works. Cydney didn't have the heart to fix it. She had just left it, cursing him every time it sprayed a stream up into her face. Oddly, it was those things that had eased her pain more than anything.

It was all a distant memory, her happy marriage that once was. Cydney turned on the kitchen faucet, now wise enough to dodge the spray that came up at her. Olivia was beating a hasty retreat from the kitchen like the coward that she was, knowing it was chore time. Cydney called her back to load up the dishwasher. While Olivia begrudgingly loaded, her mother cleaned the stovetop.

"So tell me more about what you found out on the Internet," Cydney tried to make conversation.

Olivia slammed a glass against the dishwasher, nearly breaking it. "It was just basically the same stuff you told me about the Savernake guy donating it. Because it was stashed away for so long, no one seems to know a whole heck of a lot about it. Do you think I can see it?"

"I don't see why not. Maybe tomorrow after school."

"Sweet!" Olivia chirped. She closed the dishwasher and started it. "Can I bring some friends?"

"You may not. They'll have to wait for the opening like everyone else."

Olivia dried off her hands. Agent Orange slinked into the room and she grabbed the fat tabby before it could get away.

"I read some other stuff about the robe." She sat at the table and stroked the cat. "There are a few websites that claim the Savernake dude didn't buy it from gypsies. They say he stole it from the Knights Templar when the King of France wiped them out on Friday, October the 13th. Did you know that's why everyone thinks Friday the 13th is so unlucky?"

Her mother shook her head. "Because of the Templars?"

"That's the day the king ordered their arrest."

"Interesting. What else did your websites say?"

"That Jesus didn't die on the cross. The Templars believed that someone else died in his place."

Cydney cocked an eyebrow. "Weird."

"Not really." Olivia let the cat slide to the floor. "One website said that Judas didn't betray Jesus in the Garden of Gethsemane and that he betrayed one of the disciples, instead."

"Which one?"

"James, Jesus' brother." Olivia was very matter-of-fact about it all. "The disciples had it all arranged so that Jesus would escape, marry Mary Magdalene, and live happily ever after."

Cydney paused in cleaning the stove. "You know, if you lived in the middle ages, they'd burn you at the stake for saying this kind of thing."

Olivia grinned. "The bottom line is that even if you were able to get some DNA from that tooth and compare it with DNA from Mary's descendants, it would still come back a match because James and Jesus had the same mother."

Cydney threw away the used paper towel and washed her hands. "Now you're making my head hurt. I forbid you to tell Grandma about all of this, do you hear? One word about Jesus running out and leaving his brother to die on the cross and she'll have an exorcism performed on you. You know how religious she is."

Olivia, pleased she had bewildered her mother yet again, went off in search of the television. Exhausted, Cydney retired to her bedroom and was about to put on her pajamas when the doorbell rang.

It rang again, shortly after the first chime. Olivia was up, moving for the front door, oblivious to the fact that it was almost nine o'clock at night. Before Cydney could stop her, she opened the door.

The porch light was on, illuminating a tall man with dark hair. He said something to Olivia through the screen door as

Cydney approached, but she didn't quite hear what he said. When she drew close, the man focused on her and the first thing Cydney noticed was his stunning good looks. Had she seen him on the street, she would have given him a second glance; the guy was unbelievably gorgeous. Startled, she pulled her daughter away from the door and took her place, protectively.

"Can I help you?" she asked politely.

"Cydney, it's okay." She hadn't even noticed Hemeshuk standing slightly behind the man. He seemed oddly strained. "Sorry it's so late, but these gentlemen came to the museum after you left. I've been briefed on the reason for their visit and it is important that you are, too."

The focus returned to Mr. Tall, Dark and Handsome. He and Cydney gazed at each other a moment, sizing one another up. There was instant curiosity, and perhaps interest, in the air.

"My name is Special Agent Ethan Serreaux, Federal Bureau of Investigation," the man flipped his badge up against the screen; he pronounced his last name 'Sir-row'. "This is my partner, Special Agent James Lowell. Mr. Hemeshuk was nice enough to drive my partner and me over here. Sorry it's so late, but it is fairly important we speak with you."

Cydney noticed the third man, standing back in the shadows. He was very tall and very blond. Opening the door, she led them into the living room. The agents took the couch and Hemeshuk took the overstuffed chair. Cydney was left standing with wide-eyed Olivia hovering just out of sight. The atmosphere was odd and uncomfortable.

Cydney couldn't help but wonder why the FBI wanted to speak with her. Maybe they had a hot relic in the museum.

"What can I help you with, gentlemen?" she asked.

Agent Serreaux sat casually against the back of the couch. "I know it's late, so I'll get to the point. Mr. Hemeshuk tells us that you're the Director of Operations for the Western Pacific Museum of Art and Antiquities."

"I am."

"Then you are responsible for security of The Lucius Robe."

Cydney glanced at Milt before continuing. "Yes, I am. Why?"

Serreaux paused. "Everything I am about to tell you is privileged information, Mrs. Hetherington. It does not go beyond these walls."

Her curiosity was turning to dread. "Okay."

Serreaux's gaze lingered on her before continuing. "As you know, our country has been at elevated or better terror alert for the past few years. The Bureau makes it our business to know what's going on in the nation, friendly or otherwise, and, as such, have reason to believe that The Lucius Robe may become a target of a wave of religious fanaticism."

Cydney stood with her arms folded protectively across her chest, her expression a mask of doubt. "What kind of a target?"

"Theft."

Cydney was silent a moment. The reason wasn't as bad as she thought it would be. She pulled a chair out of the dining room and sat.

"Theft is always a concern for the museum," she said patiently. "We are aware of it on a daily basis and my security people are trained to observe and deter. Did you go into the exhibit gallery when you were there earlier tonight?"

"Yes."

"Did you see the special viewing case we had the robe in?"

"We did."

"The attack of a small army notwithstanding, that thing is rigged to endure a lot. You don't think it will be enough to deter a thief?"

"We're talking about zealots," Serreaux said. "This is more than simple stealing. It has a purpose; their object has a purpose. They'll stop at nothing to get to it."

There was something about the way he said it that made her blood run cold. "Like what?"

Serreaux shrugged. "Like resorting to arson, or maybe even bombs, to get through that case. They might even kill anyone who tried to stop them."

Her doubt turned to shock. "You must be kidding."

"I wish I was."

Cydney suddenly stood up from her chair. "Agent Serreaux, all I have as a security force are a bunch of retirees, a few college students and one ex-Marine. My security force isn't structured to prevent a major theft from religious fanatics. They're more like schoolyard proctors, strategically placed to deter unauthorized activity more than to actually protect life and property. If there really are some idiots that want to steal The Lucius Robe, then I can tell you right now that our security is inadequate. That's why we built that case; it's shatter-proof and hermetically sealed. I don't want my people putting their lives on the line."

Serreaux's gaze was steady, his dark eyes appraising her. Cydney couldn't help but stare back, noticing his very square jaw and long nose. His nearly-black hair was stylishly cut, spiky tendrils flopping over his forehead. He didn't look like any FBI agent she'd ever seen, other than in the movies. He was a tall man, several inches over six feet, and filled out his dark suit quite nicely. He had enormously wide shoulders but wasn't bulky; he was simply beautifully and athletically built. She was so wrapped up in appraising his perfect male looks that when he spoke, she jumped at the sound of his voice.

"I understand your concerns," he said. "My purpose here is to make sure you're aware of a potential situation, not predict impending disaster. It's a worst-case scenario, but it is possible. You need to know."

"I didn't think the FBI got involved in anything that is simply a need-to-know basis."

"In this case, we did."

"Why?" A thought occurred to her and she cocked her head. "I may be off base, but I'm thinking that there's something else behind this that you're not letting on. There's got to be; otherwise, this whole thing just doesn't make any sense. Since when does the FBI show up just to warn about a theft?"

Serreaux's face was like stone. "We've had trouble with this group before."

"What kind of trouble?"

"That's irrelevant. Suffice it to say that the chatter we've been hearing over the past few weeks has mentioned the robe by name and we felt it necessary to inform the museum that there may be trouble. Would you rather we just not tell you and hope that nothing happens?"

No, she didn't wish that. Cydney's frustration reached a boiling point as she thought about the times she had sat across from Milt and the Board, telling them how inadequate the museum's security force was. It seemed like she went over it every six months when the Board convened. They were sick of hearing it from her, but they never took any action. They didn't want to spend the money. She glanced at Milt as she spoke.

"That's great," she couldn't help the sarcasm. "So now I know. But it does me absolutely no good because I still have the same security force I had when you walked in the door. Nothing has changed except for the fact that now we may have a real threat on our hands and I'm extremely concerned for the safety of my employees."

"That's understandable," Serreaux replied. "Perhaps Mr.

Hemeshuk should consider hiring a professional security company for this exhibit. It might help."

Cydney looked directly at Milt, hearing her own words reflected in Serreaux's suggestion. But Milt didn't do anything except stare back at her. *Say something, you idiot!* she thought. Cydney's gaze returned to the agents, resigned to the fact that Hemeshuk wasn't going to do a damn thing, as always.

"Well, I suppose I should thank you for letting us know," she said. "Can I at least brief my people and let them know what we might expect?"

Serreaux spoke. "I'll do it. We'll be at the museum tomorrow morning and I can tell them for you."

"My security people don't come in until Thursday morning, when the exhibit opens."

Serreaux glanced at Lowell; it was obvious he was mentally chewing on something. "Well," he finally sighed. "My partner and I may be able to help, at least for a few days. Since this is considered a credible threat involving goods or products from an allied nation, we can request to remain on the case for a few days to see if anything goes down."

Cydney felt better. FBI help was better than no help at all. "I'd appreciate that."

"We can probably hang around through the weekend."

"We're only open Thursday through Monday."

"Then we'll stay through Monday and go from there." Serreaux abruptly stood up, signaling that their meeting had come to a close. "Thanks again for letting us intrude tonight. Agent Lowell and I will see you first thing in the morning and we can go over your security arrangements. Maybe we can help."

Cydney walked the group to the door, lingering on the conversation, more apprehensive than she had ever been in her eleven years at the museum. All of it left a bad taste in her mouth and she knew that she wasn't getting the entire story. The FBI didn't come around warning private entities about trouble if they didn't have a damn good reason. Serreaux, she sensed, was withholding something.

The agents were through the door, out onto the porch. Milt brushed by her without looking at her.

"Goodnight, Cydney."

"Goodnight." *You jerk.*

Cydney shut the door and locked it. She stood there for a second, allowing herself a moment to collect her thoughts. It was all fairly overwhelming. When she finally turned around, she saw that her daughter was standing there, her green eyes wide with everything she had absorbed.

"Terrorists!" Olivia hissed.

Cydney shook her head. "No, sweetpea. Just freaks out to see what they can get away with. Don't worry about it."

There was no way Olivia couldn't worry about it, nor could Cydney, although she tried. She forced her daughter to bed and followed shortly thereafter.

But sleep was hard to come by. Cydney kept thinking of her security personnel, of Stu, putting their lives on the line when the mere thought was ridiculous. They shouldn't even be in this situation. They were a small antiquities museum, not the Louvre. They just weren't geared for this kind of thing.

The Resurrection exhibit was taking an ominous turn.

TWO

LOS ANGELES WASN'T an old city, relatively speaking. Although settlement of the area began back in the late eighteenth century in the area known as the Pueblo, in the grand scheme of cities, L.A. was an infant; a very large infant with more than its share of adult problems. Functionally speaking, Los Angeles was an enormous cripple of crime, glamour, money and power.

The city was so vast that even the alleys had alleys. The homeless had their own zip code. There were an infinite number of nooks and crannies into which one could fade into oblivion, never to be heard from again. Lots of people came to the city for just that reason. Skyscrapers soared into the smoggy atmosphere, riding the earthquake faults like a surfer on a monster wave. It was in this mixture of risk, thrill and oblivion that millions of people existed.

Olvera Street was in the heart of the Pueblo area, across the freeway from the Federal Courthouse and not too far from the heart of the city. It was a hive of closely knit booths, each containing the treasures of Mexico to be sold to the throngs of tourists that visited the city. It was like going to Tijuana without having to make the trip or without having to deal with the orphans selling gum on the street. It was safer, without the depression inherent to a third world nation. Every day was a busy day, safe in the bosom of America's most diverse city.

There were several Mexican food restaurants in and around Olvera Street. One in particular faced Union Station, the main thoroughfare for rail traffic in and out of the city. The restaurant was small, with a few tables outside at which to sit. It was always busy at lunchtime and people crowded around the tables and counter, breathing in the smog and ambiance of the historic City of Angels. This particular day, the temperatures reached the high eighties and the smog index level reached the unhealthful stage. It was just another day in Los Angeles.

A man in a designer shirt and dark slacks sat under a tree, alone, at one of the tables. He wore Oakley sunglasses and smoked a cigarette. In front of him sat a half-empty bottle of beer and he took a sip as another man joined him at the table. The second man brought food, carnitas, and delved into the concoction with gusto. He didn't offer any to his companion.

"You shouldn't eat the food here," the man with the beer said. "All of these restaurants grade low on the health inspection scale."

The second man chewed loudly. "Tastes all right to me."

The first man toyed with his beer bottle, watching his companion eat. "So," he said casually. "I understand we are successfully in."

"I start the job on Thursday."

The man with the beer nodded his head with satisfaction. He gazed up at the trees, watching the birds above them. Bird feces fell on the table and he wisely moved his bottle.

"His Eminence will be pleased," he said. "He is very anxious to move forward."

"I'm moving as fast as I can," the man with the mouthful swallowed. "I'll be there Thursday."

The first man took another sip of his Mexican beer. "With the relaxed security the museum has, we shouldn't have any problems," he said. "Please, whatever you do, don't act alone. We'll do any planning that needs to be done."

"I know."

"I'm very interested to know what kind of upgraded security they'll have for this exhibit."

"We'll find out soon enough." The Eater finished his *carnitas* in four bites and was now downing his soda. "This just all seems so weird to me."

"How's that?"

The Eater wiped his fingers on a paper napkin. "Because this is something my grandfather's grandfather talked about, plotted and planned for. I heard this stuff all of my life. Now that it's finally coming to fruition, it just seems unbelievable."

The man with the beer looked at him. "I thought you'd be happy."

"I am."

He didn't look happy. The beer drinker leaned forward in his chair, his voice soft against the roar of traffic.

"This is it, my friend," he muttered. "Your time has finally come. Your family's time has come and we will be here to realize it. Think of all of the people who have died in the quest for this dream and of those who have devoted their entire lives so that the dream might be realized. It is an incredible honor to finally be here, at the end of times, don't you think?"

The Eater looked at him, doubt on his face. Even though he had been groomed for this moment all of his life, Joseph d'Orleans wasn't as passionate as the rest of them were. That was sad, considering he should have been the most passionate of all. He felt like he was letting them all down if he didn't follow through. Because it was expected of him, his family's legacy for almost a thousand years, he would do what he must. A more reluctant emperor had never existed.

"I'll talk to you Thursday night," he finally said. "Give me the day to check out the layout."

The man with the nearly empty beer nodded. He knew Joseph's reservations, but he couldn't let that stop them. There was a destiny to be fulfilled and it was his responsibility to make it happen. The entire brotherhood was depending on it and Joseph's reluctance was inconsequential.

"Of course," he said. "And, by the way, just so you know, she'll be there."

Joseph's brow furrowed. "Who will be there?"

"You know. Her."

Joseph stared at him a moment before realization dawned. "Oh, right," he muttered. "What are you planning? Do we have a detailed schedule?"

"Not yet. But I know she's been in contact with His Eminence about our next step. Watch her closely. She may have a message for you."

"You're sure she's going to be there?"

"She has already bought a pre-sale ticket. She'll be there, don't worry."

Joseph stood up, wiping his mouth one last time. In his late twenties, he had an athletic physique in spite of his love of greasy Mexican food. With his mussed brown hair and smoldering good looks, one might have taken him for a scruffy male model. He lifted an eyebrow at his companion.

"If you say so," he said.

"No worries. Good luck."

"Talk to you later."

The man with the empty beer watched Joseph disappear into the cluttered booths that filled Olvera Street. Like a stubborn mule, Nat Payne knew he was going to have to kick Joseph a few times to get him into the rhythm. He'd never been as enthusiastic about this as the rest of them.

They had come too far to let the primary focus of their objective get cold feet.

———

Ethan stood looking at The Lucius Robe for the longest time. He couldn't explain it, but there had been an odd sense of déjà vu since the moment he first saw it. Something about it struck a chord in him, something deep in his chest, to the point of making his palms sweat. It was extremely odd but something he attributed to the rumor of the robe's origin. It was a pretty fascinating piece of work. It took him a long time to move away from it and inspect the rest of the exhibit.

If Cydney and Stu noticed the FBI agent's fascination with The Lucius Robe, they didn't say a word about it. As Serreaux and Lowell moved through the exhibit to more closely inspect it, Cydney and Stu followed them around, hoping they weren't going to have to rebuild the entire Resurrection exhibit because the FBI thought the security measures were too lax. But the agents didn't say a word about the cases or security measures at the moment; they were still deep into their assessment.

Stu was obviously impatient, but Cydney kept her cool, waiting for the men to conclude their findings. Being so close to relics all the time, she often lost her perspective of wonder about them. She had to remember that those not in the business were still captivated by two thousand-year-old objects.

"Incredible." Serreaux finally unfolded himself from where he had been huddled over a case filled with Roman coins and turned to Cydney. "So you're telling me that these coins have the head of Pontius Pilate?"

Cydney nodded. "They do, indeed. Pretty cool stuff."

Serreaux smiled with agreement. He had an incredibly attractive smile of straight, white teeth. "Very cool."

Stu was watching the exchange. He didn't like the way the FBI agent smiled at Cydney. In fact, he hadn't liked anything about the guy from the moment he had met him that morning. Too much testosterone in the same room tended to make the double Y chromosome human beings bitter adversaries, like Neanderthals competing for mating rights. This guy was in Stu's territory and the man wasn't taking it well.

Oblivious to Stu's mental chest-beating, Cydney led them into the next gallery where the exhibit spread into the less spectacular relics. A pot here, an ancient pair of shoes there, both excavated from the biblical city of Jericho. She pointed them out and Serreaux and Lowell went to investigate.

She watched the agents inspect the collection, still trying to gauge how she felt about the situation. She had fallen asleep with Serreaux and his prophesy of doom on her mind and had awoken to the very same thoughts. Only her thoughts seemed to center more around Serreaux himself than the message he bore. For eight years, she'd struggled against the idea of male companionship of any sort. To replace Brad was just too painful. Now, she felt odd and uncomfortable with the attractive agent on her mind. It was ridiculous, she told herself. She didn't even know anything about him.

"They're more interested in the collection than in the robe," Stu muttered. "They said something about helping us review security. When do they plan to start doing that?"

"They're probably reviewing it right now," she replied. "Do you think they're really just looking at the collection because they like the pretty colors? I'm sure they're checking out the details of the cases, among other things."

Stu grunted. Cydney passed a long look at him, noticing his

displeasure for the first time that morning. He seemed all coiled up.

"What's wrong with you?" she asked.

He looked like an angry kid. "Nothing. I just think it's stupid that they're here. Since when does the FBI get involved in the threat of a theft?"

"They told you the same thing they told me."

"I know."

"And I had the same question."

"I know, I know," he was beginning to get testy with her. "It's just... hell, did anyone even check their credentials? All they flashed us was in identification card. Do we even really know they are who they say they are?"

Cydney shook her head. "I haven't had time and I'm sure Milt hasn't done it. Maybe you should slip away and see what you can find out."

"Hallelujah," he muttered. "Finally, words of wisdom. If you don't need me to baby sit with you, I'll go see what I can do."

Cydney watched him walk off towards the elevator that would take him down to the business offices. She understood his annoyance at having the agents at the museum, stepping on his toes. But Stu wasn't usually the irritated type; he was the most easy-going man she had ever met.

Thoughts of Stu's demeanor aside, she continued to watch over the agents as they perused the collection. She found her gaze drawn more to Serreaux's butt in his dress slacks. It was nice and round. She had to keep looking away. But then she'd look back and think that Special Agent Lowell had a nice butt, too, but not nearly so nice as Serreaux's. Feeling incredibly ridiculous, she wandered up next to them in an attempt to pay more attention to what they were looking at rather than focusing on their male backsides.

"What you're looking at here are the remains of a first century crucifixion," she said, as if they couldn't read the sign on the case. "Those are someone's ankle bones. Nasty way to die."

Serreaux simply nodded, glancing at her, his eyes lingering on her. There was curious warmth there, like tendrils, reaching out to inspect her. Startled, mesmerized, Cydney took a step back, away from the case. Maybe standing behind him and staring at his backside was a better idea.

As Cydney tried to regroup, Anne-Michelle came up the stairs in the center of the lobby. Her gaze fell on Cydney and she made her way over. Cydney smiled weakly at the curator, glad to be distracted from the agent.

"Good morning," Anne-Michelle said. Her brown eyes lingered on the two men at the display case. "Our FBI guys?"

"That's them."

"I heard all about it from Milt. What are they doing?"

Cydney shrugged. "Looking at the relics, I guess. Also inspecting the security of the cases, I would think."

Anne-Michelle nodded her head. After a moment, she leaned into Cydney and lowered her voice.

"I was able to get a hold of the curator for the Bristol Museum early this morning," she said. "I didn't tell him what we thought we saw, of course, but I made up some story and asked if we might remove the robe from the case and non-invasively examine it."

"And?"

"He said he would prefer we didn't. The acrylic case is hermetically sealed and he's afraid what the open air might do to the fiber of the robes."

Cydney thought a moment. "I'm no expert, of course, but realistically, how long would it take for the material to show any effects of exposure if we were to remove it from the case?"

Anne-Michelle cocked her head thoughtfully. "Probably a few days."

"We could remove that tooth in a few seconds."

The curator shook her head. "Honestly, I should be fired for even thinking of violating a contract like that. But if I didn't think there was an undeniably good reason, I wouldn't have made the attempt. I don't want to do anything illegal or unethical."

"So what do we do?"

"I'm not sure. I'll have to think about it. I may have to call the curator back and divulge what we thought we saw. It might be enough of a prompting to gain his permission to examine it."

"Why didn't you tell him the first time?"

She looked at Cydney as if the woman had gone mad. "Tell him we thought we saw a tooth? Christ's tooth? He'd think I'd gone nuts."

"But we did see a tooth."

"And that's another thing. The Bristol Museum has had it for a while. Why didn't any of their personnel see it?"

Cydney shrugged. "I don't know. But if you don't figure out a way to remove that robe and get a hold of that tooth, I guarantee you that Olivia will be down here on the weekend to find a way to bust into that acrylic."

"Your daughter is going to make a great terrorist."

"You're telling me."

Stu joined them, having just come off the elevator from the lower administrative floor. He didn't look pleased.

"What's up, Stu?" Cydney asked.

His blue eyes were locked on the two agents. "I just talked to Milt. He said he was contacted by the FBI field office in West Los Angeles and that these guys are legit."

"Then why the long face?" Anne-Michelle asked.

"Stu is upset because he doesn't get to throw them out,"

Cydney told her, winking at Stu when he glared at her. "Oh, lighten up, Stu. You're still the big man around here."

As Stu wandered away, towards the two agents as if stalking them, Cydney decided to leave Anne-Michelle and follow her security chief. The two of them came upon the agents just as the men were turning away from the crucifixion case.

"Well," Serreaux began, "it looks like everything is well thought out. You've done a good job."

"Thanks," Cydney said. An awkward silence settled and she spoke again. "Look, I don't mean to be nosey, but can you tell me more about these zealots? I would really like to know what we may be up against. I think it's only fair."

Serreaux gazed at her, the split-second of silence confirming what she had suspected the night before. He knew more than what he was telling her. She wanted answers and she wanted the truth.

"Please?" she begged quietly, lifting her eyebrows for emphasis.

Ethan watched her expression, noting the delicate lift of the brow and the way her hazel eyes glistened. In fact, he'd done little else but check her out since nearly the moment he met her.

Cydney Hetherington had been nothing that he had expected. Although he wasn't sure what he had expected as head of museum operations, a gorgeous blond hadn't been an option. From the bottom of her pretty feet to the top of her spectacular blond head, she looked like an angel. That was his first thought when he had laid eyes on her last night. Everything about the woman was perfect. He particularly liked the sound of her voice; soft and low and sultry like an actress from old Hollywood. It was very, very sexy. The longer he stared at her, the more he could feel himself relenting. Maybe she was right.

After a moment, he nodded his head.

"Let's go to your office," he said, throwing a look over his shoulder to Lowell, who was still studying the contents of the case. "I'll be right back."

Stu tried to follow them but Serreaux waved him off. Furious, Stu struggled not to demand that he be allowed to go. Just short of throwing a temper tantrum in the middle of the gallery, he stormed off in the opposite direction and disappeared into another wing.

Lowell, somewhat caught in the middle of the power play, wasn't unaware of the security chief's reaction but he was more interested in watching Serreaux follow the hot museum director to the elevator. He wasn't oblivious to the way Ethan had looked at the woman, both last night and today. He'd known Ethan Serreaux for nine years; for four of those years they had been partners. Since Ethan's ex-wife had left him eight years ago, taking their young son with her back to the east coast, Ethan had not been a particularly joyful man to be around. There was something inherently bitter about him, especially towards women.

Lowell shook his head faintly and turned back to the case, hoping wherever they were going and whatever was going to be said, that Ethan would not drive yet another woman to tears. He was particularly good at that when the mood struck him.

Cydney was oblivious to that particular personality trait of Special Agent Serreaux as they took the elevator down to the bottom floor in silence. When the doors opened, she led him down the long, cold, concrete hallway until they reached her office.

Entering the room, it smelled slightly rotted, evidence of the rain they'd had the previous night that had seeped into the walls of the basement. The concrete was porous and soaked up the ground water like a sponge; hence, it always smelled like a swamp.

Cydney ignore the smell, indicating her guest chair as she

rounded her desk. "Have a seat," she told him. "Can I get you some coffee or water?"

"Thank you, no," Ethan replied. "Mind if I take off my coat?"

Cydney shook her head, eyeing him as he peeled off his expensive suit jacket and laid it across the other chair. She tried not to stare at his arms, the muscles straining against the dress shirt. The man had a seriously muscular build on him but she tore her eyes away, furious at herself for taking any interest. But it made her cheeks warm simply to think about those muscular arms. Sitting down in her chair, she faced him with a certain degree of self-preservation.

"I didn't know anyone wore suits anymore," she commented.

Ethan gave her a crooked smile as he made sure the coat draped so it wouldn't wrinkle. "The Bureau is still old-school that way," he said. "I've got a suit for every day of the week."

"Your mother must be proud."

It was a surprising attempt at humor. His smile broke through and he chuckled softly.

"Yes, my mother and father are extremely proud of my ability to dress appropriately." He settled his big frame into the chair. "Now," he took a deep breath as he composed his thoughts. "What more, exactly, do you want to know about this situation? I've told you as much as I can."

She lifted a well-shaped brow as her smile faded. "You may have told me as much as you can, but you certainly haven't told me all that you know." She held up a hand before he could perjure himself. "I can see it in your expression every time we discuss it. You've got a good poker face; I'll give you credit. But it's *too* good, if you know what I mean. You're too emotionless to be totally convincing."

A smile played on his lips. "I think you have an active imagination."

His statement should have infuriated her, but instead, she found herself fighting off a grin again just because he was.

"Bull," she snapped. "What do you think I'm going to do? Tell the enemy everything you tell me to make their job easier when they try to rob my museum? I think it's unfair for you not to tell me absolutely everything you know so at least we know what we're up against."

He sat back in his chair casually, his dark eyes fixed on her. "And do what?"

"What do you mean?"

"Just that," he insisted with a flick of his hand. "Even if you know everything, is that going to make your security tighter or your people better able to deal with it?"

"It might."

He held her gaze a moment longer, realizing that he was thinking about more than just her question. He was thinking of the soft pout of her lips and the way her eyelashes brushed against her brow bone. He was thinking about just how beautiful she really was. He already knew he was going to answer her question. He was just debating how much to tell her without frightening her.

"All right," he finally said, sitting forward in the chair. "Fair enough. I will answer your questions specifically but I won't volunteer any more information than necessary. So what's your first question?"

His response puzzled her slightly but she didn't take the time to analyze it. She was afraid he might rescind his offer.

"Is the threat against us specifically or just general?" she asked. "Last night you mentioned zealots. Any zealots in particular?"

He nodded. "Yes."

"Who?"

He cocked his head slightly. "They call themselves *Die Auhänger*."

Her brow furrowed as she translated the words. Having worked in museums for much of her adult life, it was necessary to have a working knowledge of several languages, German included.

"The Disciples?"

"Yes."

She stared at him. "Like... like Jesus' disciples?"

He nodded slowly. "Yes."

"So they want the robe because it's rumored to have belonged to Jesus?"

"Sort of."

"What do you mean 'sort of'? You said someone was going to try and steal it."

He could see that she was growing agitated and he put up a calming hand.

"They want the robe because it is their intention, we believe, to bring on a new Holy Roman Empire, one that uses holy relics to feed its followers." He watched the emotions ripple across her beautiful face. "Nothing is more powerful than a holy relic to a devoted believer. Such things could raise armies of millions. Intelligence leads us to believe that they want this robe to crown a new Holy Roman Emperor and, being religious zealots, they'll stop at nothing to get it."

There it was; the simple, straightforward truth. Cydney stared at him, mouth agape. "Are you serious?"

"Yes."

She stared at him a moment longer before letting out a hiss. "Oh, my God," she breathed. "That sounds like something out of a novel. Are you sure about all of this?"

He was amused at her disbelief. "Pretty sure." He probably

shouldn't have told her any more but he found himself doing so. "They plan to call their empire *'Der viert Reich de Erieuchtung'* or The Fourth Reich of Enlightenment. It's their goal to crown a new Holy Roman Emperor, take over Europe and create a new empire." His humor abruptly faded and he sat forward in the chair, his dark eyes suddenly very hard. "Mrs. Hetherington, I know this seems far-fetched, but believe me when I tell you that it is a real enough threat that the FBI considers it extremely serious. I wouldn't be here if they didn't. Therefore, it would make my job considerably easier if you stop asking so many questions and just trust that I know what needs to be done. And that goes for your ex-Marine security chief, too. I don't need that guy chest-beating every time I get around him. I need your cooperation and will accept nothing less or this could be a very bad situation for all of us."

All of the good humor they had experienced over the past few minutes was gone. Cydney sensed hardness and borderline hostility from him and struggled not to be offended by it.

"I will give you all of the cooperation you require," she said steadily. "But if this is so serious, then why doesn't the FBI have more men on the case?"

His dark eyes remained hard a moment longer before oddly easing. "We will," he assured her. "Starting Thursday, we're going to have about a dozen agents on the grounds, watching every move. You'll never see them, of course. They'll blend in like ordinary visitors so if something goes down we'll be able to get a handle on it quickly."

"Why didn't you tell me any of this before?"

"Because I was sent to scope this out and based upon my report as of today, the FBI is going to be heavily involved." He jerked his head in the direction of the galleries above him. "No offense, Mrs. Hetherington, but your little museum isn't built to withstand an attack from Boy Scouts much less people who really want to do some damage. I think you need help and that's exactly what I'm going to tell my superiors."

She sighed, half-insulted, half in agreement. "What about my security people?" she wanted to know. "I told you last night that they're mostly retirees and college students. I don't want anyone getting hurt."

"No one will if they do what I tell them," he told her. "I'll be here Thursday morning before the galleries open to brief your people."

"And Stu?" she asked. "He can handle a gun. Should he be packing a weapon?"

Ethan shook his head. "No, definitely not," he replied. "Someone might mistake him for a bad guy. Remember that my people will only know their fellow agents. They won't have any idea who some big guy with a gun is and he might get hurt."

Cydney nodded silently. She was beginning to feel like the situation was slipping out of her hands and she didn't like it one bit. She was protective of her employees and Serreaux threatened to take that control away. Without anything more to say, she simply nodded and lowered her gaze, pretending to focus on her desk, her computer, anything to avoid looking at him. She found herself wishing he would just go away.

"Thank you for your honesty, Special Agent Serreaux," she said, although she didn't sound like she meant it. "As I said, you will have the museum's full cooperation."

She was ending the conversation but Ethan wasn't going anywhere. He watched her fidget with her desk, a pen, pretending to be busy when he knew very well that she wasn't. He thought that perhaps she needed some time alone to digest everything he had told her. He dutifully rose from the chair and collected his suit coat.

"If you have any other questions, I'll be around here most of the day observing the layout," he told her, digging in his pocket to produce a business card. He laid it on her desk. "My cellular phone number is on the card. You can call me."

She passed a glance at the card. "Cell phones don't work in this building. No reception."

"Keep it anyway." He put his coat on and moved to the door. "Thanks for your time, Mrs. Hetherington."

"Stop calling me that," Cydney suddenly burst, embarrassed as the words left her mouth. She tried not to look sheepish as she recovered. "I... just Cydney will do."

Ethan paused at the door. "Sorry," he said. "I didn't mean to offend you. Mr. Hemeshuk called you Mrs. Hetherington. Isn't that your name?"

Cydney was feeling irritated, disoriented, wishing fervently that he would just leave. He had her rattled and her defenses weren't as strong as they usually were. She found herself speaking before she could stop herself.

"Not anymore," she muttered, logging on to her email in an attempt to busy herself. "You can call me Cydney and just leave it at that."

Ethan knew it wasn't his business to follow up on her comment. The way she said it had a painful ring to it. *Must be a divorce,* he thought to himself, *but what idiot would divorce a woman like that?* With a lingering glance at her blond head, he left her office and quietly closed the door behind him.

When Cydney was positive he was gone, she lowered her head and struggled not to cry.

THREE

"MOM!" Olivia was dancing around in Cydney's office. "Come on. What are you doing?"

Cydney was finishing an email to a museum patron, an elderly gentleman who visited almost daily and had unofficially adopted Cydney as his next wife. Somehow he had gotten her email address and sent her notes constantly. Everyone laughed about it but Cydney had to be careful about how she handled the man, considering he donated tens of thousands of dollars to the museum every year. She didn't want to tick off a source of revenue.

"Coming," she replied, hitting the "send" button. Standing up, she put her hands on her hips and watched her daughter wriggle uncontrollably. "Good lord, Liv. You act like you're going backstage at a concert."

Olivia didn't have time for her mother's delays. She grabbed the woman by the hand and began to yank her from her office.

"Mrs. Marquez is waiting in the car in the parking lot," she told her mom. "I told her that I would only be a half hour."

"And that's another thing," Cydney said as she followed her daughter into the cold hallway. "I can't believe you coerced that sweet old woman to drive all the way over here. She does enough just picking you up from school."

Olivia apparently didn't have the same concern her mother did. "Mrs. Marquez has no kids and no life. She doesn't mind driving me over here."

Cydney pursed her lips in disapproval. "Little did my unsuspecting neighbor know when I asked her to pick you up from school that she was reducing herself to a life of servitude to a selfish young girl."

"You said I could see the robe today."

"Yes, I did, but I didn't say hijack the neighbor's car to get here."

"How else was I supposed to get here?"

"That's not the point."

"Can I come see it tomorrow at the grand opening, too?"

Cydney just growled at her. Olivia pulled her mother the length of the cold, cement hallway to the elevator that led up to the galleries. Olivia pushed the "Up" button about a dozen times before the door finally creaked open, admitting the excited girl and her mother. Olivia twitched and fidgeted until the elevator opened again and spit them both out into the main gallery.

Olivia knew the museum layout like the back of her hand. She had been coming to her mother's work since she was very young, at a time when she considered it very boring. Now was not the case. When she looked at her mother eagerly, Cydney pointed in the direction of the west gallery and Olivia was off like a shot.

The western gallery was the largest gallery in the building, painted in a muted gold tone with a dramatic plaster ceiling and specially-coated skylights that blocked the UV rays to protect the artwork. Olivia walked, very quickly, into the gallery, to the far end where the Resurrection exhibit was set up. She was so excited that she wasn't paying attention to where she was going. Abruptly rounding a corner, she plowed into Ethan Serreaux.

He was just exiting the gallery after having done a final walk-through of analysis and logistics. When she bounced off of him, he grabbed her quickly so she wouldn't fall back against something priceless.

"Whoa, there," he peered down at the young lady, now rubbing her smashed nose. "Are you all right?"

Olivia cast him an annoyed look. "I'm fine," she mumbled. "Sorry."

He let go of her, his dark eyes moving over her fine-featured face. "You're Cydney Hetherington's daughter, aren't you?"

Olivia nodded. "How did you know that?"

"Because I saw you last night at your house."

"Oh." Olivia was surprised he recognized her. He had only caught a fleeting glimpse of her before she had bolted into hiding. She stopped rubbing her nose long enough to study him. "I remember you, too. You're the FBI guy."

"That's right."

"Are you really with the FBI?"

He gave her a half-grin. "Don't you believe me? Do you think I just walk around at night giving women that line and hope they'll let me into their home?"

She snorted. "No," she said almost mockingly. "I've just never met anyone who works for the FBI. I have been thinking about joining when I get out of college."

His dark eyebrows lifted. "Is that so?" He crossed his big arms thoughtfully. "What college are you planning on attending?"

"Which one did you attend?"

"University of Michigan."

She lost some of her smug expression. "Really?" She was

genuinely interested. "I have been thinking about the University of Michigan. But I really want to go to Harvard."

He wriggled his eyebrows. "I hope your grades are good."

Now she was insulted. "I graduated Valedictorian of my eighth grade," she flatly informed him. "And I have gotten straight A's ever since. I'm taking two AP classes right now."

"What grade are you in?"

"I'm a sophomore."

"Wow," he stroked his chin. "You must really be smart."

"I passed the high school exit exam on the first try with a perfect score."

He emitted a soft whistle between his teeth. "Then the University of Michigan isn't good enough. Harvard and Yale will be battling it out to see who gets you."

That brought back her grin. "Do you really think so? I want to double-major in International Relations and Law."

"She wants to double-major in International Relations and Law so when she takes over the world, no one can sue her." Cydney came upon their conversation, smiling at her daughter as the girl turned to her. "Trying to pull Agent Serreaux into your plot of world domination?"

Olivia shook her head. "He went to the University of Michigan. I'm thinking about going there, too."

As Cydney nodded, Ethan spoke up. "It sounds like you won't have any trouble getting into any college you want."

"I hope not," Olivia replied. She seemed to be more and more drawn to him as the seconds passed, interested in this man who was all of the things she was aspiring to be. "What was your major?"

"Political Science. Then I got my law degree at Stanford."

"Really?" Olivia's face lit up. "So you're a lawyer?"

Ethan grinned modestly, looking between Olivia and her

mother. "I'm registered with the California and New York Bar Associations, but I don't practice."

"Did you think about going to any other colleges?" Olivia pressed. "I've been looking at colleges overseas, too. Like Oxford."

Ethan nodded. "Great school," he said. "I did a semester at the University of York, another great school. Great city, actually."

Olivia was enthralled by the thought of an exotic international college. "Did you like England?"

"Loved it. Made some great friends there. Some of them American, if you can believe it."

"But you came home?"

He nodded. "I did," he said. "England was great, but I like America. Plus, I love what I do and my family is here, so it made sense."

Cydney was observing the conversation. He seemed genuinely friendly towards Olivia and that oddly touched her. Other than her grandfathers, uncle and, on occasion, Stu, Olivia didn't have much opportunity to speak or interact with men, mostly because Cydney was so protective over her only child. But the conversation with Ethan seemed harmless enough.

"Lucky for the FBI that you picked them over a lucrative law practice," she raised her eyebrows at Ethan, a twinkle in her eye. Then she put her hand on Olivia's shoulder and tried to shove the girl past Serreaux. "I thought you wanted to see the exhibit. You can't keep Mrs. Marquez waiting in the parking lot forever."

"Okay, okay." Olivia wouldn't be pushed away so easily; she was still gazing up at Ethan's handsome face. "Would you tell me sometime how you got into college and went into the FBI? I'd like to know how you did it."

Ethan shrugged easily. "Sure, anytime."

Cydney was still pushing, trying to move her daughter into the gallery she had been so fired up to see. But she paused long enough to give Ethan a now-you've-done-it expression.

"She's on to your scent now," she told him. "You'll never get rid of her. It's like feeding a cat. She'll make you tell her everything until she's sucked your brain dry."

Ethan laughed and turned to follow them. He had actually been heading out to make a phone call but quickly decided the phone call to the West Los Angeles FBI office could wait. Cydney and her daughter, at the moment, had his attention cornered.

"I have nephew like that," he told Cydney as they entered the main part of the gallery. "The kid wants to know everything about life and he wants to know it right now. He's four going on forty."

Cydney grinned at him as Olivia suddenly remembered what had lured her to the gallery in the first place and very quickly picked up the pace, leaving Cydney walking behind with Serreaux.

When Cydney realized they were alone again, the unsettling feeling from their earlier conversation returned. More than that, she realized she was somewhat nervous to be around him.

"In my family, it's just Olivia." She tried to focus on his statement to keep her mind off her jiggling nerves. "She's the only grandchild. I have a younger brother and he doesn't have any children yet, much to my mother's disappointment."

"How old is he?"

"Thirty-four."

"Give him time." Ethan watched Olivia plant herself in front of The Lucius Robe case. "He's still young."

Cydney pursed her lips. "You don't know my mother," she snorted. "She came from a big family. She could never understand why Brad and I only had one child. Honestly, it was just because we were both so busy with school and careers. Then when Brad passed, my mother only gave me a year before she was harping on me about remarrying again and having more...."

She abruptly stopped, realizing she had divulged far more information than she was comfortable doing. It had all come spilling out. Awkwardly, she cleared her throat and struggled not to feel like a complete idiot.

"Anyway," she cleared her throat again. "I'm sorry; I didn't mean to get into anything heavy. Just... well, thanks for being so kind to my daughter. I appreciate it."

Ethan was gazing down at her, his dark eyes riveted to her. There was an odd expression on his face, a mixture of appreciation, sympathy and interest. When Cydney finally dared to look up at him, she was struck by his countenance.

"When did your husband pass?" he asked gently.

Staring into his deep brown eyes, she couldn't have pulled herself away from him if she tried. She didn't want to talk about Brad but it came out anyway.

"Eight years ago," she told him. "Car accident."

He sighed faintly. "Wow," he said. "I'm really sorry. I'm also sorry if I stirred up any feelings earlier by calling you Mrs. Hetherington. I didn't mean to."

She waved him off, struggling against the intense emotion the man seemed to provoke. "Don't worry about it," she said, thinking now would be a very good time to go and join Olivia. "I shouldn't be so touchy, but... well, if it makes any sense, my husband used to call me Mrs. Hetherington. It was like a nickname and... and, anyway, don't worry about it. Calling me Cydney will be just fine."

Ethan smiled warmly at her, the first time he had done so since their association. "Whatever you want, Cydney."

Giving him a somewhat awkward grin, she joined her daughter by The Lucius Robe case. Ethan watched her walk away, thinking she filled out the faux-suede skirt quite nicely. In fact, she filled out all of her clothing quite nicely. She was an incredibly beautiful woman. With just the brief conversations he had with her, he was coming to understand her a little and liking it so far.

"Hey," Agent Lowell was suddenly beside him, nudging him in the arm. "Dickerson just called me. He said you're not picking up your phone."

Ethan's gaze lingered on Cydney a moment longer before moving to take his cell phone out of his pocket. He looked at the display with the missed call and shrugged.

"No reception in these thick walls," he replied. "I was just heading outside to call him."

Lowell hadn't missed the look that Ethan gave Cydney. He'd been doing it for the better part of the day. In fact, the man was still looking at her and Lowell grunted.

"Hey," he bobbed his head in Cydney's direction. "What's the deal?"

Ethan looked at him. "What deal?"

"With Hetherington."

Ethan's brow furrowed. "No deal," he shook his head, heading back towards the front door to the museum as if suddenly anxious to get out of there. "I'll be right back."

Lowell didn't believe him for a minute, on either account.

———

"The chatter has died down and that's very concerning on many different levels."

John David Dickerson had been a terrorist expert with the Federal Bureau of Investigation for fifteen years. A good-looking African-American in his late thirties, he had first been interested in international intelligence when he had watched sixty-six Americans being released from the Iranian Embassy in nine-teen eighty-one. The whole incident had captured his interest and carried on even now. He was one of the best in the business in isolating and identifying terrorist threats, specializing in obscure religious sects and extremists. The threat to the Western Pacific Museum of Art and Antiquities had been iden-tified and developed by J.D. Dickerson and he had a very strong interest in the situation on a minute to minute basis.

On the other end of the line, Ethan was trying to move to an area of the park-like entry of the museum that didn't have quite so much street noise.

"Why is that?" he asked.

At his desk in West Los Angeles, J.D. kicked back in his chair. "Because it probably means they already have their plan set. It means they are organized and have shut down any further discussion. I don't like it."

"So what are we expecting?"

"I'm not sure," Dickerson dug into his bowl of M&M's and popped a candy into his mouth. "We've already been through the briefing for this; this group has been known to do fairly sophisticated stuff in Europe, political assassinations and stuff like that. It always seems to be well organized and financed. Remember that they've been around for at least fifty years that we can deduce, ever since the end of World War II. But we think that was just the emergence; evidence suggests the group has secretly been around for centuries. It was the Nazis that brought them out into the open. Three of their leaders are descended from documented Nazi families but, more impor-tantly, they have very powerful support. They have connections both financially and within the political world that most radicals couldn't dream of."

"And we have no idea who the connections are?"

"None," J.D. went on. "They keep the identity of their

leader very well hidden but if I had to guess, I'd say it was someone of extreme political or even religious power. This group is too well-supported for their leader not to be someone of tremendous importance. Anyway, there's been a lot of chatter from this group about The Lucius Robe and the fact that it's in a relatively unprotected place. They have been deeply interested in it for about six months. To that end, I would expect something sudden and violent; maybe even an armed incursion. They've made it obvious that they want it."

"And we've determined these guys aren't your run-of-the-mill skinheads?"

"Not at all. They're smarter and better financed. Like I said, they've got money and people coming out of their asses but we can't figure out where it's coming from."

Ethan inhaled slowly. "I'll tell you, this place just isn't set up to handle an organized assault. It's even worse than we initially thought. Old people and college students comprise their security force, plus they've got big, unreinforced, plate glass windows, unreinforced skylights...."

"Exactly, which is why I recommended shutting the museum down."

"And I told you that I suggested that to Mr. Hemeshuk but he said they couldn't afford it. He said that they had pre-sold a lot of tickets to this exhibit and was determined to see it through."

J.D. snorted. "So it's all about the money. That's just great."

Ethan couldn't disagree at the sarcasm. "I'll need to have a meeting with the FBI team tomorrow morning before I go in and brief the museum's regular security force," he said. "I've set up the observation posts and need to give everyone their assignments before the regular museum personnel go on duty."

"So that's it?"

"That's what we've got to work with."

J.D. grunted. "All right," he said begrudgingly. "I'll be there, too.'"

Ethan smirked. "You're coming? Since when do you do field assignments?"

"Since this one might turn out to be a pretty damn big one." J.D.'s feet came off the desk. "Besides, it's the best place for me. Right in the middle of it."

Ethan's grin broke through. "J.D., I've known you for nine years. You're an analyst. You spend most of your time deciphering intelligence and bossing the rest of us around. You have never, in all the time I've known you, come out into the field."

J.D. lifted a dark brow. "And I'm going to come out in to the field and kick your ass if you don't shut up. I'm not so old that I can't take you down, Serreaux."

Ethan laughed. "You couldn't take me down even when you had the chance."

J.D.'s eyebrows rose as he pretended to be outraged. "I see how it is," he snarled. "You just couldn't let it go. You had to bring that up."

Ethan was laughing harder. "It wasn't my team that got its butt whipped in the '93 Rose Bowl. I seem to distinctly remember running through your defensive line to score a touchdown. So, clearly, you can't take me down."

"If I'd known back then that I'd be working with you today, I would have broken your legs."

"You'd have to catch me first and we know that's not going to happen."

"I'm driving over there right now to take your smug-ass down."

Ethan hooted. "No, don't do that," he said. "I apologize. I don't want an ex-linebacker after me."

"Too late. If we survive the museum opening, it's on between you and me."

Ethan shook his head. J.D. had always been sensitive about the '93 Rose Bowl when Ethan's team had beaten the Washington Huskies, J.D.'s alma mater.

Ethan and J.D. hadn't known each other back then. J.D. had been a linebacker in that game; Ethan had been a wide receiver because at six foot four and a half inches, he had the triple-whammy advantage of height, a long wingspan and astonishing speed. He had also been a big boy to boot at around two hundred thirty pounds; an offensive coach's dream. He'd been Homecoming King in high school, Class President, team captain and every other accolade that could be bestowed upon him for his good looks, athletic prowess, academic achievements and good character. He'd had a full ride to the University of Michigan and a month after graduating from college, he had returned home to marry his high school sweetheart. She had rewarded him a few years later by divorcing him and taking their son three thousand miles away.

It was something Ethan didn't think about as much as he used to. He'd just put it from his mind. As he listened to J.D. rant about the slow and painful death he had planned for him, Ethan found himself remembering those college days and not particularly missing them.

"The museum opens at ten," he interrupted J.D.'s bullying. "Employees arrive by nine, so I will want to brief them as soon as they arrive. What time will you be here?"

"I'll be there at seven a.m. with the rest of the team," J.D. was successfully diverted. "We'll want to walk the galleries and property perimeter."

"Already done," Ethan told him. "I'll take you around and show you what I feel would be the best solutions."

"Good enough," J.D. replied. "Can we get access at seven a.m.?"

Ethan immediately thought of Cydney, the Director of

Operations who he would undoubtedly be working more closely with by virtue of the sheer nature of the assignment. The thought did not distress him.

"I think so," he replied. "I'll get back to you on that."

"The sooner the better. I have to let everyone know."

"Understood."

"Do you want to watch the Lakers tonight at Mahoney's?"

He was referring to the bar they all hung out at in Westwood. It had become their department's home away from home and they spent more time there than they probably should have. But Ethan shook his head.

"Not tonight," he replied. "I think I might just go home and crash. Long day tomorrow."

"All right." J.D. stood up from his chair, ready to end the call. "Let me know about early morning access."

"You got it."

Ethan hung up the phone, heading back inside the museum to track down a certain Director of Operations.

FOUR

HER NAME WAS Coral Chastity Aames.

The woman was a world-famous televangelist, complete with a pink-hued blond hair, heavy makeup and gaudy clothing. She had hour-long programs every Sunday from her church in Costa Mesa, California, where she did everything from tell jokes to perform what she claimed to be miracles. The blind were made to see, the crippled to walk, and she would weep dramatically through the entire program as if her husband had just left her. She was a boil on the butt of God-fearing Christians but, for some reason, the woman made millions and people flocked to her. It was this woman who was the very first in line when the museum doors opened on Thursday morning.

Dressed in a navy blue sheath dress with matching pumps and looking particularly sharp, Cydney was up in the gallery when security personnel finally opened the doors. There was quite a crowd outside and thanks to Stu's logistical planning, the museum was prepared. People gave their tickets and were immediately funneled into a chute to await their turn to enter the gallery and inspect the collection. Cydney caught sight of Coral Chastity Aames at the head of the queue and, after a moment's surprise, shook her head in resignation. So it was going to be that kind of a day.

Cydney had made the decision a few weeks prior to stick with the maximum capacity of the gallery, which was limited to two hundred thirty people at any given time. They weren't going to try and cram any more in because they didn't want the Fire Marshall to shut them down, so security personnel kept close tabs on how many entered the gallery and how may left.

The Resurrection exhibit was ready for prime time. Spotlights blasted their brilliance upon the case containing The Lucius Robe while strategic lighting and paint color lent ambiance and mystery to the rest of the relics. Cydney was standing with Stu just inside the gallery entrance when Coral Chastity Aames was finally admitted entrance into the gallery. The woman in the bright pink and white jumpsuit went straight to the case containing The Lucius Robe.

"Oh," she held up her quivering hands, wanting to touch the Plexiglas but not wanting to get in trouble for it. "Lord Jesus, we praise you for your sacrifice at the cross. Glory to God! Sweet Jesus!"

Cydney and Stu couldn't help but stare at the woman as she began to pray loudly in front of the case. People around her looked rather uncertain but she didn't seem to create any real disturbance. It was just odd and, frankly, comical the way the woman carried on. It was quite a show.

"Do you want me to run her off?" Stu leaned close to Cydney's ear. He was dressed in a crisp black suit and red tie and looked like an undertaker. "We can't have that kind of disruption in the gallery. Milt will have a fit."

Cydney shrugged lamely. "She's really not doing anything," she whispered at him. "Maybe she'll just pray for a couple of minutes and leave."

Stu snorted. "Have you seen her?" he griped. "She weeps

and carries on for hours. I went to a church retreat once where we studied her for an entire day. Man, the things that woman is in to. You'd be surprised. She's one giant bundle of menopausal hysteria."

Cydney giggled and looked at him. "What would you know about menopausal hysteria?"

He pursed his lips irritably at her. "Lots. My mother has it all the time."

As Cydney continued to snicker, Coral Chastity Aames continued to pray. Anne-Michelle entered the gallery, her brown eyes wide at the performance going on in front of The Lucius Robe as she made her way over to Cydney and Stu. By the time she reached them, she was pointing a slender finger at the spectacle.

"I've seen that lady on television," she hissed. "What's her name?"

"Coral Chastity Aames," Cydney said. "She has that big yellow-painted church in Costa Mesa."

"Oh, right." Anne-Michelle crossed her arms, still watching the display. After a moment, she lifted her eyebrows at all of the crying going on and looked at Cydney. "Other than the religious hysteria, is everything okay so far? Milt wants a report."

Cydney shook her head. "The gallery has only been open ten minutes. Tell Milt that the entire terrorist world has not come crashing down upon us. At least, not yet."

Anne-Michelle grinned. "Where are all the FBI guys?"

Cydney began looking around. "To tell you the truth, I'm not really sure," she admitted. "I just saw three of them this morning when they briefed our security people. The rest, as I understand it, are mingling with the crowd. Plus, there are four of them walking the property perimeter with dogs. I saw them out in the parking lot this morning."

"All right," Anne-Michelle said as she cast a lingering gaze at the televangelist. "I wonder if I should mention that woman to Milt."

Cydney shook her head. "No, don't," she said. "He'll come racing up here and create a big scene. Just leave it alone. She won't be here too much longer."

With a grin, Anne-Michelle left the gallery to report her findings. Stu grumbled something undeniably unkind and went about his business, checking on his people throughout the gallery and heading for the ticket-takers at the entrance. Cydney continued to stand there, observing the crowd and finding a few familiar faces of regular museum patrons, when a figure was suddenly beside her. Startled, she found herself looking into a Dali-like canvas of black mascara and blue eye shadow.

"Excuse me." Coral Chastity Aames was standing next to her. "Do you work here?"

Cydney tried not to stare at the garish makeup. "Yes, I do."

"What do you do?"

"I'm the Director of Operations. My name is Cydney Hetherington. How can I help you?"

"Miss Hetherington," Coral extended a hand with two inch long red nails. "My name is Coral Chastity Aames. I'm an evangelist from Costa Mesa."

Cydney took the woman's hand and shook it. "I know who you are," she said. "It was nice of you to come."

Coral's big blue eyes welled with tears again. "I would not have missed this for the world," she sniffed. "To think that the robe in that case was actually the robe worn by Christ during his trial before Pilate is simply overwhelming. I am overcome with joy and glory."

Cydney smiled weakly. "Well, I'm glad you enjoyed it."

Coral grasped Cydney's wrist, raking her with the red nails. "But it's more than enjoyment. It's... it's everything a Christian prays for; a great holy relic to support our faith. Did you have the opportunity to touch it, Miss Hetherington?"

Cydney shook her head, discreetly removing her wrist from the woman's grip. "No, I didn't," she answered. "It came to us sealed up in the box. We're not allowed to open it."

Coral's raccoon-eyed gaze moved to the case several dozen feet away. "You're not allowed to open it at all?"

"I'm afraid not. The Bristol Museum was quite specific. They're afraid that exposure to the air and pollutants will damage it."

Coral gazed at the acrylic case as if seeing something that the rest of them couldn't see. She was staring at it with unnatural intensity. But Cydney didn't notice the odd gleam or the way her eyelid twitched with tension. Everything about the woman was odd so one more bizarre ingredient didn't make a difference. Finally, the woman looked back to Cydney and dabbed at her wet eyes.

"How unfortunate," she said quietly. "I was hoping... well, I was hoping that you would allow me to inspect it outside of the case."

It was a bold request, something that rubbed Cydney the wrong way. She didn't like pushy people and she could tell, just by that statement, that Coral Chastity Aames expected special treatment from the rest of the adoring masses.

"No one can touch it," she repeated. "But we're glad you were able to come and see it on opening day. We've had quite a lot of buzz about it."

Coral stared at Cydney a moment before breaking into a plastic-looking smile. "You're sure I can't touch it?"

"Very sure."

"Then I thank you, Miss Hetherington," she said politely. "I appreciate your time."

Cydney merely nodded and the woman headed off towards

the entrance. Cydney watched her until she reached the door before refocusing her attention on the gallery again. She didn't think twice about the woman or her aggressive request. It was just another visitor on an unusually busy day.

Out in the sunny parking lot, Coral removed her cell phone from her purse and hit the speed dial. Putting it to her ear, she was almost to her car by the time the other end answered.

"I didn't see Joseph but I think I have a brilliant idea." She forewent any greeting and went straight to the point. "Look up the name Cydney Hetherington. See if you can get an address. Then I want you to call Joseph and tell him to seek her out." There was a pause. "Because she has access that a security guard wouldn't. Perhaps if properly persuaded, she would agree to our wishes. More than that, I want to know where the woman lives. Perhaps she has family, if you know what I mean." Another pause. "All right, let me know. We're very close now and I'll leave nothing to chance."

She shut off the call and climbed into her white Mercedes E Class. Driving out of the parking lot, she headed towards the freeway.

———

Joseph was positioned in another area of the museum on his first day on the job. Most of the experienced guards were in the gallery where the Resurrection exhibit was being held, leaving the very old and the very new guards stationed in other galleries.

Dressed in his maroon blazer with a navy and maroon striped tie, just like everyone else, he was disgruntled at not being stationed in the big exhibit. But he stood dutifully in the corner of the East Asian exhibit, watching a few people trickle in and examine the sculptures. Unfortunately, from this position, he was unable to see any of his colleagues as they came to view the robe. Down in the lower floor of the museum, he was both hidden and blind.

He began to pace around the room, pretending to watch the few patrons that were there, but mostly he was just trying to figure out how he could get moved into the main gallery upstairs. Granted, he was new and hadn't had the experience of most of the other security personnel, but he was young and bright and figured that those attributes would work in his favor. Moreover, there was a bigger issue that no one but him was aware of; the FBI had made their presence known and he was anxious to see what they were up to in the gallery above.

A Special Agent had briefed security personnel before the museum opened to generically inform them that there were potential threats directed at the controversial relic and to be alert. Joseph had sat through the speech like everyone else, pretending to care when what he really wanted to do was laugh. He knew that there were no plans that he was aware of for any type of activity today or even in the next few days.

Their plan was still taking shape. The biggest factor in that plan to date had been to get Joseph a job at the museum where he would have a global picture of the robe and learn the intricacies of the security surrounding it. Based on his observations, *Die Auhänger* would plan their next move. There were just a few of them, anyway. The majority of the group was overseas, waiting. Much rested on the California cell and there was a significant amount of pressure.

Two hours into his shift, an old woman with bad dentures and black orthopedic shoes relieved him for his break. Joseph found his way to the employee lounge in the underbelly of the museum but he very soon realized that he had no cell phone reception. Wandering his way out through the main offices, he went out into the employee parking lot.

Reception was better in the open and he saw that he already

had two missed calls. Both were from Nat. He hit redial and held the phone to his ear.

"So," Nat picked it up on the second ring, recognizing the incoming number and foregoing any greeting. "How is your first day?"

"Uneventful," Joseph replied. "But we may have a problem."

"What's that?"

"The FBI is here."

There was a slight pause. "Are you sure?"

"Absolutely. There were at least three agents here this morning."

"How much do they know?"

Joseph shook his head. "I have no idea. An agent spoke to the security guards this morning before we went on duty to let us know that there had been threats directed at the robe and to be on the alert. Beyond that, I have no idea what they know. But if they are here, then it must be something fairly significant."

"Possibly," Nat said, trying not to sound like an alarmist. He changed the subject. "She was there this morning, by the way."

"She?" The statement didn't register with Joseph for moment. Then realization dawned. "Oh, right," he replied. "I didn't see her. I have been assigned to the East Asian exhibit down in the bowels of the museum."

"That's not good," Nat pointed out. "We need you in the main exhibit hall."

"I know. What did she say? Anything of use? Damn, I don't have eyes or ears anywhere near the exhibit."

"She did mention something useful, in fact," Nat said. "Do you know who Cydney Hetherington is?"

Joseph shook his head slowly. "No, I...," he paused. "Wait a minute. I've heard the name. I think she's an exhibit

68 KAT LE VEQUE

manager or something. There was a woman at the security briefing this morning. It might have been her. What about her?"

"I'm told she is the Director of Operations and that you need to get to know her," the man replied. "She could be very useful."

Joseph wasn't sure he liked the sound of that. "What do you mean?"

"She has access to the robe, Joe," Nat explained quietly. "Perhaps if you were to come to know her, it might make this endeavor considerably... easier."

"How do you want me to know her? Do you want me to date her? Sleep with her? Marry her?"

"I think a romantic acquaintance might do. You're a good-looking guy, use your charm. See where it takes you."

"So you want me to prostitute myself."

"That's a little harsh but, yes, essentially."

Joseph thought back to the woman that morning at the security briefing. She was a beautiful woman with long, layered blond hair and big hazel eyes. If that was Cydney Hetherington, then he was okay with the directive. It could prove a more pleasant part of this entire undertaking although he was more reluctant than he was interested. Unfortunately, he just didn't have the win-at-all-costs instincts like his comrades did. What he did, he did because his family demanded it; nothing more, nothing less.

"All right," he said after a moment. "I'll see what I can do."

"Good," Nat said. "Meanwhile, we've found an address for her. She lives in Arcadia, about fifteen miles from the museum. I'm heading over there now."

"What are you going to do?"

Nat laughed. "I'm not sure yet."

Joseph didn't like the sound of that, either.

———

Ethan and J.D. were on the roof of the museum. They saw the woman in the bright pink pantsuit leave just as they saw many other people come and go. There was nothing unusual about anyone's actions so far. But there was quite a crowd lining up to get into the museum so they kept an eye on the masses as they gathered around the well-pruned juniper trees in the entry. Above them, the Southern California sky was already heating up and the old roof was becoming increasingly hot.

J.D. was scanning the parking lot and nearby main boulevard with binoculars. He wore a dark pinstripe suit and expensive designer sunglasses. Ethan stood next to him in his standard dark gray suit, casually watching the crowd below. From the angle of the roof parapets, they could not be seen by the people milling about below. Two other agents roamed the roof, back in the shade where enormous eucalyptus trees grew around a lily pond that had been designed to look like a Monet painting.

As J.D. scanned, Ethan shifted on his long legs and unwound his arms.

"I'm going to head down to the main gallery to see what's going on down there," he said.

"All right." J.D. lowered the binoculars. "Talk to museum personnel. See if they have noticed anything unusual. They'll know the crowds better than we will."

Ethan nodded and went to the small spiral stairs that led into the attic of the museum. From there, a narrow staircase led down in an 'Employees Only' area near the elevator. Ethan removed his sunglasses and emerged into the main cupola area, heading towards the western gallery.

Already, he could see a roped-off queue area stuffed with eager patrons patiently waiting their turn to enter the gallery. As he continued on, the golden hues of the western gallery came into view and the magnificent relics of the Resurrection exhibit filled his field of vision. Strategic spotlights made it appear as if the light of God was shining down on all things holy and ancient. He passed lingering glances at the ankle bone with the spike through it and a tablet inscribed with Latin as he made his way down the gallery.

As he rounded a case that contained part of pillar from an ancient temple just outside of Jerusalem, his dark eyes came to rest on a woman in a navy dress that fit her body like a glove. He took a moment to appreciate the curve of her buttocks as they ascended into a narrow waist. The spiked pumps made her beautiful legs look even better. He was looking at her calves when she turned and caught sight of him.

Slightly embarrassed that he had been caught appraising her figure, Ethan smiled weakly as he drew close. Cydney smiled back.

"Mr. Serreaux," she greeted pleasantly. "What can I do for you?"

He stood just a few inches from her, his muscular height in sharp contrast to her petite curves.

"Don't call me Mr. Serreaux," he whispered for her ears only. "That's my dad."

She lifted an eyebrow at him. He was fairly close as he leaned down to talk to her and she found herself watching the way his mouth moved. "Sorry. I meant Agent Serreaux but I didn't want to say that too loud."

"It's Ethan," he informed her, "and you can tell me how it's going in here."

She shrugged and looked back over the crowd. "No problems whatsoever."

"Good." He looked over the crowd, too, but he really wanted to look at her. "Notice anything out of the ordinary?"

She shook her head. "Not a thing. Have you?"

He peered down at her. "Nope," he said. "But you might have a better idea of what is extraordinary around here than I would. Where's Mr. Longe?"

"He went to check on his personnel." She turned to him. "I'm thinking I might as well go back to my office. There doesn't seem to be any reason for me to be here. Everything is under control."

Ethan lifted his eyebrow as he scanned the crowd once more. "Give it a few more minutes. The museum has only been open an hour. Shouldn't it be busier as the day goes on?"

"Usually."

"Then why don't you walk with me and pretend we're just admiring the artwork when what we're really doing is checking out the crowd."

She looked at him with a grin. "I'm not security. I don't normally walk the floor checking on the crowd."

"Then how about if you just accompany me as I check them out?"

"Why?"

"Because I want to hear more about your genius daughter. And I'd like to hear more about you, too."

Cydney's grin faded as she stared up at him. Ethan's dark eyes glimmered warmly. As she realized what he meant, her first reaction was to refuse. She was almost outraged. But that reaction was tempered by genuine, delighted interest. Still, she'd been in self-preservation mode for so long that it was difficult to think otherwise.

"Uh...," she cleared her throat softly, suddenly unable to look at him. "I... I don't know. I think it's better if we keep our conversation strictly business related for now."

His heart sank a little but he nodded. "You're right," he tried to make it sound like it was no big deal. "I wasn't trying to suggest anything inappropriate. I apologize."

Cydney suddenly felt very bad for turning him down. She very much wanted to get to know him but she was torn. She hadn't even thought about another man since Brad was killed. But Ethan Serreaux had changed that from almost the moment she met him. After an awkward pause, she grasped his elbow.

"Come on," she said.

He noticed she was still holding on to him as she started to walk. "Where are we going?"

"To walk the gallery so you can check it for assassins."

Fighting off a grin, he followed.

They didn't say anything to each other for a few moments as they paced the massive gallery. Soft voices of thrilled museum visitors filled the air around them, but the air between them was silent. The dull sound of shoes hitting wood laminate floors was nearly the only audible resonance in their world.

"I was born and raised in Pasadena, California and I have a younger brother," Cydney finally said in a quiet voice. "I got married, had Olivia, went to California State University at Northridge, and received my degree in Civil Engineering."

He looked down at her. "You're a civil engineer?"

"Yes."

"Why did you choose that field?"

"Because I have a knack for math."

"You don't look like any engineer I've ever seen."

"Seen a lot of engineers, have you?"

Ethan grinned. "I just meant you're very pretty. I must not be very good at giving compliments if you didn't get that."

It had been a long time since she'd heard a compliment that she actually cared to hear and her cheeks flushed delicately. "You're doing okay," she said.

"Really?" He was enjoying the art of the gentle flirt. It had been ages since he'd played that game. "Are my pick up lines working?"

She laughed and shook her head, flushing brighter when he bent over and tried to look her in the eye.

"If that is an example of your pick up lines, then I think you're in trouble," she said, avoiding his grinning gaze. "I can tell you must not use them too often."

He shook his head. "No, not too often," his smile faded. "Not often at all. I'm a little rusty."

She looked up at him now that he wasn't trying to deliberately fix her in the eye. "Me, too," she admitted. "How long has it been for you?"

He lifted an eyebrow thoughtfully. "At least seven or eight years," he said. "To be honest, I really wouldn't want to date a woman who is a sucker for a pick up line."

Cydney clasped her hands behind her back as they neared the end of the massive gallery. "I know what you mean," she said. After a moment, she cast him a long look. "*Quid pro quo*, Agent Serreaux."

He looked at her, the smile returning to his face. "All right," he agreed. "I'll tell you something about me and you tell me something about you."

She paused at the end of the gallery, standing before the massive floor to ceiling windows that faced the serene Monet water garden beyond. Soft light filtered in around them as they stood a foot or so apart, inspecting one another. It was the first time they had openly done so.

"I've already told you about me," she said. "It's your turn."

He nodded in agreement. "Okay," he thought a moment. "I was born in Australia but grew up in Virginia, went to college at the University of Michigan and at Stanford, and have been employed with the FBI for thirteen years."

"You were born in Australia? You don't have an accent."

"I came to America when I was two years old. I never really had one."

"And your family?"

His smile faded slightly. "I have a mother, father and two younger brothers," he said. "I was also married years ago and I have a son who is fourteen."

"Really?" Cydney showed interest in the part about the son. "What's his name?"

"Tyler."

"What grade is he in?"

"Ninth."

"Does he go to school locally?"

Ethan shook his head. "He lives in Washington D.C. with his mother."

"Oh," Cydney sensed that Ethan wasn't particularly happy about that. His mood seemed to sink when discussing his son. "And you? Do you live locally?"

"Glendale; about ten miles west of the museum."

The sun was shining in through the coated windows, creating a glistening effect as the rays fell upon the wood floor. Ethan gazed at Cydney, watching the way her hair glittered in the muted light. The more he talked to her, the more he liked her. She was smart, witty and good at conversation. She was also extremely hot. He hadn't felt this much attraction to a woman since he first met his ex-wife and, even then, he wasn't sure he felt what he was feeling now. In all places and during the course of a job, he knew it wasn't entirely appropriate. But he really didn't care.

"I didn't find any assassins." He dipped his head in the direction of the gallery. "We have to walk back through just to be sure."

She gave him a very sweet smile and turned to retrace their steps. Enchanted, Ethan followed.

"I have to ask you this even though I'm pretty sure what the answer is," he ventured.

Cydney was walking with her hands behind her back, watching her navy pumps hit the floor. "What?"

"Are you seeing anyone?"

She looked up at him as if surprised by the question. "No."

"Would you like to?"

She came to a halt and stared at him. After a moment, her grin returned. "Your pick up lines are getting better."

"I've had a lot of practice in the past several minutes. Are they working yet?"

She laughed softly. "Maybe."

She had a beautiful smile, one he found extremely alluring. "What more can I say to close this deal?" he asked quietly.

She continued to laugh. "Deal, is it? Don't you think that whatever happens ought to happen without high-pressure sales?"

He gave her a lopsided grin. "Absolutely. Sorry, I got carried away."

Her hazel eyes twinkled as she gazed up at him. "No harm done."

"I hope not." His dark eyes were riveted to her. "Maybe we can discuss it over dinner if that would make it easier for you."

Her smile, the laughter, continued. "You're certainly persistent."

He scratched his head. "I'm not sure how else to be," he admitted. "This doesn't happen to me very often."

"What's that?"

His expression made her heart leap. "Meeting a woman I'd like to get to know."

It had been years since she had been out to dinner with a man who wasn't her husband, brother or father. The thought was thrilling and a little intimidating. Ethan Serreaux was succeeding in charming the socks off of her and she was a little frightened to think what the man could talk her in to if she had a couple of drinks in her. Thoughts of self-preservation were still there but they were fading fast. A greater part of her was ready to move on with her life under the right circumstances so she threw caution to the wind.

"All right," she agreed. "Provided those assassins you are on the lookout for don't strike, I think we could do dinner."

A smile of genuine pleasure spread across his face. "Good."

They resumed walking through the gallery. Ethan couldn't ever remember feeling so light of heart. He almost felt giddy. It had been years since he had experienced such joy. Every few steps he would look at Cydney, who would look back at him, and they would both grin like fools.

He never did find any assassins.

———

Olivia missed her usual three o'clock call. Cydney had been in her office for a couple of hours, trying to finish up some paperwork, and she called her daughter three times between three and three-thirty. She called twice on the house phone and once on the cell phone. There was no answer. She wanted to tell Olivia that she was going to be late because Ethan had talked her into dinner that night. But when Olivia still wasn't picking up the phone by four-thirty, Cydney called Mrs. Marquez.

Mrs. Marquez was the neighbor that lived down the street and picked Olivia up from school daily. Mrs. Marquez wasn't answering her phone, either, and the woman didn't own a cell phone, so as the clock neared five, Cydney went in search of Ethan.

She found him up in the main gallery with Stu. Surprisingly, Stu didn't seem to be posturing like a territorial caveman and actually seemed to be holding a decent conversation with the agent. When she approached them as the security personnel were ushering the last museum visitors from the gallery, both men turned to her with a smile.

"Hey, Cyd," Stu greeted her pleasantly. "Another day and no crazy zealots messing up our museum. I'd say that's a good day."

Cydney laughed. "It's always a good day when everything remains intact," she agreed. "We okay for the night?"

Stu nodded, his attention moving to the guards who had just shut the main doors behind the last visitor. There were four guards, all over seventy years of age and, as he watched, two of them wrestled with the massive doors. Stu sighed.

"We're fine" he said. "I'm going to check the doors myself."

"Go get 'em, Stu."

He smirked as he walked off and left Ethan and Cydney standing alone. The sun was setting outside and the ambient light in the museum was growing dim, giving it a rather romantic feel. Art, culture and two people standing alone. Ethan turned to Cydney before she could speak.

"Ready to go?" he asked.

She made a face. "You're going to think I'm paranoid, but I haven't been able to get a hold of my daughter all afternoon," she said. "She is supposed to call me every day when she gets home from school but she didn't today and I can't get a hold of her. I want to run home just to make sure everything is okay."

He gave her a gently reproving look. "I don't think you're paranoid. I think you're an attentive mother. What if I follow you home and then take you and Olivia out to eat?"

It was a sweet offer and Cydney smiled gratefully. "You don't need to do that. Olivia only eats macaroni and cheese and garlic bread, anyway."

"Then we'll find a place that has macaroni and cheese on the menu." He put his hand on her back and turned her in the direction of the elevator. "Come on, let's get out of here."

They were almost to the elevator when J.D. and Agent Lowell entered the gallery from the employee-only area. They had been up on the roof and had secured it for the night. J.D. was still carrying his binoculars and James had a flashlight.

"All secure down here?" J.D. asked Ethan but his eyes were on Cydney.

"Just locking up for the night," Ethan noticed where J.D.'s attention was. "J.D., you met Cydney Hetherington this morning, right?"

J.D. nodded. "Yes, I did, in passing," he shook her hand. "Good to see you again."

"Likewise," Cydney removed her hand. "Thanks for keeping our collection and people safe."

J.D. wriggled his eyebrows. "Well, hopefully it will remain calm for the duration of the exhibit," he said. "How long will it be on display again?"

"Four months."

J.D. made a face. "Terrific. Then you'd better get used to seeing us around for the next four months."

Cydney didn't dare look at Ethan. She didn't think four months with the FBI was a bad thing at all. "I guess it's the price we have to pay," she sighed with feigned drama.

J.D. agreed without much enthusiasm while Ethan wasn't horrendously disappointed at the thought, either. However, when he tried to accompany Cydney down to her office, J.D. stopped him.

"Ethan, we need to go over a few things," he said. "I need you to stick around up here."

Ethan let Cydney get on to the elevator without him. "Sure," he said to J.D., then turned to Cydney. "I'll see you at your house, all right?"

She nodded, smiling at him as the elevator doors shut. When Ethan turned around, J.D. and James were looking at him as if he had just robbed a bank. Their surprise, if not their outrage, was obvious.

"What in the hell was that about?" J.D. demanded.

Ethan lifted an eyebrow. "I'm taking her out to dinner."

Lowell just shook his head as J.D.'s mouth popped open. "You're *what?*" he gasped. "Since when do you ask a woman out; a woman you are working with, no less?"

Ethan wouldn't back down. "I am allowed to see anyone I want to on my own time," he pointed out. "And I don't work with her."

"This is not a good idea and you know it."

"I appreciate that. But cut me some slack, will you? I'm a big boy. I can handle myself."

J.D. put up his hands. "Wait a minute," he said, grabbing Ethan's broad shoulder. "Brother, I've been around you when you interact with women. You can be abrupt, condescending and flat-out insulting. We've got to work with that woman for the next four months and I don't want you ruining our good rapport."

Ethan knew he was right in the normal sense, but not this time. This was different. "It's not like that," he lowered his voice. "The last thing I want to do is insult or demean Cydney. She... well, she's different. She's special. Look, I know I can be an ass, but that's the last thing I'd be with her. Trust me."

J.D. lost some of his indignation. "Special? What do you mean?"

"He likes her," James piped up. "He's liked her from the start."

Now J.D. was shocked. "Really?" He looked between James and Ethan. "So you don't want to emotionally bully the woman?"

Ethan shook his head. "Not even close."

When they were supposed to be debriefing, Ethan had to

listen to an hour of J.D. Dickerson's psycho-babble on Ethan's relationship with the female sex over the past eight years. Ethan couldn't disagree. But this time, he knew J.D. was wrong.

———

After trying to call Olivia one more time from the office, Cydney made a dash for her car. She was growing more worried by the minute. Saying goodnight to the security guard as she quit the offices, she dug in her purse for her keys as she crossed the brightly lit parking lot. The mercury vapor lamps were buzzing overhead in the early dusk as she neared her car.

As she approached the vehicle, a figure emerged from between the cars, nearly running her over. Startled, Cydney stumbled back and ended up almost laying over a car hood. Her purse scattered over the asphalt.

"Whoa," the man she bumped into grabbed her wrist and pulled her off the car. "Sorry about that. I didn't see you."

"That's okay," Cydney yanked her hand away. "No problem."

The man bent over to help her pick up her purse. Cydney didn't want anyone else touching her things so she kept snatching stuff out of his hands as fast as he collected it. After a moment, she dared to look into the man's face and found a pair of sultry blue eyes gazing back at her.

"You're Cydney Hetherington, right?" he asked. When she didn't respond right away, he grinned. "Sorry. I'm Joe. I'm a security guard here. Actually, this was my first day."

Cydney nodded. "I think I saw you this morning during the briefing," she said. "Sorry, but there are so many new hires I don't keep track of everyone."

Joseph picked up a pack of gum that was still on the ground

and handed it to her. "That's okay," he said. "I didn't expect you to know me. That's why I introduced myself."

Cydney took the gum and put it back in her purse, rising from her crouched position. "Thank you for helping me pick up my purse," she said. "It was nice to meet you."

"You, too," Joseph stood up next to her. He realized the conversation was coming to a close and hastened to keep it going. That was, after all, his assignment. "Are you here on the weekends, too?"

She shook her head. "No," she replied. "Just during the week."

"I hear it gets really busy on the weekends."

"It sure does."

"Will you be here this weekend since it's opening weekend for the exhibit?"

She shrugged. "Probably."

Cydney hit the remote unlock, listening to the car beep with Joseph still hanging on behind her.

"Have you worked here long?" he persisted.

She was uncomfortable with this man, no matter how good looking or polite he was, following her to her car.

"Almost eleven years," she replied. She glanced at him as she opened the car door. "Well, best of luck to you with your new job. I'm sure we'll see each other around."

"Hopefully."

He said it in a seductive voice, hoping she would catch it. All it succeeded in doing was frightening her. She bolted into her car with a final wave, slamming the door shut and locking it.

Joseph watched Cydney drive out of the parking lot as if the Devil was chasing her. He had a feeling he had failed to impress.

FIVE

THERE WERE three cop cars in front of the house when he pulled up.

Ethan was looking forward to a wonderful evening until the moment he turned onto Cydney's street and was greeted with the sight of two black and whites and a plain clothes unit parked right in front of her house. Then the fear set in and all thoughts of dinner with two lovely women fled from his mind. He kept his apprehension in check as he parked his BMW X5 and calmly walked to the front porch. The door was open and he could see a uniform standing just inside. Reaching into his pocket, he pulled out his FBI identification card.

He held it out as he walked into the house. The uniformed officer turned to him but he spoke before the man could question him.

"Special Agent Serreaux, FBI" he held up his identification card in plain sight. "Where's Mrs. Hetherington?"

The words were barely out of his mouth when he heard someone calling his name. Cydney was sitting on her couch with a crewcut detective next to her and another uniform standing over her. Ethan glanced around and saw at least two other uniformed officers walking through other rooms of the house. It was clear they were dusting for prints. He went straight for Cydney.

"Cydney?" he asked with soft urgency. "What happened?"

Cydney looked as if she had been bawling her eyes out; the beautiful hazel eyes were red and swollen. A wad of Kleenex was in her hand. She tried to open her mouth to speak but all that came out was a sob. Ethan shoved the identification card in his pocket, sat down beside her and put his arms around her. He didn't know what else to do.

Cydney clung to him and sobbed. Ethan put a hand on her head comfortingly, holding her close against his chest. His gaze found the detective seated on the other side of Cydney.

"What happened?" he tried to sound professional and not overly concerned.

"Are you a friend of the family?" the detective asked.

Ethan nodded because to say anything else would have been too complicated. "What's going on?"

The detective glanced at the notebook in his hand. "Well, according to Mrs. Hetherington, she came home after work to find several rooms of the house in some disarray and her fifteen-year-old daughter missing. She seems to think her daughter has been kidnapped."

"Of course she's been kidnapped," Cydney suddenly came to life. "Can't you see there has been a struggle all over this house? Someone broke in and took her!"

Ethan shushed her soothingly. "Cydney, look at me." He put his hands on her face and forced her to fix on him. "Tell me what happened when you came home."

She was struggling but made a good effort to control herself. "I... I came home and the front door was open," she gasped and sniffled. "When I touched the door, it just opened. It wasn't even latched. And the kitchen was all upended, as if a herd of cattle had run through it. Olivia's book bag was on her bed where she had put it when she came home from school, but nothing was touched. Ethan, she always does her homework first when she comes home from school. *Always*."

Ethan could feel her panic. In truth, he had some of his own. He hadn't known this woman more than three days but already, she was under his skin. So was her daughter. It didn't matter if he had known them for three days or three years. As a parent and a human being, he felt her pain.

"Did you try calling all of her friends?" he asked.

She nodded, tears overflowing onto her cheeks. "They saw her leave with Mrs. Marquez, my neighbor. She normally picks Olivia up from school. But Mrs. Marquez says she dropped her off like normal and watched her walk into the house. That's the last anyone has seen of her."

Ethan inhaled slowly, thoughtfully. His mind was working furiously. Cydney was weeping softly and his hands were still on her cheeks. Kissing her forehead gently, he stood up and pulled her with him.

"Come on," he directed. "Walk with me."

She obeyed, the wadded tissue against her mouth as she stifled her sobs. He held her right hand tightly with his right hand while his left arm went around her shoulders.

"I need you to calm down and talk to me," he said firmly. "Tell me why you think she's been abducted."

Cydney sniffled and swallowed. "Because Olivia would not have just run off," she said flatly. "She's a creature of habit; she comes home, does her homework and makes macaroni and cheese because it's the only thing she likes to eat. I come home to it every night."

They paused in the hallway as a cop dusted the door knob of Olivia's bedroom. Ethan caught a glimpse of school portraits of Olivia on the wall as he turned to Cydney.

"You're sure she couldn't be anywhere else?" he pressed gently. "What about your parents? Do they live around here and could they possibly have her?"

She shook her head. "My parents are in Northern California right now visiting friends and my brother lives in Santa Monica. He wouldn't have her. Even if he did, he would have called me to let me know."

"She's never run away before, has she?"

"Never."

The detective who had been sitting on the couch was now walking up behind them. He still had his notepad out and a pen in his hand. He was listening to her answers as he walked up.

"Mrs. Hetherington," the detective interrupted their conversation. "Is there anyone you can think of that would want to harm you or Olivia? Any threats?"

Cydney blinked. *Threats.* She didn't know why, but she suddenly thought of the threat against The Lucius Robe. It was the entire reason for Ethan's presence. She looked right at him, her eyes wide with horror.

"Threat," she hissed. "Is it possible... possible this has anything to do with The Lucius Robe? You said there was a specific threat. Is it possible while everyone was focused on the museum, your Disciple group or whatever they call themselves was trying to infiltrate the museum another way?"

Ethan's brow furrowed slightly. "By threatening the families of museum employees?"

"What *if*, Ethan?" she looked stricken. "What if they are trying to get the robe another way?"

Ethan just looked at her. Then he reached into his pocket and pulled out his cell phone.

"I'll be right back."

Cydney and the detective watched him walk out the front door. The detective, sharp and seasoned, looked at her.

"Do you want to tell me what this is all about?" he asked frankly. "What's the FBI doing here?"

Cydney told him what she knew. The detective made notes in his book, looking both annoyed and skeptical. As Cydney spit out the last of the story, her cell phone suddenly rang. Jolted, she raced for her purse in the entry. It was sitting on a decorative table which she knocked over in her haste. Yanking the phone out of her purse, she looked at the incoming number and realized that it was Olivia's phone. She answered it on the fifth ring.

"Hello?" she almost shouted.

There was a long pause. "Mom?"

Cydney burst into tears of relief and terror. "Olivia, where are you?"

"Um...." Olivia faded off and the next voice that came on the line was not that of her daughter. "Mrs. Hetherington?"

Cydney's blood ran cold. It was a male voice she did not recognize. "Who is this?" she demanded. "Where is my daughter?"

"Your daughter is perfectly safe," the man replied. "In fact, I called just to let you know that Olivia is safe, warm and fed, and will be my guest for a time. She's completely sound and whole providing you do as you are told."

Cydney felt a jolt of terror, as if all of her fears had just been confirmed. By this time, Ethan had come back in the house and the detective motioned to Cydney and the phone. Understanding the gist of the man's hand signals, Ethan got up alongside her and put his head against hers, his ear against her cell phone so he could try and hear some of the conversation. He looked at the detective and mouthed the words.

Get a trace.

Pressed against Ethan, Cydney was trembling as she struggled to not fall apart completely. "What do you want me to do?"

she asked, fighting off the sobs. "God, please don't hurt her. She's all I have. She's just a little girl."

"And she's perfectly safe," the man reiterated calmly. "She had macaroni and cheese for dinner, although she didn't eat very much of it. She seemed to want to talk more than she wanted to eat."

"Talk?" Cydney repeated. "Talk about what?"

"The Lucius Robe, of course. She says that she has seen it up close. She also says that you are in charge of its security."

Cydney's heart sank. She could feel Ethan's muscular arm go around her, giving her an encouraging squeeze.

"I'm in charge of the exhibit," she answered with a quivering voice. "Security is included with that. Please, can you just bring her home? Or drop her off somewhere and I'll pick her up. I swear I won't press charges."

The man laughed. "Somehow, I think that would be out of your hands."

"Then what do you want? I don't have a lot of money, but I'll do whatever it takes. Just don't hurt her."

She was starting to cry again and Ethan hugged her gently. The man on the other end of the phone didn't seem moved by her tears.

"I don't want money," he said frankly. "But I do want your help."

"Help with what?"

"The Lucius Robe."

"What do you want me to do?"

"Give it to me."

"*Give* it to you?" Cydney repeated, growing agitated. "But it doesn't belong to me or even my museum. It belongs to the Bristol Museum of Antiquities. We only have it on a four-month loan."

"Is it worth the life of your daughter?"

"Oh, my God!" Cydney shrieked. "You would kill her if you don't get it?"

The man on the other end of the phone remained quite calm in the face of her hysteria. "She's perfectly safe. But if you can't provide me with the robe, I cannot vouch for what will happen to her." His voice suddenly turned hard. "Olivia for the robe, Mrs. Hetherington. And if you involve those FBI agents in this, you'll never see your child again."

The line abruptly went dead. Ethan pulled the phone from her grip, handing it over to the detective as Cydney let out a scream of horror. Ethan put his arms around her, picked her up, and began to carry her down the hall. He called back over his shoulder to the detective.

"See if they were able to get a cell tower reading on that call," he said. "Hurry up, they're more than likely on the move."

The detective flew into action and got on the radio to dispatch. Meanwhile, Ethan carried a very hysterical woman down the hall, peering in the open doors until he came to what he correctly assumed was her bedroom. He kicked the door open wide, listening to it bounce off the wall and slam shut behind him. He fell with Cydney onto the bed, keeping her wrapped up in his powerful embrace.

"Calm down," he murmured. "Nothing's going to happen to Olivia. We'll get her back safe, I promise."

"Let me go," she demanded while she struggled furiously. "I have to go get my daughter!"

"We will," he insisted, trying not to get elbowed. "But we have to have a starting point. The cops are tracing that call so we can see what cell tower she transmitted from. It will tell us where to begin our search."

Cydney had moved beyond hysterical gasping and was now crying as if her heart were breaking.

"Oh, my God, my baby," she sobbed. "You were right. Those

zealots really do want the robe. They kidnapped my daughter to get it."

Ethan sighed heavily, tightening his grip on her now that she wasn't struggling so much. "It never occurred to any of us that they would go after museum personnel and certainly not their families," he said quietly. "This is something completely new for this bunch."

Cydney continued weeping into his chest, getting mascara and lipstick on his white dress shirt.

"They have my baby," she wept.

He shushed her softly, stroking her head with one hand and feeling particularly helpless at the moment. There was nothing he could do until the cell tower was traced.

"Yes, they have her, but she's unharmed, she's been fed, and I'm sure they will treat her very well as long as they think they can get what they want by holding her," he was trying to sound positive. "Olivia is a smart girl; she can take care of herself and I suspect she'll have no problem telling these guys what she thinks of all of this. If anything, I'd worry for the kidnappers. Little do they know they've abducted the next ruler of the world."

Cydney's sobs turned into weepy giggles as she heard her words echoed in his statement. She was on an emotional roller coaster as she pulled her head from his chest and gazed up at him with her wet, beautiful eyes.

"Oh, no," she sniffled. "What happens if she turns the tables on them and bends them to her will? She'll have a bunch of religious zealots at her command and we'll all be in trouble."

Ethan grinned at her, thinking that she was an incredibly lovely woman. He stroked her head, gazing into her magnificent eyes and pleased that her pluck hadn't left her completely. It told him a lot about her strength of character.

"I hope I'm on her good side, then," he confided. "For now,

however, I need for you to be strong. We'll get through this but you have to trust that we'll get her back unharmed. I really need that confidence. Okay?"

Her tears were fading as she gazed up into his handsome face. She felt an odd spark in her chest, something warm and thrilling that she hadn't felt in years. In the midst of a crisis, it was hardly the time for such selfish feelings. But something about Ethan Serreaux had touched her from the beginning and now in her time of crisis, he was a strong and calming rock. She didn't know a whole lot about the man, but at the moment, she was grateful for him.

"I... I'll try." She tried to sniffle away the last of her tears. "I'm just really terrified for my daughter."

"I know." He stroked her head again. "But you're going to have to trust me, all right? This is my job."

"I trust you."

He smiled and patted her head. Gazing into her lovely face, he felt an overwhelming urge to kiss her that could not have been more poorly timed. So he let her go and climbed out of the overstuffed bed.

"Where's your medicine cabinet?" he asked.

She pointed to the adjoining master bathroom. Ethan took off his suit jacket, laid it on the end of the bed, and went into the bathroom. Turning on the light, he opened the medicine cabinet and read a couple of prescription bottles, coming to a halt when he found a bottle of Tylenol PM. Popping two into his palm, he put some water in a glass that he found next to the sink and went back into the bedroom.

Cydney was sitting up by now, watching him curiously. He sat down on the edge of the bed.

"Here." He handed her the pills. "Take these."

She peered at the tablets. "Why?"

"Because you need to sleep and calm down, and I need to get together with my unit and figure out what our next move is."

Reluctantly, she popped the pills and drank the water. Setting the glass down on the night stand, she turned to him somewhat calmer.

"Now what?"

"Go to sleep. I'll talk to you in the morning."

"Are you leaving?" She grabbed him by the arm. "What if those people come back?"

He shook his head and patted her hand. "I'm not leaving," he told her. "I'll be out in the living room all night. There's no way I'm leaving you alone."

She felt a tremendous amount of comfort with that statement. "All right," she lay back down on the bed but the tears were welling again. "Thanks for staying. I feel better."

He smiled at her, standing up so he could wrap her up in the coverlet. When she was properly swaddled, he stood over her with his hands on hips.

"Go to sleep," he commanded gently. "I'll be outside if you need me."

He was nearly to the door when she called out to him. "Ethan?"

He paused. "Yes?"

He heard her sigh. "The cat," she said. "I have to feed Olivia's cat."

"I'll do it. Where's the cat food?"

"Pantry."

"I'll feed it. Now go to sleep."

"Okay. But... Ethan?"

"Yes, honey?"

"Olivia... I can't help think about where she's sleeping tonight. Do you think she has a bed or is she all tied up in the back of someone's car?"

He didn't want to upset her, not now when she was calming. He tried to be careful with his reply. "I would suspect that she is being well cared for and probably has a nice bed somewhere."

"Not tied up?"

"I would seriously doubt it." He tried not to sound too harsh. "Cydney, honey, this is one of those things you have no control over. I seriously doubt that Olivia is being mistreated. In any case, you just need to tell yourself that she's fed and she's unharmed. Given the circumstances, that's an excellent thing to focus on right now. The rest we'll deal with as it comes. Okay?"

She was sniffling. "Okay."

He was just closing the door when she suddenly sat upright in bed. "Ethan!"

The abrupt tone started him and he shoved the door open wide. "What's wrong?"

Her face was slack with surprise. "Oh, God... I don't know why this didn't occur to me from the start, but Olivia has GPS tracking on her phone." She began tossing back the covers. "I got it as a feature but I've just never used it. I'd completely forgotten that she has it. We can track her through the cell phone provider. You just input the phone number and it locates her phone."

She could have told him that five minutes ago but he didn't really blame her; she had been too hysterical to focus. He yelled over his shoulder to the detective down the hall.

"Anyone have a laptop?" he called.

"I do," Cydney began climbing out of bed. "It's here on my desk."

Ethan could see it in the darkness. He went to the desk and picked it up before she could reach it. With one hand, he turned her around for the bed.

"Get back in bed," he told her firmly. "I'll handle this."

She squirmed away from him, out of his reach. "Please," she begged. "Please let me see where she is."

He just looked at her. She sounded so horribly pathetic and he knew there was no way he could refuse her.

"All right," he set the computer back on the desk and flipped on the light. "Boot it up and let's see what we can see."

Now that she was actually taking some action towards finding her daughter, Cydney was much calmer. The laptop booted up and she logged on to the Internet, going immediately to her cell service provider. On the homepage was a GPS link; Cydney entered Olivia's phone number and wait with bated breath.

She didn't realize that Ethan, the detective, and two uniforms were standing over her shoulder, watching the map of the San Gabriel Valley load. Immediately, the cell phone was located in Pasadena near the Old Town district. Wherever it was, it was stationary and sitting at a major intersection. The detective immediately got on the radio, contacted dispatch, and advised the Watch Commander of the situation. But Ethan put a stop to any further police action.

As Cydney sat with her eyes glued to the tracking screen, Ethan made it clear to the detective that this was a federal matter given the association to The Lucius Robe. It was obviously a terrorist act and beyond the jurisdiction of the local police department. Just as he and the detective began to get into a verbal altercation, more voices were heard entering the home and one loud voice in particular. J.D. Dickerson had arrived and he was infuriated that the terrorists he was supposed to know had pulled a fast one.

Cydney remained at her desk, watching the screen, as Ethan and the detective left her bedroom and went into the living room, where they had a spirited debate about federal jurisdiction as it related to the local police department with J.D.

in the middle of it. Cydney heard the loud, sometimes agitated voices, disturbed that no one seemed to be too intent on finding her child. The more they argued, the more disturbed she became.

With the GPS screen still up, she rose from the chair and quietly closed the bedroom door. She hoped that they would think the closed door meant she was sleeping. Quietly, she changed into a casual jogging suit and a pair of sneakers. Unplugging the computer, she hoped her battery had enough life for her to track down her daughter. If all of those cops in her living room weren't going to do anything about this, then she was. She had to get to Olivia.

Cydney opened her bedroom window that faced out onto her driveway. It was at the opposite end of the house from the living room. Grabbing the extra set of car keys and a credit card she never used from her vanity drawer, she picked up the computer and slipped from the window. There was about a six foot drop to the ground but she managed to make the drop without falling and without damaging her still-running computer. It was nearly dark out with the neighborhood settling in for the night. In stealth mode, she made it to the car and got in.

She was fairly certain they would hear her car start but she couldn't let that stop her. Starting the car as quietly as she could, she quickly backed out and took off down the street, away from her house and away from the arguing cops. It was a simple move to make a turn and end up on the street that she wanted to take to the freeway.

Once on the boulevard, she gunned it.

———

Olivia glared at the lady with the hugely made-up eyes and pink-hued hair. She looked like a clown. The woman had been trying to communicate with her for the better part of a half-hour, ever since she had arrived at the upscale hotel. But Olivia didn't want anything to do with her or any of the other people in the hotel suite. She was finished being scared of the strangers who had abducted her; now, she was just angry.

It had been an odd journey to this moment in time. Right after she had gotten home from school, a man had knocked at the door and asked for Brad Hetherington. Olivia had told the man that her father had died years ago and the man had seemed very distraught; he explained he had been an old friend of Brad's and hadn't known about his death. The man had been so pathetic that Olivia had let him in. She had taken him into the kitchen and given him a glass of water, whereupon the man directed the conversation from Brad to Cydney and they had ended up on the subject of the Western Pacific Museum of Art and Antiquities.

They had talked a lot about the museum and the new exhibit. The man had seen the advertisement for the Resurrection exhibit. Olivia had told him all about The Lucius Robe and her mother's role in the exhibition. The man had been very interested, very attentive, until Olivia had run out of things to say. Then the man had smiled, grabbed her by the wrist, tied up her hands and bound her mouth.

Olivia had put up a fierce struggle. The kitchen had been a wreck by the time he finally secured her. She tried to scream and yell but he had stuffed something into her mouth and then taped it shut so that no sound could come out. Then he had pressed something against her nose, something with a strange metallic smell. After a few whiffs of that stuff she had passed out.

When she woke up, she found herself in a hotel suite with

some other people. One of them was a crazily made-up woman who looked vaguely familiar. There was another guy, in the kitchen, who kept opening and closing the refrigerator. Groggy, a little nauseous, Olivia sat impatiently through some questions until someone asked her what she wanted to eat. Repeated refusals finally brought forth a macaroni and cheese admission. So they had produced a gourmet macaroni and cheese with strong-tasting cheese sauce that Olivia didn't like very much. And, of course, more questions while she ate.

Then they had produced her cell phone, which had about fifteen missed calls on it, all from the same number. The man who had kidnapped her hit the redial on the number and not surprisingly, Cydney had answered.

Olivia had been allowed to say one or two words to her mother before the man who kidnapped her took over. He had wandered into a nearby bedroom, still on the phone with Cydney, and Olivia had been left alone in the living room with the weird-looking woman.

"You're such a beautiful girl," Coral Chastity Aames sat across from Olivia in the penthouse suite of the Hilton Hotel in Pasadena. "What grade are you in?"

"I'm a sophomore in high school," she said. "And when can I go home? I've told you everything I know about my mom and the museum. Can I please go home now?"

Coral smiled with her bright pink lips. "Olivia, would you like to go on an adventure?"

Olivia frowned. "An adventure? Not really. I just want to go home. I have a math test tomorrow."

Coral laughed. "I'm sure your teacher will allow you to make it up," she said. Her smile faded. "I know you have talked to my friend, Nat. But did he tell you why we have asked you to be our guest for a while?"

Olivia's frown deepened. "I'm not your guest; you

kidnapped me. That guy on the phone to my mother broke into my house and tied up my hands. I have a ton of homework and I need to get home."

It was clear that Olivia was a brave girl; never once during her ordeal had she cried or panicked. She had been very stoic through everything and even now was acting like she was in charge. Coral thought perhaps she really didn't realize the serious of the situation, like this was some kind of prank. But it was clearly no prank.

"Let me tell you a little story and perhaps it will help you understand why you are here," Coral glanced up at Joseph as he walked into the room from the kitchen. He had a soda in his hand and sat down on the far end of the couch across from Olivia. Coral's gaze lingered on him before continuing. "Back in the time after Jesus was crucified, men wrote different texts about Jesus and his followers and their deeds. Some even wrote texts about the future and predictions. Most of these texts, or books, ended up in the Holy Bible. Men from the Catholic Church chose what books would be put into the Bible and what books would not."

Olivia was staring at her with an unhappy face. Coral continued. "One of those texts, the Apocryphon of James, suggested that Jesus did not die upon the cross but was rather spirited away out of the city and someone else was crucified in his place. It was told that Jesus married Mary of Magdalene and, together, they escaped by boat to the southern coast of France. There, they had a daughter. This daughter married and had children. It is said that the royal family of France, the Merovingian royal bloodlines from the twelfth century that fed directly into the kings of France all the way up through the nineteenth century, are directly descended from Jesus' daughter."

Olivia gave the woman an impatient expression. "I've heard

all of this, lady. I saw that Holy Grail movie, too, and I read the book. This is nothing new."

Coral's smile turned somewhat stiff. She sat forward, her blue eyes suddenly hard and serious.

"Olivia," Coral sounded as if she was seriously preaching to the girl. "I know all of that is common knowledge. But did you know that the bloodline of the French kings continues even today? Even though France has a Prime Minister, still, the royal family exists."

"So?"

Coral cocked her head. "That means that Jesus still exists. And he should be the Holy Ruler of Mankind."

Olivia made a face. "So why are you telling me? I don't care about any of this."

"But you should," Coral said passionately. "Because you are going to help us crown a new Holy Roman Emperor."

"What?" Olivia rolled her eyes, thinking that this strange woman had completely lost her mind. "I have no idea what you're talking about, lady. Can I please just go home?"

"Olivia," Coral smacked her hand against the coffee table. "You don't seem to understand, sweetheart. You are going to be a big part of God's new kingdom on earth. It is through you that the king will be crowned."

"Through me? What are you talking about?"

Coral was on her feet, her eyes riveted to Olivia. "You are going to help us get the robe to place upon the king's shoulders."

"Huh?"

Coral nodded eagerly and sat on the edge of the coffee table, her face full of the joy of her endeavor. "Remember I told you that the French royal family still exists; that the direct descendants of Jesus still exist?"

Olivia didn't like the way the woman was looking at her. "Uh... yes."

Coral threw an arm in the direction of Joseph. "That young man is a direct descendent of French kings, which means that he is a descendent of Jesus," she announced. "He will be our next Holy Roman Emperor and you will help bring about a new age of glory, Olivia. Isn't that exciting?"

Olivia looked at the good-looking young man seated a few feet away from her. She looked utterly skeptical.

"Who are you?" she asked.

Joseph smiled faintly. "I'm Joe," he said. When she continued to eye him critically, he elaborated. "My name is Joseph Henri Phillipe Andreas d'Orleans. My grandfather is widely considered the heir to the throne of France, being able to trace his lineage to the second century after Christ. My heritage is Merovingian, descendants of Jesus and Mary's daughter, Sarah."

Olivia was growing increasingly apprehensive; no longer angry, or scared, or just plain bored. There was something more now, an added element that had her very edgy. She began to lose some of her confidence.

"I had to do a project for my French class last year about the French Royal Family," she said, her gaze shifting back and forth between Joseph and Coral. "I remember reading that although the d'Orleans laid claim to the throne, they're really just an offshoot of the House of Bourbon. The Bourbon kings ruled in the fourteenth century, I think, and they were descended from the House of Capet, who themselves descended from the Carolingians, who descended from the Merovingians. That's the family that supposedly descended from Jesus' daughter."

Joseph grinned at her. "You're a smart girl. I can hardly remember that stuff."

Olivia wasn't falling for his charm. "Can I please go home now?"

"Don't you want to help?" Coral asked her, diverting her

attention from Joseph. "After everything we've told you, don't you want to help?"

For the first time since her captivity, tears filled Olivia's eyes. "No," she said flatly. "I want to go home. I want to see my mom."

The tears spilled over her cheeks and she lowered her head, wiping them away as quickly as they fell. Coral reached out to touch her blond head but Olivia smacked her hand away, recoiling from the strange woman's touch.

"Don't touch me!" she cried. "Let me go home. If you don't let me go home, I'll scream so loud that they call the police. I swear I will!"

Joseph moved across the couch, closer to her but not close enough to touch her. She was in a panic.

"It's okay," he said, guilty that this girl had been kidnapped on his behalf. "No one is going to hurt you, I promise."

Olivia was huddled in the corner of the couch. "Let me go home."

Joseph's dusky blue eyes were riveted to the pretty young girl. "We will," he said. "But we'd really like to have you as our guest for a while."

Coral rose from the white chair she was sitting in, moving closer to Olivia. "My dear, you must understand that this endeavor is bigger than all of us," she insisted. "We have support from the Church itself. Many, many people want to see a new world order where Jesus' descendant will rule. Don't you want to be a part of this glory?"

Olivia flipped over the back of the couch and landed on her knees. "No," she screamed. "I want to go home. I don't care about a new world or kings."

"But you are a part of us already," Nat came out of the bedroom with Olivia's cell phone in his hand. He had just hung up on the girl's mother. "You are key to obtaining the robe."

Olivia shied away from the man who had kidnapped her, backing herself into a wall. She just sat there and cried.

"If... if I tell you a secret about the robe, will you please let me go?" she begged.

Coral, Joseph and Nat showed definite interest in the question. "What secret?" Joseph asked gently.

Olivia was trying to calm herself, wiping at her face. "Promise me I can go home now if I tell you."

"I promise," Joseph said before the others could speak. "What's the secret?"

Olivia looked at the other two people in the room. Coral had her hand at her throat waiting for the most divine information while Nat, the mean man, watched her impassively. Olivia swallowed hard and focused on Joseph.

"Take me home right now and I'll tell you."

"Tell us now or I'll drive to your house right now and kill your mother," Nat replied evenly.

Olivia's eyes widened. "No," she gasped, the tears returning full force. "Please don't hurt my mother."

"Tell me your secret or I'll kill your mother tonight."

He had only succeeded in creating a hysterical child. Joseph cast him a disapproving glare as he inched closer to Olivia, hoping to calm her down.

"Tell us your secret and your mother will be fine," he insisted kindly. "Please, Olivia. It's important."

Olivia sobbed and hiccupped, wiping her face of snot and tears. Her big eyes moved back and forth between Nat and Joseph.

"Swear you won't hurt my mom if I tell you?" she whispered.

"I swear," Joseph said. "What's the secret?"

Olivia gazed into his handsome face, realizing the bargaining chip she had tried to use had been used against her.

She was terrified they would do what they said if she didn't tell them. She had no choice.

"Okay," she sniffled, wiping at her nose again. "My mom said that when they removed the robe from the crate and were putting it in the display, that they saw a tooth stuck in the material."

The reaction was varied; Joseph's eyes widened, Coral's mouth popped open, and Nat remained characteristically unmoving. It was Coral who finally spoke.

"A... a tooth?" she repeated.

Olivia nodded firmly. But the expressions of the three strangers made her feel more terrified than ever before.

SIX

THE DOORBELL RANG. It rang again. Finally, the man dozing on the couch with the muted television flickering in the background rose wearily and stumbled through the dark, coming to the door and resting his hand on the latch. The bell rang again and he snapped.

"Who the hell is it?" he demanded.

"It's me," came a muffled voice from the other end.

Kyle Winter's eyebrows lifted and he unbolted the door of his apartment, yanking it open to see his only sister standing there. She was disheveled and pale, and his annoyance immediately turned to concern.

"Cyd?" he opened the door wide and waved her in. "What are you doing here? What's wrong?"

Cydney tried to stay calm as she told him the tale but she ended up weeping through most of it. By this time, Kyle's wife Megan, a lovely brunette, was awake and had her arms around Cydney as the woman finished her story. When Cydney was done, Kyle looked both dumbfounded and grave.

"Are you serious?" he half-demanded, half-pleaded. "I can't

believe what I'm hearing. Livvy's been kidnapped by a bunch of extremists because of the new exhibit at the museum?"

Cydney wiped her nose with the tissue that Megan had handed her. "It's true," she assured him. "Kyle, I need your help. I need to get my daughter and those cops just stand around and fight about whose jurisdiction it is. I know where she is. The GPS in her phone says she's at Los Robles Avenue and Walnut Street in Pasadena. I need to go and get her and I need you to help me."

By this time, Kyle was on his feet, pacing thoughtfully. A big man at a few inches over six feet, he was thirteen months younger than his sister. Growing up, they had gone to the same schools and had the same friends. Oddly, they hadn't fought or hated each other like most siblings do. They had actually gotten along. Kyle was the one person her entire life that Cydney could always count on. He was big, smart and resourceful. She needed to count on him now.

"Cyd," Kyle raked his fingers through his messy blond hair. "I don't know what we can do. If these religious freaks really have her, then it's possible that they're armed. You might be placing her in more jeopardy by going in recklessly and trying to save her. More than that, you might get yourself killed. Did you think about that?"

Cydney's tears were back. "She's all I have, Kyle," she began to sob. "I have to get my baby back. If you won't help me, then I'll do it myself."

Megan hugged Cydney and tried to comfort her as Kyle knelt down in front of his sister.

"You know I would give up my life for you or Liv," he said, more gently. "But you're not thinking. You said the cops and the FBI are in on this, so you have to let these guys do their thing. You'll just mess it all up if you go rushing in. Is that what you want? To make things worse?"

Cydney just sobbed. Kyle sighed, patted his sister's hand, and stood up. He looked at his wife.

"I'll drive her home in her car," he told her. "You follow me in ours."

Megan's brown eyes were wide. "Is that it? You're just going to take her home?"

Kyle lifted an eyebrow at her. "Don't start."

"You need to do something," Megan insisted.

Kyle threw up his arms. "What do you want me to do?" he shot back. "I'm not a cop. I'm not going to go busting into this hideout or whatever it is at Los Robles and Walnut and get my ass blown off. It's stupid to even try. She needs to let the cops do their job. They're trained for this stuff; we're not."

Megan wouldn't give up as Cydney continued to weep. "At least call your dad and see what he says about it."

Kyle rolled his eyes. "My dad would say the same thing. It's my mom I'd worry about; she'd get the shotgun from the safe and go down there herself, guns blazing. She'd shoot first and ask questions later and probably end up in jail on a murder charge. There's no way I'm calling either of them about this. They can't know. Okay?"

His last word was emphasized at his wife. Megan made a face at him, knowing he was more than likely right. As her husband changed into jeans, Megan held Cydney and tried to comfort her. The woman was overwrought and terrified, a condition that was catching. Megan was pretty terrified herself. The whole thing seemed very surreal but, coming from level-headed Cydney, it had to be the truth. Cydney didn't have a big imagination and she wasn't a liar.

When Kyle was dressed, they got Cydney into her car. She protested at first and even tried to run off, but she seemed so weary and disoriented that she couldn't seem to coordinate herself. Deeply concerned, Kyle drove off with Megan following in the Mustang, traversing the dark freeways until they reached Arcadia.

It was surface streets to the two-bedroom bungalow with the yellow flowers bordering the walkway. Cydney had stopped weeping on the ride home and they were nearly to her house when Kyle realized she had fallen asleep. Pulling into his sister's driveway, he could see the black and white parked on the street and people in the house. It only served to validate his sister's story. He tried to wake her up when he parked the car but she wouldn't budge.

Exiting her car, he admonished his wife to stay in the Mustang as he went to the door. He only pounded once before the door was flying open.

Cops had him by the arm, yanking him in and shoving him against the wall. Kyle threw up his hands in a show of no resistance.

"Hey, take it easy!" he protested. "I'm Kyle Winter, Cydney's brother. I have Cydney in the car."

Ethan was suddenly standing next to him; he didn't even say a word. With a lingering glance at Kyle, he raced down the hallway and threw open the bedroom door. The bed was messy and empty and the window next to the headboard was open with the screen removed. The cool night air blew in gently, lifting the curtains. Muttering a curse, he retraced his steps down the hall.

"Damn it," he hissed, his dark gaze focused on Kyle. "Where is she?"

Kyle threw his thumb in the direction of the driveway. "I told you; in her car, dead asleep."

Ethan was out the door, jogging across the lawn with Kyle and the detective on his heels. He reached the newer model Acura and saw Cydney slumped in the passenger seat.

Unlocking the door from the driver's side, he circled around and opened the passenger door.

Cydney almost fell out but he caught her before she could tumble. She awoke briefly, mumbled something, but promptly fell back asleep in Ethan's strong arms. Shifting his grip, he picked her up and carried her back into the house. Kyle, the detective, and Megan followed.

"Is it true that Olivia has been kidnapped?" Kyle wanted to know as they entered the house. "She drove all the way to my house asking me to help her rescue her daughter. What in the hell is really going on?"

Ethan took Cydney down the hall, being careful not to bump her head into the wall, and carried her into her darkened bedroom. Megan was right behind him and she pulled back the covers as Ethan gently laid Cydney on the bed. Cydney did nothing more than sigh contently and snuggle down into the pillows as Ethan covered her up. With a lingering glance at her blond head, he shut the window, locked it, and ushered Megan and Kyle out of the room. Quietly, he shut the door.

"Olivia has unfortunately been abducted," Ethan explained to the big blond man who faintly resembled his beauteous sister. "We are working on a recovery plan."

Kyle sized up the good-looking man who seemed to behave very kindly towards his sister. "Who are you?" he asked.

"Special Agent Ethan Serreaux," Ethan replied. "I'm with the FBI."

"Did the cops call you in on this?"

Ethan shook his head. "I was already here." His gaze moved between Kyle and the pretty brunette standing next to him. "Cydney told me she had a brother. I didn't know you lived locally."

"I don't," Kyle said flatly. "I'm about twenty miles from here. Look, do you want to tell me what in the hell is really going on here? My sister shows up at my door, hysterical, with stories of her daughter being abducted, and I bring her home to find the cops here and the FBI and...," he suddenly threw up his hands as if at the end of his wits. "This is crazy. What's going on?"

Ethan gestured in the direction of the living room, a hint which both Kyle and Megan took. They went into the living room with Ethan on their heels. A big African-American agent came in from the kitchen and stood next to Ethan, introducing himself as J.D. Dickerson. Kyle sat on the couch with Megan close against him. They made an apprehensive pair.

"I'm sorry we can't tell you more, Mr. Winter," Ethan said in a genuinely apologetic tone. "Suffice it to say that your niece has been kidnapped and we're doing all we can to recover her."

Kyle lifted a blond eyebrow. "No offense, but Cyd said that all you guys were doing was arguing over whose jurisdiction it was. Why do you think she was so scared and frustrated that she drove all the way to my house to find help?"

Ethan cleared his throat, glancing at J.D. as he spoke. "There's no problem," he replied. "We have agents on it right now, staking out the location indicated on Olivia's GPS. That's about all I can tell you. We're doing our best to get Olivia back."

Kyle gazed at the two men a moment before shaking his head. "You guys just don't get it," he lowered his voice, now more concerned than angry. "Olivia is all my sister has. Her husband was killed eight years ago changing a tire on the freeway. The guy was hit by a bobtail truck. He was so messed up that she couldn't have an open casket but she still insisted on going to the morgue and seeing him. I went with her and the memory of my sister holding this broken up bag of bones that used to be her husband is something I'll never get out of my mind. Then, to top it all off, Brad's dad had a heart attack during the funeral and died later the same day." Kyle paused and took a breath, the horrible memories of Brad Hetherington's death catching up with him. "My sister has been through more in her life than anyone should have to go through. You have to get Olivia back in one piece. I just can't tell you how important it is. My sister can't go through another tragedy."

By the time he was finished, J.D. looked somber and Ethan appeared just plain distraught. The mood in the room was sorrowful and dark, thoughts of Cydney Hetherington's crushed husband and funeral tragedy heavy on their minds. Ethan finally drew in a long, deep breath and put his hands on his slender hips in a gesture of determination.

"I swear we'll get Olivia back unharmed," he quietly assured Kyle. "I won't let your sister go through hell again. I promise."

There was something about the way he said it that made Megan take another look at him, her woman's intuition kicking in, but Kyle was oblivious to the inflections in his tone. He was more concerned with what the man was saying.

"I really hope you mean that," he said sincerely. "She's been through enough."

Ethan nodded, prevented from replying as his cell phone rang and he excused himself to answer it. J.D. was left with the pair and he sat slowly on the armchair across from them. Kyle studied the big man.

"Do religious fanatics really have my niece?" he asked quietly.

J.D. looked up from his hands. "Yes," he said after a moment.

Kyle nodded in acceptance. "Cyd said they were after some artifact in the museum's exhibit."

"They are."

"She said they want to make a trade."

"I'm not trading anyone for anything."

"Then what do you plan to do?"

J.D. sat back in the chair, nodding slowly. "It's in the works, Mr. Winter. You're going to have to trust us."

Kyle sighed heavily and looked at his wife, who smiled timidly. With nothing more to say, he stood up.

"Can I get something to drink, please?" he asked. "I don't want to mess up your crime scene here, but I really need a beer."

"Help yourself."

J.D. motioned towards the kitchen and Kyle went to the refrigerator. He could see the other agent midway down the dark hall, talking on the cell phone. Although the men were professional, Kyle didn't feel any true sense of urgency from them. It was frustrating and he hated feeling so helpless. Didn't these guys understand that Cydney couldn't take anymore?

It's going to be a long night, he thought.

Down the hall, Ethan was on the phone to one of the field agents that had converged on the intersection of Los Robles and Walnut. A major hotel was on the southwest corner, businesses and a gas station covering the others. He was getting a report on the general conditions of the location when he suddenly caught movement out of the corner of his eye. Cydney was staggering through the bedroom door, looking like a zombie. He didn't even think her eyes were open.

"I'll call you right back," Ethan told the agent.

He hung up the phone and intercepted Cydney before she could take two steps from the room. He turned her back around for the bedroom.

"Back to bed, honey," he said.

Cydney was disoriented and mumbling. Ethan thought she might even be sleepwalking. He directed her back into the bedroom but she weakly resisted. He kicked the door closed behind them in case she made a break for it; at least the shut door would stop her until he could grab her.

"I have to go pick up Olivia," she muttered.

Ethan had her at the bed. "I'll go get her. You go back to sleep."

"But I have to go get her."

Ethan could tell by the way she was talking that she wasn't fully awake. He went to push her down onto the bed but she somehow got a foot in behind his knee and he ended up falling on top of her. Cydney suddenly twisted and wrapped her arms and legs around him.

Very quickly, Ethan found himself in an extremely intimate position with her. Had they not both been clothed, it would have been a love-making position. She held him tightly and refused to let go.

"Cyd, honey, loosen up," he tried to pry her arms from his neck. "Let me go."

Her response was to squeeze tighter and bury her face in his neck. "You smell so good," she murmured. Then she kissed him on the neck, so softly that it sent a bolt of excitement shooting through his big body. "You taste good, too."

Ethan's heart was thumping against his ribs and his palms began to sweat. He could feel her supple body pressed up against him, warm and soft, and her luscious legs were wrapped around his hips. Having no luck removing her arms, he tried to unwind her legs.

"Cydney," he tried to sound firm. "Let go, please."

She shook her head. "I don't want to let go," she whispered. "I don't ever want to let you go."

She suddenly pulled her face from his neck and planted her soft, warm lips on his. Her hands were in his hair, her delicious body pressed up against him, and Ethan knew he was a dead man. With is last shred of self-control, he tried to pull away from her.

"Cydney," he spoke even though her lips were on his mouth. "Honey, let me go. You need to get some rest and...."

She plunged her tongue into his mouth and Ethan lost his fight. He knew she was not fully awake, he knew she was distraught, but he also knew she was the sexiest, most beautiful woman he had ever seen. He couldn't help his physical reaction to her, as wrong as he knew it was. He responded quickly and with equal fervor, like a dam bursting with everything gushing out all over the place. Soon he was taking the aggressor role and not at all distressed about it. The more he tasted, the more he wanted.

Cydney was like a woman possessed. She kissed him furiously, her hands moving through his dark hair, down his wide shoulders, and the length of his back. The sleeping pills were having a very bizarre effect on her; they had erased her inhibitions and everything she felt for the man, all of the animal attraction, was bursting through like a fire hose. More than that, she hadn't been intimate with anyone since Brad. Eight years of sexual inactivity was finding release. Her natural reserve was running wild with help from her emotions and medication.

Cydney's hands went to his shirt and she began unbuttoning it. Ethan tried to stop her but she latched on to his earlobe and suckled furiously. With a growl, he surrendered, feeling her fingers as they danced over his flesh, submitting completely when she ripped the shirt open, rolled him onto his back, and began kissing his chest. He lay there, staring at the ceiling and savoring every moment of her heated mouth and soft hands.

He knew it was wrong. He knew it was as unprofessional and wrong as it could possibly be. But he felt such a strong attraction to the woman that he couldn't stop her or himself, no matter how unwise it was. The fire was overtaking him and he couldn't seem to stop it. But when Cydney moved to unfasten his belt, he came to his senses one last time.

"No, Cyd," he grabbed her hands to still them. "Don't do it;

you'll regret it and I don't want anything to ruin what we've started."

She gazed back at him with her luscious hazel eyes. She suddenly didn't look so overmedicated or sleepy. In fact, she looked rather lucid. On all fours, she crawled up on him, perched over his body as her hair draped down over the both of them.

"I won't regret anything," she purred in her sweet, sultry voice. "But if you will, I'll stop."

He exhaled, coming out as something of a grunt. "It's not that," he murmured. "It's just that this isn't happening naturally. It's not the result of a natural progression; it's because you're emotional and doped up on sleeping pills and I've got an attraction to you that I can't control. It's lust, Cyd. I don't want what we have growing between us to be cheapened by it."

She sat back on his flat belly, her gaze steady as she studied his face and absorbed his words. Suddenly, she unzipped her jogging suit jacket and threw it to the ground. She was only wearing a tank top beneath and quick as a flash, she pulled it over her head. Ethan found himself staring at breasts that were more beautiful than anything he could have imagined. They were full and perfect and wildly arousing, and oblivion began to close in around him again.

"Oh, my God," he breathed.

Cydney took his hands and put them on her breasts. "Are you saying you don't want any of this?"

Ethan could hardly speak. He wanted to clamp down on her soft flesh but didn't dare move. Still holding his hands to her breasts, Cydney leaned down and gently, erotically, suckled his lower lip.

"Well?" she whispered.

Ethan closed his eyes; he had to. He knew, deep down, that he simply couldn't take advantage of her. Sure, he could make love to her right now and get it out of his system. But it would wreck everything he was working to establish with her. He had to be strong. He had to be in control, for both their sakes. To be intimate with her now simply wasn't the right time.

Opening his eyes, he gazed up into her beautiful hazel orbs. Carefully, he rolled her onto her back so that he was in the dominate position. Without a word, he removed his hands from her breasts and kissed her mouth, gently at first but then with a wild roar of passion before abruptly pulling away. The swiftness of it left them both breathless.

"You cannot possibly know how badly I want you right now," he admitted. "But I just can't do it. It's not the right time for us, Cyd. We haven't even been on a first date yet but I swear to you, this night is only a foretaste of what's to come. I plan to come to know you very, very well and then I plan to make love to you every night for the rest of my life. But for now, you need to sleep and I need to find your daughter." He gently cupped her head and kissed her sweetly. "Do you understand me?"

She gazed up at him, feeling rejected and flattered at the same time. Her mind wasn't quite right, not enough to realize that he was doing what was best for them both. But she nodded her head.

"I understand you."

"All right?"

"All right."

He smiled faintly and kissed her again. Sitting up and looking around, he spied her tank top and gently pulled it back over her head. Once she was decently dressed again, he pulled the covers over her and tenderly tucked her in. Then he kissed her again, lingering on her sweet lips.

"Go back to sleep, honey," he rubbed his nose against hers. "I'll be out in the living room if you need me."

She signed contentedly and promptly fell asleep. Ethan

watched her for a moment, blowing out his cheeks with a heavy sigh and reminding himself to never again give her any sleeping pills. They made her crazy. Going into the bathroom, he buttoned his shirt back up, put cold water on his face, and struggled to compose himself.

It took fifteen minutes and applications of cold washcloths on his privates to achieve it and even after everything was settled down, he still wandered outside, into the night air where it was cool and quiet except for the traffic up on Duarte Road. That was a main thoroughfare through Arcadia and as he stood on the curb, looking up at the distant road, his mind was still racing with thoughts of Cydney. How he could find himself so emotionally caught up with a woman after only knowing her for a few days was beyond his comprehension. But he was.

Maybe he was just going crazy.

A cold night wind blew and Ethan took a couple of deep breaths, shoving his hands into his pockets. His cell phone was in his right pocket and he pulled it out, thinking that maybe he needed some advice from someone who wasn't close to the situation. That might help him think more clearly. He dialed a number he knew by heart and had for years.

A familiar voice answered on the sixth ring.

"What's up, Ethan? Long time, no see."

Ethan drew comfort from the sound of a man he'd been friends with for a very long time. "Hey, Beck," he said quietly. "You must be stateside if you're answering the phone."

"I am," Beck Seavington replied. "But who knows about tomorrow."

"Still loving the Navy?"

"Still loving it."

"Can't talk you into coming to work with me?"

Beck was a Navy SEAL, a man who had once been called a true American hero. He was a legacy Naval officer, following in the footsteps of his father and even his grandfather, so the Navy was really the only career he'd ever considered and Ethan knew it.

But he still liked to give him shit about it.

"What would I do in a cushy office all day long?" Beck said. "Getting soft and fat like you? That would drive me crazy."

Ethan's good humor faded. "It hasn't been so cushy lately."

"Really?" Beck said with some interest. "What's going on?"

Ethan didn't even know where to begin. "So much," he finally said. "Things are... weird. Let's just leave it there for a minute. But I think I have a problem and I need some advice."

"Sure," Beck said. "What kind of a problem?"

"Woman problems."

Beck grunted softly. "I think I'm the last person to give you advice on women," he muttered. "I've got some of my own."

"You?" Ethan said, surprised. "Sharon again?"

"Surprisingly, no," Beck said. "I've met someone. It's been a hell of a whirlwind and to say I'm crazy about her is an understatement."

"Seriously?" Ethan said incredulously. "Beck, I'm happy for you, man. That's great."

He could hear Beck sigh heavily. "It is," he said. "Really, it is, but tonight I did something... I was way out of line. I'm out driving around trying to clear my head about it."

"Oh," Ethan said, less enthusiastic in his reply because Beck seemed upset. "What happened?"

"I don't really know," Beck said. Then, he paused. "Yes, I do. I was an ass. We want to get married and she has assets. A lot of them. She asked me to sign a prenup. For protection, she said. It would keep our finances separate and protect me if anything happened on her end. And it would protect me if anything happened on her end. I don't know, Ethan... every time I hear prenup, I hear pre-divorce."

Ethan frowned. "You can't look at it that way," he said. "She's right – it makes smart financial sense to protect everyone's assets. You've worked hard for what you have and it sounds like she wants to make sure that's all protected. It's no big deal. But you should have your lawyer look it over."

Beck grunted again. "Not you, too."

"What?"

"That's what she said."

"She sounds like a smart lady, Beck. You might want to listen to her."

Beck sighed heavily again. "Like I said," he said. "I was an ass about it. But enough about me – what about you? You've got woman trouble and I want to hear about it."

Ethan shrugged. "I met her on the job," he said. "There's a lot of crazy stuff going on that involves her, stuff I really can't talk about, but the truth is that my boss is starting to catch on that there's something there."

"No fraternizing, eh?"

"Exactly."

"Well," Beck said slowly, "it's not a fling, is it? Like, the woman is crazy-hot and you just want to sleep with her?"

Ethan was shaking his head before the man was even finished. "No, nothing like that," he said. "I feel like... like this is the real deal, Beck. It's not a whim. I don't work that way."

"I know you don't," Beck said. "But I have to be honest, Ethan – when it comes to women, you are one of the most closed off people I've ever seen. I've seen you get downright nasty. I'd be shocked if this was just an impulse."

"I know," Ethan said, his gaze moving back to the house. "But not with her. Not with Cydney."

"You feel like this could go somewhere?"

"I really do."

"Then I suggest you take it slow," Beck said. "You can't take another Kimberly."

He was referring to Ethan's ex-wife. "I think it might kill me if it was with Cydney," Ethan said quietly. "But I really do want to explore whatever's happening."

"Then you should," Beck said. "Hell, I met Blakesley when I saved her daughter from nearly drowning. In our professions, sometimes we don't always meet people in the best of circumstances. But it's what arises from those circumstances that count, no matter what your boss says about it. If it's real, it's real. You can't deny it."

"Says the man who calls himself an ass when it comes to women."

They shared a chuckle as the front door to the house opened up and Ethan could see J.D. standing there, the light from the living room creating a silhouette behind him.

"Speaking of bosses," he muttered. "I need to go. But thanks. You've given me something to think about."

"Good luck," Beck said. "And whatever's going on with your job, I wish you well."

"Thanks," Ethan said. "As for your lady – just grab her some flowers and apologize. You're not an ass by nature, Beck. If she loves you, she'll forgive you."

"I hope so."

Ethan signed off and hung up the phone, tucking it back in his pocket as he headed for the house. J.D. wanted him back inside where he belonged and that was okay with him. Cydney was inside and even if she was asleep, he wanted to be where she was.

If it's real, it's real. You can't deny it.

Ethan was coming to think that truer words were never spoken.

SEVEN

IT WAS DAWN. The pink and gray sky was growing lighter over the San Gabriel Mountains, a beautiful view from the hotel suite where Nat and Joseph and Coral now sat at the breakfast bar. None of them had slept the night before even though Olivia was passed out on the couch. It had been a strategy session between the three of them; given the information Olivia had provided last night, the scheme had changed considerably. A call to their leader overseas had confirmed it.

Nat had been on the phone for the better part of an hour as Coral and Joseph talked quietly between them. At one point, Joseph went into the small kitchen of the suite and made coffee, returning with a mug for himself and Coral. By this time, Nat was off the phone.

"Well?" Joseph sat down. "Are we set?"

Nat nodded. "His Eminence is extremely pleased with what we have accomplished and he agrees with the change in plans," he said. "Let's go over it one more time."

Coral nodded, her heavy makeup smeared from being up all night. "I'll take the girl with me to the airport and wait for you both. But you know she won't go quietly. How do we plan to keep her quiet?"

They had already been over this during the course of the night and Nat had little patience with the woman who had sunk millions of dollars into their cause. It was the only reason he tolerated her; that, and the fact that their superior had instructed him to do so. Deep in the bowels of the Vatican, their leader gave directions that were meant to be followed.

The man known as Cardinal Bishop Baldemar Wildegrav was an extremely powerful man and the Supreme Sovereign of The Fourth Reich of Enlightenment. It was at his bequest they had come for The Lucius Robe. One did not deny the Cardinal and live to tell the tale.

"I have something to give her that will make her sleep," Nat replied patiently. "You'll get her to the airport and onto the plane and wait for us. We'll be there shortly."

"What about a passport?" Coral persisted. "Won't they want to see her passport?"

Nat's patience was fading. "Coral, it's your plane at a private hanger at Los Angeles International Airport. The plane and the hanger are registered under your corporation, Izan Enterprises," he gestured with his hands as if she were an idiot. "The limo will be here in a half hour; you'll go to the hanger, get on the plane, and wait. Joe and I will be there as soon as we can. Don't worry about any passports other than your own."

"But what about a flight plan? Where are we going? We won't be able to get the child into any country without a passport."

"His Eminence is taking care of that. Our first stop is de Gaulle Airport in Paris and we will be given instructions on proceeding once we arrive. Many supporters are in France and we'll have no problem making it through Customs without a passport for the girl."

Coral fell silent, contemplating what the day would bring. Her smeared-makeup gaze traveled to the sleeping bundle on the couch.

"I just don't understand why we need to take her," she muttered, sipping her coffee. "She told us all she knows. She'll be a burden we simply don't need."

Nat had had enough. He was tired and irritated with Coral and smacked the table with his open palm, causing both Coral and Joseph to jump at the sharp sound.

"We went through this all night," he hissed. "Must I go through this again? What she told us last night brings an entirely new element to this situation. After informing His Eminence about what the girl told us, we were instructed to do anything necessary to secure that robe immediately. We're not going to wait for the mother to turn it over. That could take days or weeks and, inevitably, the FBI will get involved in spite of our warning. It's simply a matter of time. Joseph and I are, therefore, going to take matters into our own hands and take the robe when the museum first opens, before it gets particularly crowded. We will have a car waiting to take us to the airport where we will meet you and the girl and take off for France. No one will suspect what your private jet will carry; you are not linked with Die Auhänger in any way. We need the girl to prevent the cops from doing anything rash or stupid. They'll think twice with a young girl as our hostage. Now, do you finally understand?"

Coral nodded, wide-eyed. Nat was quick tempered, violent and unpredictable. But they were all working towards the same goal, she told herself. Besides, she was afraid of him; too afraid to attempt to pull out or do anything foolish.

Moreover, her instructions on this matter, as they had from the beginning, were coming from a higher source. The Cardinal had her within his control as well with promises of a high position when the new Reich finally came to power. The television evangelist that everyone laughed at would finally have the last laugh. Those who ridiculed her for her dramatic ways and clown-like makeup would finally bow in her presence. She would make them pay.

"All right," she whispered. "I'd better get ready, then."

Coral rose from the table and disappeared into one of the bedrooms. Joseph's dusky eyes were on the sleeping girl on the couch. Nat caught his expression and turned to see Olivia sleeping quite soundly.

"I'll wait until right before we leave before sedating her," he said. "It will do us no good if she wakes up before she gets to the airport."

Joseph wasn't particularly happy that Olivia was being forced to accompany them on their travels, but his instructions were coming from higher up as well. They had no choice. Still, he felt very sorry for the bright young lady, caught up in something she could hardly comprehend.

"What are you using on her?" he asked.

"Halothane. It's a general anesthetic. A few good whiffs and she'll be out for a while."

"How'd you get that stuff?"

Nat shrugged. "It's amazing what you can get in Mexico for the right price. Halothane, and other narcotics, come in very handy when needed."

"So you always carry stuff like that with you?"

"You know what the Boy Scouts say; be prepared."

Joseph nodded, raking his fingers through his dark hair and glancing to the warming mountains out the window. He could feel his trepidation begin to mount at the thought of what lay ahead.

"Well," he grunted as he stood up. "I'd better get ready for work. Are we clear on what's going to happen today?"

Nat nodded. "Clear as rain."

Joseph didn't ask any more questions. If Nat said he was clear, he was. The only problem was that Joseph hoped he had the nerve to carry out what he must.

———

"Damn it," Stu growled. "Why didn't you call me?"

Cydney sat her desk, gazing up at a very angry security chief. She was dressed in attractive black slacks and a black shirt that clung deliciously to her shapely body. Her blond hair was pulled back, revealing her lovely if not exhausted face. When she told Stu the wild story of the previous night, it was apparent why she was so exhausted. Even though she had been told not to divulge what had happened, she felt the need to confide in Stu. He was her friend as well as security chief and Stu was positively beside himself at the news.

"Because you couldn't have done anything," she put her head in her hands, groggy from the sleeping pills and sick to her stomach with worry. "Nobody can know what happened, Stu, especially not Milt. Promise me you won't tell anyone. Olivia's life could be in danger if you do. I'm only telling you so you know how serious this threat is."

Stu was gearing up for another rage but he could see by the look on Cydney's face that she couldn't take it. So he huffed and puffed and sat heavily in her visitor's chair. He watched her as she toyed with a pen, seemingly verging on tears. He didn't blame her; he realized he was fairly upset as well.

"So what are they doing to find her?" he asked hoarsely.

Cydney shook her head. "They were working on it all night," she said faintly. "When I woke up this morning, there were a couple of cops and Agent Lowell in my kitchen. Kyle and Megan spent the night in Olivia's room and then Kyle drove me to work. Agent Lowell said I needed to pretend that every-thing was normal, so here I am. But I don't feel normal. I feel... I feel like my life is hanging on a precipice. One good shove and off I go."

Stu sighed heavily; he had known Cydney for ten years and remembered when her husband had been killed. He didn't want to see her go through that again but he was frustrated that he couldn't do anything to help her.

"The FBI won't let that happen," he reassured her although he wasn't sure he believed it. "I'm sure they're doing everything they can."

Cydney nodded, still toying with the pen. Then she burst into tears and lay her head down on the desk. Stu, seized with sorrow and sympathy, grasped the hand lingering on the desk-top. She held it tightly and he squeezed hard, wishing he could be of some comfort. It hurt his heart to see her like this. Just as he opened his mouth to give her what comfort he could, the door to the library opened and Serreaux and Dickerson entered. Stu watched them through the glass windows of Cydney's office as they approached.

Ethan paused in the doorway of Cydney's office, his eyes on her blond head as it lay on her desktop. He could hear her sobbing softly. He looked at Stu, standing next to the desk holding Cydney's hand, and jerked his head in the direction of the door.

"Give us a minute," he said quietly to Stu. "We need to speak with Cydney."

Stu nodded reluctantly, giving Cydney's hand a final squeeze before releasing it and leaving the office. J.D. closed the office door behind him as Cydney picked herself up off the desk and struggled to compose herself. She wouldn't look either agent in the eye as she wiped at her face.

"Sorry," she whispered. "I know I'm supposed to act normal but I just can't seem to get the hang of it. I'll try harder."

Ethan sighed faintly and sat in her visitor's chair, his dark eyes heavy with sympathy. "Cyd, I know it's tough but I need you to be strong just a little longer," he said. "We've got some news."

Cydney's head shot up, her big hazel eyes red-rimmed. "You found her?"

Ethan shook his head. "No, not yet."

Her face threatened to crumple again. "Then what?"

Ethan reached out and took her hand gently, a gesture not missed by J.D. It seemed to him that Ethan was having some trouble explaining the situation to the distraught mother so he took charge.

"We staked out the hotel on the corner of Los Robles and Walnut, the location that the GPS in Olivia's phone told us was her location," he said, watching Ethan caress the woman's hand. "We were able to pin down the exact location of the phone and, just after dawn, we raided a hotel suite. But your daughter wasn't there. In fact, no one was there. But her phone was on the kitchen counter."

Cydney stared at him, struggling to absorb what he was telling her. "Is that why you guys were gone when I woke up this morning?"

J.D. nodded. "We had a strike team move in to the hotel. I wanted to make sure we were on hand when your daughter was located."

Cydney continued to process what had happened. Ethan had said they were working on it and it was apparent they had. They had left her to sleep while they had gone about their job. She looked at Ethan, still caressing her hand.

"She wasn't there?" she repeated.

Ethan shook his head. "No," he said gently. "They must have moved her."

"But they left her phone behind."

He nodded. "There was really no reason for them to take it. It was on the counter next to a bowl of half-eaten cereal."

"What kind?"

He shrugged. "Cornflakes, I think."

Cydney's face screwed into tears. "That's her favorite," she sobbed. "Where in the hell did they take my baby?"

J.D. closed the office door as Cydney had another meltdown. He didn't want anyone to hear her sobs. Ethan rose and went to her, kneeling down beside the chair and putting his arm around her shoulders.

"Honey, get hold of yourself," he kissed her forehead, causing J.D.'s eyes to nearly burst from his skull. "I need your calm, level head right now. I can't focus if you're hysterical. Please?"

She nodded, sobbing into her hand and struggling to stop. "Where did they take her, Ethan?"

He kissed her forehead again. "I don't know," he said honestly. "But we're working on it. Remember what I said before? I need your trust. We'll find Olivia but you have to trust me. Okay?"

She nodded, wiping the tears from her face and gazing into his dark eyes. "I'm just so scared for her," she whispered.

He smiled gently. "I know."

The looks between them were tender and passionate, both at the same time. It was evident to an observer that there was much more between them than met the eye. At this point, J.D. cleared his throat.

"Special Agent Serreaux," he said quietly. "A word, please."

Ethan winked at Cydney and stood up, following J.D. out into the library. J.D. closed the door to Cydney's office and took

Ethan to the other side of the room where he faced him with a concerned expression.

"What in the hell are you doing?" J.D. demanded in a harsh whisper.

"What do you mean?"

J.D.'s eyes bugged as he waved his hands around. "Kissing her, that's what I mean. Have you lost your damn mind?"

Ethan cleared his throat, scratching his neck and turning to see if Cydney was watching them. She was busy wiping her face with a tissue. Ethan turned back to J.D.

"Look," he held out a hand. "I know it's not professional behavior. But I've been feeling something unprofessional for that woman for a couple of days now. In the privacy of her office, I'll comfort her in any way that I want to. Out in public in front of people, I'd never do anything like what you just saw."

"I was in her office!" J.D. was doing a very odd yell-whisper. "You were doing it in front of me. You can't kiss that woman!"

"I'm going to marry that woman."

J.D. stopped dead in his tracks. "Oh my God," he muttered, putting his hand over his heart. "I think I'm going to be sick."

Ethan snorted, amused. "Why? Because I found someone I want to spend the rest of my life with?"

J.D. was back to be agitated and animated; it was comical as his jerky hands moved all over the place. "You're insane," he hissed. "If you don't watch yourself, I'm going to take you off this case. I can't have you mixing business with pleasure like this."

Ethan's smile vanished. "You're not going to take me off this case," he growled. "But I will refrain from showing her any affection in front of anyone. I wasn't trying to be an exhibitionist, but I couldn't help myself. She's really distraught and has every right to be."

J.D. had his hand over his mouth, regarding Ethan through strained eyes.

"Ethan," he struggled to calm down. "Please tell me you aren't toying with this woman. Please tell me this isn't some kind of infatuation because if it is, I think the best thing would be to pull you off this case."

Ethan had never been more serious. "I know it sounds crazy, but I think I'm in love with her."

"You've only known her a couple of days. How can you know that?"

Ethan shrugged. "What can I say? She's perfect and I think I love her."

"It's not because you feel sorry for her, is it? You took the required psychology classes. You know how lines can be crossed when you're particularly sympathetic with a victim."

Ethan held out a hand, nodding his head emphatically. "I know, I know," he said. "I've been an agent for thirteen years. I think I know how to draw the line between sympathy and interest."

J.D. stared at him, trying to determine if he was telling the truth. After a moment, he puffed out his cheeks and shook his head.

"All right," he threw up his hands. "I'm not going to argue with you about this. But watch the kissing, okay? And any other public displays of affection. I don't want anything to be perceived as inappropriate."

"Point taken."

"Good." They began to walk back towards Cydney's office. "So you're really going to marry her?"

Ethan suppressed a grin. "That depends; I have to ask her first."

"I'm already planning the bachelor party."

Ethan cast him a reluctant, if not somewhat fearful glance

just as James Lowell entered the library. Immediately, their attention was drawn to the tall, blond agent.

"We're good to go upstairs," James told them. "We've got agents stationed next to The Lucius Robe case."

Ethan and J.D. checked their watches. "All right," J.D. replied. "The museum opens in fifteen minutes. Let's get to our posts."

Ethan nodded, glancing over at Cydney, who was now on the computer. He watched her through the glass window. "You want her upstairs?"

J.D. looked at the pale woman in the office. "Yes," he said reluctantly. "Get her up there. We need her eyes to notice anything out of the ordinary."

Ethan nodded and headed towards Cydney's office as J.D. and James left the library. Ethan opened Cydney's door, watching her as she typed. He studied the curve of her face, the way her lashes fanned out against her cheek when she blinked. After a couple of moments, she stopped and looked up at him.

"Hi," she smiled weakly.

He smiled back. "Hi," he replied. "Feeling better?"

She shrugged. "I guess," she said. Then the smile faded from her face. "Did J.D. leave?"

"Yes."

"Good." She stood up and walked around her desk, going to her office door and shutting it. Her reluctant gaze met Ethan's dark eyes as she leaned back against the door. "I just want to apologize for my behavior last night. I was out of control and that's really not like me at all. I'm really sorry... well, if I said or did anything uncomfortable."

His eyes glimmered warmly at her. "No need to apologize. You didn't say or do anything uncomfortable in the least."

She rolled her eyes at him, letting her embarrassment slip through. "Like hell I didn't," she scratched her head, refusing to look at him. "I practically molested you and I am really, really sorry about that. I don't have any excuse except I was just out of my mind. I hope you don't think too badly of me. I'm not usually such a loose woman."

He laughed. "In case you didn't realize it, I wasn't exactly resisting you."

She shrugged, nodded, and broke into a grin when he continued laughing. "It's not funny," she told him.

"No, it's not," he stopped snorting and looked at her. "It's very serious, in fact. And I'm very serious about you."

She gazed up at him, wide-eyed. "What do you mean?"

He cocked his head. "Let me ask you something," he said. "Did you say anything last night that you didn't mean?"

She looked somewhat dumbfounded, trying to remember what she had said. The drugs had muddled her mind. "I... I don't think so," she replied. "Like what?"

"You said that you didn't ever want to let me go. Did you mean that?"

She blinked with surprise and perhaps some chagrin. "I... I don't know. I guess so. I don't know."

He took a step closer to her, gazing down into her lovely face, and lowered his voice. "I hope you meant it. Because I have no intention of ever letting you go, either."

Cydney's limbs went to warm mush and she slumped back against the door. It was like a dream, these words from his mouth that she could have never imagined to hear from him. "Seriously?" she asked weakly. "Why would you say that?"

He moved closer but didn't touch her, cognizant of the open library door. He didn't want someone coming in and seeing them in a compromising position through the glass windows of her office.

"Because I'm falling for you, Cyd," he murmured. "In spite of this crazy situation we find ourselves in, the chaos and sorrow,

I have found the woman of my dreams in the most unexpected place and I have no intention of letting her go."

She just stared up at him. Then, the corner of her mouth twitched and, as he watched, a smile spread across her luscious lips. Her pale cheeks regained some color.

"Thank you," she murmured.

He smiled tenderly at her. "For what?"

"For bringing some light into my darkness."

Ethan couldn't help himself; he reached up and gently stroked her cheek. "Now tell me," he whispered. "Did you mean what you said?"

She nodded, so emphatically that tendrils escaped from her ponytail. "Every word."

His grin broadened. "Good," he said as he took her hand, kissed it, and let it drop. "Now, the gallery is opening in about ten minutes and we would like you on the floor when it does. Do you feel up to it?"

She nodded, pushing herself off the door and opening it. "Yes," she squared her shoulders. "I can do this."

"That's my girl."

It had been a long time since Cydney had been called anybody's girl. It made her feel comforted and wanted. They walked in warm silence from the office, down the corridor to the elevator, and up to the gallery above.

EIGHT

THE GALLERY WAS bright with the morning sun as it poured through the skylights and the security personnel were in place as Cydney took up position against the gallery wall to watch the visitors. Stu came to join her a short while later, very concerned for her mental state but noticing she seemed in better spirits. He stood beside her and made small talk as the museum doors opened for another sell-out day.

J.D. and Ethan had gone up to the roof where they had been the day before, leaving Lowell and several agents in the gallery below. Two men were stationed next to The Lucius Robe case, FBI agents dressed in the navy slacks and maroon blazer of museum security staff.

J.D. had made the decision to move security closer to the case due to the events of the previous night. He wasn't sure what to expect but he wanted to be prepared. Even the local cops had been called in and the Pasadena Police sent three black and whites, all strategically placed around the museum's perimeter. When the museum opened, they would be ready.

The patrons were already lining up in the queue to view the collection and Stu left Cydney standing against the wall as he moved forward to let the first twenty people in. Cameras and large bags were not allowed, so people dropped their oversized bags and cameras off at the security desk and crowded around the displays, softly voicing their excitement over the artifacts and being deterred by security from taking pictures with their cell phones. It seemed like another normal day.

So normal, in fact, that Cydney wasn't paying any attention to the well-dressed man making his way toward The Lucius Robe case. Truth be told, Cydney wasn't very alert; her mind was focused on her missing daughter and she wasn't able to concentrate on much else.

When she heard the first pop of a gun, she had no idea what it was. It sounded weak and muted. But she turned in the direction of the noise just in time to see one of the FBI agents guarding The Lucius Robe fall to the floor. The second agent was just drawing his weapon when the gunman turned his weapon on the agent, sending a bullet through the man's head. It happened so fast that it was like watching it all in fast motion, a scene out of a movie that was horrific and abrupt. There was hardly time to take a breath as it all went down.

Chaos erupted and Cydney found herself sprinting towards the case. All she could think of was protecting the robe. The gunman planted three armor-piercing rounds into the acrylic case in rapid succession, splitting the corner seam of the case and knocking the entire display onto the floor. People were screaming and undercover FBI agents were running towards the case from all directions. The hermetically sealed, vandal-proof case was cracked open and the gunman reached in and yanked out the ancient robe.

With the robe in one hand, the gunman proceeded to lift his weapon and cap off several rounds at the FBI agents closing in on him. The men dove for cover as the explosive-tipped rounds exploded against the walls and priceless artwork. Cydney screamed at the museum security force to hit the ground or run away, reaching the shattered case about the same time Stu did. The gunman turned on them both and shot Stu in the shoulder as the man put himself between Cydney and certain death.

Cydney shrieked as Stu went down. Looking up, she found herself looking down the barrel of a gun and into very dark, wicked eyes. The gunman stared back at her for a split-second before giving her a wink and turning the gun on two other agents who were running at him from the south gallery. He continued firing his weapon as he began to run, hitting another agent in the chest. People were falling to the ground all over the place as the gunman capped off round after explosive round, doing severe damage to the gallery as he fled toward the front doors.

Suddenly, a museum security guard ran right at the man and Cydney yelled at the guard to back down. She was positive he was going to be killed. But the man wasn't listening to her. In fact, he pulled out a gun of his own and took down an agent who had just stepped off the elevator and into their path. Now there were two gunmen, firing their weapons wildly and hitting walls, artwork and, on occasion, people. Cydney dropped to the floor when a bullet whizzed past her head, moving to Stu and throwing herself over him protectively. As she watched in horror, the two gunmen fled out of the front door with The Lucius Robe in their possession.

They could hear more shots fired outside and people screaming in the parking lot. People in the museum, lying on the floor, began to stir but Cydney loudly and calmly ordered them to stay down. Abruptly, the door from the roof access stairs shot open and Ethan, followed by J.D., bolted across the gallery entry and out the front door. Cydney could see Ethan as he ran down the long entry courtyard, watching him in the distance as he suddenly dropped to one knee and fired off several rounds into the parking lot. Then he, and several agents who had been outside of the museum, ran out of her sight.

It was suddenly still in the gallery. Like a switch thrown, everything went from bedlam to deafening quiet all in an instant. Dust and smoke were everywhere. People were crying, some were moaning.

Stunned, Cydney looked down to see Stu's blue eyes gazing up at her. He was bleeding profusely from the shoulder wound.

"Oh, my God," she breathed, looking around for something to stop the bleeding with. "Stu, you're going to be okay. It doesn't look that bad."

There was a woman a few feet away with a sweat jacket around her waist. Cydney reached out and pulled at the jacket. The woman saw what she was doing and untied the garment, throwing it to her. Cydney pressed it hard against Stu's shoulder.

"You're going to be all right," she repeated, pressing the jacket against his shoulder with one hand and stroking his forehead with the other. "Say something, Stu. Can you hear me?"

Stu was staring up at the ceiling now. He nodded his head faintly. "I was just thinking," he muttered. "Two tours in Iraq and I finally get it in a museum of all places. This really sucks."

Cydney smiled. "You're not going to get it yet," she said firmly. "It's just a shoulder wound. You'll be fine."

She said it but she wasn't sure she believed it. She wasn't a doctor. Around them, people were picking themselves up off the floor. Anne-Michelle suddenly appeared from the stairwell that led from the lower levels and her brown eyes widened at the horror and destruction. She clapped a hand over her mouth as if to hold back the scream at the sight of all the blood and damage.

Behind Anne-Michelle appeared three of the preparators, young men with wide eyes and open mouths. It looked like a war zone. Anne-Michelle's gaze finally fell on Cydney and the Director of Operations waved her over.

Anne-Michelle was shaking violently by the time she reached Cydney. Then she saw Stu on the ground and she fell to her knees.

"Oh, my God," she gasped. "Stu, are you all right? What happened? We could hear the noise downstairs."

Cydney took Anne-Michelle's hands and placed them on the sweatshirt covering Stu's shoulder wound.

"Gunmen," she told the woman in a low voice. "One of them was dressed like a museum security guard."

Anne-Michelle looked horrified. "An inside job?"

Cydney shrugged grimly and Anne-Michelle looked as if she were about to cry. As she put pressure on Stu's shoulder, her dark gaze fell on the remains of The Lucius Robe case.

"The robe," she breathed. "My God, they took it."

Cydney stood on unsteady legs, her gaze falling on the shattered case. She couldn't even speak. Numb, stunned, she went to the agent who had been hit first by the gunman, seeing that the man had been hit in the stomach. Two museum patrons, elderly women, were putting their sweaters over his wound in an attempt to stop the bleeding.

Already, Cydney could hear the sounds of sirens as she moved to the second agent who had been hit in the head. The handsome African-American lay prone on the floor, a hole in his forehead and blood and brain matter on the ground underneath him. Cydney didn't know what else to do but take a jacket from an elderly man nearby and put it over the agent's head. She struggled not to vomit.

People were crying and trying to move outside but Cydney stopped them. She stood in the middle of the gallery and lifted her voice.

"Please, everyone," she said loudly. "If you are hurt in any way, please come over by the stairs and sit down. I'm sure the paramedics are on their way. If you're not hurt, please move into the south gallery and stay there. I'm sure the police don't want anyone to leave right now. Please go have a seat and we'll have coffee and water brought to you."

People were reluctant to stay but did as they were told. Several people had been nicked by bullets or flying debris and the injured moved to the area near the staircase and sat down against the wall. One elderly man had a bullet burn across his forehead but he was in surprisingly good spirits. He even helped the preparators as they tried to assist the wounded.

Those who were unharmed moved with sobs and whispers into the southern gallery while some remained behind to help with the injured. Cydney sent one of the preparators downstairs to make sure the fire department were on their way. She also instructed the young man to grab all of the office personnel he could find to bring water and coffee up to the uninjured.

As the dust began to clear and those who were mobile began to move to their designated areas, Cydney got a clearer picture of the carnage. There were at least five dead and almost double the amount wounded. Taking some jackets from a group of uninjured ladies, she moved to the dead agent near the elevator and gently placed a jacket over his face. Then she moved to the agent who had raced in from the south gallery to cover him, only to realize that it was James Lowell. The explosive-tipped bullet had entered his chest and blown a hole the size of a basketball out of his back. It was an awful wound. When she realized who it was, the tears came. Gently touching the man's head, she placed a pink ladies' jacket over his face. She was just rising to her feet when strong hands grabbed her.

Startled, she found herself looking into Ethan's face. The man's expression was taut, his jaw ticking faintly.

"Are you all right?" he asked, his voice hoarse with emotion.

She nodded but her lower lip was trembling. "I'm okay," she replied in a whisper. "Are you okay?"

He exhaled heavily, nodding his head. "I'm fine." Then he did what he told J.D. he would not do; he put on a public display of affection by pulling Cydney into his arms and holding her tightly.

Cydney clung to him, her terror finding comfort in his powerful embrace. It took her a moment to realize that he was shaking. She pulled back, putting her hands on his cheeks to better study his face.

"Are you sure you're okay?" she asked, sniffling away her tears and caressing his cheeks with her thumbs.

He nodded again, closing his eyes at the tenderness of her touch. "Fine."

"What happened out there?"

He shook his head. "They disappeared into the heavy brush that runs between the museum property and the freeway. They must have had a car waiting on the other side because by the time we got there, they were gone. They somehow lost themselves in hundreds and hundreds of cars on the freeway."

Cydney closed her eyes, sickened at the thought. "And now they have the robe," she mumbled. "Those must be the same people who have my daughter."

Ethan didn't want to frighten her any more than she already was. He rubbed her arms gently, trying to distract her. "You're safe and that's all I'm concerned with right now."

Cydney knew he was diverting the subject but she let it go. She couldn't possibly become any more upset than she already was. She was feeling very numb and disoriented but a glimpse of Lowell's arm down by her foot brought her back to reality. The tears returned.

"Ethan, I'm so sorry," she moved aside, pointing to the body at her feet. "It's your partner."

Ethan's jaw flexed tightly as he gazed down at the prone body with the pink jacket over its face. After a moment's hesitation, he crouched down and lifted the jacket. When he saw it was James, he almost became physically ill but he fought it. He carefully replaced the jacket and stood up.

"The police are sending a command post over here and we've got a helicopter on the way," he told her, struggling to ignore his grief. "I want you to go down to your office and stay there. I don't want you up here in this mess."

She shook her head. "I had a front row seat to all of this," she said. "I don't want to go hide in my office. There are a lot of people up here who need help and I feel strongly that I'm needed here. Besides, Museum Operations is my jurisdiction. Someone really messed up my operations and I need to assess the damage."

He sighed heavily. "All right," he agreed. "I don't like it, but I understand what you're saying."

She smiled at him and he winked at her as they moved into the main gallery. Anne-Michelle and one of the preparators were helping Stu, giving him some water and putting wads of gauze from the First Aid kit on his shoulder. Ethan saw Stu and headed straight for him.

"Is it bad?" he asked whoever could answer.

Cydney replied. "It's a shoulder wound. I don't know how bad it is." She looked up at Ethan and lowered her voice. "He put himself between me and the gunman, Ethan. He took a bullet meant for me."

Ethan didn't know what to say. When the first of the paramedics began to arrive, Ethan told them to take care of Stu first. The ex-Marine was the first one to get medical care before being transported to the local trauma hospital. More and more paramedics arrived, some from neighboring cities, and soon the main gallery was filled with medical personnel, cops and firemen, all efficiently working as one big team.

The day progressed and the news media arrived. Reporters and their choppers were everywhere as emergency personnel tried to work around them. The Pasadena Police pulled a massive newer-model, state-of-the-art, forty foot American Coach into the parking lot, setting up their command post. The FBI also brought in a mobile crime investigation unit that wasn't nearly as large as what the police had, but it had more gadgets. There was some serious police envy going on as a result. As noon approached, the wounded were moved out of the gallery but the dead were left in order to better map out the chain of events.

Cydney was key to the investigation. She had lost sight of Ethan somewhere around mid-morning and spent the rest of the day with the Pasadena Police detectives and then the FBI investigators. She told her tale a hundred different times without any variations, including the part about the other gunman in a museum security jacket. Other security personnel were also questioned repeatedly and released one by one when they could no longer produce any useful infor-mation. But Cydney was left in the gallery with two uniformed officers, never out of their sight, as the FBI ran her through the events second by second. By the time early evening rolled around, she was tired, irritated and hungry and her patience was growing thin. Still, she did her best to cooperate.

At nearly nine o'clock, Ethan entered the gallery with a bag of food in his hand. He headed for Cydney, telling the uniformed officers to get lost and then politely asking his fellow agents the same. The men vacated as Ethan sat down next to Cydney on the bench in the main gallery and handed her the bag with grease stains.

"Thank God," Cydney muttered as she opened the bag. "I'm starving."

Ethan watched her pull a burger out of the bag before reaching in and claiming his own.

"I thought you would be," he said. "Sorry I couldn't do better with dinner."

Cydney took a big bite of the loaded burger. "You did just fine," she said with a full mouth. "Where have you been all day?"

Ethan took a massive bite of his burger. "Where haven't I been is more the question," he replied, chewing. "There's a lot going on and a lot to do."

Cydney took another bite of her burger, savoring it. Ethan pulled the fries out of the bag and handed her a soda from the two he had brought with him.

"How's Stu?" he asked.

"In surgery the last I heard," Cydney replied, her mouth full. "Anne-Michelle called his mother this morning to let her know what was happening, but I haven't heard anything else."

"Anne-Michelle?"

"The curator."

"Oh." He sucked down half his soda. "You know, when I asked you out to dinner last night, this really wasn't what I had in mind. I hope you don't think I'm a cheap date."

She grinned at him. "I would never think that."

He returned her smile, taking a moment to relax and enjoy her. The day had been hellish but somehow, when he looked at her, he felt as if his heart was lighter.

"I guess this is our first date, then," he said.

She wriggled her eyebrows. "You sure know how to show a girl a good time. Blood, guts, excitement and burgers."

He laughed. "I'll try to do better next time."

She just smiled at him, feeling better than she had in a

while. But thoughts of her daughter weren't far from her mind and they settled heavily upon her, once again, as she thought of the hotel sweep at dawn that failed to produce her child.

"Where do you suppose Olivia is?" she asked. "Do you think they'll release her now that they have the robe?"

Ethan looked at her, seeing that she had stopped chewing, stopped eating, and was once again verging on tears. He gently pushed the burger towards her mouth.

"Eat," he commanded. "Then we'll talk about Olivia."

She blinked and tears spattered on her cheeks but she dutifully took a bite of the burger, chewing slowly. Ethan wolfed down the rest of his burger, sitting with her while she finished most of hers. When she couldn't eat the rest, he took it from her and threw all of the trash away. Returning to the bench, he sat down very close to her.

"Now," he began. "As for your daughter, that's what we've been trying to determine for the majority of the day. We've got a lot of people looking for her and the guys who did this. If I could guess as to where Olivia is, I would say that she's been moved to another safe house somewhere. I'm sure she's unharmed, fed, and probably bored out of her mind. I don't think these people are out to hurt your little girl. They're just out to use her for leverage and an injured or abused child is not going to get them what they want. It just pisses people off and turns the tide against them. Does that make any sense?"

Cydney nodded, wiping the remainder of her tears away. "It makes a lot of sense." She looked up at him. "Thank you for putting it into those words. It helps a lot."

He smiled at her. "Good," he sighed, studying her fine features in the dim light. "So I think the investigators are done with you for the day. Let me take you home, okay?"

She shook her head. "I would love to let you take me home, but I've got an entire gallery I have to assess for damage. I think the Rembrandt case has been hit and the Degas towards the end of the gallery took a few hits as well. God knows what our damages are going to amount to."

"So you're going to spend all night here?"

"Probably. The insurance people are arriving tomorrow and I need to have a report."

"Has anyone called the museum that you borrowed the robe from?"

"Anne-Michelle did. I don't know what the ensuing conversation was like but it couldn't be good."

He nodded, looking around the gallery to all of the bullet holes in the beautiful golden walls. He sighed faintly.

"I'm sorry we couldn't prevent this," he said quietly. "We tried. We thought we had everything in place to prevent it."

She shrugged. "Had you guys not been here, I'm sure it would have been a lot worse." She gazed at his strong profile. "I'm really sorry about James. Have you known him a long time?"

Ethan nodded, his gaze moving over the wrecked gallery. "Nine years. He was my friend."

"I'm truly, truly sorry."

Ethan's eyes seemed to take on a distant look. "I drove out to his house around noon to tell his wife. I was a groomsman at the wedding two years ago. She didn't take the news too well. So I spent the afternoon with her and picked up burgers for you and me on the way back." He turned to look at her. "You wanted to know where I was all day. That's where I was."

Cydney's eyes began to well again; her emotions were very much on the surface for the past couple of days.

"I know what it's like to bury a husband," she murmured. "I feel her pain."

Ethan broke his promise to J.D. for the second time that day. He wrapped his arms around her and held her close, so close that he knew he was crushing her. But she didn't resist and he didn't care. It felt so good to have her warm and alive in his arms, the faint scent of her hair filling his nostrils. After a moment, he began to rock her gently, his cheek against the side of her head, drawing strength from her. After years of loneliness and bitterness, the new-found excitement was consuming him.

They stayed that way for a while as night settled and the distant voices of cops and agents moving through the galleries filled the air. The thunder of news copters could be heard overhead, but wrapped in each other's arms in the midst of the destroyed gallery, it was as if only the two of them existed. Ethan gave her a final squeeze and released her.

"Let me take you home to at least change your clothes and maybe get a shower," he said. "I'll bring you back and you can do what you need to do."

She still had her head on his chest. "All right," she murmured. "That sounds good."

Ethan kissed her forehead, hoping no one was watching. But when she turned her face up to him, he couldn't resist kissing her lips as well. It was a sweet, gentle, hormone-charged kiss. He pulled away reluctantly, smiling at her.

"I'll be in trouble if J.D. sees that," he said.

Her brow furrowed gently. "Why?"

"Because I'm on the job. I told him I wouldn't touch you during work hours."

"Then you're in big trouble, buster."

Ethan laughed. Just as he stood up and pulled her to her feet, a uniformed officer entered the gallery and headed straight for them.

"Are you Cydney Hetherington?" He was looking at Cydney.

She nodded, slightly apprehensive. "Yes."

The cop came to a stop and jabbed a thumb in the direction

of the entrance. "There's some guy at the driveway claiming he's your brother. He says he's here to pick you up."

"Name?" Ethan asked.

"Kyle Winter."

"Let him pass."

The uniform walked away. Ethan turned to Cydney. "It looks like your brother has come to take you home, instead."

She nodded. "He brought me to work this morning. With everything that's gone on, I completely forgot to call him."

They began to walk towards the elevator leading to the lower level. "He seems very protective of you," Ethan commented. "I spoke with him briefly last night."

"He is," she replied. "He's a good guy. I don't know what I'd do without him."

They reached the elevator and Ethan pushed the button. "That's the way I feel about my brothers. We'd all kill or die for each other."

"And who are these other Serreaux brothers that you've mentioned before?"

"Peyton and Alex."

"Are they local?"

He nodded. "Peyton is also with the FBI and Alex is a firefighter with the City of Los Angeles. They're both big and blond, believe it or not. Other than our height, we don't look too much alike," he confessed. "Come to think of it, they look more like your brother than they do me."

She laughed at his comment. "So we both have big, blond brothers."

He grinned. "No joke," he said, scratching his head. "Believe it or not, they're bigger than I am."

"With your size? Are you kidding?"

"No kidding," he assured her. "I don't know what my mom fed us as kids, but I'm the shortest at six feet four inches. Peyton is an inch taller and Alex is almost two inches taller. I'm the runt."

"So am I."

He snorted. "You're not a runt." His eyes were warm on her. "You're just right."

She smiled her thanks, thinking of her brother and how close she was to him. "We're lucky to have families that support each other," she commented, casting him a warm gaze. "And if you still want to take me home, you can. Kyle doesn't need to be shuttling me all over the place so far out of his way."

The elevator doors opened and they stepped in. As soon as the door closed, Ethan swooped in on her and kissed her deeply. Cydney responded with equal passion and it was a hot, lusty kiss. But when the elevator jerked to a stop, Ethan quickly released her. When the doors opened, they were standing about two feet apart and walked out into the corridor as if nothing was amiss. Together, they proceeded down the corridor and on into the library that contained Cydney's office.

Kyle was waiting in Cydney's office. He leapt up from her visitor's chair and met her in the doorway.

"Jesus Christ!" he exclaimed, looking his sister up and down. "Are you all right? The museum heist is all over the damn news!"

Cydney patted her brother's arm. "I'm fine," she said patiently. "I'm sorry I didn't call you earlier."

Kyle wouldn't be put off so easily. "What in the hell happened?"

Cydney eyed Ethan, now standing beside and slightly behind her brother. "You remember Ethan Serreaux, don't you?"

Kyle turned to the FBI agent who was about an inch taller than he was. "How are you doing, dude?" He shook Ethan's hand in a hurried and distracted gesture before turning to his sister again. "Mom and Dad are having a fit. You'd better call them right now. Where's your cell phone?"

Cydney's gaze fixed on Ethan. "The FBI has it," she said quietly. "It was the last number that Olivia contacted me on so they're keeping it in case she calls again."

Kyle understood but he lifted an eyebrow at his sister. "Then you better come up with a good story for Mom and Dad. They just got back home today from vacationing up north and saw all this stuff about the museum all over the news," he shook a finger at her. "They keep calling your cell phone and some guy answers and tells them they have the wrong number."

Cydney nodded wearily. "I'll do it now," she told him, heading towards her office. "I don't need you to take me home, Kyle. Ethan will drive me home."

Her last sentence trailed off as she entered her office and picked up the phone. Kyle looked at Ethan, who gazed steadily back at him. He took a second look at the handsome, athletic agent and immediately became suspicious as a good brother would.

"Why are you taking her home?" he wanted to know.

Ethan smiled weakly. "I'm assigned to protect her until this threat is over."

Kyle nodded although it was apparent he didn't believe him. "You were at her house last night, too."

"Yes, I was."

"My wife thinks you've got a thing for my sister."

Ethan blinked, not sure how to address the blunt statement. Given how Cydney's brother had reacted last night to everything, he suspected the guy's sense of protectiveness was working overtime. Not that he blamed him. He further suspected that any truths at the moment would not be well met and it wasn't his place to tell him anything at all, certainly not this early in the game.

He scratched his head in a nervous gesture that almost gave him away. "My relationship with your sister is purely professional," he replied steadily. "There was a credible threat against the museum and she falls under the scope of federal protection, especially since Olivia's abduction."

Kyle simply grunted, watching Cydney as she talked on the phone with their parents. He could see that she was wiping her eyes and his suspicious posturing left him. He turned to Ethan on more of a conversational level.

"It's like I told you last night," he said. "She can't take any more tragedy and I need to make sure she doesn't have to."

Ethan could see that he genuinely cared for his sister. "I respect that. But you have to respect the fact that there are certain things beyond your control and this happens to be one of them. I promise that I'll take care of her and Olivia. I won't let you down."

Kyle didn't have the opportunity to reply. Cydney came out of her office wiping her eyes. She looked straight at Ethan.

"I want to go see my mom and dad before I go home," she sniffled. "Can you please drive me over there?"

As Ethan nodded, Kyle stepped in. "I'll take you."

Cydney gave her brother a pointed look. "No, thanks," she said. "You need to go home. You spent all night at my house and I feel bad enough about it. Go home and hang with your wife and I'll call you if I need you, okay?"

Kyle wasn't happy. "Are you sure?"

She stood on her toes and kissed her brother's cheek. "Yes," she said. "I love you, Kyle. Thanks for being there for me."

There wasn't much more Kyle could say. He backed off and followed Cydney and Ethan out to the parking lot. The night was deepening when they got outside, the warmth of the Southern California day having faded into a balmy night. The mercury vapor lamps were buzzing overhead and they were nearly to Ethan's car when his cell phone rang.

"Serreaux," he answered.

J.D. was on the other line. "Ethan, where are you?"

"In the lower parking lot getting ready to take Cydney home. Why?"

J.D. was in the FBI command post in the upper parking lot. "Don't let Cydney know this yet, but we got another call from Olivia on her cell phone. Bring her up to the command post, okay?"

Ethan reacted coolly as his training had taught him. "We're on our way."

He hung up the phone and looked at Cydney. "J.D. has something he wants to discuss. Let's head up to the command post for a minute."

He was very casual and raised no alarm with either Cydney or Kyle. Cydney nodded, going to her brother and giving him a big hug.

"Thanks again, Kyle," she said. "I'll talk to you tomorrow."

"All right." Kyle cast a long glance at Ethan before moving to his car. "I'll talk to you later."

Cydney waved at him as he walked off. "Okay."

Ethan watched the tall blond man climb into his turbo-charged Mustang. When Kyle gunned the engine and peeled out of the parking lot, he looked at Cydney.

"Like I said before," he commented, "he's very protective of you."

Cydney turned to him. "We've always taken care of each other. And he doesn't like other guys around me; he feels like he needs to protect me from anyone of the male species."

"Is that so?" Ethan grinned. "How did he handle your husband?"

She laughed. "Brad was a lot shorter than Kyle but built like a bulldog. In high school, he was a linebacker and a wrestler. His nickname was "Mad Dog". It didn't take long for Kyle to figure out he couldn't beat him up or intimidate him, so you know what they say; if you can't beat 'em, join 'em."

"How long do you think it will take him to realize that he can't beat me up, either?"

"He's probably already realized it," she chuckled. "Did you have any crazy nicknames in school? Anything to scare him off with?"

He wriggled his eyebrows. "Nothing I would repeat to you."

Her soft laughter joined Ethan's. After the chuckles died down, he nodded his head in the direction of the upper parking lot. "Shall we?"

Cydney returned his smile and took his hand as they trekked across the lower parking lot towards the stairs that led to the upper lot. Ethan kissed her hand before letting it go as they mounted the stairs. She had no idea what she was really walking in to until a few minutes later.

NINE

OLIVIA WOKE up in Joseph's arms.

Her first awareness was of lights passing overhead, one after another. She could hear noise and echoes of voices around her, like she was in a big room. It was bright and harsh. Stirring slightly, she turned to see that that they were in some sort of public place. She didn't recognize it. But the second she moved, Nat leaned down and whispered in her ear.

"If you scream or make any cry for help, your mother will be dead by morning," he hissed. "Do you understand?"

Instinctively, she recoiled from the man, putting her hands over her ears and dissolving into tears. Joseph told Nat to back off and the man put some distance between himself and the girl. But Olivia was still upset, disoriented and not feeling particularly well. She had no idea where she was or what had happened. She wiped at her eyes, noticing that there were signs overhead. She saw the words Terminaux a few times and Station de taxis. She finally lifted her head when she knew that Nat was far enough away not to threaten her again.

"Where are we?" she asked Joseph.

He smiled down at her with his messy good looks. "In a magic land far, far away."

"France?"

"That's a good guess. What makes you say that?"

"Because I can read the French on the signs. Are we at an airport or something?"

Joseph's smile broadened. "You slept all the way across the Atlantic. Have you ever been overseas before?"

Olivia heart sank. She looked around at all of the people with their luggage, their coffees, their families. The airport was crowded.

"What airport is this?" she asked.

"We're in Paris."

Olivia looked at him, shocked. "Paris? Really?"

Joseph nodded. "Really."

Olivia looked around again, identifying a sign that pointed to the AirFrance terminal. She could smell bread and other scents wafting from a nearby patisserie and it made her stomach hurt more. People were speaking French all around her and it only fueled her disorientation.

"Can I walk, please?" she begged.

Joseph stopped and set her down. Coral, coming up from behind with her white leather carryon with gold trim, smiled at Olivia with lipstick-stained teeth.

"Hello, sweetheart," she said. "So you're awake now, are you? Are you hungry?"

Olivia didn't like Coral. She shied away from the woman, bumping into Joseph in the process. "No," she looked around. "Can I go to the bathroom, please? I don't feel very well."

Nat was several paces up ahead, glaring impatiently at them when he realized they had come to a halt. Joseph made a motion towards the restrooms off to the right, indicating why they had stopped, but Nat continued to glare.

"You'd better hurry up," Joseph told Coral. "Take her and go."

Coral grabbed Olivia by the hand but Olivia pulled away. "I can walk by myself," she insisted irritably.

Coral followed Olivia into the restroom, which had a lounge attached to it with a black vinyl couch and bright fluorescent lights. As Olivia wandered towards the white-tiled toilets, Coral moved towards the couch.

"I'm going to sit here and wait for you, sweetheart," Coral said. "Hurry up and do your business."

Olivia watched Coral sit on the couch, sigh heavily, and reach into her carry on bag. Olivia took a few more steps towards the toilets but didn't go completely in; she was looking to see what Coral was digging for. The woman pulled out a makeup bag, a cell phone, a hair brush, a bottle of pills and a small bottle of vodka. Coral popped three of the long white pills and chased them down with the contents of the vodka bottle. Then she pulled out another bottle of alcohol and drained that one as well. As Olivia watched curiously, Coral picked up her makeup bag, opened it, and then lay her head back against the couch and closed her eyes. In a matter of seconds she was snoring.

Olivia watched the woman steadily. It had been a very odd happening and she waited for Coral to open her eyes and continue with whatever she was doing. But Coral remained stone-cold asleep. Olivia's gaze inevitably trailed to the cell phone, sitting on top of the carry on. People were coming in and out of the restroom, not paying any attention to her. She wondered if she could get to the cell phone before Coral opened her eyes. She realized that she had to try. Slowly, she moved into the lounge, making her way towards the white leather carry on bag. The cell phone was her goal. If she could only get to it....

Coral was sleeping like the dead. Olivia snatched the cell

phone from the top of the bag and very quickly raced into the farthest toilet stall she could find from the lounge. She had no idea how to make an international call so she pressed "oo" for the operator and prayed the call would connect. Her hands were shaking as she held the phone to her ear, realizing she was very close to tears.

The numbers "oo" took her to a French speaking operator with Verizon Wireless International. Olivia was in a panic trying to explain that she needed to call the United States when the woman politely transferred her to an English speaking operator. Olivia was whispering and flushing the toilet at the same time so no one could hear her, but the problem was that the operator couldn't hear her, either. Finally, Olivia was able to get her mother's number across and the call was connected. The relief she felt at that moment was immeasurable.

The phone rang six times. Olivia counted. Then a man answered.

"H-Hello?" Olivia didn't recognize the man. "I'm calling for my mom. I need to talk to Cydney Hetherington."

The man seemed stunned. "Is this Olivia?"

"Yes. Who is this?"

On the other end of the line, J.D. nearly fell off his chair with surprise. But he maintained his cool.

"My name is J.D.," he said evenly. "I'm with the FBI. I have your mother's phone in case you called again. Where are you?"

Olivia knew she didn't have much time. "In France," she told him. "We're in the airport in Paris."

J.D. was motioning to some of the other agents in the trailer and the men flew into action, putting the wheels in motion to trace the phone number of the caller and then put a GPS tracker on it. It was difficult but not impossible. J.D. intended to keep her on the line as long as he could so his people could work.

"Paris?" he repeated. "How long have you been there?"

"I don't know," Olivia replied. "I slept the whole way over here. I think they gave me something to make me sleep because I feel like I did when I had my teeth pulled. I don't feel very good."

"But you're all right?" J.D. pressed. "They haven't harmed you, have they?"

In the stall, Olivia flushed the toilet again just to keep up the illusion that she was still using the restroom. "No," her lip began to tremble. "But they told me if I don't cooperate, they'll kill my mom. She's okay, isn't she?"

"She's fine, baby," J.D. said, more gently. He could hear how scared she was. "There's no way they can hurt her. But I want you to continue to cooperate, okay? It's important. Do you know where you're going?"

Olivia was struggling not to cry. "No," she sniffed. "I don't even know why I'm here. They told me last night that they wanted The Lucius Robe from the museum so they could crown a new Holy Roman Emperor. There's a guy with them named Joseph who is descended from the House of d'Orleans. They told me he is a direct descendent from the Merovingian line of kings. They said he descends from Jesus so he should be the next Holy Roman Emperor."

By now, several agents were listening to the phone conversation, taking furious notes about what she was saying. J.D. was trying to formulate questions that would bring about the most information but he was reeling with her revelations; Holy Roman Emperor.

"Have they told you anything else? Names, perhaps? Do you recognize any of them?"

Olivia was silent a moment. "There's a lady with them that I think I've seen on television," she said hesitantly. "Like, when I'm flipping through the channels, she's there sometimes. I think she's some kind of pastor or something. She cries a lot."

J.D.'s ears perked up. "Do you know her name?"

"Coral," Olivia said. "She wears a lot of makeup and I really don't like her."

Two of the agents fled with that information while three more remained with J.D. writing down everything Olivia was saying. J.D. thought he knew the woman Olivia was describing. In fact, he'd heard tale that Coral Chastity Aames had visited the Resurrection exhibit on opening day. Ethan had made mention of it in his daily report. The coincidence was just too striking for it to be random.

"Coral Chastity Aames," he breathed. "She's a part of this? I'll be damned."

On the other end of the line, Olivia was flushing the toilet for the eighth time. "What did you say?"

"Nothing," J.D. caught himself and focused once more. "Is there anything else you can tell us, baby? Any other names or places or things you may have picked up in conversation?"

Olivia thought hard. She knew her time was running out and she wanted to tell them as much as she could. But her fears were overtaking her, making it difficult to focus.

"Are you guys going to come and get me?" she asked.

J.D. had to remember that he was dealing with a young girl, a hostage that was caught up in something big and terrifying. "Absolutely," he said firmly. "Don't give up. Stay strong and cooperate. And if you can call us again from this number, do it."

"Okay," Olivia's tears broke through. "Can you please tell my mom that I love her? And can you make sure she's feeding my cat?"

"Of course I will, baby girl," J.D. said. "She misses you a lot and she's very worried. But she knows we're doing everything we can go get you back and you're very brave to call us."

Olivia sniffled. "I'd better go," she said. "I stole this phone and I'd better go put it back before they notice."

"Okay," J.D. said. "You're very brave, Olivia. Keep on being brave. I promise we won't stop until we find you, okay?"

She was weeping softly. "Okay."

"Do you believe me?"

"Yes."

"Good girl. Now go put the phone back where you found it and don't ever let them know you made this call, all right?"

"I won't."

The phone went dead. Olivia wiped her face and scrolled through the screen to delete the outgoing call. Slowly, she emerged from the stall. The restroom was fairly empty but for a few women passing in and out and she quietly made her way back to the lounge only to find Coral still sleeping where she had left her. With a silent prayer of thanks, Olivia put the phone back where she had found it and slipped back into the restroom to actually use it.

When she reemerged a short time later, Coral was awake and reapplying her makeup under the harsh glare of the fluorescent tubes, none the wiser to what had occurred just a few minutes before.

Olivia could not believe her luck.

———

Cydney walked right into it.

Ethan escorted her to the FBI mobile command post and helped her into a chair. J.D. was watching the way Ethan acted around the woman, the chivalry and gentleness. He never thought he'd see that kind of behavior from Ethan Serreaux, not ever. He couldn't help the roll of his eyes when their gazes met but just as quickly, J.D. planted himself in front of Cydney.

"Cydney," he said. "I asked Ethan to bring you here. I knew you would want to know that we received another call from Olivia."

The smile on Cydney's face vanished. "Oh, my God," she breathed. "Is she okay? Where is she?"

J.D. drew in a long, deep breath. "Well," he scratched the back of his neck. "This whole situation is getting stranger by the moment. Olivia says she's in Paris."

"Paris!" Cydney shrieked, leaping to her feet. Ethan's hands went on her shoulders to firmly put her back in the chair as J.D. grabbed her hands. "What in the hell is she doing in Paris?"

"I'm not sure yet," J.D. said. "But the main thing is that your daughter is fine. She says that they have not harmed her and she sounds healthy and alert. She's just confused, as you would imagine, and wants to come home. I told her we're doing everything we can."

Cydney was staring at him with panicked expression, expecting him to say more about her child. When he didn't, she lifted her eyebrows.

"Is that it?" she demanded. "She didn't say anything else?"

J.D. shook his head. "Not much else. She was calling on a cell phone that she stole so there wasn't much time."

"A stolen cell phone?" Cydney repeated, looking as if she were about to become ill. "Oh, my God. My poor baby."

J.D. watched her for a moment, careful about how he worded his next sentence. "I need to ask you something, Cydney," he said slowly. "Yesterday, were there any notable visitors who came to view The Lucius Robe? Anyone at all?"

Cydney wasn't following him, too focused on her daughter's plight. "Notable visitors? Like who?"

"Anyone at all; politicians, celebrities... anyone."

Cydney was struggling to think. "The only one I saw was

that televangelist," she said. "Why? Was there someone else? What does that have to do with anything?"

"The televangelist," J.D. repeated. "Who was it?"

"Coral Chastity Aames. You know, that woman who cries on television and begs for money. My grandmother watches her sometimes. Why?"

J.D. glanced at Ethan, who was gazing down at him with a grim expression. "Because," J.D. refocused on Cydney, wondering how she was going to take the news. "She's with your daughter right now."

For the second time in as many minutes, Cydney shot up from her chair. "What?" she yelped. "That woman has my daughter?"

Ethan and J.D. were struggling to sit her down again. "Did Coral Aames say anything to you, Cydney?" J.D. persisted. "Did you speak with her?"

Cydney nodded, shaken and furious. "She wanted to see The Lucius Robe. She wanted me to take it out of the case and I told her no."

"Was there anything else? Did you tell her your name or exchange any information?"

Cydney nodded. "She asked who I was and I told her."

J.D. looked up at Ethan. "So she gets her name and finds out where she lives...."

Ethan was following him; he cocked an eyebrow in understanding. "And sent someone to her house when Olivia happened to be there."

"Bingo," J.D. said. "Get the daughter and use her for leverage."

"Wait a minute," Cydney interrupted, agitated. "You're saying that woman was here to find out about me and my daughter?"

"No," J.D. shook his head. "It probably could have been

anyone. It just happened to be you. Had she run into any other museum manager, the curator for instance, she probably would have pulled the same thing."

Cydney went pale, her agitation lessening as the seriousness of the situation settled. "So this bitch is part of that Disciple group? And she kidnapped my daughter in hopes that I'd turn over the robe?" she shook her head furiously. "But they already have the robe. Why do they still have my daughter?"

J.D. felt sorry for the woman, he really did. He squeezed her hands gently. "Olivia said that they need her to crown the next Holy Roman Emperor. Beyond that, I'm not sure. But you can sure as hell believe I'm going to find out."

Cydney stared at him, dumbfounded and numb, as Ethan gently rubbed her shoulders. J.D. gave her a weak smile and stood up.

"I'll let you know if I hear anything else," he said to them both. "I've got a dozen people working on this right now so hopefully I'll have some news for you soon."

Cydney was beyond grief at the moment. All she could think of was Olivia with that overly-made up woman, caught up in some bizarre scheme of emperors and robes. It made her sick to her stomach.

"Surely you have a ton of information about Coral Chastity Aames," she looked up at J.D. "She should be easy to track, right?"

J.D. nodded. "We're working on it," he said. "We filed a motion with the U.S. District Court about a half hour ago to freeze all of her assets and bank accounts in the United States. As we speak, agents are preparing to raid her television studios down in Orange County and we have another group preparing to serve a search warrant at her home in Corona de Mar. The IRS is already moving in to start auditing accounts."

Cydney felt better that they were moving quickly. But it

didn't bring her daughter home any sooner. Olivia was a half a world away and Cydney was growing more distraught by the moment. But she rose from the chair, feeling Ethan's strong hands on her arms to steady her.

"Thank you for telling me," she said. "I appreciate all you've done for us, really."

J.D. reached out and shook her hand, holding it big longer than necessary. "There's one more thing," he said softly. "Olivia asked me to tell you that she loved you and wants to make sure you're feeding her cat."

Cydney's composure took a direct hit. She crumpled up and sobbed, feeling Ethan's powerful arms go around her. This time, J.D. didn't scold him for his public display of affection.

TEN

THERE WAS one uniformed officer at Cydney's house when Ethan and Cydney pulled into the driveway. Climbing out of the car, the night was cool and dark around them as night birds sang in the sky overhead. Somewhere, night blooming jasmine was growing and the heady scent wafted on the air. It would have been a very romantic night had their minds not been elsewhere. Ethan took Cydney's hand as they crossed the yard and onto the front porch.

The officer met them at the door. Ethan had seen the guy from the previous night so they knew each other on sight. He told the officer it was all right for him to leave and that the FBI would be taking over until morning. The uniform bid him a good night and left.

Cydney had already gone back to her bedroom by the time Ethan closed the front door and locked it. He shut off the living room light just as a fat orange tabby rubbed up against his leg and meowed loudly.

"Cydney?" he called. "There's a large carnivorous creature out here and I think it's hungry."

Back down the hall, he could hear her giggle wearily. She

suddenly appeared clad in only her bra and panties, walking up the hallway and into the kitchen. When she saw the expression on Ethan's face as he stood there looking at her, she suddenly stopped. He looked rather startled and she looked down at herself.

"Oh," she muttered, apologetic. "Sorry. It's a houseful of women and I just wasn't thinking. I'll be right back."

She turned back around and walked exhaustedly down the hall. But it gave Ethan an excellent view of her shapely body; flat belly, rounded buttocks and delicious thighs. He'd already seen her breasts and they were magnificent. He watched her walk down the hallway, inspecting her shape, not at all self-conscious about it because he knew she didn't know he was watching her. He was allowed to watch her openly with no one, especially J.D., to tell him to keep it under control. When she disappeared into the bedroom, he had to wipe the drool off his lips.

She emerged a short time later in a nightshirt that nearly knocked him off his feet. The scanty underwear had been more concealing; the nightshirt was loose fitting with a plunging v-neck and see-through fabric. And he could see that she wasn't wearing anything underneath it. But Cydney was oblivious to the fact that he was checking her out; she went about feeding the big orange cat now purring at her feet.

"Hey," he leaned against the kitchen doorjamb and crossed his big arms across his chest. "I thought you were heading back to the museum."

She shook her head. "Not right now," she said quietly. "After the news about Olivia, I really just want to lay down for a while. I can go back over around five a.m. or so and start my assessment. The insurance people aren't due until noon, anyway."

Ethan nodded faintly, watching her put cat food on a plate.

"Good," he said. "I'm glad you've decided to take it easy for a few hours. You've had a pretty busy day."

She set the plate in front of the cat and looked up at him. "So have you," she walked over to him, inspecting his handsome face in the dim light. Faintly, she smiled. "You really don't have to stay and babysit me. I can drive myself to the museum in the morning. I don't think you've been home since this whole thing started."

He gazed down at her, the gentle toss of her blond hair and the slight tilt of her amazing hazel eyes. The picture was soft, beautiful, and ethereal.

"There's no place I'd rather be than right here," he murmured.

Her smile broadened. "We've already had our first date," she said. "I guess it's okay for you to hang out here."

His smile broadened as well. "Can I ask you something?"

"What?"

"Do you have a boyfriend?"

She laughed. "Not yet."

"I'd like to apply for the position."

"Really?" she said with mock skepticism. "It's a fairly rigorous interview process."

"I'm confident I can pass."

Her eyes twinkled at him as her gaze moved over his powerful form. "I think you can, too."

Ethan unfolded his arms from across his chest and pulled Cydney against him. Her arms wound around his neck and their lips met, softly at first. But that momentary gentleness was replaced by passion so strong that Ethan swept her up into his arms and held her against him tightly. Their lips, their tongues, clashed and melded and began the intimate dance of desire. Before either one of them realized it, they were on Cydney's bed and Ethan's clothes were coming off.

There weren't any sleeping pills this time or a question of the right or wrongness of it. Ethan knew very well what he wanted and he further knew that she wanted it, too. There was such a powerful attraction between them that went beyond the physical. There was emotion involved and a magnetic pull he'd never before felt. Every time he looked at her, he felt as if she already belonged to him. He felt as if he'd known her all of his life. Her quick wit, sultry voice and gentle humor had him spellbound. He never wanted to be parted from her.

Ethan took his time with her. His mouth and hands never left her body. He felt like a starving man, gorging himself on her flesh. It was the most amazing experience he could have imagined and listening to Cydney's soft gasps told him she was experiencing the magic, too.

Their passion went long into the night. Agent Orange parked himself in the open doorway, listening to the animal grunts of pleasure and sniffing the musk of lovemaking in the air. Around four o'clock in the morning, Cydney and Ethan finally fell asleep entangled in each other's arms.

Ethan's ringing cell phone woke them up.

———

Olivia didn't own a passport. She'd never needed one. But during a taxi ride from the Charles de Gaulle Airport into Paris, she heard Nat and Coral speak of the need to get her one. Nat had been directed by his superiors to take her to a location where a fraudulent French passport would be made. As the town car drove slowly in traffic down the Rue Royale, Olivia strained to catch a glimpse of the sights. She could see the Place de la Concorde through the windshield with the big gold-tipped obelisk, but the car made a left onto Rue de Rivoli before she could get a good look at the obelisk.

It was early morning and the sun was just beginning to rise over Paris as the car made its way down the Rue de Rivoli. Olivia, seated between Joseph and Nat, almost forgot the fact that she was an abduction victim. She was actually excited to be in Paris. To their right was the Jardin des Tuileries, the garden designed by Louis the Sun King, and she could see the early morning sunlight casting brilliant light on the myriad of flowers. A big fountain spit a clear water fount up into the air. Directly to the east was the Louvre.

"Oh," she gasped as she caught sight of the glistening pyramid at the Louvre entrance. "The Louvre. I've always wanted to go there."

The car suddenly made a quick left on the Rue St. Roche and she lost sight of the dazzling pyramid. It was a tiny street, no bigger than an alley, and Nat exited the car and went inside a small tour company business that faced out to the street. It was called L'Ami du Voyageur and they had several national flag stickers on the big plate window. Olivia climbed up on the seat and looked out of the back window catching a small portion of the Sun King's garden and part of the fountain in her field of vision. The area itself was filled with small shops, mostly tourist traps and t-shirt shops, with dingy little apartments overhead. She turned to Joseph, sitting next to her.

"I've been in the same clothes for two days," she said. "I haven't taken a shower and I feel really gross. Can I at least get some clothes to change into and maybe a toothbrush?"

Joseph nodded. "I don't see why not." He looked at Coral, seated across from them and looking rather wary about the suggestion. "Do you want to go and get her some things?"

"No," Olivia said before Coral could answer. She eyed the woman balefully before refocusing on Joseph. "I don't want her to. I would rather have you get them for me. You might actually get me something I like."

Joseph fought off a grin. "Okay, munchkin," he said. "I'll see what I can do."

"Joseph," Coral grasped his arm as he got out of the car. "I don't think it's a good idea to...."

Joseph cut her off. "She's right," he said rather firmly. "She's been in the same clothes for two days. Tell Nat I'll be right back."

Coral opened her mouth to protest but he was gone, slamming the car door and heading off towards the Rue de Rivoli where shops were starting to open for the day. Olivia watched him disappear on the avenue, realizing she was alone with Coral in the car. The woman was weak and stupid. And slow. A thought began to occur to her. She might not ever have another chance like this. This wasn't like stealing a cell phone; this was much more serious.

There wasn't time to think about it, consequences or results. Quick as lightning, she threw open the car door, slamming it into the curb. As Coral shrieked, Olivia bolted from the car and ran in the opposite direction that Joseph had gone. It was a narrow little street that was bisected by another alley about fifty feet from the car. Olivia darted to her right and just kept running.

She was feeling glee and terror and everything else she could possibly feel. The pavement flew under her feet. She couldn't even look behind her, terrified that Nat was in hot pursuit and she would never make it to freedom. When another little alleyway came up, she darted off to the left and bolted as fast as she could. Her heart was pumping and her chest aching with exertion, but she continued running. She had to put as much distance as she could between herself and those people with their weird scheme. She had to run or die trying.

The next street she came to was a major boulevard. She turned left and ran as if the devil was chasing her. The day was awakening and there were people about heading to work, and she tore past them with tremendous speed. Oddly enough, no one gave her a second look, as if they saw that kind of thing every day. Paris was, if nothing else, a relaxed city. They didn't get excited very easily. Coming up to another major intersection, she turned left and continued her run. But her stamina was beginning to wane. Off to her right, she could see a big hotel. It was a major American chain and she headed for it.

The building loomed ahead of her, already busy with guests at this early morning hour, and she began to see it as a beacon of safety. Hyatt. Something from home, something she recognized. Surely they would help her. The tears began to come because she was losing steam. Her legs were burning, her chest ready to explode. But she managed to run onto the sidewalk, avoid two taxis that nearly hit her, and plow headlong into the lobby.

The lobby was luxurious and modern. Olivia ran through the lobby, past the main desk and concierge, and on into a small hallway. There happened to be a restroom in an alcove and she bolted into it. A woman who had just finished cleaning the restroom and saw her run past, followed out of curiosity, and found her huddled in the very last stall.

"Le miel, êtes-vous bien?" the woman asked timidly.

Olivia was weeping and shaking. She looked up at the round woman and wiped the mussed hair from her eyes.

"Please help me," she whispered. "Bad people are after me."

The woman frowned, not entirely understanding her, but she knew that something was seriously amiss. She put her hands out soothingly.

"Ne pas déplacer," she said gently. "Je retournerai."

Olivia had no idea what the woman said but she wasn't about to go anywhere. She was absolutely terrified. Hot, fearful tears came and she sobbed into her hands. The next thing she realized, another woman with a crisp dark bob and glasses was opening the stall door and kneeling down in front of her.

"Are you all right?" the woman asked with a heavy French accent. "What is wrong?"

Olivia was sobbing so heavily that she could barely speak. But she managed to answer.

"People are chasing me," she said. "They kidnapped me but I got away. Please help me."

The woman looked both concerned and dubious. She muttered something in French to the maid still standing behind her and the woman darted off. She returned her focus to Olivia.

"We will help you," she assured her. "What is your name?"

"Olivia."

"Olivia, can you please tell me what happened?"

Olivia put her hands on the woman's wrists, grabbing hold, emphasizing her fears. "Lady, please put me in a room somewhere, someplace safe. You need to call the cops and hide me. Please. I'm afraid these people will kill me if they find me again."

The woman could feel her fear but she still wasn't sure if she was telling the truth. After a moment, she patted Olivia's hand gently. "You're American, are you not?"

Olivia nodded. "Please help me."

The woman nodded patiently. "Of course I will, have no fear." Her gaze moved over the shaking, terrified girl and she realized she had to do something. Even if the girl was crazy, or a runaway, she felt compelled to do something. "Come with me, Olivia."

Gently, she pulled Olivia to her feet. "Where are we going?" Olivia asked, panic in her voice.

The woman put her arm around Olivia's shoulders. "Someplace you can rest until the police come."

Olivia's grip on the woman tightened. "You called them?"

"Someone is calling them right now."

"Thank you," Olivia was in tears again. "Can you please call my mother?"

"Where is she?"

"In California." When the woman looked reluctant, Olivia spoke quickly. "Please? She'll pay for the phone call, I promise."

The woman's brow furrowed slightly but she eventually nodded. "Very well," she agreed. "Do you know her number?"

Olivia did. The woman took her to a second floor room where she let her make a phone call to Cydney's cell phone. J.D. answered again and this time, Olivia was not surprised. In fact, she felt rather comforted to hear the man's voice. It somehow made her believe that this whole nightmare was over. After telling him the story, J.D. had Olivia put the hotel employee on the phone so he explained the situation to her. The woman went from somewhat doubtful to deeply surprised with the FBI man on the other end of the line. But when she hung up the phone, she brought Olivia a robe, let her take a shower, and then fed her pancakes from room service. She also bolted the door to the room.

By the time officers from the Prefecture of Police arrived, Olivia was fast asleep. But she was finally safe.

———

"I'm going to Paris to get my daughter and I'll kill you if you try to stop me," Cydney jabbed a finger at him. "Don't give me that crap about letting the police handle this. We're talking about my child and I'll get to Paris if I have to cross the Atlantic in a canoe."

Ethan was struggling not to laugh at her because he knew she was serious.

"Honey, I didn't say that we weren't going to go and get

her," he said patiently. "What I told you was that agents from the Washington Bureau are already en route to Paris to take custody of her. The Prefecture of Police has her right now and J.D. has already spoken with one of the Inspectors. She's perfectly safe but they are doing some preliminary investigating until our Washington agents get there. As soon as we can get a flight booked, we're gone."

"Prefecture of Police?"

"It's the Paris Police Department."

"Aren't they called Gendarmes?"

He grinned. "Maybe three hundred years ago they were."

Cydney was standing in her kitchen in the see-through nightshirt that had excited Ethan so much the night before. The sun was barely over the horizon and the phone call twenty minutes before that had awoken them had been J.D. with outstanding news: Olivia had escaped her kidnappers and was now in the custody of the Paris Police. But Cydney was so over-whelmed that her daughter had been found, safe, that she couldn't process anything else. She was even having difficulty making coffee so Ethan took the filter out of her hand and resumed making the coffee. Meanwhile, Cydney wandered around the kitchen, her mind a jumble of emotions and thoughts.

"Why are agents from Washington going to take custody of her?" she wanted to know. "Why can't we go right now?"

"Even if we go right now, we're still at least twelve hours away," he measured coffee into the machine. "The Washington agents are only six hours away and we want to get her into FBI custody as soon as possible."

Cydney continued to pace, digesting his explanation. "My poor baby," she ran her fingers through her messy blond hair. "This whole experience has been a nightmare. Do you think she'll be scarred the rest of her life?"

Ethan poured the water into the machine and turned it on. "No," he turned to her, eyeing her supple body through the sheer fabric. "She's young and resilient. I think, with time, she'll be fine."

Cydney suddenly came to a halt. "Oh, my God," her eyes were wide at him. "You don't think... think they molested her, do you?"

He shook his head, walking over to her and putting his hands on her shoulders.

"She said she was unharmed," he said. "Besides, that's not what this group is after. They wanted her for leverage, not sex."

Cydney scratched her head, thinking on his words. "J.D. said that she escaped them," she muttered, her mind completely wrapped around her daughter's plight. "She must have been so scared, Ethan. Can you imagine being fifteen years old and running from kidnappers? Kidnappers who took you to Paris, no less. She's never even been to Paris. How did she know where to go, where to find safety?"

He pulled her close and kissed her forehead. "J.D. will be here shortly and he can answer your questions." He looked down at the outline of her breasts through the nightshirt. "You might want to consider changing before he gets here."

She looked down at herself as if her state of dress had just occurred to her. Then she gazed up at him, his incredibly handsome face in the early morning light. Thoughts shifted from Olivia to Ethan. What she had experienced with him last night could only be described as purely magical and all reserve, all inhibitions, had vanished. She felt like a new woman. She pressed up against him, her arms around his tight waist.

"Any regrets about last night?" she asked.

He wrapped his arms around her, trapping her against him. "Are you kidding?" he said. "That was the most amazing night of my life. Thank God for The Lucius Robe and Die Auhänger. I would have never met you otherwise."

Cydney lifted her eyebrows. "I'm not sure that my daughter's abduction was a fair trade-off, but I know what you mean. There's no way we would have met otherwise. I don't hang out in Glendale and I'm pretty sure you don't get over this way."

He shook his head, kissing her forehead tenderly. "They say that everything happens for a reason," he murmured as his lips moved across her flesh. "I really thought I would never be happy again but the past two days have seen that opinion drastically changed."

"Really?"

"Really."

She closed her eyes as his mouth moved down her left temple to her cheek. "I never even thought of another man since Brad died," she whispered. "It was just too painful. Not only did I not want to expose my emotions again, but I almost felt as if I were betraying his memory by thinking of another man."

"And now?"

Her head lolled back as his lips suckled her neck and chin. "He wouldn't want me to be alone the rest of my life," she breathed. "And I think he would have liked you."

"So you're okay with us? I don't want to rush you if you're not ready."

She could feel the heat in her body rise as his mouth moved to her collar bone and his right hand began caressing a full breast. "I'm ready," she murmured, capturing his wandering mouth with her soft lips. "Oh, God, I am completely ready."

The kiss was blazing with passion and raw emotion. Ethan picked her up and she wrapped her slender legs around his waist, hanging on to him. Carrying her over to the kitchen table, he laid her down on the surface and made love to her.

It was fortunate for them that J.D. rang the doorbell just

seconds after they finished. They stared at each other in shock, like teenagers who just got caught behind the bleachers. When the doorbell rang again, Cydney began to giggle uncontrollably and Ethan pulled her up from the table and put his hand over her mouth.

"Shush," he hissed. "Do you want to get me fired?"

She continued to giggle and he picked her up bodily and carried her down the hall, setting her down when he reached her bedroom.

"Hurry up and get some clothes on," he told her as he rapidly pulled on his dress slacks from the night before; it was all he had to wear. "I'll keep him busy while you get dressed."

She fell onto the bed like a rag doll. "I don't think I can get dressed," she mumbled into the pillows. "I feel so... good."

He struggled not to grin at her and slapped her bottom lightly. "Get dressed," he commanded. "I'll see you out in the kitchen."

She suddenly flipped over. "Ethan!" she gasped. "The table... make sure there's no remnant of... well, you know...."

He nodded patiently. "I'll make sure."

"And if he asks what that smell is in there, just tell him the cat farted."

He burst into laughter, trying not to be too loud. "Don't worry; the smell of brewing coffee should cover up any smells of sex."

She grinned at him as the doorbell rang again. He went over to her and tried to pull her up from the bed but it was like trying to grab hold of spaghetti; she was falling every which way and giggling.

"Get dressed before I get in trouble." He had her by the wrists. "He's here to talk about Olivia, remember?"

Her smile vanished and he was sorry to see it go. He loved it when the happy and carefree Cydney emerged. She was dressed in yoga pants and a sexy little tank top almost immediately as Ethan pulled on his white t-shirt from the day before and went to the door to open it.

J.D. was standing on the porch looking at his feet. When he looked up and saw Ethan only in his t-shirt and dress pants, he shook his head and closed his eyes.

"I don't want to know what you've been doing," he put up a hand as if to stop any explanation that came out of Ethan's mouth. "But I can guess."

Ethan stepped back and ushered him into the house. "How did Olivia sound when you talked to her?" he wisely changed the subject.

J.D. smelled the coffee and went straight into the kitchen. "Scared," he said frankly. "But her story is amazing. Where's Cydney?"

"Here," Cydney entered the kitchen, heading for the coffee pot. J.D. had just poured himself a cup and she took it right out of his hand. "Thanks."

He pursed his lips irritably at her and hunted around for another cup. He spoke as he poured. "I have to give you all the credit in the world, Mrs. Hetherington," he said. "Your daughter is one courageous kid."

Cydney ignored the formal name address, but oddly, it didn't upset her as much as it once had. "Tell me everything."

J.D. took a healthy swig of the strong black brew and turned to her. "Well," he started. "It seems that she escaped a car when it came to a stop. According to your daughter, she ran in circles trying to lose them until she came upon a Hyatt Hotel. She ran in the lobby and asked for help. Fortunately, they didn't think she was crazy and sheltered her until the police came."

By this time, Cydney was watching him with tears in her eyes. "But she's okay?"

J.D. nodded, a twinkle in his dark eyes. "She's fine. The

police have her in a safe location and a couple of agents from the Washington Bureau are just a few hours away. She'll be in our hands very soon, so don't worry. She's fine."

Cydney couldn't stop the tears that flowed freely down her cheeks. She put her hand over her mouth as she spoke. "Can I speak to her? Can we call her?"

J.D. nodded. "Sure."

He picked up the roam phone on the kitchen counter and dialed. After a few words, he paused as if waiting to be transferred and smiled at Cydney. By now, Ethan had come up behind her and wrapped his big arms around her. J.D. tried not to stare as Ethan buried his face in the side of her head, murmuring soft words to comfort her. He was, frankly, astonished. He would have never guessed such a surly and bitter man towards the opposite sex could be so sweet and gentle. He was distracted from his observations when another voice came over the line. After a few short words, J.D. waved Ethan over.

"Come here," he held out the phone. "I don't think the guy speaks English and my French isn't good enough. Tell him what we want."

Ethan took the phone and put it up to his ear. "Ceci est Serreaux Spécial d'Agent avec le Bureau Fédéral d'Investigation," he said in perfect French. "Peux-je parler avec Dulay d'Inspecteur, s'il vous plaît?"

Cydney, very impressed that he was fluent in French, watched him carefully as he spoke to the person on the other end of the line. After a couple of seconds, it was evident that someone else came on the phone.

"Ceci est Serreaux Spécial d'Agent," he repeated. "Qui est ceci?"

Cydney came closer, listening to the male voice on the other line. The words were English; Cydney could hear a few she recognized. Their eyes met as Ethan spoke.

"Inspector Dulay," he said. "Very nice to meet you. I have Olivia Hetherington's mother with me and she would like to speak to Olivia if she's available."

After a pause, Ethan handed the phone to Cydney. The next voice she heard was Olivia's.

"Mom?"

Cydney broke down. "Hi, baby," she wept. "How are you? Are you all right?"

Olivia began to cry, too. "I'm fine," she sobbed. "I want to come home."

"I know, sweetheart," Cydney could feel Ethan's arm go around her shoulders comfortingly. "Ethan and I are getting a flight to Paris as soon as we can. Meanwhile, a couple of FBI agents are going to be there soon and stay with you until we arrive."

Olivia wiped her cheeks. "You know," she chuckled through her tears. "I've always wanted to come to Paris. Now they won't let me go to the Louvre."

Cydney laughed, wiping away her own tears. "I promise we'll go when I get there."

"Good," Olivia was calming now that the emotions of the initial reunion were fading. "I've been eating since this morning. You wouldn't believe the food they have here. The restaurant in the hotel had thirty different kinds of goose liver."

Cydney launched into a conversation with her daughter about the French foods she would, and would not eat, as Ethan leaned back against the kitchen counter and listened to the happy chatter. Every once in a while he'd look over at J.D. as the man stood aside and sipped his coffee, gazing into his onyx eyes and suspecting that there was more on J.D.'s mind than just this happy reunion. It was enough to get him off the counter and motion to J.D. with a discreet nod of the head. J.D. followed him into the living room.

"What's up?" he asked the man.

J.D. shook his head. "What do you mean?"

"I mean I've seen that look on you before. What else is there that you haven't told Cydney?"

J.D. shook his head. "Nothing, really, but we asked Olivia about the robe," he said quietly. "She doesn't know anything about it. They never showed it to her, which makes me wonder if they even have it. But she did confirm that Coral Chastity Aames was with her the entire time. We traced the cell phone call Olivia originally made to us and the number comes back registered to Aames' company, Izan Enterprises."

Ethan stared at him a moment before his dark eyes widened. "Jesus," he hissed, smacking himself on the forehead. "I don't know why this never occurred to us before. Think about this, J.D.; Izan Enterprises?"

"What?" J.D. wasn't following him.

Ethan shook his head ominously. "I've spent a lot of time on airplanes and, consequently, a lot of time doing crossword puzzles. I remember seeing this once in puzzle. Izan is 'Nazi' spelled backwards."

J.D.'s eyes bugged as the full impact of Ethan's statement hit him. He made the connection immediately. "The Fourth Reich of Enlightenment."

"She's been linked to this all along and we never realized it," Ethan said. "Who's going to pay attention to a televangelist that no one takes seriously anyway? She'd be the last person suspected of being linked to a radical sect."

J.D. nodded, blowing out his cheeks as the realization settled. "Why didn't I see that before?" he demanded to no one in particular. Then he looked at Ethan. "We've moved the IRS in to audit her companies since yesterday. Maybe that will bring up some kind of shady dealings, like monies deposited to individuals or other companies that can be traced that support this radical sect."

Ethan opened his mouth but J.D.'s smart phone rang and he answered. As Ethan listened to Cydney on the phone with Olivia in the kitchen and J.D. on the phone to someone he couldn't identify, he went back into the bedroom and put on his dress shirt.

He had just finished securing his tie when J.D. wandered back into the bedroom. The man was so preoccupied he couldn't even make a comment about the fact that all of the covers were off the bed and the mattress was askew. He looked straight at Ethan.

"You're not going to believe this," he said.

Ethan wasn't sure he wanted to know. "What?"

"That was the IRS," he said. "I talked to an auditor named Ruddins and she has spent the better part of twenty-four hours auditing Izan's international capital accounts. She had a little question."

"What question was that?"

"Under the 2001 Banks and Companies Trust Law, Cayman accounts aren't as private as they once were. You can find out certain information under the right circumstances," he lifted his eyebrows. "Ruddins wanted to know if we know why Izan is depositing huge amounts of money into a Cayman Islands account with a Vatican City address."

Ethan just stared at him, torn between confusion and surprise. "What?" he finally blurted.

J.D. nodded his head in a knowing gesture. "That's exactly what I said. What in the world would a deeply religious corporation that adheres to the strict Southern Baptist Admission of Faith doctrine be doing depositing money into an account controlled by the Roman Catholic Church?"

Ethan continued to stare at the man as a feeling of tremendous foreboding closed in around him. "With everything we've learned about Die Auhänger over the past few years, with all of the evidence about it, I have a couple of questions for you," his quiet tone took on a tinge of irony. "Remember when we were speculating where they get all of their financial support from?"

"Looks like we're finally figuring it out."

"And historically, who crowns the new Holy Roman Emperor?"

J.D. just shook his head. "The Pope."

"So she's depositing money into an account with a Vatican City address?"

"Is it possible this sect has bigger ties than we could have imagined?"

"Like, all the way to the top of the Catholic Church?"

"How do we fight the Pope?"

J.D. didn't know. At the moment, he realized he didn't know nearly as much as he should have. He saw some Bailey's liqueur on the dining room sideboard and poured a couple of ounces into his morning coffee in the hopes it would either help him think or dull the sense of dread he was feeling.

The mystery was deepening.

ELEVEN

INSPECTOR DULAY of the Paris Prefecture of Police was a man in his mid-forties, tall and lanky, with dark hair and big brown eyes. He lived on the Rue de Navarin on the north end of Paris in a five-story apartment building that had been built in the early eighteen hundreds. It was everything a Paris apartment building should be with its distinct provincial architecture and sharply angled roof. He lived in his six-room flat with his wife, an interior designer, and their twins who had just celebrated their fourth birthday. His wife was German and the toddlers spent all day at the German school that sat alongside the picturesque St. Martin canal that ran through the Paris suburbs.

The young American kidnap victim had been assigned to Dulay. Two agents from the Washington D.C. Federal Bureau of Investigation had come to take custody of her until her mother arrived, but Olivia was still very upset and the introduction of two new strangers wasn't helping her anxiety. She clung to Dulay because he had been one of the first officers on the scene at the Hyatt when the police had been called. Because of that, she was very attached to him and the American agents, after calling their field supervisor with the news that Olivia cried every time they came around her, were sent back home. Dulay was officially put in charge of her.

She became his responsibility until the Los Angeles agents, along with the mother, arrived. Other than put Olivia up at a hotel for a couple of days, Christophe wasn't quite sure what to do with her. She was a sweet, intelligent girl and he felt rather bad at the ordeal she had endured. It was a harrowing, and somewhat crazy, tale. Putting her up in a hotel seemed so cold but, more than that, he would have to provide around the clock protection for her which could get expensive.

After some deliberation, he thought it best to bring her home with him so he could keep a constant eye on her. There was something about this whole case that seemed very strange and he wanted to keep her close.

His wife, Elise, was thrilled with the visitor and went out of her way to be extremely gracious even though she didn't speak a word of English. Olivia had taken French for two years and knew some conversational French, so there was some amount of communication going on.

The twins, Arthur and Vivienne, were enamored with their American visitor. Because of American cartoons, they spoke better English than their mother. The afternoon that Christophe brought Olivia home, she lay on the floor with the twins and drew pictures with them for hours. It was a normal, safe place for the teenager and she was desperate for something safe and normal. Christophe and Elise thought it was one of the sweeter things in life that they had witnessed. Beyond being a girl in trouble, or a guest, Olivia Hetherington was an average young lady and they naturally felt protective over her.

That night, after speaking with her mother, it was particularly difficult for Olivia. She lay on the leather couch in the living room, the large French doors open to let some air in, listening to the unfamiliar sounds outside the window. She couldn't sleep even though she was exhausted. Finally, she got up and stood in the open doorway, feeling the spring breeze on her face and experiencing some of the fascination that was Paris. Christophe, getting up after midnight to check on the twins, found her standing in the open doorway.

He came up behind her, listening to the faded sounds of night and feeling the soft breeze on his face. Olivia noticed him and smiled sheepishly.

"I can't sleep," she said. "I didn't wake you, did I?"

Christophe shook his head. "Not at all," he replied. "Would you like some hot chocolate? Tea, perhaps?"

Olivia shook her head. She gazed across the rooftops, up to the moonlit sky. "Have you been a cop a long time?" she asked.

He stood next to her in the doorway, looking at the street below as she looked up at the sky. "A long time," he murmured. "Almost twenty-five years."

"Have you seen a lot of kidnap victims?"

Christophe shrugged his lanky shoulders. "I've seen enough," he replied. "It is one of the aspects of my job."

"Do people ever feel safe again?"

He looked at her. "They do," he replied. "From what I understand about your kidnapping, you were not the true target. You were a victim of convenience."

Olivia gazed up and him and cocked her head. "La victime de convenance," she grinned when he nodded his approval. "Je suis le président Du Club français de mon école. J'aime pratiquer mon français."

"You are doing a very good job."

She grinned. "I'm trying. You speak much better English than I speak French."

He smiled. "I have had more years of practice than you have."

"Très vrai."

He laughed at her attempts to speak his language. But Olivia's smile faded as her gaze turned to the street below, now still and quiet in the dark.

"Do you think they're still out there?" she asked with concern. "The people who kidnapped me, I mean. Is that why you brought me here? So they couldn't find me?"

He lifted a dark eyebrow. "Would you have rather stayed at the police station?"

"No. But you didn't answer my question. Do you think they're looking for me?"

He gazed steadily at her. "I think you need to go to bed."

All warmth faded from her features. "I know," she sighed. "But I'm kind of scared right now. It's hard for me to sleep."

He put his hand on her shoulder and turned her around for the couch. "I understand," he said in understanding. "But you are safe here, I promise. I won't let anyone get you."

Olivia let him steer her towards the couch and she sat down, laying down when he practically shoved her onto her back. He pulled up the sheet.

"Pretend I'm your father and do what I say," he commanded gently. "Go to sleep now. You will have a busy day tomorrow."

She gazed up at him with her big green eyes, very reminiscent of her mother. "My father died eight years ago," she said. "It's just me and my mother."

A ripple of sorrow crossed Christophe's features. "I am sorry to hear that," he said. "Then pretend I am your uncle and do as I say. *Sleep.*"

"Is the door locked?"

"The front door has two big bolts on it. You're safe, Olivia. I promise."

She didn't say anything as she pulled the sheet up and snuggled down. As Christophe left the room, he could hear the distinct sound of tears.

———

The first flight they could get out of Los Angeles International Airport direct to Paris was an AirFrance flight that departed at three-thirty in the afternoon the next day. It was a flight with a stopover in New York before continuing on to Paris. Cydney was frantic that it would be two days before she got to her daughter, but it was the best they could do. J.D. booked himself, Ethan, Cydney and two other special agents onto the flight.

The day was busy with preparations for the coming trip. Cydney had been forced to let Milt in on what had happened because she needed to request immediate time off. Milt had been greatly disturbed but seemed more concerned that word would leak to the press about the abduction.

It was bad enough that the news of the museum heist had spread all over the world and the Bristol Museum of Antiquities was extremely unhappy that The Lucius Robe had been the target of the theft, so Milt and Anne-Michelle had been thrust to the forefront of damage control for the incident. The abduction of Cydney's daughter only added to Milt's stress. He gave the time off without a fight.

Cydney's second task of the day was to check up on Stu, who was recovering from surgery at Huntington Memorial Hospital in Pasadena, just a stone's throw from the museum. He was in good spirits, hated the hospital food, and was upset because Cydney was going to Paris while he was stuck in a hospital. Cydney mentioned she was going with four FBI agents and he seemed better with that. At least she was adequately protected. But when he found out that Ethan was one of the agents, he grew inordinately quiet. Cydney suspected that she knew why but she let it go. Stu was a dear friend and, to her, that was all he would ever be.

The rest of the day before she left was spent packing. She packed a big bag for Olivia and a massive suitcase for herself. Ethan had spent the entire day with her, watching her do laundry and make herself busy in preparation for the trip. He knew her anxiety was making her rush around like a madwoman, anxious to reach her child, so he helped her as much as he could and didn't say a word when she packed the biggest suitcase he had ever seen. She had enough clothes for a six month sojourn.

Somewhere towards mid-afternoon, Kyle and Megan came over and Ethan used that time to return home so he could take a shower, change clothes and pack. He didn't want to leave Cydney alone and was grateful for Kyle's appearance. He left Cydney with a delicious kiss, not missed by Kyle or Megan. While Megan grinned happily, Kyle looked as if his sister had just been kissed by an ape.

But Megan made her husband keep his mouth shut. It was the first time in eight years that Cydney had a boyfriend and she refused to let him ruin what appeared to be a very happy circumstance.

When Kyle wanted to go to Paris also, Cydney firmly shut him down. She appreciated the offer, but she suspected that Kyle would be so concerned for Olivia that it might interfere with what the police were attempting to accomplish and perhaps the case in general. He was overprotective of his only niece so Cydney, very nicely, convinced him to stay home and wait for their return. With a begrudging agreement, Kyle went into the kitchen to find the chips and salsa while Megan helped Cydney finish packing.

Ethan had jetted home in record time. Arriving at his townhome in Glendale, he parked in the underground structure of the modern townhomes and raced to his front door.

Entering the home he had lived in for seven years, he realized that it felt very empty and bleak. Although the decor was his taste and he'd spent a good deal of money and time decorating it in grays, blacks and fine artwork, it suddenly felt very cold to him. He'd only spent two days in Cydney's warm and lovely home and already, he missed it. He missed *her*.

Taking the stairs to his second floor master bedroom with its giant king bed and giant black silk comforter, he stripped off his clothes and turned on the shower. As he pulled out his shaving cream, he began to realize there was a certain scent about. He could smell it, vaguely, but couldn't quite make it out. Then he smelled his hands and realized he could smell Cydney on his flesh. She was all over him. He sniffed all down his arms and his hands again, inhaling her sweet, musky scent. It sent his heart fluttering madly. The hot shower turned into a long, cold one.

Freshly cleaned and shaved, he turned on the television as he began to pack his black leather Kenneth Cole suitcase. The top story on the four o'clock news was about yesterday's museum heist and he watched it as he packed, realizing it was the first time he had seen the news story. As he listened to the newscaster's dramatic take on the subject, his cell phone rang. He looked at the incoming number and quickly answered.

"Hey, Ty," he stopped what he was doing and sat on the edge of the bed. "How are you?"

On the other end of the line was the voice of a boy verging on manhood. "Hi, Dad. I'm good."

Ethan felt indescribable joy at the sound of his son's voice. "What's up? Long time, no see."

"I know," Tyler Serreaux replied. "That's why I called. I wanted to remind you that I have Spring Break next week. Mom wanted to know what the travel plans were."

Ethan's joy was replaced by the dull thump of disappointment. "Spring Break is next week?"

"Yeah," Tyler answered. "Remember? I gave you the dates last fall."

"Oh, right," Ethan felt like a fool. "I didn't forget, Ty, but I've got a problem. Something's come up with work and I'm going to be out of town for a while. I'm not sure when I'm getting back."

"Oh," Tyler's disappointment was obvious. "Where are you going?"

"Paris," Ethan replied. "I'm really sorry, buddy. It's out of my hands."

"I know," Tyler replied, although he didn't mean it. He only got to see his dad on major school breaks and during the summer and his disappointment was extreme. "Well, I guess I'll just stick around here then. The weather's been good; some of my friends are talking about going to Myrtle Beach but I don't think mom will let me go with them. No parents to chaperone."

Ethan listened to his son pretend their missed time together didn't matter, but the truth was, it mattered very much to them both. Ethan didn't want to miss time with his son and his mind was working quickly as he thought of a solution.

"I can do better than Myrtle Beach," he said. "How would you like to come to Paris with me?"

"Really?" Tyler perked up immediately. "That's cool. I'll go."

"When do you get out for Break?"

"Thursday."

Two days away. Ethan suspected it wouldn't be that big of an issue to take Tyler out of school a day early; more than that, he wouldn't be working the entire time he was in Paris. He would have some time to spend with Cydney and Olivia, and now, especially, Tyler. He found himself looking forward to introducing the ladies to his son. It was one of the most joyful things he could imagine.

"Put your mother on the phone," he told his son. "I need to make some arrangements with her."

Tyler passed off the phone to Kimberly Serreaux, who agreed to take Tyler out of school a day early and make sure he got to New York for his flight to Paris. Oddly, Ethan didn't feel any emotion while speaking to his ex-wife. Normally, he felt a great degree of bitterness and anger, even after all these years. Kimberly noticed that Ethan wasn't even remotely brusque with her, which was surprising. She wondered what could make the man change after all these years and truthfully had no idea. But she was glad, nonetheless.

So Tyler joined Ethan, Cydney, J.D. and two other agents on AirFrance Flight Sixty-Five departing John F. Kennedy Airport at nine forty-seven pm on Wednesday night. He sat by the window as Ethan sat in the middle seat between his son and Cydney. Although it was extremely uncomfortable for a man of his height to sit not only in a middle seat, but a non-exit row aisle, he could bear it. With Cydney on one side and Tyler on the other, Ethan couldn't imagine a more perfect situation. He was in heaven.

J.D. sat behind the three of them and snored like a bear the entire way to Paris.

————

They were in their hotel suite at the Hilton situated along the Seine River. After a day and night of searching for their escapee, Nat had been forced to call Cardinal Wildegrav and inform the man that their hostage had escaped. The Cardinal did not take the news well and after a search failed to turn up Olivia, he made a few phone calls and put Nat in touch with an informant of the Prefecture of Police in Paris. Nat was waiting for the man to call him back.

Overshadowing the fact that the American teenager had escaped, the Cardinal was nonetheless thrilled that they had the robe in their possession. Olivia Hetherington was secondary and, in fact, no longer vitally important to what they were doing. The only reason the Cardinal thought it would be better to find her was because, thanks to her three captors, she knew the inner workings of what they were attempting to accomplish. It would be better to have the girl until all was said and done, and Joseph seemed particularly concerned that she was out running around in a strange city. The fact remained, however, that they had what they wanted. They had The Lucius Robe.

"Paris is a big city," Joseph said. "I don't think we're going to find her."

Coral was a weeping mess. "Where could she have gone?"

"Who knows?" Nat was sucking on a cigarette, pacing the room. He jabbed a finger at Coral. "It's your fault that she's gone. You're absolutely useless."

Coral was weeping mostly because Nat had been browbeating her since Olivia's escape. Joseph didn't even try to intervene; he was more concerned about Olivia. She was such a pretty young thing, now alone in a strange city. He cursed himself for being stupid enough to leave her alone with the weak and ineffectual Coral.

"No," Joseph muttered. "It's my fault. I shouldn't have left the car."

Nat raised his eyebrows in agreement but said nothing. He continued to drag on the cigarette. And he also kept glancing at the large black suitcase they had propped up against the wall. He'd been eyeing it or the better part of the afternoon. Finally, he put the cigarette down.

Going to the suitcase, he laid it on its side and unzipped it.

Joseph noticed what he was doing and went over to stand next to him as he opened the case and pulled forth a large sealed garment bag. Nat took the bag to the small dining table and turned on the light.

By this time, Coral was up and wiping the mascara and tears from her face. She wandered to the table and stood behind Joseph as Nat unzipped the garment bag. Under the weak light of the sixty watt bulb, the faded remains of The Lucius Robe were revealed.

"I didn't even look at it when we put it in there," Joseph said, somewhat in awe as he gazed at the garment. "Was it damaged when we grabbed it?"

Nat pushed the garment bag to the floor and carefully laid the robe on the table. "I don't know," he muttered, gazing down at the faded cloth. "Look at it; this is the most amazing thing I've ever seen."

Coral dared to move up alongside Joseph and inspect the robe for herself. Her smudged blue eyes moved over the collar line and she gingerly touched the fabric, feeling the rough fibers against her fingers. It was a truly magical moment and the most prevalent sense was that of the smell. It smelled like dust and mold and, perhaps, smoke. It was a strong, musty scent that hinted of the centuries that had passed beneath it. Touching the ancient fabric gave her chills.

"La Vestaglia di Lucius," she mumbled.

Nat ignored her as he moved the robe around, lifting the sleeves, opening up the front. The interior of the robe was lined with coarse linen, faded brown spots near the neck. Suddenly, he paused as if fixed on something; reaching out, he pulled something free of the fabric. It actually came loose with a small pop. He held the object up to the light as Joseph and Coral strained to see what it was.

The soft bulb revealed the target of their fascination. Nat smiled.

"A tooth," he muttered. "I'll be damned. It really *is* a tooth."

Coral suddenly turned away, whispering furious prayers. Joseph took the tooth from Nat and put it in the palm of his hand, inspecting it closely.

"It's got two roots on it," he said as he flipped it over. "I wonder what kind of tooth it is."

"A molar, I guess," Nat said, still eyeing the prize. "His Eminence will be extremely pleased to hear that what the girl told us was true."

"Maybe so, but what does he intend on doing with it?" Joseph ventured. "Another Holy Relic for the Vatican archives?"

"Maybe the Holy Relic to end all Holy Relics," Nat said. "It might even be possible to extract DNA from the tooth."

Joseph looked at him, curious. "For what purpose?"

Nat's dark eyes glittered as an idea took hold. "Think about it," he said. "Perhaps science and theology has been wrong all along. Perhaps we really can create God."

Joseph's brow furrowed with confusion. "What are you talking about?"

A smile joined Nat's wondrous expression. "Cloning, Joe. The DNA can be used to clone," he looked back at the tooth, almost crazed with delight. "I'm not a scientist, but if DNA can be extracted, then perhaps it can be used in the laboratory to clone a human being."

Joseph looked at him as if he were out of his mind. "How would you do that?"

Nat shrugged, taking the tooth from Joseph and looking at it again. "I think you need an unfertilized human egg to do it." He suddenly looked up at Joseph. "Like one that a fifteen-year-old girl could provide."

Joseph's horror grew. "You don't know what you're talking about. You're not scientist – you said so yourself. You have no idea about cloning."

Nat shook his head, not at all disturbed by Joseph's words. "No, I really don't," he said slowly. "But there are a lot of people who do. I think His Eminence will be very interested to know my thoughts on the matter."

By this time, Coral had stopped praying and was listening apprehensively to the conversation between Joseph and Nat. Joseph, however, was apprehensive for another reason; Nat was unpredictable at best. He wouldn't put it past the man to kill them all in the quest to fulfill his own agenda. He didn't like where this conversation was going.

"Then maybe you should let the Cardinal decide what's to be done," he said. "Right now, we have a job to fulfill. I'll call him and tell him we have the tooth and see what he wants to do about it."

"No," Nat said firmly. "I'll call him."

Joseph surrendered and walked away. The plan for The Lucius Robe was growing by leaps and bounds. No longer was it only intended to crown the next Holy Roman Emperor and bring on a new Age of Enlightenment. The discovery of the tooth in the folds of the robe now brought about an entirely new set of issues and possibilities.

Joseph wasn't sure he liked the new twist. Just as he was mulling over the ominous turn of events, the phone rang. Nat picked it up and introduced himself to their contact at the Prefecture of Police for the City of Paris.

TWELVE

CYDNEY COULD HARDLY BELIEVE she was in Paris again. She and Brad had come here on their honeymoon, but that had been sixteen years ago and she didn't remember a lot about it. They had spent too much time in their hotel room or in bars getting drunk. Also, she was concerned that returning to the place of her honeymoon might bring on some melancholy. But there was none; the fact that she was there with Ethan brought about the excitement of seeing the city in a whole new light.

After going through Customs and baggage claim, they made their way outside to the curb where two shiny black town cars from the United States Embassy were waiting. It was a brilliant day with a vibrant blue sky and puffy clouds scattering on a light breeze. The temperature was in the mid-seventies.

"Ah," Cydney drew in a deep breath. "Paris in the spring."

Ethan was helping his son with a suitcase with a malfunctioning wheel. He leaned over and murmured to her, "You know what they say about Paris in the spring."

She grinned at him but Tyler heard him also. "What do they say?" he asked.

Both Cydney and Ethan looked to him. Tyler was a very tall boy for fourteen; he was just at six feet tall and weighed in at about one hundred thirty pounds. Considering his father's impressive height, it was no wonder he was as tall as he was. Cydney hadn't gotten a chance to talk to him on the flight over, as she deliberately stayed out of the conversation and let Ethan and Tyler get caught up. But now, there was time to talk to the light-haired, blue-eyed boy with his father's good looks.

"It just means that romance is in the air," she told him. "Paris is called the City of Light and the City of Romance, among other things."

Tyler cocked his head in much the same way his father did. "I told my History teacher that I was coming here on Spring Break and she told me to bring her back a report of the Louvre," he said, looking at his father. "When are we going?"

"We're going to make a quick stop at the hotel to drop every-thing off," Ethan replied as the embassy driver began loading their baggage into the car. "Then we need to head to the Prefec-ture of Police to pick up Cydney's daughter."

Tyler looked at Cydney again, who smiled at him. The attention from a lovely woman seemed to fluster him and he averted his gaze, taking his suitcase to the trunk of the car. As Tyler helped the driver load baggage, Ethan turned to Cydney.

"I'm so glad he's here," he said quietly. "Thanks for being such a good sport about it."

She lifted her eyebrows. "Good sport?" she repeated. "Ethan, he's your son. Of course he's welcome to come. He seems like a very sweet kid."

"He is," Ethan gazed fondly at his lanky boy as the youth enthusiastically threw a suitcase into the trunk and nearly shot it over the side of the car. "He's grown so much since I saw him last."

"When was that?"

"Christmas," Ethan replied, still watching his son. "The custody arrangement has him with me on major school breaks and all summer. The rest of the time he spends with his mother."

With J.D. talking to the driver of the first car several feet away and the other two FBI agents already in the second car, Cydney dared to put her hand on Ethan's back in a gentle, affectionate gesture. No one was watching them and she had been dying to touch the man since they left Los Angeles. The entire flight had been full of discreet leg touches and the brush of a hand here and there.

"Why did his mother move to Washington?" she asked.

He looked at her. "She had a job offer from the State Department," he said. "It was just something she felt she had to do and she wanted out of our marriage, anyway."

"And you didn't move to Washington, too, just to be near Tyler?"

"My job was rooted on the West Coast. I couldn't go."

Cydney sighed sadly, stroked his back one more time, and dropped her hand.

"Well, you've both done a good job raising him," she said. "This will be a great opportunity for you to spend some quality time with him."

His dark eyes glimmered at her. "I want to spend quality time with you, too."

She smiled. "You will, don't worry," she nodded her head in Tyler's direction. "But he comes first."

Ethan's eyes continued to glitter at her. "You have no idea how badly I want to kiss you right now."

"You must be reading my mind."

The trunk of the car slammed and Tyler leapt back over to

his father, interrupting the increasingly heated discussion with Cydney.

"Dad," he said. "Can I sit up front with the driver?"

"Sure," Ethan told him.

Tyler bounded into the passenger side of the front seat of the first car while Cydney, J.D. and Ethan piled into the back seat. Cydney sat between the two men and when everyone was settled, both cars took off from the curb and headed south towards the city.

The Charles de Gaulle Airport was located northeast of the City of Paris. Cydney sat between Ethan and J.D., watching the scenery go by and the French suburbs that were quaint and typically French. Coming closer into the city, there was a good deal of graffiti and they passed through an area that was run down and dirty, but other than that, everything was delightful and beautiful as they moved into the City of Light.

The decision had been made early on to drop everything off at the hotel first before heading to the Prefecture of Police, something that Cydney had initially resisted. She wanted to get to Olivia immediately, but J.D. wanted to drop their baggage and equipment off at the hotel first before making their way to the Prefecture. Olivia was in good hands and he had already received the first report of the girl's testimony from the French police, so he didn't see that a fifteen minute delay would be an issue. Ethan tried to convince him otherwise but, not being a parent and given the fact that everything was under control, J.D. stuck to his guns. They were heading to the hotel first.

Therefore, Cydney had to fight down her anxiety as Ethan and J.D. made small talk as the landscape of France roared past the window. Up in the front seat, Tyler announced when he could finally see the top of the Eiffel Tower off in the distance. The kid was so excited that it made everyone in the car grin as he announced soccer fields, tiny little cars, schools that didn't look like anything he had ever seen before, and the landmark in the distance.

They finally entered the outskirts of the city proper and headed for their hotel. They were booked into the Hotel Crowne Plaza Paris Republique, a four-star hotel near the St. Martin canal. J.D. had booked single rooms for himself and the two other agents, but Ethan had upgraded with his travel points from his credit card and got a two-bedroom suite for him, Cydney, Olivia and Tyler.

J.D. had protested initially and was again concerned with the perception of an agent on a job bunking up with someone he was supposed to be working with, but his protests eventually died because he knew it would do no good. He knew the man was in love with Cydney. It wasn't just lust or sympathy that fed his emotions; it was attraction and chemistry, pure and simple. J.D. couldn't fight an affair of the heart.

Soon they entered the narrow Paris streets. The traffic was crazy and it looked as if it were a free-for-all, but there really was a method to the madness. The taxis were the worst, shooting in and out of traffic and cutting people off. Cydney finally switched seats with Ethan so she could look out the window, pressed against the glass just as Tyler was. The city was a magical sight. After a few more twists and turns, they were finally at the Crown Plaza Paris Republique.

It was an enormous hotel that looked like a French palace. Her first glimpse of it towering against the blue sky was that of a fairy princess castle; it was magnificent. The two town cars pulled into the lavish drive and immediately, bell boys in dark suits were opening the trunks and removing the luggage.

J.D. got out of the car, followed by Ethan, who held out his hand to Cydney and helped her from the car. He took a moment to study her. Even though she'd been traveling for about fifteen hours, she looked fantastic in her slender jeans and three-inch heels. She had a casual top on that clung to her shapely breasts and her hair looked great. He realized he was extremely proud to have her with him and when they moved into the hotel, he took her casually by the elbow and escorted her inside. Truth was, he just wanted to touch her.

"We're just going to drop our luggage off and go straight to the police station, right?" Cydney clarified anxiously. "I need to get to my daughter as soon as possible."

Ethan nodded. "I know," he assured her. "We're going to check in, drop the luggage off, and go straight to the Prefecture. It'll take us ten minutes at the most. I might leave Tyler here as well. In fact, there's no reason for him to go with us."

Cydney watched the boy race ahead. "He might wreck the place if you leave him here. Maybe we'd better take him."

Ethan grinned in response. Tyler was rushing towards the Check-In desk and Ethan had to call out a couple of times to slow him down. The young man waited long enough for them to catch up with him before promptly dropping his suitcase on his father's foot and running off to the gift shop. The kid was all over the map.

Ethan tried to check in and keep an eye on his son at the same time, but Cydney finally took pity on him and went to find Tyler. She found the boy thumbing through some very expensive knick-knacks in the posh gift shop.

"There you are," she said pleasantly. "Your dad was wondering where you'd run off to."

Tyler glanced at her before returning to his treasure hunt. "I want to find my mom something," he said. "I told her I'd bring her back a present."

Cydney nodded in understanding. "Well," she began to look at the necklaces. "What does she like? Jewelry?"

"Naw," Tyler shook his head. "She has enough of that stuff.

Her boyfriend buys her all sorts of stuff. I want to get her something he won't think about buying her."

"Okay," Cydney turned around and started looking at the purses and very expensive designer outfits on the mannequins. "How about a wallet? Or a hat?"

Again, the boy shook his head. "I want to get her something nice."

Cydney looked around a bit more and finally put her hands on her hips. "Why don't we look around at other places," she suggested. "We're going to be doing a lot of sightseeing and you can get her something nice from the Louvre or another place. Does she like perfume?"

Tyler stopped pawing through the merchandise and cocked his head thoughtfully. "I think so," he ventured. "That might be something good to get her."

"Also, we'll take a picture of you in front of the Eiffel Tower, blow it up, and you can give it to her in a nice frame. She might like that."

A smile formed on his lips. "Yeah," he nodded in agreement. "That would be cool."

Cydney smiled back. "Good," she said. "Now, why don't we go find your dad and go up to our room? I need to drop off the luggage so we can go get my daughter."

Ethan was just coming to get them when they exited the swanky gift shop. He eyed his son. "You didn't spend your inheritance in there, did you?"

Tyler grinned; Cydney noticed that he looked just like his father when he did. "No," he said much in a way that Olivia replied when annoyed. "I was just looking for something for Mom."

"Did you find anything?"

The boy shook his head. "No," he replied. "But Cydney said

we could take a big picture of me in front of the Eiffel Tower and put it in a frame for her."

Ethan put his hand on his son's shoulder and began to lead him back toward the front desk. He looked over his shoulder at Cydney and winked at her.

"I think that's a great idea," he said. "I'm sure your mom would like that."

Tyler picked up his suitcase and his big duffle bag from where he had left it in the lobby, slinging the duffle bag over his shoulder. Cydney collected her enormous suitcase while Ethan took Olivia's bag plus his own two bags. He grunted under the weight.

"I feel like a Sherpa," he muttered.

Cydney smiled at him as they moved down the corridor to the elevator banks. The lobby was unbelievably gorgeous with its modern décor and expensive artwork. J.D. and the other two agents were on the third floor while Ethan, Cydney and Tyler were on the eighth. They got off the elevator and found their way down the lavish hall to a beautiful dark pair of double doors with stainless steel hardware. Ethan used his key card to open the door.

It was a beautiful modern suite of rooms. The kitchenette was immediately to the right and the living/dining room combination beyond. To the left off the living room was a decorative entry attached to a bedroom. As they walked into the living area, to their right was an identical entry leading into a second bedroom.

"Dibs!" Tyler bolted towards the bedroom on the right. "I get the bed near the window!"

Ethan watched as his son raced into the room and began throwing his stuff around. Helplessly, he looked at Cydney.

"I was hoping...," he whispered. "Well, I guess it was a stupid hope."

Cydney read his mind. "Did you really think we'd be able to share a bedroom?" she whispered back, a grin on her face. "Furthermore, do you really think I'd let my daughter bunk with a teenage boy?"

He sighed heavily. "I was hoping we'd at least..." He trailed off when Tyler yelled at him. He called in return: "Coming, bud!"

He took a moment to kiss Cydney quite seductively before following his son into the room. It was the first time since they had left her house that he had been provided with the opportunity to kiss her. He suckled her bottom lip gently, responding to her hungry reaction. He was about to drop the bags in his arms and pull her against him when she abruptly pulled away.

"Go," she murmured, "before he comes out looking for you."

Ethan growled low in his throat. "Cyd, I don't know how I'm going to handle not being able to touch you every waking moment."

"We'll figure out something," she assured him.

"But it's more than that. I just want to shout to the world how happy I am right now. And I just want to be with you."

She smiled and touched his cheek. "Me, too," she whispered. "Honestly, this has been pretty difficult for me with Olivia on one hand and you on the other. I'm so concerned for my daughter, yet now I have this new-found relationship with you and I don't know whether to cry or laugh. I just feel so... lucky. Really, really lucky."

He kissed the hand that was against his cheek and she turned away with a wink, meandering off towards the other bedroom. His gaze lingered on her, her great butt inside her tight jeans and the way her hair fell so gracefully against her back. When Tyler yelled again about a "free" robe in the bathroom, Ethan finally went to tend his son. But not before he stopped briefly at the phone in the living room and called down to the front desk. The concierge picked up.

"Ceci est la suite huit quinze," he said in his perfect French. "Il y a des magasins de bijouterie dans le voisinage?"

"I speak English if that is your pleasure, sir," the concierge said.

"Either language is fine," Ethan said, but caught sight of his son out of the corner of his eye and lapsed back into French. "Il y a des magasins de bijouterie dans le secteur?"

"Oui, monsieur," the woman replied. "Il y a Dubail dans cet hôtel et il y a deux très biens magasins dans quelques kilomètres. Peux-je vous aider avec quelque chose?"

Ethan watched Tyler as the kid yanked back the curtains of the room so hard that he nearly pulled them off the rod.

"Yes, I think you can help me," he lowered his voice and switched back to English. "Would you call those jewelry stores and see if they'll send a choice of rings to the hotel? Diamonds. Engagement rings. See if they'll deliver them to you and I'll come down and take a look when I have a chance."

"Of course, sir," the woman replied. "I'm sure Dubail, located in the hotel, would provide you with a lovely selection. Would you not like for me to send them to your room?"

"No," he said quickly, startled when Tyler bolted out of the room, zipped past him, and began yanking open the curtains in the living room. "Garder les sonneries avec vous et je viendrai les voir quand je peux. Ceci est une surprise."

"I understand, sir."

Cydney suddenly stuck her head out from the bedroom and looked straight at him, making him feel like he just got caught with his hand in the cookie jar. His first reaction was to slam the phone down but that would make it way too obvious. So he just stood there and looked at her.

"Is that the front desk?" she asked.

He nodded dumbly. "Yes," he tried not to stammer. "I wanted to find out about... um, renting a car, maybe for later."

She bought it. There was no reason not to. "Can you ask them about sending up another bathrobe?" she asked. "There's only one in here and I need one for Olivia."

"Sure," he said, relieved beyond words that he hadn't been caught in his covert deeds. He asked the concierge in French for another bathrobe, with Cydney still watching him, and hung up the phone.

She cocked her head as he went to pick up his luggage again. "Where in the world did you learn to speak such fluent French?" she asked. "That's a very impressive talent."

He lifted an eyebrow at her. "My last name is Serreaux," he stated the obvious. "It's an old and distinguished French name. We can trace our family back for hundreds of years, through the French Revolution and even further than that. Justine and Jean-Pierre Serreaux, my grandparents, only spoke French, as did my mother, the former Charlotte de Saulet, for many years. I learned French before I learned English."

Her features screwed up with confusion. "Your French parents relocated to Australia and then to America?"

"Dad worked for the French Embassy. He was a diplomat. He went where they sent him."

"Then you've been to Paris before?"

He nodded. "Many times. My grandmother still lives in France in the old family homestead."

Cydney's eyebrows lifted. "Really? A lovely French castle?"

She thought she was teasing him, but it was close to the truth. He grinned. "If I told you, you wouldn't believe me."

"Try me."

"Yes, a lovely French castle," he said, "built five hundred years ago."

Cydney's eyes widened. "Seriously? Can we visit?"

He shrugged. "Maybe," he replied. "I'd like Ty to see it. It's his heritage, after all."

Excited at the prospect, Cydney disappeared back into her bedroom and Ethan went into the other bedroom as his son opened the windows and turned on the television. Just as he was lifting his suitcase up onto the suitcase stand, he heard Cydney call for him again.

"In here," he called back.

She came into the room, shoes off and hairbrush in hand. He was unzipping his suitcase but smiled at her as she moved towards him.

"I know I said I wanted to get Olivia right away, but I need to change my clothes first," she fingered her blouse. "I slept in this thing and I just noticed a big stain on it."

He shrugged. "Sure; whatever you want. J.D. was going to call Inspector Dulay as soon as we got here to let him know we're on our way."

She began to scoot away. "Then give me five minutes to change and I'll be ready to go."

"No worries," he said, eyeing her shapely body. "Do you need any help changing?"

She paused in the doorway, grinning devilishly. "I'd love it. But I don't think we could adequately explain that little encounter to your son."

He smiled and turned back to his suitcase. "Then get out of here before I lose control."

She laughed and padded out of the room on her bare feet. Tyler bolted past Cydney as she exited the room, nearly bowling her over as he took a flying leap and landed on the bed nearest the window. As Cydney giggled and proceeded on to her room, Ethan frowned.

"Hey, man," he said, soft and stern. "Take it easy. There are women about."

Tyler was lying with his hands behind his head, all stretched out over the overstuffed bed.

"This is a really cool hotel," he said. "I'm going to have to tell Mom about it."

"Why?" Ethan looked up from taking his shoes out of his suitcase. "Does she want to come to Paris?"

"Sort of; because she might want to come here after she marries Dan," Tyler rolled onto his side and looked at his father. "I've heard them talking about coming here on their honeymoon."

Ethan gazed steadily at his son, pausing for a brief moment before continuing. "That guy she's been dating for the past year?"

Tyler couldn't lie still long; he resumed rolling around on the bed. "Yeah," he said. "They're getting married this summer."

"Really?" Ethan didn't know why he felt a great deal of relief at that news, but he did. "That's great. Dan's a pretty good guy, isn't he?"

He shrugged. "He's okay," he said, wrinkling his nose. "He tries to tell me what to do but I don't listen."

"When he's your stepdad, you're going to have to listen."

"Why?" Tyler sat up and looked at him. "You're my dad and I don't need another. I don't want to listen to some guy just because he married my mother."

Ethan could see some rebellion in his son, something he hadn't seen in him yet. Tyler was just finishing his first year of high school now and he was growing up, becoming a young man. He was coming to know his own mind and strengths. Ethan thought carefully of how to handle this as he pulled off his tie and began to remove his shirt.

"Dan's a cop, right?" he asked.

"Yeah, why?"

"Doesn't he have two boys?"

"Yeah. They're okay. Pretty cool, I guess."

Ethan lifted an eyebrow at his son. "I'm sure Dan is an okay guy, Tyler. I'm sure he doesn't tell you what to do just to boss you around. He tells you because it's for your own good. Son, your mom and I have been divorced for eight years. Life goes on. She'll get remarried and I will, too, someday. You'll have a new stepdad, a new stepmom, and who knows how many stepbrothers, sisters, half-brothers or sisters... do you see where I'm going with this? You are my son. You will always be my son. Just because Dan marries your mom, it doesn't take that away from us. It's okay to listen to him and to do what he says. I would like to know that my son is being respectful and kind, not rebellious. That means a lot to me."

By this time, Tyler was sitting up and staring at him with wide eyes. "You're getting married, too?"

Ethan averted his eyes and pulled his white t-shirt over his head, revealing his magnificent build. If Cydney was going to change, he thought it might be a good idea for him to as well.

"I'm not getting married right this second," he didn't want to lie to the boy but he wasn't going to spill anything, either. "I'm just saying that life goes on. You will have stepparents in your life at some point and I would like for you to always be respectful."

Tyler scratched his light head. "I wasn't trying to be mean," he said, though there was no force behind it. "I just meant that you're my dad. I want to live with you, not Mom and Dan. Can I come live with you in California?"

Ethan looked at his son, feeling more happiness at that question than he could comprehend. For eight long years he had been waiting for that inquiry. He went over to the boy and put a big hand on his head.

"You'd like that?" he asked.

"Uh-huh."

"But it would move you away from your friends. You'd have to start a new school and everything."

"I don't care. I don't want to live with mom anymore. I want to be with you."

Ethan ruffled the light hair and moved towards the bathroom. "Okay, bud," he said. "Let's get through this vacation and then we'll talk about it."

They quickly unpacked in relative silence as they waited for Cydney to change. Tyler's unpacking was more of just opening his suitcase and throwing stuff around, while Ethan was neat as he put his clothes into the closet and into the drawers.

When they were finished, they went into the living room to wait. J.D. called a short time later and told them he would meet them downstairs in a few minutes, as they had a car coming to take them to the Prefecture of Police. Ethan relayed that information to Cydney through the closed bedroom door and she assured him that she was ready to go, anxious to get to her child.

When she emerged from the bedroom a minute later in black slacks, a black blouse with a strategically placed ruffle along the neckline and black pumps, she looked absolutely marvelous. Her blond hair was pulled back into an attractive casual ponytail and Ethan gazed at her like a man who had fallen in love. He had, in fact.

"Ready?" he asked her.

She nodded, grabbing her black and silver designer purse and stepping through the front door when Ethan opened it.

"What's going to happen once we get to the police station?" Cydney asked Ethan as they waited for the elevator.

He gazed down at her, still feeling that giddy warmth that he had moments earlier when she had stepped from the bedroom.

"I'm not sure at this point," he said. "She has been thoroughly interrogated by the French Police but we need to do our own investigation, hence the two other agents we brought with us. They'll be interrogating and recording."

"Interrogating?" she eyed him warily as the elevator doors opened and they stepped in. "I don't like the sound of that word."

He smiled and hit the button for the lobby. "Just a figure of speech. It's really just an interview to get her side of the story."

"How long will this take?"

"Hard to say. We'll be there most of the afternoon, probably."

"Me, too?" Tyler wanted to know.

Ethan lifted his shoulders. "You knew I was working today, Ty. You can sit and watch television somewhere until we're done."

He snorted with displeasure. "Why is her daughter at the police station?"

Cydney looked up at Ethan; she would let him answer that question. Ethan's gaze lingered on Cydney a moment before turning to his son.

"Because Cydney's daughter was the victim of a kidnapping," he said quietly. "Cydney and her daughter are part of the case I've been working on."

Tyler thought a moment about that. "Why did she get kidnapped?"

The doors to the elevator opened. "That is a long story for another time, son," Ethan replied.

He put his hand on the boy's shoulder and guided him out into the modern deco lobby before he could ask any more questions. The boy changed focus quickly and asked for some money to go to the gift shop and buy a soda. Ethan handed him a few Euros and sent him on his way. Cydney and Ethan stood together and watched him disappear into the crowded shop.

"I knew he'd ask that question sooner or later," he muttered. "I've been debating how much to tell him."

Cydney shrugged. "You did fine," she said. "I'm sure he'll learn more as the days pass, especially when we end up spending time together with the kids. They'll get to know each other and Olivia will eventually talk."

Ethan nodded in agreement, watching his son at the counter paying for a big bottle of soda and an assortment of smaller snack bags. "Olivia is a year older than he is," he snorted. "I wonder if he likes older women,"

Cydney cast him a baleful glare but she was grinning. "Don't even think it."

He laughed at her expression. "Considering how I react to you, he might react the same way towards your daughter. He has my genes, after all. They react strongly to yours."

"You're awful," she sniffed.

He was enjoying teasing her. "Oh, être des jeunes et dans l'amour."

She looked up at him with a lifted eyebrow. "Et oh, être le père d'un jeune garçon avec les hormones de raging et non contrôle automatiquement."

Ethan's smile vanished and his jaw dropped. "You didn't tell me you spoke French."

She grinned at him. "You didn't ask."

He put his hands on his hips and gave her his best suspicious look. "How in the hell do you know it?"

She laughed. "I work in a world-class art museum. Don't forget that French is the common art language all over the world. Sometimes I have to deal with international art galleries and if they don't speak English, they definitely speak French. It's come in very handy over the past eleven years."

He pursed his lips into a flat line. "Il y a aucuns autres secrets que vous voulez me dire?"

Her smile faded as she gazed up at him. "We've only known each other seven days, Ethan," she said. "Every day will be a day of discovery for us. There are lots of things you don't know about me simply because we haven't had the time to discover them yet. But in answer to your question, no, I don't have any secrets in the least."

His mock irritation fled. "I know, honey," he said for her ears only. "I really wasn't mad. I'm just perpetually amazed at your talents."

She winked at him. "I know you weren't really mad," she whispered as Tyler finished paying for his booty and headed back in their direction. "And I also know something else."

"What?

"That you weren't calling the front desk earlier about rental cars."

He tried to keep a poker face. "Why do you say that?"

"Because I could understand a word here and there. You said something about a store, although I didn't catch all of it. What's the big secret?"

"If I wanted you to know, I would tell you."

"Are we going shopping somewhere expensive and fabulous?"

He clapped a hand over his face. "Do you mean to tell me that I can't even connive or scheme without you knowing everything? Christ, I'm going to have to learn Spanish now."

Her hazel eyes twinkled at him. "Vaya el derecho adelante. Puedo comprender eso, también."

His face went slack with shock. "Oh, no way...."

"Did I mention that my minor in college was Languages?" she said innocently.

Tyler was upon them and they were distracted from their conversation. Ethan looked at all of the junk food and shook his head.

"Ty, you had a big breakfast on the plane right before we landed," he knew it was of no use to point it out but he did anyway. "What's up with all of that crap?"

Tyler ripped open a bag of red hot jelly beans. "I'm hungry," he said simply.

Cydney just grinned as Ethan shook his head and looked around for J.D. and the other FBI men. The man wasn't long in coming and within a minute or two, stepped off the elevator with the other two special agents in tow.

Special Agent John Daniels and Special Agent Woody Penryn had been introduced to Cydney before they boarded the flight from Los Angeles but the two had stayed silent and out of the way the entire trip. They were young, only in the bureau for a couple of years, and on their first overseas assignment. With J.D. Dickerson and Ethan Serreaux leading the team, they were somewhat in awe of their surroundings. Dickerson and Serreaux were well-known agents in the Los Angeles bureau with solid reputations. This was the big time.

A limousine was waiting this time, big enough for everyone to fit into. Cydney climbed in first, followed by the men except for Tyler. He wanted to ride with the driver again. When the doors slammed, the driver pulled out and onto the Boulevard de Magenta. Cydney once again sat in between Ethan and J.D., oblivious to the fact that Special Agent Penryn, having been unobtrusive during the entire trip, was now checking her out. She was more interested in watching the city pass by.

But Ethan was aware; when he realized that Special Agent Penryn seemed to be taking an interest in the woman seated next to him, he shot the man such a withering look that it was all Penryn could do not to open the door and leap from the car just to get away. One did not provoke the wrath of Serreaux and live to tell the tale.

————

"Right there. See her?"

Joseph was straining to catch a glimpse of what Nat was talking about. He had parked the car so far away from the Paris Police Headquarters that it was difficult to make out features on people walking in and out of the massive building, which emulated a French palace to a certain extent. The light gray stones and severely gabled roof were both elegant and imposing.

"No," he squinted. "Where?"

Nat was sitting in the driver's seat of their rented Vauxhall sedan, sunglasses on as he casually pointed. "Right there, in black," he said. "She's just stepping up on the curb. There are about four or five agents with her."

Joseph squinted a moment longer before nodding his head. "Yes," he said slowly. "Now I see her."

"Then our contact was right," Nat said with satisfaction. "Olivia is in the station. Now the FBI and her mother are here to get her."

Joseph sat back in his seat and puffed out his cheeks, both wearily and in anticipation of what was to come. He scratched his head, a gesture of uncertainty.

"So when do we enact this plan?" he asked, not particularly excited about it.

"When Olivia comes outside," he said. "It would be stupid to try anything while she's inside the station, obviously. We need to wait until she comes outside."

"All right," Joseph looked away from the station, out over the Paris street that was busy with people going about their day. It was clear that there was much on his mind. "Nat... I'm not sure this is such a good idea."

Nat never took his eyes off the police station. "Why not?"

Joseph rolled his eyes with frustration. "Because this whole plan is going in directions that were never originally intended," he looked at Nat. "We were just supposed to get the robe; that's it. Now there's a whole new element to this that is taking on really ominous tones and it all centers around that damn tooth."

Nat looked at him. "What are you worried about? You will still be crowned. The tooth is for Wildegrav."

"And the girl, too?" Joseph gestured angrily. "After you told him about that crazy idea of yours, he bought it. He liked your idea of cloning."

"The possibilities are staggering."

"They're crazy. That's not what we had originally planned."

"Plans change." Nat looked back at the police station. "We're supposed to have backup here but I haven't seen anyone I recognize. We'll just have to assume they're here. Our contact was supposed to arrange it."

Joseph just shook his head at Nat's changing of the subject, completely disagreeing with everything that was happening. "Who is this contact, anyway?"

Nat remained uncommonly cool considering what was about to go down.

"A watch commander with the Paris Police," he said. "A man extremely loyal to the church and to His Eminence. Wildegrav says he has been a faithful servant for years."

Joseph sighed. "Whatever," he said. "Look, just give me a chance to get near Olivia before you start shooting. I want to be able to grab her in time and I don't want to get hit. I don't want her to get hit, either."

"She won't," Nat said steadily. "I'll be aiming for the agents around her."

"Don't hit the mother, either."

Nat wriggled his eyebrows. "No, definitely not. She's quite beautiful."

Joseph cast him a long look before turning away again and

gazing out of the car window. He wasn't focused on anything in particular except the scheme looming on the horizon.

"Thank God Coral is already at the train station," he muttered. "Why in the hell is she still with us, anyway? We don't need her any longer."

Nat's dark eyes watched everyone coming in and out of the station in the distance. "She's money, pure and simple. Don't so easily cast her aside; she has financed a good deal of your quest for the throne."

"It's not my quest; it's my family's quest."

"But the throne is yours."

Joseph lifted an eyebrow, his gaze taking on a distant, displeased, look. "Yes," he said slowly. "It's mine. All of this is mine."

The conversation was interrupted by Nat's cell phone. It rang once and he hit the answer button. Joseph listened disinterestedly to his one-word replies until Nat finally hung up the phone. He pulled his sunglasses off and began cleaning them.

"It seems that we are to create a diversion," he said casually.

Joseph looked at him. "Diversion?"

Nat nodded. "That was our contact inside the prefecture. We need to create a diversion out here and he'll take care of Olivia for us. It seems she is surrounded and a covert extraction is our best option for success."

Joseph sighed heavily, shaking his head. "What in the hell does that mean?"

Nat was watching the front of the building. When he didn't reply immediately, Joseph looked to see what had the man's attention cornered. He was staring at the building as if seeing something no one else could.

Nat was a genius, a psychotic mastermind, and someone that Joseph feared more than he respected. His family had served the d'Orleans family for three hundred years. On this particular venture, since the days before the opening of the Resurrection exhibit, Joseph was getting more than he bargained for. More and more, he was feeling reluctant to see the mission through. It had been his family's dream, not his personal quest. But this quest had already been costly; he was fearful just how costly it would eventually become.

"I have an idea," Nat finally murmured.

Joseph looked at him with some trepidation. When Nat had an idea, it usually involved violence and death.

Joseph's reluctance grew.

THIRTEEN

OLIVIA RAN at her mother and hit her so hard that she knocked her over into Ethan, who had to grab them both to keep them from falling over. Olivia wept hysterically in her mother's arms while Cydney, surprisingly, kept her cool. She held her daughter tightly and whispered in her ear, over and over.

"It's okay, baby," she murmured. "You're safe now. You're safe."

Christophe had been walking with Olivia down a carpeted hallway but Olivia had bolted ahead of him when she saw her mother. He came up behind the hugging pair, extending a hand to J.D. because Ethan's hands were full at the moment as he tried to keep the women from toppling.

"Inspector Dulay," he introduced himself with a smile.

J.D. shook his hand. "Special Agent Dickerson," he indicated Ethan, Daniels and Penryn, in that order. "Special Agents Serreaux, Daniels and Penryn. And that woman being mugged is Cydney Hetherington, Olivia's mother."

Christophe smiled as he watched the pair. "I would have never guessed."

By this time, Ethan was able to release the women because

they were moderately steady. He extended a hand to Christophe.

"C'est un plaisir pour vous rencontrer," he said; his French was very rapid and very comfortable. "Merci pour tout vous avez fait."

Christophe shook his head. "C'était mon plaisir. Elle est une fille douce."

J.D. interrupted. "No offense, gentlemen, but this sounds like the United Nations and I don't speak the language nearly as well as the two of you."

Christophe laughed as Ethan grinned. "Sorry," Christophe replied, indicating a door just a few feet away. "Shall we go in and sit?"

Daniels and Penryn went with Christophe into the small but comfortable interrogation room, followed by J.D. while Ethan lingered behind with Cydney and Olivia as they fiercely embraced. He put his hands on them both gently.

"Come on, ladies," he said, trying to steer them towards the room. "Let's go sit down."

Cydney whispered soothingly to Olivia to get her going and they moved into the room. Ethan, with his wide-eyed son, went in after them and closed the door.

Cydney and Olivia sat on the couch with Tyler while Ethan, J.D., Christophe and the two other agents sat around the table and chatted. Most chatter was about the case but nothing in-depth because of the three civilians in the room. But within several minutes they had wasted enough time and were at the point where they needed to get down to business.

Ethan was dreading this moment, mostly because he knew how Cydney would react. Since she wasn't directly involved with the details of the case, she would not be allowed to be in the room while the FBI questioned Olivia. He stood up and went over to the couch where Olivia sat cradled in her mother's arms.

He knelt next to the couch, smiling at Olivia when the girl looked at him with her red-rimmed eyes. She was calm now for the most part and he put his hand on her knee.

"Olivia," he said gently. "I know you answered a lot of questions with the Paris Police, but I need to ask you some questions now, too. Are you up to it?"

Olivia hiccupped and nodded, wiping at her nose. "Yes."

He patted her knee. "Good girl," he looked at Cydney. "Can I talk to you outside a moment?"

Cydney nodded, kissing Olivia on the forehead as she released her daughter. As Cydney walked from the room, Ethan pulled Tyler from the couch and made him leave with them.

When the three of them were in the corridor, Ethan shut the door to the interrogation room quietly and sent his son down the hall to the vending machine. Alone with Cydney, he stood very close to her and lowered his voice.

"We need to speak with Olivia alone for a bit," he said, cutting her off before she could protest. "The reason is simple; she may say things to us that she wouldn't say if you were in the room. You're an emotional crutch for her and in her current state, she'd be focused more on you than on us if you were to stay in the room. I need for her to focus on me right now because we really need to figure out what happened. I promise I won't let anything happen to her and I promise I'll try my best not to upset her too much. Okay?"

Cydney was deeply displeased. "But she's a minor. Isn't she allowed to have a parent present?"

"She's not being accused of a crime. We just want to find out, in detail, what happened. I promise I'll take care of her, Cyd. Please trust me."

Cydney still looked doubtful and Ethan dared to steal a kiss. "Okay?" he pressed gently.

She sighed faintly. "All right," she said. "But she's so fragile, Ethan. I...."

"I know, honey," he whispered, moving to kiss her again but noticing that his son was heading in his direction with two sodas in his hand. He backed off of Cydney. "Just trust me. I'll take care of Olivia. And I need you to take care of Tyler until we're done."

At this point, Tyler had reached them and handed a diet soda to Cydney, who took it gratefully. Ethan focused on his son.

"Ty, I need you to hang out with Cydney for a while," Ethan instructed. "I don't like leaving women alone. Will you be a gentleman and stay with her while I work, please?"

Tyler looked at Cydney and nodded. "Sure."

Cydney, still not happy that she was not permitted to be with her daughter while the FBI questioned her, nonetheless smiled weakly at Tyler.

"Thanks, Ty," she said without much enthusiasm. "Maybe we can go outside and walk around and see the sights. Notre Dame isn't too far away."

"Good idea," Ethan said. "We should be a couple of hours at least. Come back by five o'clock."

"Okay," Cydney cast Ethan a long look as she turned to walk away. "See you later."

"Thanks," Ethan winked at her, blowing her a kiss when his son wasn't looking. He watched the two of them until they disappeared down the main stairwell.

It was a very long and very emotional afternoon. And it was only going to get worse.

———

The police station was about a block from Notre Dame Cathedral. Cydney and Tyler had walked over to the massive church, taking pictures and daring to go inside. There was a tour going on that they attached themselves to, laughing between themselves because it was a group of Germans and Tyler didn't understand one word. Cydney understood what was being said, but mostly, they just wanted to walk around and see the cathedral.

Cydney came to discover that Tyler was a very smart, very considerate young man. He reminded her of Ethan to a fault. When they went through a doorway, he always hung back and let her go first. When they passed by a kiosk outside that had water and sodas, he asked her if she wanted something. He was also very funny, doing a great imitation of their tour guide. Cydney decided early on that she liked Tyler Serreaux very much. He was a charming kid.

When they were finally finished with the massive structure that was Notre Dame, it was almost time to head back to the police station. But they still had a few minutes to kill and went to the river walk. Boats of all kinds were jetting up and down the Seine River and they stood on the sidewalk, leaning against the guardrails as the soft wind blew and watching the boats.

Cydney asked Tyler about school and he was more than happy to tell her how much he hated math, how much he loved football, and that he and four of his friends had a garage band named "Fun Bags." Cydney burst out laughing and asked him if he knew what that really meant, to which he assured her that he did. Did his mother approve? No, he said. He told his mother that they just called the band "Bags."

Closer to five o'clock, Cydney and Tyler pulled themselves away from the river and began their block and a half walk back to the police station. The wind had picked up a little and

Cydney wished she had brought a jacket. It was growing chilly and clouds were beginning to gather overhead.

Arms wrapped around her torso, Cydney listened to Tyler talk about his dream of being a rock star as they walked along the busy street. Cydney admired the architecture as they went along, gorgeously designed buildings that were unbelievably intricate or complicated. Paris was a lovely place and, so far, she was enjoying the trip very much. She couldn't wait to collect Olivia and get her mind off what had happened over the past few days.

Tyler was describing his new drum set by the time they hit the street that the police station was on. Cydney listened with great interest although her mind was on Olivia in the building up ahead. There were people coming in and out of the building and there were many cars parked along the street. Just as they neared the police station, she glanced up to see if their limousine was still waiting for them. It was, across the street. The driver even waved at her.

As Tyler chatted and they turned to enter the building, Cydney's gaze scanned the crowd for no particular reason. She was just looking at the people. But one person in particular seemed familiar and her pace slowed as she studied the man seated a few feet away with sunglasses on, reading a French newspaper. Tyler was slightly ahead of her, still talking. When the man reading the newspaper looked up at her and smiled, Cydney's blood ran cold. She knew that smile. She had seen it, once, at the museum.

Panic seized her. She began to run after Tyler, shoving the boy towards the police station entrance to get him moving.

"Run, Tyler," she screamed. "Run for your dad. Go!"

Tyler was startled and started to ask questions but Cydney shoved him again, so hard that he tripped. But he was dutifully picking up the pace.

"Run!" Cydney screamed again. "Get your dad!"

Tyler took off like a shot. Cydney, at a distinct disadvantage in high heels, heard the shots ring over her head and shrieked, running for the nearest cover, which happened to be a tree. Bullets started flying and the people coming in and out of the Prefecture of Police began screaming and diving for cover.

The tree she was hiding behind wasn't wide enough and another bullet sang by, grazing the tree before grazing her arm. Cydney screamed and ducked, hand over her arm now beginning to run with a small stream of blood. She could see cops flying out of the police station and beginning to engage in a gunfight. The bullets were flying fast and heavy now. Crouching as low as she could go, she put her arms over her head and prayed.

Inside the police station, people were shouting, grabbing their weapons, and beginning to empty outside. Tyler ran through the lobby, past the information desk and up the stairs. He knew where his father was and he could hear the bullets flying behind him.

Terrified, he ran through police officers who were going the opposite way in their quest to take on whoever was attacking the police station. No one bothered to stop a frightened young teenager; they were too busy focusing on the gun battle outside. Just as Tyler reached the interrogation room where he last saw his father, the door flew open and Christophe, J.D. and Ethan spilled into the corridor. Tyler ran straight for his father.

"Dad!" he hollered. "You've got to come! They're shooting and Cydney is out there!"

Ethan bolted faster than he had ever moved in his life. "Tyler, stay with Olivia," he ordered. "Get back in that room and shut the door."

Tyler nodded, terrified, as J.D. unholstered his service weapon and ran past him. Agents Penryn and Daniels followed very quickly. Only Christophe was left, shouting in French to one of the men who happened to be standing near him. It was the watch commander of the swing shift, directing his men to go and see what the trouble was. Christophe gestured to the man.

"Watch these children," he commanded in French. "Make sure they stay in that room."

The watch commander waved him off. "Will do, Inspector."

Christophe shoved Tyler into the room with Olivia and slammed the door. The two teenagers stared at each other for a moment, terrified, until Tyler finally took a seat across the table from Olivia and lifted his hand in a weak greeting. He didn't know what else to do.

"Hey," he said.

"Hey," Olivia replied.

They could hear the distant sounds of gunshots and Olivia looked particularly horrified. "My mom is out there somewhere?"

Tyler gazed into her pretty green eyes, not knowing what to say. "Yeah," he finally grunted. "But my dad went to help her. She'll be fine."

Olivia just nodded and lowered her head. It took Tyler a moment to realize that she was weeping. Concerned, he leaned across the table.

"Hey," he tried to sound comforting but this was a new situation for him; he'd never had to comfort a weeping girl. "She'll be fine. There are lots of places to hide out there. Besides, my dad will save her. He does that kind of thing all the time."

Olivia just nodded, wiping at her nose. She lowered her head, fiddling with the cup in her lap that had once held water. Tyler watched her lowered head.

"So," he ventured awkwardly. "What grade are you in?"

Olivia looked up at him with her watery eyes. "Sophomore. What grade are you in?"

"Freshman. Do you play any sports?"

She shook her head. "No," she replied. "But I'm in the marching band and the French Club. I'm also the ASB Recording Secretary. Do you play sports?"

Tyler nodded. "Football and baseball. I made the varsity team this year for both."

"You must be really good."

"I guess so. I want to be like my dad and go to college on an athletic scholarship."

Olivia nodded and the conversation died. Tyler watched her for a moment, fiddled with a pen on the table, and then suggested he go see what was happening. Olivia thought it wasn't a good idea so he sat back down again. Suddenly, the door opened and a man with thinning hair and a police uniform entered and closed the door behind him. He had a strange look on his face, one that Olivia was uncomfortable with. When he took out his baton and whacked Tyler over the head with it, Olivia started screaming.

The baton came down on her, too, and everything went black.

———

Cydney was trapped behind a tree, arms over her head as the bullets flew all around her. She could hear them ricocheting off the old stone walls of the prefecture. Her eyes were closed and her head lowered, praying that she would live through this mess, when a warm body was suddenly next to her and powerful arms were going around her body. Startled, she started to scream until she looked up into Ethan's handsome face.

He was in a flak vest he had borrowed from Dulay. His expression was grim as he tried to hide his bulk behind the tree with Cydney.

"Are you all right?" he asked, ducking his head when a bullet flew into the tree and bark rained down on them.

She nodded but her bloody arm said otherwise. "I'm all right," she said. "I just got nicked."

He looked at her arm, his jaw flexing with concern as he did so. "It doesn't look bad," he looked around, trying to see where they could go to get better cover and not get their asses shot off in the process. "I've got to get you out of here."

"Ethan," she grabbed him by the collar before he could move. "I saw the museum guard here, the same one who ran off with the guy who stole the robe. He was sitting on a bench over there. I think he's the one doing all of the shooting."

Ethan tried to look around the tree without getting hit. "Are you sure?"

"Positive," she said. "In fact, the night Olivia was kidnapped, that same guard talked to me out in the parking lot but I don't remember his name. I think he said it was Joe. I told the cops about him the day the museum was robbed."

Another bullet sang overhead and huge amounts of bark exploded off the tree. Ethan put his arms around Cydney's head to protect her, pulling her onto his lap and trying to cover her with his body as much as possible. He leaned back against the tree, looking over to the steps near the entry to see J.D., Christophe and about three dozen cops firing off rounds towards the street. He yelled to J.D. to get his attention.

"Hey!" he hollered. "Cover me! I'm bringing her back over!"

J.D. acknowledged him, said a few words to the cops around him, and they all began rapid-firing at their target. Ethan practically picked Cydney up and raced all the way back to the steps, flying into the entry as the bullets zinged around them. Once inside, they were finally safe and he took a closer look at her bloodied arm.

"It doesn't look too bad but we're going to take you to the

hospital anyway," he said calmly. "Let's go put something on it to stop the bleeding."

"It's not bleeding too badly," she insisted. "I'd really like to see Olivia."

"She's fine," Ethan insisted, pulling her into the station and asking the first person he came across for a First Aid kit. "I left her with Tyler to keep her company. They're probably having a great time right now, getting drunk and having a wild party."

Cydney smiled weakly as a policewoman quickly brought out a First Aid kit from what looked like a small coffee bar. She handed it to Ethan, who pulled out the antibiotic wipes and cleaned off Cydney's nick. After the blood was wiped away, it was a tiny little scratch. But there was alcohol in the wipe and she danced around in pain while he tried to clean her up. He smirked at her as she made faces at the sting of the wipe. Finally, he managed to get a big gauze pad on her wound.

"Good Lord, woman," he hissed, throwing away the wipe. "Are you always such a baby?"

She nodded. "Remember what I said? We're on a path of discovery for us. Today, you've learned that I speak fluent French, Spanish, and that I'm a huge baby when it comes to injuries."

He laughed at her. "How did you deal with childbirth?"

She lifted an eyebrow and made a comical face. "Lots of drugs."

He laughed heartily; she was a character and every moment that passed saw him falling more deeply in love with her. Since there was no one around of consequence, he pulled her into his arms and kissed her deeply. Then he hugged her tightly.

"I'm so glad you're okay," he murmured, kissing the side of her head before letting her go. "I have to tell you; that really scared the crap out of me out there."

She gazed up at him with her big hazel eyes. "Me, too," she

admitted. "You were quite the hero coming after me like you did."

His expression grew serious. "I'd walk through fire for you, Cyd. There's absolutely nothing I wouldn't do for you."

She put her hands on his cheeks and he pulled her into his arms again, holding her close.

"You're very sweet." She stood on her toes and kissed him tenderly. "I think I could become quite fond of you."

"Really?"

"Really."

He smiled at her and kissed her again. "I'm already quite fond of you," he murmured against her lips.

People were starting to enter through the front doors so he let her go, not wanting anyone of consequence to see them in a clutch. They headed back towards the stairs that led to the second floor where Tyler and Olivia were, with a respectable distance between them.

"I understand that your son is quite the rock star," she made conversation as they mounted the stairs.

Ethan grinned at her. "So he told you about Fun Bags?"

She nodded with some disapproval. "I asked him if he knew what it meant."

He chuckled. "He's a teenage boy, Cyd. He knows what it means."

"Did you tell him?"

"Hell no," he said as they mounted the top of the stairs. "I didn't have to. Kids know a lot about sexuality these days. When I had the father-to-son talk with him about three years ago, he already knew pretty much everything."

"And you're telling me that you left my daughter alone with a kid who plays in a rock band called Fun Bags and knows everything there is to know about sex?" she feigned horror. "I may have an issue with that, Special Agent Serreaux."

He struggled not to laugh. "I already warned you," he said. "I told you that he has my genes and my genes are very attracted to your genes."

Cydney just shook her head, grinning as Ethan continued to chuckle at her. They neared the door to the room where they had left the teenagers.

"We had a nice time, anyway," she said. "He's a pretty neat kid."

Ethan's dark eyes glimmered at her as he put his hand on the doorknob and turned. "I think so."

She smiled at him as he opened the door for her. But the moment she set foot inside, one look at Tyler picking himself off the floor and she shrieked.

"Tyler!" she exclaimed as Ethan pushed past her on his way to aid his son.

Tyler had his hand to his head, a trickle of blood coming from his right ear. Ethan grabbed his son and helped guide him into a chair.

"Ty," Ethan's voice was full of concern. "What in the hell happened?"

Before Tyler could answer, Cydney was looking around the room. "Where's Olivia?" she demanded.

Tyler was having a difficult time sitting up. "I don't know," the light hurt his eyes and he had a huge headache. "Somebody whacked me on the head. I don't know what happened to Olivia."

Ethan looked at Cydney, who had a supreme expression of panic on her face. "Oh, my God," she breathed. "Ethan, not again."

She was bolting for the hallway but Ethan let go of Tyler and was on her in a flash. "No," he commanded firmly. "You stay with Tyler and see what you can do to help him. I'll find Olivia."

Cydney was starting to panic but Ethan grabbed her by both arms and forced her to look at him. "Cyd, honey," he shook her gently before she could get up a head of steam. "Look at me; help Tyler. Stay here. I will find Olivia. All right?"

She nodded, terrified. Ethan rushed out of the door and she stood there a moment, trying not to get hysterical. Behind her, Tyler groaned and she turned around, her gaze falling on the injured young man. He was hurt and needed help. Pushing aside her panic, she went to him.

Bags of ice and a couch to lie down on helped Tyler tremendously. Focusing on Tyler helped Cydney calm because she had something else to hold her attention. The door to the interrogation room was open and she could see police personnel rushing up and down the hall but she couldn't tell what they were saying. Some phrases here and there weren't even about Olivia and she was beginning to grow concerned again because she never heard her daughter's name. She assumed that Ethan would have the entire prefecture looking for a fifteen-year-old girl.

Tyler had a horrible headache and she gave him a couple of aspirin from her purse. He tried to get comfortable on the couch but his head was hurting too badly. Cydney tried to make him more comfortable and then sat down beside him and began to stroke his dark head. She didn't even ask permission; he was so uncomfortable that, as a mother, she inherently wanted to help him. He didn't protest. As she stroked his head and gently massaged his left temple, the young man fell into an exhausted sleep.

Still stroking Tyler's head, Cydney wept when she knew that no one could see her tears.

———

The gunmen who had started the battle had gotten away. Estimates were that there had been as many as a dozen men, but they had fled one by one, disappearing into the city as the Paris Police gave chase. While half of the precinct was involved in the city-wide search, Ethan, J.D., Christophe and a host of other officers turned the prefecture upside down in the hunt for Olivia Hetherington. No stone was unturned. They went into bathrooms, janitor's closets and kitchens. But mostly, Christophe and his men were looking for the watch comman-der, Sgt. Michel, who was missing as well. Christophe had known the man for years and was genuinely concerned for his welfare.

After combing the massive building with an internal manhunt, one of the officers happened to look out of a doorway that led to a tree-lined walkway behind the building. He caught sight of a man struggling in the bushes and ran outside to investigate.

Sgt. Michel was picking himself up out of the brush, his head so bloodied that one eye was swollen shut. The police officer helped the Sergeant to stand and practically carried the man into the station. He began yelling for Inspector Dulay, sending men running for Christophe and finding him with Ethan and J.D. near the information desk. The three of them ran into the back offices of the first floor, running headlong into Sgt. Michel as he leaned heavily on the other officer.

"Paul," Christophe grabbed the man urgently. "What happened?"

The sergeant spoke in stammering French. "A man struck me," he said. "I don't know who he was. I was standing near the interrogation room where the children were and was hit from behind. I must have blacked out because when I came to, I heard the girl screaming. I followed the sounds and ended up out towards the walkway on the north side of the building. But I was so weak... I couldn't run and I fell into the bushes. I don't know how long I lay there until Depris here found me."

Ethan was already bolting out of the back of the prefecture building. There was a tree-lined walkway that paralleled the river on the north side of the island and absolutely nobody was upon it. It was completely empty for about a quarter mile in either direction. The sun was setting and it felt oddly empty and spooky. Experiencing more panic than he could describe, Ethan began to run towards the west.

Someone was yelling behind him, a booming voice that finally broke through his anxiety. He slowly came to a halt, breathing heavily as he realized there was no point in him running. Olivia was long gone by now; there had been plenty of time to take her, get her into a car, and speed away. It was painful to realize that whatever happened at the front of the building must have been a ruse. The plan was well-executed and they all fell for it. He couldn't see any other explanation. Nauseous, he turned around to see J.D. walking towards him.

"She's gone," J.D. told him. "Don't waste your time. She's out in the city now."

Ethan was pale, his nostrils flaring with exertion and emotion. "That gun battle out front was a diversion," he said furiously. "It pulled us away from Olivia so they could get at her."

J.D. put up a hand. "We don't know that for sure."

"Bull," Ethan burst. "J.D., this sect has fingers in every damn aspect of our world. They had to have a contact inside this station who told them where she was and how well she was guarded. We were pulled away from her by this gun battle, giving Die Auhänger the opportunity to kidnap her again. Why in the hell do they want her so badly? Just tell me that!"

"I don't know."

"You're the damn expert!"

"I don't know. I'm sorry, but I just don't know."

Ethan thrust a finger in his face. "I'll tell you why. This goes beyond that damn robe and all of this Holy Roman Empire crap. There's more to it that we're not seeing and it's going to cost Cydney and Olivia dearly if we don't figure it out."

J.D. knew he was upset. And he felt like he had failed both the museum and Cydney Hetherington in particular. He felt bad enough without Ethan blowing up at him.

"Look," he said calmly. "Let's go back inside and see what we can...."

Ethan suddenly pushed past him. "That sergeant," he growled. "He was the one who was supposed to be watching her. He let her get away."

J.D. was behind him. "That guy got the crap beat out of him," he insisted. "What are you thinking? That he just let them take her without a fight?"

Ethan was so furious that he couldn't answer. J.D. suddenly grabbed him and forced him to a halt.

"Ethan, stop a minute," he snapped. "Listen to me. I know you're upset, but you're also a Special Agent in Charge with the Federal Bureau of Investigation and right now, you're exhibiting conduct unbecoming that position. I realize your lady friend's daughter is involved and you are understandably emotional, but get a hold of yourself. Your behavior isn't going to do anyone any good. I need your level head right now. I gotta have it, man. Do you understand me?"

Ethan was still furious but J.D.'s words were sinking in. After a few moments, he took a deep breath and tried to calm himself. He pulled himself from J.D.'s grasp.

"I understand." He took another deep breath, raking his fingers through his dark hair and struggling for composure. "I know you're right. But those bastards hurt my son in their quest to get Olivia. They couldn't have just walked into that station unchallenged. Someone would have seen them. Everyone in that place has an I.D. badge, even visitors. They couldn't have just slipped in unseen and made off with a fifteen-year-old girl and nobody noticed. Someone had to let them in."

J.D. nodded slowly. "I know that," he said evenly. "But that sergeant is the only one who saw what happened. We need to tread carefully. If it's an inside job, then we don't know who we can trust."

Ethan was calming rapidly. "Maybe the information desk officer? Maybe the watch commander? Maybe even Dulay."

"It could be anybody."

"Goddammit," Ethan swore in anger.

He stood with J.D. a moment as the two collected their thoughts, thinking forward the next few hours. J.D. finally put his hand on his arm and steered him towards the building again.

"Go and talk to Cydney," he said. "She's going to need your comfort, not your fury. Be calm. Take her and Tyler back to the hotel and wait for me. I'm going to stay here with Daniels and Penryn and see what I can find out."

Ethan was feeling weak now that his fury had abated. The adrenalin rush was gone, replaced by an overwhelming hollowness. He just felt empty and sickened.

"Where's Cydney's cell phone?" he asked.

"I gave it back to her."

"I'd better keep that thing around in case Olivia calls again."

They reached the door leading into the prefecture. Ethan paused and took a deep breath. His hesitance was obvious.

"God," he muttered. "What am I going to tell Cydney?"

J.D. opened the door. "The truth," he replied. "Tell her the truth. I'll meet you at the hotel later."

Ethan passed through the doorway, moving to the stairs without so much as a hind glance to J.D., Christophe and the battered sergeant as he walked by them. His focus was on the woman on the second floor he was very much in love with. This wasn't news he was looking forward to delivering.

————

Upon reaching the interrogation room where Ethan had left Cydney and Tyler, he opened the door quietly to see Cydney sitting on the couch stroking Tyler's swollen head. His son was sleeping soundly. Cydney's head snapped to him, her eyes wide with expectation, and he smiled weakly. With a silent gesture beckoning her out of the room, she dutifully left Tyler sleeping and went out into the corridor with him. Ethan quietly closed the door and faced her.

"Where's Olivia?" Cydney asked.

Ethan took a deep breath. "She's gone," he said quietly. "Cyd, there's no easy way to tell you this so I just need to come out and say it. We suspect that gun battle in front of the prefecture was a ruse to pull us away from Olivia. Once we were occupied, they were able to slip in and take her again."

Cydney just stared at him. When the wait grew excessive, he began to wonder if she had even understood what he had said. Finally, she shook her head.

"No," she said flatly. "It's not true. She's here, somewhere. She was scared and ran off to hide. We just need to find her."

Ethan reached out and put his hands on her arms. "Honey, we have a witness who saw someone take her. J.D. is questioning the guy right now."

Cydney continued to stare at him. Then she shook her head again and turned away from him.

"She's here, somewhere," she said confidently as she walked towards the stairs. "I'll find her. She's just hiding."

Ethan went after her and put his arms around her. "No, honey, she's not," he murmured against her head. "I need for you and Tyler to come with me so I can have you checked out at the hospital. J.D. will work on locating Olivia."

Cydney suddenly turned into a wildcat. She violently yanked away from Ethan as he tried to hold on to her. Her hair partially came out of the ponytail, wild and askew across her face. Shocked, Ethan tried to grab her again but she swung her fists at him and wouldn't let him get a hold of her.

"No!" she shouted. "I'm not listening to you anymore. You let them take my baby twice and I won't listen to you anymore."

Ethan stopped trying to grab hold of her but continued following her down the hall.

"Cydney, please," he sounded as if he were begging. "I know you're upset but I need your calm head right now. Please, baby. I need for you to come back with me so we can get Tyler to the hospital."

Cydney's strong stance was crumbling. Tears sprang to her eyes and avalanched down her cheeks.

"You still have your child," she wept painfully. "I need to go find mine."

"No, no, baby," his heart was breaking. "We'll find her. I don't want you to...."

"Why didn't you protect her?" she interrupted him angrily. "You promised you would protect her and you didn't."

Ethan's heart went from breaking to being completely shattered. "I'm sorry," he said dejectedly. "We tried, we honestly tried. I don't know why they want her so badly, but they do. But we'll find her again, I swear it. Her and the robe."

"I don't even care about the robe anymore!" she screamed. "The robe is just an object. We're talking about my daughter and she's more valuable than any goddamn robe!"

He grabbed hold of her arm just as she hit the stairs and she ferociously reacted to his touch. She thrust herself away from him and ended up falling down about half the flight of stairs before catching herself on the railing.

Ethan began running after her but she took off, running as fast as she could past the information desk and out the front door where they were now conducting a shooting investigation. Ethan was shouting after her but she was racing wildly. She even lost both her shoes, enabling her to run even faster. She dodged around the corner and tore off to the south.

Ethan rounded the corner and watched her run, coming to an exhausted halt. He wanted desperately to go after her but he couldn't leave his son. Tyler needed to get checked out by a doctor and, at the moment, his son's welfare was the priority. But it didn't stop him from watching Cydney run into the darkness, fading off until he couldn't see her anymore.

He stood there with tears running down his cheeks.

FOURTEEN

OLIVIA WAS VAGUELY aware of a gentle rocking motion. Gradually, as she became lucid, she could hear a strange rhythmic clacking sound. It was like two sticks hitting together in regular rhythm.

Opening her eyes, she could see that she was in a supine position, looking at a window with the blinds drawn against the sunlight. Everything was moving and she thought, as she lay there, that she might be on a train. It sounded like one and she was certainly rocking around enough. Disoriented, she stirred slightly, realizing instantly that she had a monstrous headache. She groaned.

"Hey," came a soft voice. "You awake?"

Olivia blinked several times, turning slightly to see Joseph sitting next to her. He was smiling gently.

"Hi," he said as their eyes met. "We meet again."

Olivia immediately started crying. Deep, painful sobs and crocodile tears spilled out onto her face. Her head throbbed and she was nauseous and terrified.

"No, no," she wept. "I want my mom!"

Joseph tried to soothe her. They were in a private cabin on

the Artesia night train from Paris to Rome. It was a nicer train, meant for overnight travel. Nat was in the lounge car and Coral was in the dining car, leaving Joseph to watch over their young captive. He put his hand on her back gently and she screamed.

"No!" she cried. "Don't touch me!"

"Calm down, Olivia," Joseph said. "It's not as bad as you think."

She was sobbing hysterically. "Where am I?"

"On a train."

"I don't want to be on a train. I want my mom!"

He put his hands on her to forcibly calm her as she struggled to get away from him. "You'll see her soon, I promise. But you really need to cooperate."

"No!" she screamed.

She began kicking at Joseph, who put up his hands to try and deflect her frantic feet. The train swayed strongly to the right and he ended up falling on top of her, trapping her in the chair. He grabbed her tightly, forcing her to look at him.

"Look," he hissed, "I'm sorry this happened, I really am. But you and I are caught up in something that's bigger than anything you can imagine. I know you're just a kid, but you really need to understand that we're not a bunch of idiots. It's not like you got kidnapped by the Three Stooges. You have a purpose in all of this and, just like me, you need to fulfill your purpose. Olivia, do you understand me?"

She wouldn't look him in the eye but her crying had lessened. He shook her gently. "Olivia, answer me. I need you to understand what's going on and maybe you won't be so scared."

After a small eternity, she slowly opened her eyes and looked up at him. "You're squishing me," she told him.

Joseph shifted but he didn't get up. He was afraid she would fly out of control again if he wasn't physically restraining her.

"Do you remember what we told you about the Holy Roman Empire and the robe?"

She wasn't focused on that. She was only focused on her desire to get back to her mother.

"Joseph, please help me to find my mother," she countered. "I swear I won't tell them I know you or anything about you. I just want to go home."

He touched her head gently. "I wish I could, doll," he said earnestly. "But I don't make the decisions."

"But you're going to be the next Holy Roman Emperor if everything works out the way you guys said it would," she insisted. "People have to do what you say. You can tell them to let me go and they'll have to listen."

"Baby girl, it's not that simple," Joseph said. "Even I take directions from someone else."

"Who? Who is more important than you?"

Joseph gazed back at her, seeing a terrified young girl that he felt very sorry for. He still didn't agree with abducting her out of the police station but that had been beyond his control, too. All of this was out of his control and he was being swept along in the maelstrom.

For all intents and purposes, Joseph was a captive, too, and the more time passed, the more disillusioned he felt. His family lineage had not been a choice, but everything he had done until this point had, indeed, been his choice. He was beginning to deeply question his choices.

"A very important guy," he told her. "Look, we'll be in Rome soon and all of this will be over in a few days. Okay?"

She gazed up into his dark blue eyes. "Rome?" she repeated, shocked. "I don't want to go to Rome. I want to go home."

"You can when this is all over," he told her. "But right now, it's really important that you cooperate. I'm serious."

Her lips twisted angrily. "You guys can't threaten me about

killing my mom if I don't go along with you. She's with the FBI
and they'll protect her."

"We got you, didn't we?"

That seemed to stop her anger and bring about the fear
again. "Please don't hurt her."

"Then you need to do what you're told and no one will get
hurt."

"What do you want me to do?"

Joseph climbed off of her. "Right now, I want you to calm
down and eat something. We'll be in Rome in a few hours."

"Then what happens?"

He smiled thinly. "Then we finish what it's taken two thousand years to start."

Olivia had no idea what that meant. But she was sure that
she didn't like it.

―――――

Ethan returned to his hotel suite after midnight. He was hoping
to find Cydney there, but the suite seemed dark and empty as he
opened the door and ushered his son inside. Other than a bad
headache, Tyler was fine. The physician had given him some
prescription painkillers for the headache and Ethan went to the
kitchenette and got a glass of water for his son to take the pills.
The boy choked them down and went straight to bed.

Tyler fell immediately into a deep sleep. Ethan pulled the
kid's shoes off and covered him up, leaving the room and shutting the door softly behind him.

He moved for the living room with the intention of
watching television and waiting for some word from Cydney,
but he was drawn to her room, instead. He was curious to see if
she had returned at some point and taken all of her luggage with
her. He didn't blame her for her anger; she was right. He had

made promises he didn't keep. Heartbroken wasn't the right term to describe what he was feeling. He was devastated.

The door to Cydney and Olivia's bedroom was cracked open and he could see the Parisian moonlight streaming in through the open drapes, bathing the room in an unearthly glow. He stuck his head into the room, looking for Cydney's suitcase and was startled to find her lying on the bed next to the far wall.

Relief filled him in a rush, making him feel lightheaded. He actually had to grip the doorjamb to keep from swaying. Silently, he moved into the room to get a look at her, just to make sure she was all right. He just couldn't believe what he was seeing.

She was curled up on her right side, still in her black slacks and black blouse. She lay on top of the comforter, eyes closed, still and silent. Ethan walked silently into the room, reaching down to put a gentle hand on her forehead, touching her to make sure he wasn't dreaming. The moment he touched her, however, her eyes popped open.

Startled by her swift awakening, he wasn't sure what to say. He just smiled, hoping it wouldn't set her off again. Cydney gazed up at him and suddenly burst into tears.

"Oh, my God," she wept. "Ethan, I'm so sorry. I was so horrible to you and I'm so sorry. Please don't be mad at me."

He immediately fell down on the bed beside her, pulling her into his powerful embrace. Cydney wept openly against him, getting mascara and tears on his white dress shirt. He held her so tightly that he was in danger of suffocating her. Cydney clung to him.

"It's all right, honey," he couldn't begin to describe the relief of having her in his arms. "I'm not mad. But I was really worried. Are you all right?"

She nodded, sobbing pitifully. "I don't know why I said

what I did," she whispered. "It was like watching another person scream at you. It's just that Olivia... she was safe, Ethan. She was with me and she was safe. And now she's gone again and I just don't know what to do."

"I know," he kissed her forehead. "I'm so sorry, Cyd. So sorry you and Olivia have to go through this again."

She continued to sob and he held her tightly, stroking her head with one hand. She didn't seem capable of doing anything other than expending her grief and all he wanted to do was comfort her.

"Where did you go?" he asked.

"I don't know. I just ran until I was exhausted and then found a taxi to take me back here. I've been here for hours."

"Did you eat any dinner?"

She shook her head. Ethan kissed her forehead, her cheeks, and climbed off the bed. As Cydney lay there and sniffled, he picked up the phone and called Room Service. When she realized what he was doing, she tried to stop him but he ignored her, ordering a couple of sandwiches from the twenty-four hour menu and a bottle of champagne. Hanging up the phone, he gave her a wink and went into the bathroom.

The bathroom was truly a luxurious retreat. There was a shower large enough for four people, a toilet, a bidet, and a large Roman tub. Ethan went to the tub and turned on the spout. Steaming water soon began filling the tub. He looked around, spied her overnight case, and dug around until he found a tube of shower gel. He squeezed the floral-scented gel into the tub to get the bubbles going. Soon, the whole bathroom smelled like a girly treat.

By the time he went back into the bedroom, Cydney was sitting up and pulling the remainder of her pony tail out of her messy hair. The light next to the bed was on and she looked up at him as he came into the room.

"What are you doing in there?" she asked.

He gazed down at her with his hands on his hips, studying her pale, red-eyed face. "Running us a bath."

She cocked an eyebrow at him. "*Us?*"

"Yep."

"What about Tyler?"

"He's dead asleep behind a closed door. The entire building could collapse around him and he wouldn't hear it."

"Is he okay? How is his head?"

"He's got a bad headache but he's okay."

She nodded and stood up, shaking out her glorious blond hair and unbuttoning her blouse. Ethan began removing his tie, watching her as she removed her blouse and exposed her sexy body to the weak light. Unzipping her pants, she slipped them off and revealed a black lace thong. Ethan could already feel his erection. But Cydney was oblivious to his physical reaction to her; she was looking at her feet.

"I don't even know what happened to my shoes," she observed with some chagrin. "They were new."

"I have them," Ethan said. "I brought them back with me."

She looked up at him as he was unbuttoning his shirt and rolled her eyes wearily. "Oh, what those French cops must think of me," she lamented. "Cette femme Américaine folle."

He grinned as he pulled off his shirt. "I swear they didn't bat an eyelash. All in a day's work for the French."

She smiled in spite of herself. "Thanks for saving my shoes."

"It was the least I could do."

Her smile faded as she moved to unhook her bra. "Where is J.D.?" she asked. "Did he find anything out about Olivia?"

Ethan shook his head faintly. "Not yet."

"Did you ask Tyler if he saw the guy who whacked him over the head?"

"He doesn't remember a thing."

She looked dejected. "Oh."

Ethan looked her in the eye even though she removed the bra and her beautiful breasts sprang free. "J.D. is still at the prefecture working on it with Dulay and, just so you are aware, Dulay acts like they stole his own child. Olivia stayed with his family for a couple of nights and they grew very attached to her. Whatever moles or informants they may have planted in that police station, I seriously doubt Dulay is one of them. He seems on the level."

She sighed heavily and scratched her scalp, her gorgeous hair splaying over her naked shoulders and back. "Then you really think that someone inside the prefecture was behind Olivia's abduction?"

"I can't think of another explanation."

She thought on that a moment. "You haven't told me if you learned anything from your interrogation of Olivia. Did she provide you with any information that might help you figure out who these Disciples are and why they want her so badly?"

Ethan nodded faintly. "Are you sure you want to hear this right now?"

"Please," she begged. "It makes me feel like I know who she's with, like they're not just out to kill my daughter."

He shook his head. "No, they're not out to kill her," he replied. "But her tale is a really strange one. We knew, from the chatter we had been picking up for the past several months, that it was their intention to steal the robe to crown a new Holy Roman Emperor. According to what Olivia told us, what we didn't know is that they have a descendent from the House of d'Orleans with them, a young man who is apparently the man they intend to crown."

She cocked her head. "House of d'Orleans?"

He nodded. "The French Royal Family. If you believe the folklore, they are descended from Jesus of Nazareth's daughter with Mary Magdalene, Sarah, through the Merovingian blood-lines. That would make him a descendent of Jesus Christ."

"And they intend to make him the next Holy Roman Emperor?"

"As Jesus' descendent, yes."

"But isn't it the Germans who have historically ruled the Holy Roman Empire?"

"Historically, yes. But if Die Auhänger has proven one thing, it's that they're not predicable. To crown the heir to the French throne the next Holy Roman Emperor because he is a direct descendent of Jesus Christ is a new twist. Apparently, they feel the one to lead the new Fourth Reich of Enlightenment should really be holy."

"That sounds really strange."

He moved in her general direction, crossing his powerful arms as he spoke.

"It gets stranger," he lowered his voice. "Coral Chastity Aames has a big hand in this, although to what extent, we can't be sure. But the IRS has traced some deposits from her corporation, Izan, into a Cayman Islands account with a Vatican City address."

Cydney stared at him, her brow furrowing as she mulled that over. "She's not Catholic, is she?"

"No," Ethan shook his head. "She's not. But the Pope is, and the Pope is traditionally the one to crown the new Holy Roman Emperor."

"What?" Cydney's jaw dropped. "The Pope is in on this?"

"We're not sure. But there is one more oddity to this."

"Only one more?" she asked with weak, if not desperate, sarcasm.

He smiled faintly. "The name of Coral's corporation, Izan, is 'Nazi' spelled backwards."

Cydney stared at him a long moment before closing her eyes

as if to ward off the overload of information. "Oh, my God," she breathed. "This is the most bizarre thing I've ever heard."

He raised his eyebrows in agreement. "Yes, it is. But please don't repeat what I've told you, not to anyone. This is classified and the only reason I'm telling you is because Olivia is involved."

She was both stunned and frightened. "But what in the hell do they want with my daughter? There are so many pieces to this crazy puzzle that it all must be pointing to something, but I can't see what it is. Why do they want her?"

He pursed his lips regretfully. "We just don't know," he said quietly. "I'm sorry I can't tell you more than that, but we're working on it as hard as we can. J.D. is brilliant; if anyone can figure this out, he can."

Cydney just stood there, looking dazed, as Ethan stood next to her and watched her for her next reaction. He let his gaze move from her face to her luscious body, as she was still standing nude except for the naughty-looking thong. Finally, she shook her head, too overwhelmed to know how to react.

"It's all so crazy," she muttered.

"I know. But have faith. We'll find Olivia."

She nodded, knowing she had to trust him in all matters. "I know you will," she muttered, her mind so muddled that she forced herself off the subject; it wasn't doing her any good to continue stewing over it. Her thoughts moved back to Tyler as she padded into the bathroom. "Poor Tyler, getting his head smacked by some crazy person. I'm sure that's not something he expected to be part of his trip to Paris."

Ethan was following her, watching her round butt underneath her thong. "He'll be all right," he said, leaning against the doorjamb as she removed her underwear and tested the water in the tub. "He's very concerned about Olivia, though. He thinks she's pretty cute."

Cydney shot him such a look that he started chuckling. "Keep Mr. Fun Bags away from my daughter."

He was still laughing as she climbed into the tub. "You can't fault him for his good taste."

She settled down in the bubbly water. "No, I can't, but I can fault him for his taste in band names."

Ethan continued to grin as she pulled out her bath sponge. But he soon sobered "So," he ventured quietly. "I have a question for you."

"What?"

"Are *we* okay?"

She understood his meaning. "We're okay," she confirmed. "We'll always be okay."

"Good." He smiled faintly, turning away after a moment. "I'll be right back. I want to check on Ty."

Cydney let him go, settling down into the tub and laying her head against the side. Ethan left the bedroom and went to check on his son, but that wasn't his only purpose. He called the front desk from the living room phone and asked about the selection of rings he had ordered earlier. The desk clerk didn't know anything about it but she quickly tracked down the night manager who did. Ethan had the rings sent up with room service.

Ten minutes later, the food arrived with a hotel waiter and the jewelry arrived with the manager. Ethan had the waiter bring the food into the kitchenette while he stood out in the hall and looked at the rings that the manager had brought.

It wasn't a difficult selection; he knew what he was looking for. Something simple – a slender band with a big diamond, and he wanted platinum. The prices were presented with the rings and he selected a two carat Radiant-cut diamond in a size six platinum setting. It was nine thousand American dollars and an absolutely spectacular ring. He hoped Cydney would like it. More than that, he hoped she would accept his proposal.

He thanked the manager and tipped the waiter. When the door was shut and locked, he found the sandwiches and put the ring on Cydney's club sandwich, held in place by the decorative toothpick. Then he covered it back up with the stainless steel heat cover. Taking the tray with the food and champagne glasses in one hand and the wine bucket with the liquor in the other, he proceeded into the bathroom.

Cydney had doused her hair and now lay against the side of the tub with her eyes closed. Ethan set the food down on the tiled area near the tub's water spout.

"I know you're tired," he said. "Eat something and then we'll hit the sack."

She opened her eyes and sat up, watching him pop the cork from the champagne bottle and pour two glasses. She accepted one of them and they toasted.

"To us," he said. "And to Olivia."

Tears filled her eyes but she fought them as she took a long, healthy swallow and smacked her lips. "That's really good," she looked over at the still-covered food. "What did you get us?"

"Just a couple of sandwiches," he said, pulling his white t-shirt over his head. "Take the one nearest you."

She did. Reaching out, she pulled the entire thing off the tray and set it on her side of the tub. Meanwhile, she failed to notice that Ethan was now down on one knee beside the tub in all of his bare-chested glory. The man was spectacularly built. She pulled the stainless steel cover off of the sandwich and set it aside.

He watched her face as she looked at the food. He waited for her to realize that there was something on top of one of the halves. First, her brow furrowed when she spied it. Then, she cocked her head when wasn't quite sure what it was. Suddenly, her eyes widened when she reached out to confirm her observations as if her eyes were deceiving her. Her mouth fell open.

"What in the hell...?" she picked up the ring, turned it around, and was faced by the brilliant two carat diamond. "Ethan, what is this?"

He was watching her, an amused expression on his face. "What does it look like?" When she looked up at him, stunned, he reached out and took her hand. "Cydney, I know we've known each other only eight days, but I knew I loved you within the first twenty-four hours of knowing you. You are the most amazing, intelligent and beautiful woman I've ever met and every time I look at you, I fall more deeply in love with you. I know this is sudden and I know it's ridiculously soon, but I will feel the same way about you in fifty years as I do now. I would be incredibly proud to be your husband. Will you please do me the honor of becoming my wife?"

Cydney was floored; he could tell that just by looking at her. Her mouth opened into an unconscious "O" as her gaze moved between him and the ring. After several long moments, she licked her lips, struggling for the correct words.

"It's not just me," she whispered. "It's my daughter, too. We're a package deal."

"And I love her, too. I will love her as if she were my own flesh and blood."

She was back to staring at him. "Are you sure?"

"Never more sure about anything in my life."

"But we've only known each other a week."

"It only took me a day to fall in love with you."

"You *love* me? Really?"

He grinned. "Absolutely. What's not to love?"

She took her eyes off him and stared at the ring. Ethan didn't want to push her for an answer, but he was slowly dying inside. Every moment that passed was like torture. But suddenly, she was flying out of the tub and hit him squarely in the chest, her arms around his neck and her lips on his. Ethan laughed low in his throat, meeting her passionate kiss as she was wet and slippery in his arms.

"Oh, Ethan," she breathed against his lips. "I'm just blown away."

"Is that a 'Yes?'"

She nodded, giggling, and he started giggling, too. Soon they were both giggling, lustily and happily kissing one another with Cydney half-in and half-out of the tub. Ethan pulled her out of the tub completely and laid her on the cold tile of the bathroom. Her hands were on his pants, unfastening his belt, and soon they were off completely.

His big body covered her, warm and powerful, as she surrendered to his joyful attention. His tongue was in her mouth, tasting her sweetness, as one hand roved her damp body. When his mouth left hers and began to nurse hungrily at her breasts, she stopped him.

"Ethan," she breathed heavily, thrusting a hand into his face. "The ring. You'd better put it on me so we don't lose it."

He was wedged in between her legs and paused, holding his weight off of her with one elbow while taking the ring from her with his free hand. She held up her left hand and their eyes met briefly, with smiles, as he slid the ring on the third finger of her left hand. It fit perfectly.

"There," she whispered, inspecting the gorgeous ring seated upon her finger. "Now we're official."

He gazed at her, faintly shaking his head. "You have no idea how happy I am right now. I honestly didn't know how you'd react."

"Seriously?"

He wriggled his eyebrows. "I could have gone down in flames."

"Ethan?"

"Hmmm?"

"I love you, too."

She leaned forward, kissing him sweetly and he became upswept in the fire that ignited so easily between them. His hands, his mouth, told her how very much he was coming to love her as they moved over her flesh. Ethan took her twice on the floor and was preparing to take her a third time when he heard her stomach growl, very loudly.

He broke down into soft laughter. Cydney grinned up at him, somewhat embarrassed. "I haven't eaten all day," she said apologetically. "Sorry."

He sat back on his heels and pulled her up with him. "I'm the one who should apologize," he said, looking around and spying a bathrobe on the sink. He yanked it down and put it on her. "Let's eat, okay?"

She agreed and soon they were sitting on her bed, eating club sandwiches and drinking champagne. Cydney fell asleep alone in her bed when Ethan returned to the room he shared with Tyler, but she knew that she would never again be alone.

Her outlook on life suddenly didn't seem so bleak.

FIFTEEN

NAT HAD hold of Olivia's arm as they made their way off the train at the Rome Terminal Train Station. It was loud, busy, dirty and crowded. Olivia was still disoriented, now with the added pleasure of having gotten motion-sick on the train. But Nat had no sympathy for her as he pulled her across the dirty platform and into the modern train station. It was mid-morning, the day slightly overcast and humid in the ancient city of Rome.

Olivia had been allowed to shower on the train and wash her hair. Having no clothes of her own, the only option available was Coral's clothes. They were very expensive, well-made, and gaudy. Olivia was horrified but unless she wanted to wear the same jeans and t-shirt that she had been wearing since she left California, she was going to have to make do. Coral was about Olivia's weight but two or three inches shorter. Olivia picked out a pair of white Capri jeans and a bright pink t-shirt, the lesser of all of Coral's wardrobe evils. She wore her own sneakers with the pink and green skulls on them. Her still–damp hair went into two braids.

Collecting the luggage, they went out onto the curb to hail a taxi amidst the chaos of exhaust fumes and people. Olivia squinted in the glare of the overcast sky, looking around with some curiosity. Directly across the street, she noticed substantial ruins. As Nat held her arm with a death grip, she spoke to Joseph standing next to her.

"What are those ruins over there?" she asked.

Joseph shaded his eyes from the glare. "Oh, those," he smiled down at her. "The Baths of Diocletian."

Olivia's green gaze was fixed on them. She found Rome far more interesting than Paris just because of the truly ancient ruins. The smell, the feel, of the city was different, too. It smelled like exhaust fumes and dirt. There was something quite old and timeless about it, and she couldn't help her curiosity.

"Are there any more ruins around here?"

Joseph continued to smile. "Tons."

"Like what?"

"A bunch of stuff," he said as a taxi pulled up and Nat yanked Olivia towards it. "We're in Rome; everything is old."

Nat had Coral get into the car first, followed by Olivia. He followed and put Joseph in the front seat with the driver.

"Hotel Columbus de Roma, *per favore*," Joseph told the man who smelled heavily of cigarettes.

The taxi pulled away from the curb and in spite of the harrowing circumstances, Olivia couldn't help but get swept up in the glory that was Rome.

There weren't any major roads like freeways, just medium-sized roads that branched off in all directions. The taxi driver took them through a series of streets, like a maze, and every other block had a ruined basilica or other ancient ruins that Olivia found fascinating. At one point, they passed right by the Pantheon with its massive size and time-worn pillars. Tourists were clinging to the steps, like flies, taking pictures of the ancient glory.

"Wow," Olivia bumped into Coral as she strained to get a look as they drove by. "That's really cool."

Nat ignored her as did Coral for the most part. Coral was still stinging from the fact that Olivia had run from her, making her look very inept in the eyes of Nat and the Cardinal. But Joseph watched her from the front seat, grinning at her enthusiasm.

They crossed over the Tiber River on a massive bridge, past the General Hospital of the Holy Spirit, and neared Vatican City. Olivia could see the horrendous traffic up ahead and the top of St. Peter's Basilica gleaming in the muted sunlight. But before they got to the City proper, the taxi driver suddenly pulled a sharp right and entered a driveway with a terra cotta-colored building alongside of it. Curious, Olivia watched as they pulled up to the entry of the very large hotel.

Nat looked at Joseph. "Get back here and sit with her," he instructed. "Don't get out of this car and don't let her out of your sight."

Joseph nodded, climbed out of the front seat, and sat along-side Olivia when Nat got out of the car. Joseph smiled at Olivia when Nat slammed the door and, to his surprise, she smiled back. She inched closer to him so she didn't have to sit so close to Coral, drowned in some wretched perfume that was undoubtedly quite expensive. It made Olivia sneeze.

They sat in the taxi for quite some time while Nat checked them in to the hotel. At one point, Coral began rummaging around her massive Gucci purse, spilling half the contents onto the dirty floor of the taxi. Her makeup bag exploded, much to Coral's displeasure, and Olivia watched disinterestedly as she scrambled to pick everything up. She wasn't going to lift a finger to help the woman until she noticed a black eye pencil next to her white sneaker. It had just rolled there by chance. As Olivia stared at the eye pencil, a thought occurred to her.

Coral was scrambling to pick everything up from the hundreds of items now strewn over the floor and Olivia suddenly felt like helping the woman pick up her mess. She bent over, grabbing a handful of stuff and making sure to slip the black eye pencil inside her shoe.

"Thank you, Olivia," Coral said as the teenager dumped handfuls of makeup back into the purse. "This is very nice of you."

Olivia's heart was thumping, praying that Coral didn't inventory her makeup bag and know every single little piece that was in it. "You're welcome," she replied.

Coral smiled at her with her stenciled-on red lips. "You're a good girl, sweetheart," she said.

Olivia smiled without meaning it. But, at the moment, she was cooking up a plan and needed to be in Coral's good graces. She turned to Joseph.

"I don't want to be pain, but I have to go to the bathroom really bad," she said. "Do you think the hotel has a restroom in the lobby?"

Joseph glanced towards the hotel. "I'm sure it does," he said. "But we'll have to wait until Nat gets back."

Olivia began to shake her leg. "I don't think I can. I have to go really, really bad." She could see Joseph's reluctance and she sought to ease him. "I swear I won't run away. I promise. Can I please go?"

Joseph gazed at her a moment, deliberating. Olivia fixed him with a beseeching gaze. "Please, Joe," she begged. "I really need to go and I swear I won't run."

He met her stare a moment longer before reluctantly nodding his head.

"All right," he opened the door and pulled her out after him. He had her by the wrist. "Coral, get out. You'll need to take her into the women's restroom."

Coral, looking extremely reluctant, climbed out of the cab with her askew purse. Joseph, now holding Olivia's hand very tightly, led her into the truly gorgeous lobby. The architecture was classic, the colors muted shades of gold, orange and yellow. Olivia trotted after Joseph as Coral brought up the rear until they came across a sign that read *Gabinetto di Womens*.

"This way," Joseph said.

Olivia almost got whiplash as he pulled her after him in their quest to find the bathroom; she was still reading the odd sign.

"What does *Gabinetto di Womens* mean?" she asked as she scooted behind him.

"Women's bathroom," he pointed up at the door that had it posted in lovely gold letters on it. "Hurry up, now. We don't want to piss off Nat."

He opened the door and thrust her inside, followed by Coral. Coral stood uncertainly near the sinks as Olivia raced inside one of the stalls and slammed the door, locking it. The truth was that Olivia really did have to relieve herself, but she had a more self-serving goal in mind.

Removing the eye pencil from her shoe, she sat on the toilet and wrote on the stall door in big black letters. Then she flushed the pencil down the toilet to get rid of the evidence. There were no words to describe her relief as she exited the bathroom, completely calm and completely subservient.

Nat checked them into two adjoining rooms. Olivia behaved herself completely, at least for the time being. Sitting on one of the beds, she kept her head lowered so no one would see her smile as they went about their business around her. They seemed so busy with phone calls and other things that no one gave her a second look. Olivia just sat on the bed, still as stone.

Please God, she prayed over and over again. *Let the next person who sits in that stall read English.*

———

Tyler was bouncing off the walls the next morning. Having slept eleven hours, it was close to noon by the time he awoke and he wanted to go sightseeing right away. Other than a big lump on his head, he showed no ill effects from the previous day. Ethan was already up, working on his laptop, when Tyler bound into the living room and demanded, very nicely, breakfast. He threatened to eat the fake fruit on the coffee table if his father didn't feed him right away.

Ethan called room service with his son reading the room service menu and rattling off his breakfast order. Ethan ended up ordering pancakes, bacon, eggs, a roast beef sandwich and steak fries, plus oatmeal, fresh fruit and a cheese omelet. Cydney still wasn't up yet and he wanted to have something waiting for her when she woke.

The food finally arrived and Tyler ate his breakfast while watching cartoons as Ethan answered emails and sipped his espresso.

"Dad," Tyler announced with a mouth full of pancake. "They have Scooby Doo cartoons in French. They call it Scooby Doo et le Mystère Usinent."

Ethan grinned as he looked up from his computer, over his son's head to see the 1970s cartoon on the television in full color.

"Weird," he commented, looking back to the screen.

Tyler was laughing loudly at the cartoon dog speaking French. Ethan told him to hold it down a couple of times but eventually gave up; Tyler wasn't listening to him, anyway.

Sometime around high noon, the door to Cydney's room creaked open.

Ethan looked over to see her walking towards him fully dressed. She was wearing jeans, a tank top with a zip-up hoodie over it, and her lovely hair was pulled back into a loose ponytail. She smiled at him and Ethan felt like a giddy idiot; his heart was thumping and his palms began to sweat. He returned her smile as she walked over to him, leaned against him, wrapped her arms around his big shoulders and kissed him. He wrapped his arms around her waist, his face pressed in the valley between her breasts.

"Good morning," she said. "I'm sorry I slept so late."

"No worries," Ethan gazed up at her as if she were the most beautiful sight in the entire world. "Sorry if Junior over there woke you up."

She looked over at Tyler, who was glued to the television. "I'm glad he did," she said. "Otherwise, I would have missed *Scooby Doo et le Mystère Usinent.*"

Ethan laughed. "Cet aurait été dommage."

She snorted, kissing him again and noticing the food on the table. "I'm starved." She looked at it with interest. "What did you get me?"

He put the laptop aside and pulled out a seat for her. After yesterday, he wasn't sure what kind of mood she would be in and was pleased to see that she seemed happy and calm. It already made the day better.

She was hungry, too, a good sign. Cydney sat down and devoured the grapes, oranges and strawberries. Then she moved on to the oatmeal, now cool, and piled it with raisins and brown sugar. Ethan had already eaten the omelet and he sat and watched her as she ate.

"So how are you doing this morning?" he asked her.

She nodded as she took a bite of the oatmeal. "I'm all right," she replied, meeting his warm gaze as she wiped her mouth. "And you?"

He reached out and took her right hand, kissing it. "I'm awesome," he murmured.

She smiled sweetly at him and held up her left hand, inspecting the beautiful ring for the hundredth time that morning. Ethan took her left hand and kissed the ring. Now he had both hands trapped and he kissed them again.

"Did you tell Scooby Doo over there yet?" she whispered.

Ethan shook his head and let go of her hands so she could eat. "There hasn't been the opportunity," he responded quietly. "But I will today. Maybe we should do it together."

She shook her head. "No," she said. "Do it alone. He barely knows me and if he has something to say about it, he probably won't say it in front of me. This will be a surprise to him; with the two of us telling him, it looks like an ambush."

He nodded thoughtfully. "Point taken."

"Dude!" Tyler exploded over on the couch. "It's Scooby Doo meets the Monkees!"

"The Monkees?" Cydney's face screwed up. "That's a name from the past."

Ethan chuckled. "I wasn't a fan."

Cydney smiled, watching him react to his son's delight. "I loved watching them as a kid."

He looked at her, cocking his head. "It just occurred to me that I don't even know how old you are."

"Fifty-seven."

He snorted because she had dead-panned it so well. But she eventually broke down into smile. "I'm thirty-six. My birthday is May tenth. And you?"

"I'm afraid, my dear, that you are going to be married to an older man."

She feigned dread. "I *knew* it. You've got one foot in the grave, haven't you?"

He smirked. "Sometimes I feel like it. Thirty-eight seems pretty old sometimes."

Suddenly, the television went off and Tyler was bounding into the kitchenette with his dirty dishes in hand. He slammed them down on the table in his haste. Ethan caught a spoon before it could flip off the table.

"Take it easy, man," he admonished. "Don't break up the joint."

"Can we go to the Louvre today?" he asked enthusiastically. "And then can we go see the Eiffel Tower?"

Ethan opened his mouth but Cydney spoke first. "I think that would be great," she looked at Ethan as she spoke. "Tyler had a pretty rough day yesterday. I think the Louvre would be a perfect place to spend today."

Ethan gazed at her over the tabletop and she could tell that he had something more to say to that. But he spoke to his son, instead.

"Go get yourself together," he told him. "We'll leave in a bit."

Tyler was rushing back into the bedroom he shared with his dad with the grace of a runaway train. Cydney shook her head and grinned as he smacked into the dresser and tried not to use curse words to describe the pain.

Ethan just rolled his eyes. "It's like a stampede every time with that kid."

"And I'm sure you were perfect at that age, right?"

"Of course I was."

She made a face letting him know what she thought of that statement as he picked up her right hand again and kissed it.

"Are you sure about sightseeing today?" he asked. "I can't go with you. I need to go back over to the Prefecture of Police."

"I know you do, but Tyler doesn't have to and I don't think there's anything I can do over there to help find my daughter that you and J.D. aren't already doing," she sighed, watching his fingers as they played with her own. "I woke up this morning and realized that all of this is completely out of my hands. You're my daughter's best hope and I need to let you do your job without having a meltdown every five minutes."

He smiled sadly. "You're her mother. I would worry if you weren't having meltdowns once in a while."

It was apparent that she was trying to be brave. "I think spending the day with another teenager at the Louvre is just what I need right now. I'm really glad he came."

He smiled gently, stood up, and kissed her on the forehead. "All right, honey," he agreed. "Whatever you want."

She watched him walk into the bedroom he shared with his son. With a sigh, she stood up and went back to the bedroom to get her purse and money. She slipped on her walking shoes and put on her big hoop earrings. Taking a look at herself in the mirror, she suddenly felt very different. The Cydney Hetherington from eight days ago was light years away from the woman gazing back at her in the mirror. So much had happened that she was still trying to process it all.

She collected her purse and went back into the living room area. Fiddling with her earring, she barely heard the cell phone go off in her purse. Then she heard it again. Because of the situation with Olivia, she had changed her phone plan before leaving Los Angeles and now had an international plan through an international carrier. Ripping open the purse, she yanked out the cell phone.

"Ethan!" she yelped.

He suddenly appeared in the bedroom doorway, his expression full of concern. "What's wrong?"

She held up the cell phone as it went on its fourth ring. He bolted over to her, took it from her shaking hand, and answered it.

"Hello?" he sounded very calm.

There was a long pause. "Hello?" It was a woman's voice.

"Who is this?" Ethan asked.

The woman didn't say anything for a moment. "Well," she sounded strained. "This is going to sound really strange, but I saw this number on a bathroom stall."

Ethan's brow furrowed. "Excuse me? Ma'am, who are you?"

The woman sighed and grunted, as if struggling to explain her purpose. "My name is Marianne Ustel and I'm from Des Moines, Iowa. Look, I know this sounds really crazy, but something told me to call this number."

Ethan was trying not to look at Cydney's anxious face. It made him nervous to see how on edge she was. "Marianne, my name is Ethan Serreaux. I'm a special agent with the FBI. Can you please start at the beginning and tell me where you saw this number and why you called?"

The woman sighed again. "Look, I'm not crazy, but my husband and I are visiting Rome and we stopped in at a hotel near Vatican City to have lunch," she was trying to explain without sounding like she was delusional. "I used the restroom while I was there and somebody has written this number on the back of a stall door in one of the urinals with a note asking someone to call it. I wouldn't have paid any attention normally, but...."

Ethan was on pins and needles. "Marianne, can you read the message back to me? Are you in the restroom right now?"

"Yes," she said and he could hear her fumbling around. "Are you really with the FBI?"

"Yes, ma'am. Can you please read me the message?"

The woman paused. "It says, '*my name is Olivia Hetherington and I am being held captive. This isn't a joke and I won't* have a second chance to ask for help, so please please call my mother Cydney Hetherington at 626-566-3549. I swear this isn't a joke and I'm begging whoever reads this to please call my mother. This is a matter of life or death'," the woman abruptly stopped. "That's all it says. Like I said, I wouldn't normally pay attention to anything like this but this bathroom is so clean and beautiful that this graffiti looks really out of place. And it seems so urgent. So I'm sorry if this is a joke, but it's written in very beautiful handwriting. Something told me to call the number, which took me a few tries because of the international connection. I had to use an operator."

Ethan was so electrified that he was beginning to lose his cool. "You did the right thing, Mrs. Ustel. It is definitely not a joke," he dared to look at Cydney. "Can you tell me exactly where you are?"

"Yes," the woman said. "We're at the Hotel de Columbus just outside of the Vatican City."

He went over to the table where the phone and hotel stationery were and picked up a pen. "Can you please give me your contact information and I'll make sure you're reimbursed for the call?"

She was reluctant. "Well, I don't know...."

"Ma'am, this is legitimate. We may have more questions so will you at least be available by phone?"

"Uh... all right," she said. "So this message is real?"

"It's real."

The woman hissed. "Oh, my God," she said. "My husband will never believe it."

"I would prefer you not tell him, ma'am. This is an international case and I need your promise that you will not discuss this with anyone."

By the tone of her voice, he could tell she was starting to take all of this seriously. "Uh... okay."

"Thank you very much, Mrs. Ustel," he said. "You did the right thing."

Hanging up the phone, he had to close his mouth; his jaw was hanging open. He focused on Cydney again. She looked like she was about to explode.

"Well?" she demanded. "What was that all about?"

Ethan's mind was going in a hundred different directions. "That," he said, "was an American tourist in Rome who saw your cell phone number on a bathroom stall door at the Hotel de Columbus. There was a message written by your daughter begging whoever read the message to call your number."

Cydney's eyes were threatening to pop from her head. "Olivia's in Rome?"

Ethan nodded, picking up the land line. "I need to call J.D. right now."

Cydney went to stand next to him, trying to stay calm. "What are you going to do?" she asked with fear in her voice.

He put his arm around her as the phone on the other end of the line began to ring. He kissed her forehead. "We're going to Rome."

Tyler picked that moment to come out of the bedroom. He heard his father's last sentence and his big blue eyes widened.

"Rome?" he repeated, shocked. "I thought we were just going to the Louvre!"

SIXTEEN

VATICAN CITY WAS IMPOSING at night. St. Peter's Basilica rose like a great mountain in the middle of the city, its massive dome outlined against the moonlit sky. As the taxi pulled in from the south into an area with a street sign that read Largo di Porta Cavalleggeri, Olivia's face was practically pressed up against the window. There was an enormous building between the taxi and St. Peter's Basilica, blocking her view of the structure.

The taxi came to a halt and Joseph and Nat bailed out, pulling Olivia out between them. Coral was forced to climb out of the cab herself. Nat went around to the rear of the car and opened the trunk, pulling forth a large suitcase before slamming the trunk shut. Then he said something to the taxi driver in Italian and the man sped away, leaving the four of them standing there. Nat turned to the group, to Olivia in particular. His face looked eerie and evil beneath the ghostly gray moon.

"Come on," he said.

He led them past a heavily fortified guard shack next to the enormous building. He exchanged a couple of words with the guard, who ushered them through.

Once inside the grounds, it was dark and somewhat lush with the trees silhouetted against the night sky. Moisture hung heavy in the air. Joseph had Olivia's hand as they moved through the grounds. Olivia should have been terrified but she found she was more in awe of her surroundings than dialed into her fear at the moment. She could hardly believe she was at the Vatican.

"What's this big building?" she asked Joseph.

He looked over his right shoulder, up to the massive building beside them.

"That's St. Marta's Palace," he told her. "The one to the left is St. Charles' Palace."

Olivia looked between the buildings; it was difficult to make out much in the dark but she was trying. Soon they emerged from between the buildings and Nat led them across a large courtyard. There were a couple of smaller buildings and a large grassy area. But another enormous building loomed before them, this one three stories tall with two mammoth wings. It was dark and foreboding against the dark sky. When it was clear that the building was their destination, Olivia pointed at it.

"What's that?" she asked Joseph. "Where are we going?"

"The administration building," he told her. "You need to be quiet now."

She tugged on his arm. "Why are we going there?"

"*Shush.*"

She frowned at him, her fear now making a return. She didn't like the look of the big dark building and began to slow her pace. Joseph tugged on her, smiling encouragingly when their eyes met.

"It's all right," he said. "Come on."

Nat took them in a side door in the southern-most wing. There was a keypad next to the door and he input a code then laid his thumb against an electronic eye. The red beam of the eye scanned his thumbprint and the door opened. He quickly ushered the group inside.

The building was relatively empty. Olivia was disoriented in the first few feet. They walked very quickly along a corridor, up a flight of stairs, and then down another corridor until they reached a big set of double doors. They were heavy, richly carved doors and Nat opened one of them.

A big reception room was inside, complete with lush carpets, heavy and ornate furniture, and a color scheme of reds and golds. A single light was on in an elaborate lamp set upon an elaborate end table, hardly giving out any illumination for the size of the room. When Nat closed the door behind the group, a man suddenly emerged from one of the dark offices.

The man was big and bulky, with dark hair and a big belly. He wore crisp red cardinal's robes and Joseph was the first to greet him. He took the man's hand and kissed his ring.

"Your Eminence," he said. "It's good to see you again."

The man put his hand on Joseph's head, then his cheek, studying the young man's face intently. "Joseph," he murmured the name almost reverently. "I'm happy to see you."

Nat made his way forward, also kissing the man's ring. "Your Eminence," he suddenly sounded strangely exhausted. "We've finally made it."

The man nodded, his gaze falling over Coral before finally coming to rest on Olivia. His eyes were muddy brown, strange, and as Olivia gazed back she felt a distinct sense of fear. She resisted the urge to back away when the man came towards her; nonetheless, she instinctively recoiled when he came near. He smiled faintly, those muddy, disconcerting eyes intense as he gazed at her.

"You must be Olivia," he said in a voice that sent chills up Olivia's spine.

She nodded unsteadily. His smile grew. "She's lovely," he

said, but he wasn't talking to her. He seemed to be speaking to the group. "She'll do wonderfully."

Joseph ended up standing beside Olivia and the young girl pressed against him, fearful of the man whose countenance seemed to radiate something dark and deep.

"She's exhausted, Your Eminence," Joseph sounded very much like he was defending her. "We haven't taken the time to rest since all of this started so you'll have to make some allowances."

The man waved his hand as if to make no issue out of exhaustion or bad manners.

"It's of no concern," he said, his eyes still boring into Olivia. "I'm Cardinal Wildegrav, Olivia. I've heard a lot of good things about you."

Olivia gazed back at him with a mixture of trepidation and anger. "I don't know why I'm here," she said flatly. "I want to go home."

The Cardinal lifted an eyebrow as if to retort but thought better of it. He waved his hand at the group. "Why doesn't everyone take a seat and get comfortable? It seems as if the situation has been inadequately explained to young Olivia. If you all had done a better job, she would not want to go home."

Joseph tugged on Olivia's arm and sat with her on the nearest couch. Coral sat in a wing chair, fanning herself furiously, while Nat sat against the far wall. All eyes were on the man in the red robes as he turned on another light. The room grew brighter, but somehow, it also grew colder. There was something so very cold about the man and his room. He went to light a cigarette before speaking.

"Olivia," he turned to her as he blew white smoke from his nose. "Do you know who I am?"

She gazed up at him with a baleful expression. "You told me your name is Cardinal Wildegrav."

"Of course, but do you know who I am?"

She shook her head and he lifted an eyebrow. "You're not Catholic, are you?" Again, she shook her head and he went on. "Olivia, my title is Cardinal Bishop. This means I am one of the most senior cardinals in the Church. I am also the Cardinal Secretary of State, the head of the Holy See's Secretariat of State. I am the chief diplomat for the Vatican. Do you understand so far?"

Olivia's face was still dark with fear and anger but she nodded. "Why am I here?"

Baldemar held up a finger. "I'm coming to that," he said before clasping his hands behind his back. "I have been a priest for almost forty years. A very long time. And in that time, I have seen Rome, and Catholicism, go through many changes; some good, some not so good. For so long, religion, and mankind in general, has had such little hope in the future. It seems like things in our world are getting worse and worse. Do you know what I mean?"

Olivia was looking less angry and more confused. "Like with wars and stuff?"

"Exactly," the Cardinal nodded firmly. "You're a very smart girl. I know that you can see how bad things are getting. Do you know about global warming?"

She nodded. "We studied that in my environmental class."

"What did you learn about it?"

"Lots of things. Do you really want me to go through it all?"

"No, that's not necessary," he seemed to be tapping into a subject she was willing to warm to and he went with it. "And what about the animals of the planet? There are several species that will be extinct by the time you have grandchildren, like the white rhino and several types of apes. Possibly even the lowland gorilla; do you want to see them wiped off the face of the earth?"

"Of course not," she said, her brow furrowing. "But I can't

stop that stuff. No one person can. It would take everyone to try and stop that."

"And that's exactly what I want to do." The Cardinal drew closer to her, his eyes alight with the passion of his conviction. "Olivia, I know that Coral and Nat have told you of our desire to crown Joseph the next Holy Roman Emperor because of his bloodlines to Jesus Christ."

Olivia nodded unsteadily. "Y-yes."

"Do you think Jesus would allow all of these horrible things to happen to this planet?"

Olivia was thoroughly perplexed. She looked at Joseph with uncertainty. "No, I guess not," she looked back at the Cardinal. "But that still doesn't explain why I'm here. I have nothing to do with all of this."

The Cardinal backed off, his sweaty face moving in the direction of the suitcase that Nat had brought with them. He began to walk towards it.

"I assume it is in here?" he asked Nat.

Nat jumped out of his seat and began unzipping the suitcase. "Of course, Your Eminence."

He threw open the top of the suitcase to reveal the garment bag inside. He unzipped the garment bag so the Cardinal could get a look at the contents. Baldemar's muddy eyes glittered as the faded robe came into view and he took a moment to absorb the sight. After several long seconds, he reached out and hesitantly fingered the ancient, rough material. He exhaled sharply, as if he had just had a brief moment of ecstasy with the contact. He cheeks flushed.

"And the tooth?" he whispered.

"In the pocket of the suitcase, Your Eminence."

Baldemar nodded faintly and ran his finger along the old material one last time before turning to Olivia. There was something unsettling in his eyes as he focused on her and she instinctively shrank as he approached.

"Do you want to help the world, Olivia?" he asked.

She knew it was a trick question; she could just tell. "I'm not sure. What do I have to do?"

Baldemar sat down on the couch next to her. She was leaning so far away from him that she was practically sitting on Joseph's lap.

"We want you to help us create this new world that will keep it strong and save the planet," he said. "Would you like to do this?"

She wasn't sure what he was driving at; she didn't trust him. "What do I have to do?"

Baldemar seemed to ponder his reply. When he answered, it was seemingly off the subject.

"Hundreds and hundreds of years ago, my family was a great Teutonic family," he said quietly. "I was born in Germany, in fact. We can trace my family lineage back to the thirteenth century. My ancestors were Templars."

Olivia's eyes widened. "Knights?"

"Yes," Baldemar nodded. "Templars who once had that robe which is now back in my hands, back where it belongs. Two of my ancestors were at the fall of Castle Domme in Southern France when King Philip IV ordered the dissolution of the Templars. The truth was the king was heavily in debt and jealous of the property and treasures that the Templars had collected. He enlisted the help of rebel English, among others, to help him arrest the Templars and steal their property. This robe was part of that treasure."

"And you're going to crown Joseph with the robe now that you have it?"

"Something like that, yes."

Olivia digested his explanation. "But I don't understand,"

she said. "How are you going to form a new Holy Roman Empire? What about all of the other countries in Europe? They won't want to give up their independence to join up."

"We have many supporters in many countries. We will start here, in Rome, and eventually spread over the face of Europe. It will come in time. All conquest does."

She watched him a moment, carefully understanding his words. "Isn't that what Hitler wanted, too? To create a big united Germany all over Europe?"

Baldemar smiled faintly. "More or less. But Hitler did not have the backing of the Church."

"And you will? You're saying that the pope supports all of this?"

"I will support it, as the pope."

She frowned. "But there's already a pope."

"All popes must die. Sometimes at God's choosing, sometimes at the choosing of others."

"Choosing of others?" she repeated, perplexed. "How could someone choose the pope's death?"

"The issue is not how the pope dies, but when. Sometimes death is necessary to bring about a great good. Our Holy Father's time will soon come to an end and a new age will dawn."

She still wasn't quite following him; he was speaking in riddles, but riddles enough that he had her attention. "So if the pope dies, you're next in line?"

Baldemar cocked a modest eyebrow. "It is a near certainty," he said. "And as the new pope, I would have the privilege of crowing Joseph and beginning our brave new reign of Enlightenment. This will be our new world."

She didn't like the way he said it. There was danger in his tone and she shut her mouth, not wanting to take the conversation any further. Even at her young age, the implication was something very ugly. Cardinal Wildegrav frightened her on more levels than she could comprehend and she was suddenly very, very scared.

"I can't help you with any of this," she was beginning to beg. "Please let me go home."

"But you are so wrong," Baldemar said seriously. "You will help more than you realize. You, darling, will be the mother of the next Christ."

Her eyes widened. "What?" she choked. "What are you talking about?"

Baldemar rose and went to the suitcase. He began unzipping the side pocket where a small box was wedged. He drew it forth, pondering what looked like a ring box. Then he popped it open, revealing the tooth inside. He stared at it a moment, sighing faintly as he put it under the light to get a better look. After several long and tense moments, he gently closed the box and looked at Nat.

"It's perfect," he said quietly. "You are to take Olivia and the tooth over to the Hospital San Pietro Fatebenefratelli. Go to Admitting and ask for Dr. Giovanni Antonio Gioia. Tell him that I sent you. He will know how to proceed from there."

Nat nodded shortly and stood up, heading straight for Olivia. She panicked when she saw him coming.

"I'm not going anywhere," she bolted up before Joseph could grab her. "I'll scream my head off if you try and take me anywhere. I want to go home!"

Nat suddenly grabbed her around the neck, shoving her up against the wall before Joseph could stop him. Olivia's face was turning red as Nat pressed his body up against her to trap her.

"Scream and I'll kill you right now," he hissed. "There are a million other teenagers in the world that we can use for this so don't think you're special. Whether you live or die is of no difference to me. So scream if you want to. Be quiet and you'll live through this. It's your choice."

Olivia began to weep hysterically and he squeezed her neck tighter until she screamed just so she could breathe. He eased up.

"Well?" he demanded. "What's your choice?"

She was trying to speak but couldn't because of the pressure he was putting on her throat, so he eased up a little more. "Well?" he asked again.

"I'll... I'll be quiet," she whispered.

Nat let her go immediately and she collapsed against the wall, a weeping, gasping mess.

"You'd better," he growled.

The Cardinal came up behind Nat, moving him out of the way. He knelt down before the frightened girl.

"Olivia," he tried to sound kind after Nat's scare tactics. "You will bring about a whole new world. There will be a place of honor for you. Don't be frightened; be excited. You will be the key to a new world for everyone and you will secure your place in history."

She looked up at him, terrified. Her hair was hanging in her face as she spoke. "What... what are you going to do?"

Baldemar smiled and tried to touch her hand, but she yanked it away. "A very nice doctor will put you to sleep for a little while and then you will wake up. A little while later, he will put you to sleep again and you will wake up with a child inside you. That child must be brought to term so we are going to have you as our guest for a while."

Olivia's eyes widened and her tears returned en force. "A baby?" she wept. "You want me to have a baby?"

The Cardinal nodded. "You see, we plan to extract DNA from that tooth you found in The Lucius Robe. We will put the DNA in one of your unfertilized eggs and implant it in your womb when it has begun to multiply. It can be done; we have a very good fertility specialist that is willing to do this. He is a man very loyal to the Church and to what we are attempting to accomplish. But we need your cooperation."

She was a weeping, snotty mess. "I just want to go home."

"Bring the child to full term and you shall. All we ask of you is to be the mother for the new Christ. It is such an honor, Olivia. I wish you would understand that." He paused as he watched her cry. "Our Holy Mother, the Blessed Virgin Mary, was about your age when she gave birth to Jesus. You will be the new Blessed Virgin, an icon for a new age. You *are* a virgin, aren't you?"

He was asking a horribly personal question, making her more hysterical. But she nodded, embarrassed, overwhelmed. "Of course."

Baldemar smiled. "Wonderful," he said soothingly. "God will reward you, Olivia, for giving birth to another holy son. You will have a great place in His kingdom here on earth. Isn't that wonderful?"

She couldn't answer him, too far gone with hysteria. Joseph, extremely unhappy at the way Olivia was being treated, carefully pushed past the Cardinal and picked her up off the floor. Olivia clung to him and wept as he carried her from the room. Coral, mascara smears down her face, followed Joseph while Nat hung behind. Soon they were alone in the room.

By this time, Baldemar's gentle expression was vanished. "I don't care how you do it, but make sure this does not fail," he instructed in a cold voice. "If you have to drug her for the next nine months to keep her quiet, you'll do it. I want that child born healthy. Is that clear?"

Nat nodded slowly. "It is, Your Eminence."

"And send Coral home. We don't need her anymore."

"With pleasure."

The Cardinal watched Nat silently leave the room. He knew how ruthless the man was and he knew, without a doubt, that his plans would be carried out.

———

Their flight from Paris to Rome left at seven o'clock in the evening later that same day. Ethan, Cydney, Tyler, J.D., Christophe Dulay, Agents Penryn and Daniels were on it. Tyler had been able to visit the Louvre for a couple of hours with his dad and Cydney, but they had to hurry back to the hotel to collect their baggage so they could make their flight to Rome. Tyler was disappointed that he only got to see a fraction of the Louvre, but he was excited to be going to Rome. He wanted to go straight to the Colosseum when they got there. It would seem the lure of gladiators held more excitement for him than the Mona Lisa.

The flight from Paris to Rome was only a couple of hours long. They were on a smaller plane with two seats, an aisle, and then two seats, so Ethan and Tyler sat together while Cydney sat with J.D. Christophe, Penryn and Daniels were somewhere towards the back of the plane. Cydney read a magazine while J.D. snored heavily next to her.

Cydney was pensive and apprehensive. Her thoughts lingered on her daughter and the desperation the young girl must have felt writing a message on the back of a bathroom stall door. But Ethan and J.D. gave Olivia a lot of credit for her cleverness. She had, throughout this entire event, proven to be resourceful and strong. Cydney was proud of Olivia for her exhibition of strength, but she just wanted her daughter back. A fifteen-year-old girl shouldn't have to be so resourceful.

She could see Ethan's profile between the seats up ahead as he talked with his son. She watched his gorgeous features as he interacted with Tyler and she found herself staring at him for most of the first half of the flight. He was almost too good to be true, this FBI agent whom she had fallen madly, deeply in love with. She couldn't help think what her parents would say or what Kyle would say. They would be shocked initially, of course, but deep down, they would be very happy that she was moving on with her life. So, she suspected, would Brad.

Visions of Brad Hetherington popped into her mind for a moment as she listened to the drone of the engines. About five feet nine inches, Brad had been built like a fireplug with massive shoulders and a broad chest. He'd had dark blue eyes and a flashy, megawatt smile. When Olivia had been a toddler, she's had trouble with her "Ls" and Brad used to gently tease his daughter about her lazy tongue in the hopes that she would practice proper speech. The word "dollar" came out "dah-yer". "Olivia" had been pronounced "Oh-yivia". Cydney laughed to herself as she remembered the way Brad used to mimic Olivia. Olivia, of course, would squeal in protest but she knew Daddy wasn't serious. She'd very much loved her father and she'd missed him terribly for eight years.

Odd how Ethan had helped heal in eight days what eight years couldn't do. Cydney's scabbed wound had turned into a scar, strong with Ethan's healing powers. She knew Olivia would be thrilled that her mother was marrying him; she could tell that Olivia had liked him a great deal. Brad Hetherington was gone but the women he left behind were finally ready to move on. Cydney knew that Brad would have been very happy about that. It was time.

The flight attendant came around with fruit, cheese and wine for a snack. Cydney took a little tray of cheese and fruit and J.D., roused from a deep sleep by the smell of pungent cheese, woke up in time to collect his food. As the flight attendant moved on to Ethan and Tyler, J.D. rubbed his eyes and put his tray down.

"Good evening," Cydney said.

J.D. grunted. "Good evening." He took the plastic off the cup of wine. "How long have we been in the air?"

"About an hour. We should start the descent soon."

"Good," he took a drink of his wine and a big bite of the strong cheese. Chewing, he looked at Cydney as if suddenly seeing her for the first time. When their eyes met, he smiled weakly. "Sorry I haven't been good conversation."

She grinned. "As I recall, you did the same thing on the flight to Paris. You must be one of those people who react hypnotically to an airplane."

He nodded. "I do," he said. "I haven't seen a plane take off in years. I'm usually asleep by the time it rolls out from the gate."

She laughed and sipped her wine. It took her a moment to realize that J.D. was holding his cup at her.

"Congratulations," he said. "Ethan told me."

She smiled, somewhat shyly, and clinked her plastic cup against his. "Thanks," she replied. "I know it seems really, really soon, but, well...."

J.D. put up a hand to prevent any further explanation. "When it's right, it's right," he said. "From what I heard, he was attracted to you from the start. Between you and me, I'm relieved."

"Why?"

J.D. shook his head knowingly. "I've known Ethan for nine years," he lowered his voice so Ethan, seated directly in front of him, wouldn't hear. "When Kimberly left him, he was a changed man. Bitter, rude... just changed. It was like something went out of him when she left with Tyler. When he'd get around women, he usually turned into such an ass that I was afraid to let him interact with women in general. He'd usually leave them in tears."

Cydney's eyes widened. "Really?"

J.D. nodded and took another drink of wine. "I don't think he's really dated anybody in eight years and certainly not anybody seriously."

"I can't believe that; with his looks and personality? He should have women falling at his feet."

"You would think so, but he chases them all off with his surly attitude. He may look like a Greek god, but he can be the biggest jerk in the world when it comes to women. So when I heard how he was reacting to you, I didn't believe it until I saw it with my own eyes. You've changed him, whether or not you realize it. You've made him happy again and for Ethan's sake, I'm really glad. He deserves to be happy."

Cydney just stared at him, stunned. "He's such a sweet man. I've never met anyone so thoughtful or considerate."

"There are a lot of women in Los Angeles that would beg to differ with you."

Cydney raised her eyebrows in shock and took a pensive sip of her wine.

"Then I guess I'm the lucky one," she said, eyeing him after a moment. "You've known him for a long time. Other than being a jerk to women, what can you tell me about him that he wouldn't get mad at you for divulging?"

J.D. grinned. "He can get mad all he wants," he said with feigned bravery. "I can still hold my own against him." When Cydney giggled, he continued. "To me, he has always been the most loyal friend I've ever had. He'll give you the shirt off his back. He's smart, too; brilliant. That guy can do math in his head like no one I've ever seen and he speaks four languages. Who else do you know that can do that? And he's a good judge of character; he knows people and what they think. He's as honest as the day is long."

It made Cydney feel warm and cozy to hear J.D.'s praise of Ethan. Even though she felt, deep down, that he was all those things; still, it was good to hear it from someone who had known him a long time.

"What four languages does he speak?" she asked.

"English, French, Spanish and Italian. He knows 'em all."

Cydney had to laugh; J.D. caught the chuckles and his eyebrows rose. She shook her head as if to apologize for the quiet laughter. "He and I were joking about that yesterday because he was trying to pull a fast one on me by speaking in French. But I am fluent in it also so he threatened to speak Spanish next time he didn't want me to know his plans. But I speak that, too. My minor in college was Languages."

J.D. looked impressed. "We can use you for an interpreter, then. What languages do you speak?"

"English, French, Spanish, and Italian. I have a working knowledge of Russian, German, Swedish, and two Chinese dialects."

"Good lord," J.D. hissed. "You're smarter than he is."

"Not really," she shook her head. "I've just always liked foreign languages. And I don't want to read subtitles when I go to movies."

"So with all these talents, you end up working in a museum?"

"I have to work somewhere."

J.D. nodded in agreement and finished his wine. He set the cup down. "Well, I am very happy for you both," he said. "But I will say this; treat him right or you'll have to deal with me."

She grinned at him. "I promise I'll make you proud."

"Good."

They grinned at each other a moment before J.D. reached

over and stole a little hunk of gorgonzola cheese off her plate. Cydney just shook her head at him; already, they were comfortable with each other. That was a good sign.

The plane landed at the Leonardo da Vinci Airport fifty-two minutes later. Ethan grabbed his carry on and Cydney's as they departed the plane, leaving Tyler to lug his own backpack down to baggage claim.

Ethan and Cydney walked next to each other, very close, as they made their way to the baggage area. Ethan wanted very badly to hold her hand but with Dulay and the other two agents present, he didn't want to create a scene of impropriety. So he settled for carrying her bag. Truth was, as much as he loved his son, he had missed sitting next to her on the plane. J.D. walked on the other side of Cydney as Tyler walked slightly in front of them.

"Dad," Tyler turned around, walking backwards through the terminal. "Where are we going first?"

"You and Cydney are going to the hotel," Ethan replied. "J.D. and I need to head to the U.S. Embassy."

"Can I come?"

"No, bud."

Tyler made a face and turned around, walking angrily. "Can we go to the Colosseum first thing in the morning? I really want to see it."

Cydney looked at Ethan and nodded faintly, but Ethan was obvious that he wasn't pleased with his son's request.

"I'm not sure what our plans are tomorrow," he told Tyler. "We'll have to play it by ear."

"Dad," Tyler whined; the word ended coming out of his mouth with two syllables. "I don't want to sit around. Please, can I go to the Colosseum? Please?"

Ethan sighed with exasperation, refraining from being harsh

with his son by a tug on his arm. He looked down to see Cydney nodding her head firmly.

"I think that's a good idea," she told Ethan quietly. "Tyler and I will do a tour while you and J.D. take care of business."

Ethan relented. "All right," he said to her, looking at his son and lifting his eyebrows. "You can go tomorrow morning. But tonight you're going back to the hotel and going to bed. And no argument or I'll turn J.D. loose on you."

Tyler grinned at his father's friend. "Bring it on, dude."

J.D., garment bag slung over one big shoulder and a carry on in his right hand, rolled his eyes at Ethan's brave son.

"Boy, you better be faster than I am because I guarantee you won't like it if I catch you." He watched Tyler do some fancy footwork, pretending to escape him. J.D. looked over at Ethan. "He's got your moves, man."

Ethan and Cydney chuckled as Tyler's fast moves suddenly turned into a Fred Astaire-type dance across the terminal floor. It was hilarious and the adults laughed as Tyler pretended to waltz with his book bag. He jumped up on a chair and leapt gracefully off the other side like a gymnast. Then he started twirling and crashed into a wall. While Cydney, J.D. and even Christophe howled with laughter, Ethan put a stop to his son's reckless behavior.

"If you break something, I'm going to pretend I don't know you and leave you for the Italian police," he told him. "Maybe you'd better straighten up for now."

Tyler, still smiling, obeyed. "First thing in the morning we go to the Colosseum, all right?"

Ethan sighed heavily and slapped his son lightly on the side of the head. "I won't be able to go but Cydney will. You'll watch out for her, right?"

"Sure."

Ethan turned to wink at Cydney, who was still smiling at

Tyler. "He makes a great bodyguard. Or dance partner, which-
ever we decide to do," she said.

Baggage claim was jammed with people at nine o'clock at
night, but they found their baggage and made their way out to
the curb. It was humid and overcast. The U.S. Embassy had
sent over a car and the driver found them just as they began to
set their baggage down on sidewalk.

Tyler switched into Sky Cap mode again and grabbed
Cydney's bags along with his own, dragging them over to the car
and swinging them into the open trunk. Ethan sighed with exasperation and was opening his mouth to mildly rebuke the boy
but Cydney stopped him.

"It's okay," she tried not to laugh as she watched Tyler
create an unorganized mess in the trunk. "It's very sweet that
he's trying to help."

Ethan made a face as he looked at her. "Is that what you
call it?"

She laughed. "What hotel are we staying at?"

"The Hilton Rome Cavalieri," he told her. "I'm going to
send you and Tyler over there now. J.D. and I need to head over
to the hotel where Olivia's message was found. It's been
sectioned off since we received the call to keep the crime scene
untouched."

She watched him hand his bag to Tyler as the kid grabbed it
and ran back to the open trunk. "What are you going to do?" she
asked quietly.

Ethan was watching his son cram his bag into the trunk. "A
CSI team from the U.S. Embassy is already on-scene. We're
going to work in conjunction with the Rome police to see if we
can pick up any clues. We're going to go over it with a fine-
toothed comb, trust me."

Cydney was silent a moment and Ethan looked down at her,

noticing she suddenly looked extremely distressed. He nudged her gently.

"What's wrong, baby?"

She glanced up at him, tried to smile bravely but failed. "I was just thinking," she said, "that woman who called never said what the message was written in. God, please don't tell me that it was written in blood."

He went to put his arm around her but stopped when he realized he didn't want everyone to see. "No, honey," he said quietly. "I'm sure it wasn't. There was no mention of it, not in any of the phone calls since the message's discovery."

"But isn't that what a CSI team does? Looks for blood and..."

He cut her off. "A Crime Scene Investigation Team just looks for evidence, like hair or fingerprints. Haven't you ever watched those television shows? If blood is there they'll find it, too. But nothing was said about blood so I wouldn't worry about that right now."

She just nodded and he reached out to touch her hand, squeezing her fingers quickly, firmly, before releasing. Then he noticed that Tyler was in the process of trying to slam the trunk of the car, much to the driver's distress, so he left Cydney to go call his overzealous son off. Cydney climbed into the car as the men piled in after her.

The Hilton Hotel Cavalieri was a mile or so from Vatican City, a gorgeous structure with all of the Roman Italianate architecture that one would expect. The lobby alone was worthy of a world-class museum. Ethan and J.D. settled Cydney and Tyler into adjoining rooms, Ethan managing to steal a kiss from Cydney before he and J.D. went on to the Hotel Columbus.

Tyler's instructions were to go to bed right away, but in the room next door, Cydney could hear the television on well into the night. She could have opened the adjoining door and put an end to the disobedience, but she didn't have the heart.

She lay in bed, in a dark room with moonlight streaming in through the open window, wondering where Olivia was at that moment and praying that she was all right. She just wanted her daughter back, in her arms, and the tears came as she thought of the tribulations Olivia had been forced to endure. She whispered into the night as if Olivia could hear her.

I'm here, baby. I'm here and we're going to find you, just be strong.

Somewhere along the line, she must have been whispering loud enough for Tyler to hear because as she lay there, the television next door suddenly turned off and there was a soft knock at the adjoining door. She wiped at her face quickly and answered.

"Yes, Tyler?"

His voice was muffled on the other side of the door. "Can I come in?"

"Sure."

He opened the door, his handsome face hesitant as he stepped into her room. The only light was that from the moon outside so he couldn't see her red eyes or tear-stained cheeks. But just by his expression, Cydney could tell that he had heard her crying.

"I don't mean to bug you," he said quietly. "But... well, I heard you and... well, I just wanted to say that I'm sorry I couldn't stop those people from getting Olivia. I should have tried to but they whacked me on the head when my back was turned. If I'd had the chance, I would have helped her."

His expression of heroism undid her. She held out a hand to him and he came to her, taking her hand before sinking awkwardly to the floor beside the bed. Cydney held his hand tightly, gazing at the strong young face, into the boy who was growing into a fine young man like his father. She thought she could answer him without sobbing but it was a difficult struggle.

"It definitely wasn't your fault," she whispered tightly. "In fact, I'm glad you didn't try. They might have taken you, too, or worse. You might have really gotten hurt."

He wriggled his dark eyebrows at her. "Maybe," he said. "But I would have tried."

"I know," her eyes were spilling over as she gazed at him. "You're a brave young man. I really appreciate that."

He grinned modestly and averted his gaze, which happened to fall on her hand. He was holding her left hand, the one with the big ring on it. He stared at the ring and Cydney watched him a moment, waiting for the inevitable questions.

"I've never had a sister," he finally said. "I guess I'm going to have one."

She realized that Ethan must have told him on the plane. He didn't seem distressed and she smiled faintly.

"Olivia's never had a brother," she murmured. "She's always wanted one."

Tyler couldn't decide whether to nod or shrug. It looked like he was working out a kink in his neck.

"My dad seems really happy," he finally looked up at her, his blue eyes very wise. "I can't remember ever seeing my dad so happy. But he's smiling and talking about stuff, like me coming to live in California with him after you guys get married."

"Are *you* okay with that?"

Again, he half-nodded and half-shrugged. "Yeah, sure," he said. "I told him I wanted to come live with him, anyway."

"Are you okay with having a new stepmom and stepsister?"

"It's cool," he looked at her hand as it still held his. "You're cool. I'm okay with it."

She laughed softly. "Thanks, Ty," she squeezed his hand. "You're pretty cool, too. I think you'll like California."

He nodded, pausing a moment. "Can I ask you something?"

"Sure."

"Do you love my dad?"

"I do. You know what else?"

"What?"

"I kind of like you, too."

He gave her a goofy grin and she laughed. But her smile faded and she squeezed his hand again.

"Thanks for talking to me, Ty," she said. "I'm feeling kind of sad about Olivia right now."

He sobered up. "I know," he said. "I'll sit here with you for a while if you want me to."

She smiled at his sweetly chivalrous offer. "That would be nice. Thanks."

"No problem."

When Ethan returned to the hotel well after midnight, he was puzzled to find the room he shared with his son empty. Noticing that the adjoining door into Cydney's room was ajar, he entered the moonlit room silently only to find Cydney fast asleep, holding Tyler's hand as his son slept the sleep of the dead on the floor.

Ethan gazed at the two of them a moment, having never seen anything so heartwarming in his life. He had no idea how Tyler ended up in here, but it didn't matter. He was touched beyond words at the sight. Removing his jacket and tie, he lay down on the opposite bed, on top of the comforter, and fell into a deep sleep with the two people he loved best just a few feet away.

SEVENTEEN

THEY DIDN'T NEED her anymore.

Coral was still crying, even now in the bright morning of the new day. Nat told her that they didn't need her anymore and instructed her to go home. When Coral called her office to get flight arrangements, someone she didn't recognize picked up the phone.

Frightened, she hung up and called one of her operations managers, who told her that the FBI and IRS had taken over control of the company several days prior and had frozen all of her assets. The operations manager still wasn't clear why the government had moved in because they had only been forthcoming with the Chief Operations Officer and Executive Vice President, neither of whom anyone could get in touch with. The men, who had been with Izan collectively for eight years, had vanished.

Terrified and disoriented, Coral tried to use her credit cards but they were all declined. She couldn't take any money out of an ATM. Even her cellular phone had been shut off. To top it all off, she was too frightened to return to Nat and Joseph and tell them what was happening. She didn't want to get in any trouble.

The United States Government was closing in on her. She didn't want the others to know, fearful that if the Feds found her, they would find Nat and the others. She had to distance herself from them and in doing so, perhaps they would appreciate her loyalty and sense of self-sacrifice. So, hauling her considerable luggage around and using the remainder of her cash, she ended up on a city bus headed for the Colosseum. She didn't have anywhere else to go.

———

The dining room of the hotel was an exquisite lesson in culinary décor and ambiance, even at breakfast time. Cydney sat with Ethan, J.D., Christophe and Tyler at a sunny table that faced out over the expansive hotel gardens. Had the circumstances not been so harrowing, it would have been a breathtaking morning. The overcast skies had lifted, leaving a brilliant blue sky. But Cydney was having difficulty focusing this morning, thoughts of her daughter weighing more heavily than ever. She just couldn't seem to bounce back as she had the past few days. The worry, the fear, was beginning to take its toll.

Those around her could sense it, especially Ethan. He sat silently next to her, drinking his coffee as his son wolfed down everything that wasn't nailed to the table. Christophe sat next to the boy, watching him eat copious amounts of food and wondering out loud if his own son would someday eat the same way. Ethan assured him that he would.

Cydney sat through the conversation, picking at her toast and sipping her coffee. When Tyler finished inhaling his breakfast and begged to go into the gift shop located down the hall near the lobby, Ethan reluctantly agreed. Tyler begged ten Euros off of his old man and ran off in a triumphant sprint.

Christophe laughed as Tyler raced from the dining room and nearly knocked over a waiter in the process. He turned to Ethan.

"He's a lively boy," he commented.

Ethan just shook his head. "That's a nice way of putting it."

Christophe snorted into his espresso. "He's a spirited and bright young man," his gaze moved to Cydney, sitting forlorn and quiet next to Ethan. His expression softened. "I enjoy young adults. It makes me remember my own youth. So far, my experience with Tyler and Olivia has been very encouraging."

Cydney's head came up at the mention of her daughter's name. She saw that he was looking at her and she smiled faintly. "Encouraging? How?"

Christophe's dark eyes glimmered. "Mrs. Hetherington, I am not sure if you were told, but while waiting for you to arrive in Paris, Olivia stayed with my wife and me as our guest. I did not want to put a young girl in a hotel for two days, alone. That would have been cruel. So she stayed with my family."

Cydney nodded. "Yes, I was told," she replied. "I'm sorry I've not had the chance to thank you for your kindness. It was very gracious of you to take her in for a couple of days."

Christophe waved her off. "It was our pleasure, believe me," he said. "My children are enamored with her. She would lie on the floor and draw with them or watch cartoons. When I say that my experience with Tyler and Olivia is encouraging, I mean that they are intelligent and well-behaved young adults, not like some of these wild hooligans you see on MTV or stupid reality shows. It's children like those two who will make a difference in this world."

Cydney nodded, smiling. Then she burst into quiet tears and hung her head. Throwing appearances to the wind, Ethan put his arm around her shoulders and pulled her against him, his lips on her forehead. J.D. didn't bother reprimanding him and Christophe didn't look surprised. The truth was that they all had figured out what was going on, especially when Cydney began sporting a giant diamond the day before. Christophe leaned across the table and put a hand on her arm.

"Olivia is a brilliant girl," he told her. "You must not worry so much. She can take care of herself and the American FBI is looking for her. They will find her. She will be all right."

Cydney wiped at her nose, struggling to compose herself. "I know," she sniffed. "I... I just miss her."

"Of course you do," Christophe squeezed her arm and let go. "I miss her, too, and she's not even my child. I want to have a look at those bastards who took her."

Cydney smiled weakly, wiping at her eyes. "Thank you," she whispered, dabbing her face with a napkin. Then she glanced up at Ethan. "You didn't tell me what you found at the Hotel de Columbus last night."

He sighed faintly, casting J.D. a brief glance. "A message that is written in some kind of makeup pencil from what we can deduce. I brought a picture back to show you so you can confirm if it's Olivia's writing."

"Why didn't you show me last night when you came back?"

"Because you were exhausted and asleep. It could wait until this morning."

"Where is it?"

"I have it," J.D. piped up. "It's in my briefcase up in my room."

Cydney nodded. "I'd really like to see it before Tyler and I head out," she said, wiping some black mascara out from underneath her eyes and looking at Ethan as she did so. "I need to go fix my face before we leave. I'll be right back."

"Sure, honey," he replied.

The men at the table watched her walk towards the restroom at the far end of the restaurant before turning to one another. Ethan just looked distressed as J.D. blew out his cheeks.

"It's taking its toll on her," he commented quietly. "Considering everything that's gone on, she's been pretty strong up until now."

"She's still strong," Ethan said firmly. "She's a strong lady. She'll get through this."

Christophe sat across from them, watching the exchange, his mind working. "I came to help with the investigation," he said pensively. "I feel responsible for Olivia's disappearance from Paris. I take personal offense to what happened, this group of religious zealots who have a mole somewhere in my office. But when I see her mother cry, I cannot tell her what Olivia said to me."

Both Ethan and J.D. looked at him. "What did she say?" Ethan asked.

Christophe was fidgeting with his used fork on the tabletop, distractedly.

"I was one of the first on the scene when Olivia found safety at the Hyatt after fleeing her captors," he said. "I came upon this lovely young lady with a look in her eye like a chased animal. Her fear was so palpable that you could breathe it. It made me feel very protective over her, which is another reason why I took her home with me. I wanted her to feel safe with a mother and father to watch over her. But one night I found her awake when it was very late. She said she was too scared to sleep. She asked me if kidnap victims ever feel safe again. I lied and told her that they do."

Ethan stared at him a moment before letting out a sharp sigh and looking away. J.D. scratched his bald head. He looked particularly bitter.

"If we could only figure out why they want her so badly," he muttered. "There are so many pieces of this goddamn puzzle and none of them make any sense. Why is she so important to them? And where is that goddamn robe?"

Ethan, sitting in brooding silence, suddenly spoke up. "I don't want Cydney and Tyler going to the Colosseum alone," he said. "If Olivia is still in Rome and there are other Disciples around, then they may recognize Cydney. I don't want her to be in jeopardy if they figure out she's here looking for her daughter. God knows how those people operate, but they seem to be everywhere. I just don't want to take that chance."

J.D. looked at him. "I need you with me. You can't go with them."

Ethan grew snappish. "Then they stay here at the hotel. I don't want them out and about if I can't be with them."

"I'll go with them," Christophe offered.

Ethan and J.D. paused and looked at him before they could get into a verbal battle.

"But you came to help with the case," Ethan said.

Christophe shrugged. "Perhaps I will be more help if I stay with Cydney and Tyler for now," he sat forward, his dark eyes intense. "Ethan is right; if the group you are searching for has an informant inside my police station, then there's no knowing where else they have eyes and ears. There could be someone in this hotel or it could be the taxi driver. Perhaps I am needed most with Cydney and Tyler right now."

Ethan had to agree with his logic. "Thank you," he said sincerely. "If I can't be with them, then I trust you completely."

Christophe nodded shortly, feeling like he was truly helping the situation. Olivia's abduction from the Paris prefecture had been a mark against him. He felt responsible whether or not it was truly within his control. When Cydney returned to the table, she was glad to have Christophe as an escort.

Leaving the restaurant, they had to track Tyler down in the gift shop where he had purchased more soda and red hot jelly beans. Ethan couldn't even summon the energy to comment, knowing it wouldn't do any good. Tyler was an eating machine. J.D. went up to his room and retrieved the photo of the bathroom stall, showing it to Cydney who confirmed that it was, indeed, Olivia's handwriting. She almost burst into tears again but held herself in check. The photograph hammered home the seriousness of what they were facing and Cydney was feeling increasingly depressed.

Ethan put Tyler, Cydney and Christophe on the big tour bus that arrived shortly thereafter. The tour guide was an obviously homosexual male who seemed to have an eye for Ethan. It was the first time Ethan had seen Cydney laugh in days. It was good to see her laugh, even if it was at his expense. Christophe offered to get the tour guide's phone number for Ethan, an offer that was flatly turned down.

Ethan stood in the driveway, watching the bus pull out, wondering why he didn't have a particularly good feeling at the moment. He couldn't put his finger on it, but something told him to get ready for a busy day.

———

The massive building of the Colosseum was bathed in early morning light, the stones glowing golden against the warm sun. Disembarking the tour bus, Cydney shielded her eyes against the glare, awestruck by the glorious Roman ruin. Gazing up at the towering structure, she could almost hear the fans screaming for their favorite gladiator or the roar of the lions as they were released against the Christians. It was a surreal experience. She found herself wishing that Olivia was there to enjoy it. She knew her daughter would have loved it.

But Tyler's enthusiasm, for the moment, took the place of Olivia's and then some. He bailed off the bus and stood in front of the structure with a gaping mouth. Cydney urged him to follow the group and he did so, commenting on the cobbled street beneath his feet, the dust and the dirt of ancient Rome. When they finally entered the structure and passed from the bright light into the cool, sheltered darkness, he ran his hands all over the walls and wanted to know if this was where the gladiators would gather before fighting.

Christophe had a guidebook he had purchased at a kiosk outside the Colosseum and read from it as they followed the tour guide. Tyler, with the remaining money his father had given him, ran back outside to the same kiosk and purchased a big, flat wooden gladiator sword called a *rudis*.

When he rejoined the group, he was grinning like a kid at Christmas. He swatted Cydney with it and she yelped, slapping a hand over her mouth when everyone turned to look at her. Smiling wanly at the collection of curious and annoyed faces, she pinched Tyler when no one was looking. He fell down on the ground as if she had stabbed him and Christophe pretended to step on him, still reading, as he walked over him. Grinning, Tyler shot to his feet and pushed his way to the front of the group.

Entering into the Colosseum proper, it was as if an entirely new world opened up. The sun was already blaring down and tourists littered the interior of the great ruins. Cydney had a disposable camera that Ethan had given her and she snapped away, struggling to move beyond the melancholy that surrounded her.

Cydney wanted to take plenty of pictures for Olivia but, having only been at the Colosseum ten minutes, she knew that pictures would not do the place justice. One had to see it to believe it. Based on that alone, her melancholy was lifting and she was becoming very interested in her surroundings. It was a magnificent place.

The tour guide took the group to a platform that faced out over what was once the arena floor. Cydney and Tyler pushed their way up to the front, looking down at the labyrinth of columns and passageways where both animal and gladiator roamed. The people around her were very excited, chatting about the games and spectacles that had happened in this skeletal ruin.

The tour guide was going through his routine about the bloody Christian events and Cydney stopped taking pictures long enough to look out over the arena floor and imagine all of the deaths that took place there. If she believed in ghosts, this would have been a spectacular place for them.

Tyler had bolted to the other side of the group to investigate the passages where the gladiators used to congregate before going out into the arena. There were small sections that tourists could visit. Cydney followed him, as did Christophe and his book, and Tyler insisted that Cydney take several pictures of him mock-fighting with his rudis. She did, laughing at his antics, when something in the next tour group behind them caught her eye.

It was platinum blond hair with a hint of pink to it. Cydney saw it through the viewfinder of the camera first before, puzzled, lowering her camera to get a better look. There was something oddly familiar about it. The face with the hair was blocked behind some tourists but as she continued to watch, a distinct sense of uneasiness swept her. She'd seen that hair, once, on the opening day of the Resurrection exhibit. One would not forget hair like that. As Cydney waited with increasing disquiet, Coral Chastity Aames' face came into view.

Like a phantom materializing, the woman with the pink hair loomed larger than life several feet away and Cydney felt as if she'd been struck. All of her breath was suddenly sucked out of her and the horror and fury she had been feeling for days swamped her. In a panic, she grabbed Christophe and struggled to keep her wits.

"Inspector Dulay," she hissed, nearly yanking his arm off as she labored to turn him around in Coral's direction. "That woman over there; she's one of the people who kidnapped my daughter."

Christophe forgot about the book as his dark eyes focused intently on what Cydney was pointing at. "Where?"

"The pink hair."

"Are you sure?"

"Oh, my God, yes," she was near the point of hysteria. "That woman is part of the group. When Olivia called me from France, Ethan said it was from that woman's cell phone."

"How do you know her?"

Cydney couldn't get the words out fast enough. "She's on television back in the States," she was frustrated that she had to explain and that he wasn't leaping into action. "I saw her the day that my daughter was kidnapped and... oh, please do something!"

Christophe spied the pink-haired woman and he could feel his adrenaline surge. He didn't know any of Olivia's kidnappers on sight, but if Cydney said she recognized the woman, then he believed her. She was involved in this well before he was. If the woman in the pink hair was here, Christophe wondered who else from the Disciple group was here. As he'd said earlier, they had eyes and ears in many places. His police officer training kicked in and herded Cydney and Tyler together.

"Stay with me," he commanded quietly. "Do not leave my side."

Cydney obeyed, her heart thumping wildly in her chest, but

Tyler was oblivious. He had no idea what had Cydney and Christophe so spooked.

"What's up?" he asked, his head bobbing around to see what they were looking at.

Cydney grasped the boy by the arm. "Not now, Ty," she whispered urgently. "Just do what Inspector Dulay says."

"Huh?"

Cydney didn't answer; she was too busy watching Coral in the distant crowd. Dulay was on his cell phone, dialing J.D.'s number. The call was answered on the fifth ring.

"Dickerson."

"This is Dulay," Christophe was speaking quietly, rapidly. "We seem to have located one of the people who abducted Olivia."

On the other end of the line, J.D. nearly dropped the phone with surprise. "Who? Where?" he demanded.

"At the Colosseum," Christophe explained quickly. "A woman."

"Coral Chastity Aames," Cydney said helpfully.

"Coral Chastity Aames," Christophe repeated. "Mrs. Hetherington has recognized her. She appears to be with a tour group."

"Is she alone?"

Christophe shook his head. "I don't know," he looked at Cydney. "Do you see anyone else you recognize?"

Cydney's gaze roamed the crowd quickly, fearfully. "No," she said. "But I don't think I'd know anyone else on sight. I just happen to know that woman."

Christophe listened to her and then spoke into the phone. "We don't know," he said. "What do you want me to do?"

"Get her," J.D. hissed. "I don't care how you do it, but arrest her. And try not to create a scene. We're on our way."

"Right."

Christophe shut off the phone and shoved it back into his pocket, his eyes never leaving the distant pink hair. He grasped Cydney by the arm, pulling her close so he didn't have to speak too loudly. Tyler just happened to be right next to her because she had a tight hold on him. Christophe spoke in a low voice; he didn't want to be overheard.

"Listen to me," he said. "I need your help so that she doesn't get away."

Cydney looked both terrified and eager. "What do you want me to do?"

Christophe thought a moment, knowing that every moment they delayed was another moment that the woman might get away from them. He spoke quickly.

"We can't be sure that there aren't people with her, people who are involved in Olivia's disappearance," he said. "We have to assume that she's not alone. That being the case, I must approach her with stealth. She does not know me so I can get near her. I want you to move around her tour group on the other side in case she tries to run from me when I grab her."

Cydney shook her head. "But she knows me," she said. "I've met her."

Christophe took his eyes off of Coral long enough to look at Cydney. "But with your sunglasses on, she might not recognize you, at least not right way."

Cydney gazed back at him with some fear. "All right," she realized she still had hold of Tyler. "But what about Ty? We just can't leave him."

"We won't," Christophe looked at the young man. "I want you to go back out the way we came in and wait for your father. They're on their way. Flag them down and tell them to hurry."

Tyler nodded with uncertainty, trying to figure out what was going on. He could tell that Cydney was scared and that, in turn, frightened him.

"Okay," he said, looking between Cydney and Christophe. "Do you need my sword?"

Cydney, in the midst of her terror, giggled at him. She touched the boy on the cheek. "Keep it with you," she told him. "Flag your dad down with it. Hurry!"

Tyler dashed off. Christophe looked at Cydney, confidence in his expression. It made her feel confident, too, and she braced herself for what was to come.

"Ready?" he whispered.

Cydney turned to the pink hair, now moving towards the platform overlooking the maze beneath the arena floor.

"Ready," she answered.

Christophe moved off to his left, his eyes tracking the prey near the edge of the platform. As he moved into the crowd of tourists now following their guide to a different section of the Colosseum, Cydney moved off to her right, hanging back and keeping her focus on both Christophe and Coral. She wandered towards one of the ramps leading to another section of the ruins, pausing as she watched Christophe stalk. Her heart was thumping so violently against her chest that she was sure it would burst.

Coral was oblivious to what was happening. She was gazing down into the network of passages on the Colosseum floor, also apparently oblivious that her tour group was moving away. Cydney sank back behind an ancient pillar, watching with anticipation as Christophe got to within a few feet of Coral. With every second that passed, Cydney was waiting for Coral to move but the woman remained fixed in place, studying the ruins below the platform. Christophe drew closer still and Cydney's breath caught in her throat. It was like waiting for an explosion and she couldn't stand the tension. But finally, he was on her.

Christophe's hand reached out and grabbed Coral firmly

around the elbow and as Cydney watched, he leaned closed and whispered something in her ear. Coral started violently and let out a yelp, but Christophe squeezed her arm so hard that she instinctively tried to dislodge his hand.

The arguing and panic began with Coral's wild reaction and Christophe's firm, quiet voice. Cydney had all she could take. She raced up behind Coral and grabbed the woman by the neck. As Coral cried out, Cydney's furious face was filling her field of vision.

"Where's my daughter, you bitch?" Cydney cried angrily. "Tell me where she is!"

Coral's eyes widened at the sight of Olivia's mother. She began to scream but Cydney slapped a hand over her mouth and, together, she and Christophe dragged her back towards the street. Most of the tourists weren't paying attention and those who were hardly gave the struggling trio a glance. It made for an odd sight but no one seemed particularly concerned. They went back to their sightseeing. Cydney still had her hand over the woman's mouth, getting red lipstick all over her palm.

"If you don't keep quiet, you will be very sorry," Christophe growled as he continued to drag her towards the street. "You are a wanted person, Ms. Aames. Kidnapping a minor and transporting her out of the country is extremely serious."

Coral began to weep hysterically as they pulled her out of the Colosseum and onto the street. Cars whirled past and people were going about their business. Thinking that perhaps they should put Coral someplace inconspicuous until the Americans arrived, Christophe shoved her beneath one of the many arches that comprised the exterior of the Colosseum and pushed her back against the shadows of the wall.

When they were safely hidden, Cydney's hand came away from Coral's mouth and she slapped her, hard, twice before Christophe could stop her.

"Where's my daughter?" Cydney was in Coral's face like a madwoman. "What have you done with her? Where is she?"

"Cydney," Christophe had his hands full both restraining Coral and pulling Cydney off of her. "Calm down, please. Go find Tyler."

Cydney was furious, terrified, panicked. She let Christophe move her away from Coral but she wasn't finished with her yet. The tears were beginning to come.

"She's only fifteen," she burst into angry tears. "Why did you do this? Tell me why?"

"Sweet Jesus, help me," Coral sobbed.

"Tell me where my daughter is before I kill you!"

Coral was weeping hysterically with Christophe's arm across her neck to restrain her. Receiving no answer to her demand, Cydney lashed out and slapped her again before Christopher could grab her hand and firmly shove her away. It was a chaotic, heart-wrenching scene with both Cydney and Coral crying. Christophe spent more time watching the volatile Cydney than he did watching Coral; an enraged mother was never a good thing and he was concerned for her. She seemed to be going to pieces and understandably so.

But Cydney didn't try to slap Coral again. Whatever violence she seemed to be feeling had apparently spent itself. She stood a few feet away, back turned and weeping bitterly, until Tyler approached from the west. The young man was racing at top speed and as soon as he drew near, two smaller black Fiat sedans sailed around the corner behind him with the red lights rotating. Ethan was out of the passenger side of the first car before it even came to a halt.

He raced up with J.D. on his heels. Penryn and Daniels were in the second car and bailed out to assist. Ethan and J.D. grabbed Coral from Christophe and handed her off to Penryn and Daniels, who quickly escorted the hysterical woman to the first car. Christophe followed, as did J.D., but Ethan went straight to Cydney and threw his arms around her.

"It's all right," he murmured in her hair. "Come on, honey. Let's go."

Tyler was standing next to Cydney with wide eyes at all of the activity. Ethan's gaze fell on his son.

"Are you all right, bud?" he asked.

Tyler nodded. "Sure," he lifted his shoulders. "I don't even know what happened."

Ethan reached out and grabbed his son gently by the neck. "Come on," he said. "Let's get Cydney back to the hotel."

Tyler's face fell. "We have to leave?"

"Yes, for now," Ethan replied. "I've got work to do and I don't think Cydney wants to hang around here."

"But...!" Tyler began to protest.

Ethan cut him off with a stern fatherly look. "We'll come back later," he enunciated each word so there would be no room for argument. "We need to get Cydney back to the hotel and I need for you to stay with her while I work. All right?"

Tyler wasn't happy but he nodded. Ethan, his arm still around Cydney, escorted her and his son back to the second car, idling with an Italian cop in the driver's seat. He put her into the back seat and climbed in next to her as Tyler, as usual, sat next to the driver.

"Hotel Cavalieri," Ethan told the cop.

The sedan pulled out into traffic. Ethan sat in the back seat with his arms around Cydney as she struggled to recover her composure. He could feel her shaking in his arms.

"I'm all right," her voice was muffled against his coat. She lifted her face to look at him. "Where are you taking Coral?"

He smoothed the hair from her face. "Back to the Rome Police Department headquarters," he told her.

"She wouldn't tell me where Olivia was."

"You let me worry about that."

Cydney sniffled. "Ethan, I swear to you, I just wanted to kill the woman," she fell forward, her forehead against his chest. "She knows where Olivia is and...."

"Hey," he put his hand under her chin and forced her to look at him. "I told you to let me worry about that. We'll find out where Olivia is. But I need you to take Tyler back to the hotel and wait for me, okay? Just take it easy right now, please. I need for you to trust me."

Her gaze lingered on him a moment before she collapsed against him again. He gathered her up fiercely in his powerful arms, feeling her warmth and softness against him and drawing strength from it.

"I do trust you," she murmured. Her gaze found Tyler. "Poor kid; he was having such fun until all that went down."

"He'll survive."

"No, I won't," Tyler turned around, having heard almost every word. "Can Cydney and I at least go walk around a little? I'll be bored out of my mind if I have to sit around in the hotel all day."

Ethan cocked an eyebrow. "Ty, I appreciate that you didn't come on this trip to sit around, but you also know this is a special circumstance. I'm working a case and I really need for you to do what I tell you."

"We can walk around," Cydney, as usual, was trying to diffuse the situation. She smiled weakly at Tyler. "Did you show your dad your sword?"

Tyler grinned and raised his wooden weapon. "Will they let me take this on the plane?"

Ethan shook his head. "They will not. We'll have to pack it in a suitcase to get it home."

Tyler reached his sword into the back seat and tried to poke his father, which set Cydney to giggling. Leave it to Tyler to make her feel better; whether or not he realized it, he'd been doing it the entire trip. Cydney didn't know what she would have done without Tyler's comic relief; being around a child the same age as Olivia had done a tremendous amount to boost her spirits. He had been a God-send.

Ethan grabbed the sword from his son, turned it around and swatted him on the shoulder with it. Cydney started laughing as Tyler whined for his sword until Ethan finally gave it back but only on the condition that he do as he was told from this point on and not argue about it. Tyler agreed and regained his weapon.

Arriving at the hotel, Ethan had the cop wait in the car while he walked Cydney and Tyler up to the rooms. Cydney was exhausted and wanted to lay down for a bit while Tyler begrudgingly sat down to watch Italian television. Ethan made sure the two of them were settled before returning to the *Polizio de Stato,* or the Rome Police Department headquarters. Even though this was a United States case with FBI jurisdiction, the Rome police were cooperating and J.D. decided to use the facilities at the Public Security Office for their investigative purposes.

The wild morning was about to turn into a wild afternoon.

EIGHTEEN

CORAL RESISTED their attempts to question her for eighteen long, painfully drawn-out hours; J.D. tried, Ethan tried, even Christophe tried. Coral cried and shrieked through the interview attempts until J.D. got on the phone to the Justice Department and worked through some strategy with the prosecutor who had been assigned the case. When J.D. got off the phone, he had a definite scheme in mind. He pulled Ethan into the interrogation room with him as he went in for another attempt.

Coral was a mess; her makeup was under her eyes, on her neck and on the top of her yellow shirt. Her pink hair was askew and her hands were shaking as she clutched a wad of tissues. The room was minimally lit and cold, which they did on purpose. There were no windows. Coral eyed J.D. warily as the man sat down on the other side of the cold metal table that looked more like a morgue slab.

J.D. folded his hands carefully as he gazed steadily at the raccoon-eyed woman.

"Ms. Aames," he began. "I have been authorized by the Justice Department to make a deal with you in return for your honest and complete testimony."

Coral's blue eyes widened and she looked between J.D. and Ethan. "But I told you – I don't know anything."

"Yes, you do," J.D. replied evenly. "If you deny knowing anything about this case one more time, this deal is off the table. I'm finished playing games with you. I'll find something to prosecute you on and throw away the key. Do you understand?"

Coral's wide-eyed gaze cooled somewhat. She may have been dramatic and hyped, but she wasn't stupid. As they sat and watched, her personality seemed to change; her face slackened and her hands clenched. She sat back in her chair and looked away. When she spoke, her voice was oddly dull.

"I can't tell you anything," she said.

"Yes, you can and you will. I'm prepared to offer a lot in exchange for your testimony."

Coral looked at him. "You don't understand. If I tell you anything, they'll kill me."

Now they were getting somewhere. J.D. was very careful about how he approached her. "Who will kill you?"

She smiled thinly. "Them," she said simply, suddenly sitting forward and gaining a great deal of animation. "They're everywhere, Special Agent Dickerson. They're in the Paris Police department, the Federal Bureau of Investigation, Washington D.C. and anywhere else you can imagine. There's nowhere you can hide me that they won't find me. And they'll kill me."

"They'll kill you in jail, too, just to make sure you don't talk," J.D. countered. "You'd be better off telling me what you know and at least give us a chance to protect you."

Coral chewed on her red-stained lip as she thought on that. "There's nothing you can do."

J.D. wasn't going to beg. He decided to play his cards and hope that was enough of an incentive.

"I am prepared to stop all audits on your corporation and release all of your financial assets," he said. "In exchange for helping us locate Olivia Hetherington and The Lucius Robe, we will promise you complete amnesty for your testimony. Not a mark on your record. I will only make this offer once."

Coral was intrigued; that much was obvious. After several long moments of deliberation, she exhaled sharply and lowered her gaze.

"I need a cigarette," she grumbled.

Christophe, sitting on the couch at the rear of the room, produced a pack and a lighter and handed them to Ethan, who extended a cigarette to Coral. She eyed the tall, dark and handsome agent as he lit her cigarette. Taking a long drag, she inspected him from top to bottom in a way that totally destroyed her televangelist image. She looked like a cougar on the prowl.

"Do you swear you'll release my assets?" she finally said.

J.D. nodded firmly. "Everything I just told you. It's a given."

She took another drag off the cigarette and seemed to surrender somewhat. Crossing one of her bird-like legs, she blew silver smoke to the ceiling.

"Special Agent Dickerson, am I to understand that you're a terrorism expert?" she asked.

J.D. nodded. "I am."

"How much do you know about Die Auhänger?"

"Not as much as you do," he sat forward, sensing they were on the verge of a confession. "Tell me."

Coral eyed Ethan. "I'll tell you if you throw him into the package deal."

Before J.D. could respond, Ethan spoke. "Done," he said. "Now tell us where Olivia and the robe are."

Coral laughed softly and took another drag of the cigarette. "You're in for a real story, boys," she said, almost grandly. Her gaze moved between Ethan and J.D. "Die Auhänger had been around since Medieval times. My father, my grandfather, and my ancestors as far back as we can trace were members. Secretive, of course, because the origin of the sect wasn't something you wanted to spread around. The original Die Auhänger were called, among other things, the Knights Templar."

Ethan sat down next to J.D., listening intently as Coral continued.

"Die Auhänger is really just a general term," she said. "The term more popularly known in recent times is the Nazis, of which my father and grandfather were members. The Third Reich, as it were. But that dream died out with the end of World War II. There's an entirely new group of us now, more powerful than you can imagine and far more clever. We're not obvious with our determination to create a new world. We're smarter. We know we must begin small and grow, spreading the word of Enlightenment so people gradually come accustomed to it."

"Izan," Ethan asked quietly. "It's Nazi spelled backwards. So that wasn't a coincidence."

Coral shook her head. "No," she replied, taking another long drag off the cigarette. "That was my father's idea."

"Is he still alive? Is he in on this?"

"He's still alive," she nodded. "He is a part of Die Auhänger but no longer active. He's too old."

"So how does the robe come into play?" Ethan wanted to know. "Do you really intend to crown the heir to the house of d'Orleans as the next Holy Roman Emperor with it?"

She nodded. "It makes sense," she replied. "Joseph is a descendant of the Bourbons, the Carolingians and the Merovingians. The blood of Christ runs through his veins. It is imperative that the heir of Jesus rule the Fourth Reich for the sheer fact that it was Christ's destiny to rule mankind. He never got to fulfill that before the Jews and Romans were crucifying him. Joseph will take his rightful place as Jesus' heir."

"So that's where the robe comes into play?"

"Yes," Coral suddenly grew serious. "But now there's more to this than meets the eye thanks to young Olivia."

Ethan struggled not to become emotional. "Why her? What do you need with her?"

Coral smiled knowingly. "Originally, she was simply a means by which to gain the robe since her mother had access to it," she said. "But while we had Olivia as our guest, she told us something very interesting about the robe."

"What was that?"

Coral took a hit on her cigarette. "There was a tooth embedded in the folds of the robe," she replied. "Once we were told about it, the entire mission took on new depth. We were instructed to get the robe, and the tooth, at all costs and bring them both, and Olivia, to Rome."

J.D. shook his head. "What in the hell for? What do you need with Olivia?"

Coral seemed to take on a very strange countenance, an almost dreamy way of speaking. It was eerie. "Joseph d'Orleans may be a distant descendant of Christ, but think what we can do with DNA extracted from the tooth." She watched the agents' stunned expressions. "This is where our plans changed, gentlemen. With DNA extracted from the tooth, we can use an unfertilized human egg to clone Christ. Think about it; we can actually have Jesus Christ walk the earth again, born to a virgin and prepared to resume his mission on earth. Can you imagine the fantastic implications?"

J.D. and Ethan sat for a moment in shocked silence. It was Ethan who finally put the pieces of the puzzle together.

"Olivia," he hissed. "You need her unfertilized egg."

Coral nodded. "The egg fertilized with the DNA from the tooth will be implanted in her and she will carry the child to term. Christ will once again be born from a young virgin, just as our blessed Mary was a virgin. Olivia will be the Virgin Mary of our time, the mother of Christ."

Ethan had to stand up; he was having a difficult time controlling himself. He walked away from the table, struggling with his emotions. But J.D. remained calm.

"Where is she?" he asked.

"In Rome," Coral replied vaguely. "She's under the care of a fertility specialist."

"Have they gone forward with this scheme yet?"

"They took her to the hospital yesterday. I don't know what's happened since then."

J.D. hoped the men on the other side of the one-way mirror were getting all of this and moving into action. He was, frankly, still reeling from the information even if his manner remained cool. It was too crazy to believe.

"Coral, I need to know one more thing," he said. "You deposit assets into a Cayman Islands account with a Vatican City address. Who is this money for?"

"It's for our dreams."

"I get that, but who controls it?"

She seemed to lose some of her calm. "The person who makes all of our decisions, who made the decision to clone with DNA from the tooth found in the robe."

"Who?"

"The one who will be pope someday very soon. And he will crown our new Emperor."

By this time, Ethan had turned back around and was listening intently. "So it's not the current pope?"

"Of course not," Coral sucked down the last of her cigarette.

"Then who?"

"I'll tell you but you can't do anything about it."

"Who?"

She put the butt into the ashtray on the table. "Cardinal Bishop Wildegrav."

J.D.'s eyes bugged. "The Secretary of State for the Vatican?"

Coral nodded, eyeing Ethan as the man leaned over the table. His muscles were bulging and his handsome face was near, making her feel very much like talking to him.

"He's very much in control, of everything, everywhere," she said confidently. "You can't touch him. Not only does he have diplomatic immunity but he has papal immunity as well. I'll tell you something else you can't do anything about – he plans to assassinate the current pope so that he can assume the post. I don't know any details but I know that is his plan. I heard him speak of it. Wildegrav must be pope in order to crown the new Holy Roman Emperor."

J.D. sat back in his chair, shocked beyond words. Ethan continued to lean over the table, gazing into the raccoon-circled eyes and wishing he wasn't a special agent and a gentleman to boot. He would like nothing more than to throttle the woman. So he turned away, waiting for J.D. to make the next move. Frankly, they were all muddled with the information. It would take some time to process.

But time was something they didn't have. Ethan's priority was to get to Olivia. On the other hand, he found himself angry because Cydney had never mentioned a tooth embedded in The Lucius Robe. If Olivia knew about it, then Cydney certainly did. He wondered why she didn't tell him. But Coral interrupted his tumultuous thoughts; she wasn't finished with her story yet.

"Want to hear something else?" she asked, figuring she truly had nothing more to lose.

J.D. nodded. "Absolutely."

She looked at her nails casually. "Wildegrav is German by birth, the product of Nazi parents," she said. "His ancestry goes back as far as mine. He can trace his lineage back to the Templars, also. On Friday the 13th, 1307, King Philip of France ordered the arrest of all Templars and the confiscation of their wealth. The Lucius Robe was among those treasures confiscated. Now Wildegrav has the robe back in his possession just as his ancestors did almost eight hundred years ago and he plans to keep it."

"So The Lucius Robe is with the Cardinal?" Ethan asked from across the room.

Coral turned her gaze to him. "Yes," she replied. "The last I saw, it was at the Vatican in his offices. But the tooth and Olivia are at the hospital."

"Then the Cardinal is attempting to create Jesus," J.D. muttered, more to himself.

Coral sat forward, her blue eyes glittering with an odd excitement that was difficult to pinpoint. It was clearly disturbing.

"Yes," she whispered. "He wants to create God. And then he wants to control Him."

The implications were overwhelming. It was almost more than they could wrap their minds around and J.D., in particular, was having a tough time; in all his years as a terrorist analyst, he'd never heard of anything so outlandish. It was mind-boggling.

"What hospital is Olivia at?" he finally asked.

Coral's gaze turned to Ethan, boldly. "Do you truly want to know?" she was speaking to J.D. as she looked at Ethan. "You promised me a package deal. If you want the name of the hospital, I get my package right now."

"You need to tell me everything or the entire deal is off."

"Package first if you want the name of the hospital. If not, then you can find Olivia yourself and that could take days. She'll be pregnant by the time you find her."

J.D. looked at Ethan, who was fixed on the hideously smudged woman. There was a heavy uncertain pause before Ethan spoke to J.D. without looking at him.

"Go," he told him. "Shut the door behind you. And clear out the control room behind the one-way mirror."

"Ethan," J.D. hissed. "You can't...."

"Get out."

"I won't let you do anything that will compromise the integrity of this case."

"I won't. Just do what I say."

J.D.'s jaw ticked furiously but he did as he was told, motioning Christophe from the couch against the wall. The two of them quit the room, J.D. shutting the door quietly behind him. He then cleared out the observation room behind the one-way mirror, his last look at Ethan had the man still standing where he had left him. He hadn't moved a muscle.

J.D. turned away, sickened and disheartened. He couldn't even stomach what Ethan was considering doing just to gain that last little vital piece of information, so critical to them all. So critical to Cydney. The man loved her enough to do anything for her, even at great personal expense.

J.D. shut the door to the empty observation room. He didn't want to know any more.

Ethan heard the doors slam and knew that he and Coral were alone. Coral was gazing up at Ethan expectantly and he was having difficulty keeping the bile down. She wanted something, that was clear; yet so did he. He pulled out a chair and straddled it, his arms resting on the back of the chair as he faced Coral.

"Now," he said. "There's one more thing you need to do before this package deal is sealed."

She had a stupid smile on her face. "What's that?"

Ethan lifted an eyebrow. "When this is said and done, you'll be free. Free to roam the streets, free to go home... free to return to Wildegrav."

Her smile faded. "Why would I return? He'll kill me if he knows I've talked."

"He won't know right away," Ethan countered. "I want you to go back to the Cardinal and do something for me."

"What about my package deal?" Coral demanded.

"You need to give a little before I will."

"But I've already told you what I know," she insisted. "I will not divulge Olivia's location until you hold up your end of the deal."

Ethan gazed steadily at her before moving a hand to his tie. Very slowly, he began to remove it. Coral watched with wide eyes as he pulled the tie off and set it on the table.

"Answer a question for me and I'll remove something else," he said seductively.

Coral was having difficulty breathing as she gazed at his spectacular form beneath the clothes. She could only imagine what that white shirt and t-shirt concealed.

"Sweet Jesus," she gasped, swallowing hard. "She... she's at the Hospital San Pietro Fatebenefratelli."

It all came pouring out in a quickly running sentence. She couldn't seem to get it out of her mouth fast enough. Ethan smiled, a very sexy gesture that nearly toppled Coral from the chair.

"Awesome," he purred. He began to unbutton his shirt, hinting at the delights beneath. "You said she was under the care of a fertility specialist. What's his name?"

The shirt was halfway open and Coral was feeling faint with anticipation. It was difficult for her to think back and remember what Wildegrav had told Nat.

"Uh...," she drew in a deep breath. "I... I think the name is Gioia. Dr. Gioia."

The shirt was open now and he pulled it off. A clean white t-shirt lay beneath and he grabbed the bottom of it in preparation for pulling it over his head.

"Excellent," he said. "One more thing."

Coral was fanning herself with her hand. "What?"

"I want the robe back."

He pulled the t-shirt off, revealing a torso that could only be described as glorious. Coral actually thought she might faint. She stared at the tanned skin with the light matting of dark hair, her heart fluttering wildly, as he stood up. The faint scent of aftershave floated upon the stale air of the enclosed room and she closed her eyes, inhaling deeply. She opened her eyes and looked at him.

"I can't help you with that."

"I think you can."

She hesitated until he flexed a beautiful bicep. Then she lost her control completely.

"Oh, God," she gasped. "What do you want me to do?"

He told her.

———

"Cydney," Ethan was standing in her hotel room, having just switched on the light. "Wake up. We need to talk."

Cydney had been in a dead sleep but she sat up at the sound of Ethan's voice. It was morning now, the dawn of a new day. Only half awake, she rubbed her eyes and struggled to snap out of her stupor.

"What's wrong?" she was instantly frightened. "What's happened to Olivia?"

He sat on the bed opposite her, his expression impassive. "Nothing has happened to her yet," he said. "But you and I need to talk. It seems that you forgot to tell me something about

The Lucius Robe, something that has turned out to be the reason why we're chasing Olivia over half of Europe."

She was more awake now and thoroughly perplexed. "What did I forget to tell you?"

Ethan lifted a dark eyebrow. "About the tooth in The Lucius Robe."

"The tooth?' she repeated, confused. Then realization dawned and her eyes widened. "Oh, my God... the *tooth*. I completely forgot all about it. Why? What does it have to do with anything?"

Ethan could see she was being truthful but it didn't soothe his irritation.

"It has a lot to do with it," his voice was tinged with sarcasm. "Apparently, Olivia knew about the tooth embedded in The Lucius Robe and told her captors. That's why they want her."

"What?" Cydney was completely awake now, watching Ethan through horrified eyes. "I don't understand. What does that tooth have to do with my daughter?"

He didn't pull any punches although in hindsight, he should have been gentler about it. Still, he was in interrogation mode and his patience was gone. After what had just happened with Coral, he was exhausted, aggravated and preoccupied, which spelled disaster when dealing with Cydney at the moment.

"We told you that they intended to crown a new Holy Roman Emperor with the robe," his voice was low. "But when Olivia told them about the tooth, it changed the entire schematic. Somehow, somewhere, they got the crazy idea of extracting the DNA from the tooth and using it to create a clone. A clone of Christ. But for that plan to work, they need an unfertilized ovum and a surrogate mother. In their crazy and twisted world, Olivia becomes the new Virgin Mary and they plan to have her give birth to whatever they end up cloning from the DNA extracted from that tooth."

Cydney was ashen by the time he finished his speech. She stood up unsteadily, hand to her mouth.

"Oh, my God," she breathed. "They... they're going to get her pregnant?"

"Yes," Ethan nodded irritably. "You should have told me about the tooth, Cyd. It would have saved us a lot of time and hassle."

As horrified as Cydney was, she sensed his anger at her and she riled. Her emotions were on the surface as it was and she didn't need his fury for something unintentional.

"I completely forgot about the tooth," she fired back. "It never even occurred to me. Certainly, if I had thought of it, I would have told you, but it slipped my mind. I'm sorry I made your job more difficult, Ethan, I really am. It's not like I with-held vital information on purpose."

He looked at her, his jaw ticking, realizing he had been harsher with her than he should have been and she was reacting in kind. Gazing into her pale face, he realized he wasn't really angry with her. If he thought on it, it was a fairly trivial thing. Still, this trivial thing had been a major key. He wiped his hand over his eyes, a gesture of his level of exhaustion.

"I know," he relented. "I'm sorry, honey. It's just that I sat through eighteen hours of interrogation with Coral Chastity Aames and she was the one who ended up telling me about the tooth. I felt like an idiot that it had to come from her."

"Is that all you care about? Feeling like an idiot?" Cydney wasn't ready to accept his apology yet. "My daughter is in horrible danger because a group of crazy zealots want to implant her with a fertilized ovum and all you can think about is yourself?"

He sighed heavily. "I didn't mean it that way."

"Then how did you mean it?" she shot back. "Olivia is fighting for her life and all you care about is looking like a fool?"

He put up his hands. "Stop, will you?" he commanded softly. "I'm sorry; I didn't mean it the way it sounded. I just meant that I should have known already. I should have heard it from you."

"And I told you that I forgot about it," she seethed. "It never even occurred to me. I saw the thing once, mentioned it to my daughter, and that's as far as it went. I put it out of my mind."

He lifted his eyebrows at her. "Well, your daughter told her captors about it and now it's a major issue," he said pointedly. "Are there any other surprises you forgot about? Now would be a good time to tell me so I don't get blindsided again."

Frustrated, sick and furious, Cydney just turned away from him and went into the bathroom. Slamming the door, she locked it. Ethan stood there all of five seconds before he moved to the door and lifted his hand to knock. Before he could rap on the door, however, he could hear Cydney vomiting on the other side. Feeling like a massive jerk, he knocked on the door.

"Cydney, honey," he said. "Open up. I'm sorry, I really am. Please open the door."

He could hear her crying. "Cydney," he rattled the door-knob. "Open the door, baby. I'm sorry, I'm just tired. I took it out on you and I'm sorry."

Her weeping was interrupted by a series of painfully deep dry heaves. Ethan counted seven before he heard the toilet flush.

"Go away," she cried from the other side of the door. "Leave me alone."

"I'm not going away," Ethan said firmly, gently. "If you don't open this door, I'm going to break it down."

She didn't answer him. He could hear her crying on the other side of the door. Taking a step back, he lashed out a big foot and kicked the door right at the weak point where the knob and plate met. The door plate ripped out, dislodging the lock completely and the door popped open.

Ethan pulled his coat off and tossed it on the bed as he entered the bathroom. Cydney was lying on the tile floor next to the toilet, her hands over her face. He knelt down beside her, putting his lips against the hands that were covering her face.

"I'm sorry," he murmured, kissing her fingers. "I shouldn't have gotten upset with you and I'm sorry. Please forgive me."

Before Cydney could answer, they suddenly heard a young, frightened voice in the doorway.

"Dad!" Tyler was standing there in his pajamas, gaping at the broken door. "What did you do?"

Ethan looked back at his son, trying to formulate a reply, when Tyler suddenly came rushing into the bathroom where Cydney was laying on the floor. He looked accusingly at his father.

"What did you do to her?" he jabbed a finger at Cydney. "Why is she on the floor?"

Ethan opened his mouth to reply but just ended up chuckling. He looked down at Cydney, who was now gazing up at Tyler from between splayed fingers.

"You'd better help me out of this or I think my son seriously intends to hurt me," he said.

Cydney pulled her hands away from her face and wrapped her arms around Ethan's neck. He picked her up off the floor, cradling her.

"No worries, Ty," she said, laying her head on Ethan's shoulder. "The door was jammed and your dad had to bust it open."

Tyler was young but he wasn't stupid. His gaze moved between his father and Cydney. "Then why were you on the floor?"

"I slipped."

His brow furrowed. "Oh," he said. "Are you okay?"

"I'm fine. I appreciate your concern."

Tyler made a thoughtful face, looking around the bathroom before coming to rest on his father again. "Why were you guys fighting? It woke me up."

Ethan cradled Cydney against him. "It's okay, Ty," he moved to take her out of the bathroom. "Your old man was just being an ass. Everything's okay now."

Tyler followed them out of the bathroom and stood at the bottom of the bed as Ethan lay Cydney down. Cydney didn't let go of him, however, so he ended up sitting beside her with his arms wrapped around her. Tyler eventually came to sit on the bed opposite the pair, his anxious gaze moving between them.

"What did you find out about Olivia?" the boy asked.

Ethan gazed at his son a moment, debating how much to tell him. "She's being held captive not far from here," he said. "J.D. is with the Rome police right now gathering a task force together. He's also made arrangement with the U.S. Embassy for some Marines. We're going to go get her."

Cydney's head snapped up. "An armed incursion?"

Ethan gazed steadily at her. "We want to make sure we're prepared. My specific task is to get her out of wherever she is while everyone else covers me."

"It sounds like a battle."

"I won't lie to you," he said. "It may be. We just want to be prepared."

Tyler watched as Cydney's head lowered and she buried it against his father's chest. He could see the silent tears flowing. He felt as bad and confused as a fourteen-year-old could.

"Dad?" he asked.

Ethan looked at him, his hands caressing Cydney's head. "What, buddy?"

"You could get shot, right?"

"I'm a federal agent, Ty. There's always that chance no matter what."

"Have you done this kind of thing before?"

"I have."

"And you came out all right?"

"I'm here, aren't I?"

Tyler sighed faintly, trying to be a man about it but still struggling with that scared kid inside of him. He looked at Cydney, her face pressed into Ethan's chest.

"Don't worry, Cydney," he told her. "My dad's really good at what he does. I know he is."

Cydney, head still against Ethan's chest, turned to look at him. She wiped her eyes and tried to smile. "I know he is, too," she sniffled. "I'm not really worried. I just want this all to be over. I miss Olivia."

Cydney's cell phone suddenly rang. Ethan, cupping her face, kissed her on the cheek as she rose to go get it. Wiping at her nose, she pulled it out of her purse and recognized the number. Quickly, she answered.

"Stu?" she asked, surprised.

A familiar voice was on the other end. "Hey, Cyd," Stu sounded very glad to hear her voice. "How's Paris?"

Cydney laughed, stunned at the call. "What's going on?" she said. "How are you doing?"

"Good," Stu said. "They let me go home last night. I'm off work for a month. Can you believe it? Milt is having a fit. First you and now me. He says he feels like he's being deserted."

Cydney chuckled. "Perish the thought," she said. "Now he might actually have to do his job without the rest of us there to cover for him."

Stu laughed loudly on the other end. As Cydney settled in

to the conversation, Ethan and Tyler stood up and made their way out of the bedroom. Ethan grasped her by the shoulders, kissed her head, and whispered in her free ear that he was going to get Tyler some breakfast. Cydney waved at him.

"So how's Olivia?" Stu wanted to know. "We haven't heard anything. What's going on?"

Cydney shook her head. "You won't believe it," she said. "Look, I really can't get into everything right now but believe me when I say it's been crazy. Like something out of a movie plot."

"Really?" Stu was interested. "What about the robe? I think Milt's been updated about it but he wouldn't tell me anything. What's going on?"

Cydney suddenly felt very weary, thinking of her most recent conversation with Ethan.

"God, Stu," she groaned. "You just wouldn't believe it. Somehow the robe and Olivia go hand in hand and... well, I can't get into it over the phone. I'll fill you in when I get back."

"When is that?"

"I don't really know," she said honestly.

"Oh," Stu fell quiet for a moment. "Hey, Cyd... you know, I've been doing a lot of thinking while in the hospital. I had a lot of time on my hands."

"Thinking about what?"

"Life," he said. "When I got shot, my life flashed in front of my eyes. I know that sounds corny, but it's true. I saw that guy point the gun at you and all I could think about was protecting you. My own life didn't even matter at that moment."

Cydney sighed faintly. "I really appreciate it," she said quietly. "You saved my life, I think. I never had the chance to thank you, so thanks. More than you know, thanks."

"You're welcome," he replied, then paused. "But I guess the real reason why I called was to say that I've been thinking a lot about you."

"Why?"

He grunted, suddenly uncomfortable. "Well, I guess because we've known each other a long time. The first time I met you, I thought you were the most beautiful woman I'd ever seen. And we get along really well. I guess what I'm trying to say is that all of this stuff with the robe made me realize that you mean more to me than just a friend. I want us to be more than just friends."

Cydney felt very sorry for Stu. She knew his admission had been a big one. Frankly, she had been waiting for it for years and was surprised that it had taken him this long. *What rotten timing*, she thought.

"I'm flattered," she said hesitantly. "But what about your dreams of marrying a virgin Catholic girl?"

Stu snorted. "I don't think they exist," he said. "All this time I've been looking for that, I've completely overlooked you when it was you I really wanted."

On the other end of the line, Cydney made a face of regret. Clapping a hand to her forehead, she shook her head with the irony of Stu's declaration. She had to be very careful with her answer if there was any hope of salvaging their friendship.

"Stu, you are one of my dearest friends," she said gently. "You have made my job worth going to every day and I don't want to lose you for the world. But you and I... it just can't be."

"Why not?"

"Oh, Stu," she murmured. "I love you dearly, I really do. But not as a lover or a husband. That's something I never thought I would feel again after Brad died."

"I know," he said, unsure where she was going with this. "I'm not trying to take Brad's place, Cyd. But I swear I would make a good husband. I don't drink or smoke. I don't do drugs. And I love Olivia; she's a great kid. And I promise I would love you the rest of your life."

Cydney sighed heavily. "I know how hard this is for you to say," she said. "I know it takes a lot of courage and I really do love you dearly. I would never do anything to jeopardize that. But us being together just isn't possible."

"Why not?"

"Because I've gone for years convincing myself that I'd never marry again. I didn't want another husband because Brad's death just hurt too much. I couldn't open myself up like that again."

"I know."

"I know you do. But what you don't know is that someone else has changed my mind about never getting married again. I've fallen in love, Stu, and I'm so happy I can't even put it into words."

Stu was quiet a moment. "Oh, I get it," he finally said, his voice dull. "It's that FBI guy, right?"

"What makes you say that?"

"Because I saw the way he looked at you and the way you looked at him. There was something there. Even I could see it."

Cydney nodded. "Your instincts are right," she said. "Stu, he's the most amazing man I've ever met. I'm so lucky to have such a great friend like you and also to have met someone like Ethan. As flattered and touched as I am by your proposal, you need to understand that I love Ethan very much. We're getting married."

There was a long pause as Stu absorbed her words. "Stu?" Cydney asked gently. "Are you still there?"

"Yeah," he said. "I'm still here."

"Please don't be upset. I need for you to be happy for me. It means a lot to me to have your blessing."

He grunted and groaned for a moment before answering. "I guess you have it," he finally muttered. "I know how hard the last few years have been for you. I guess I really am glad you've finally found someone. I was just hoping that someone could be me."

She smiled. "I love you, Stu, I really do. Thanks for being such a rock for me. I know you'll like Ethan a lot when you get to know him."

"Maybe," Stu said, now seemingly restless and slightly embarrassed that he had put himself out there and she had essentially rejected him. "Hey, this call is costing me a small fortune. I'd better cut it off now."

"I know."

"I just wanted to make sure you and Olivia are all right."

"We're fine. Thanks for asking. I'll see you soon, okay?"

"Okay."

Stu hung up the phone and Cydney stood there a moment before shutting her phone down. She was hurting for Stu yet she knew without a doubt she was making the right choice. Her heart belonged to Ethan. There had never been any question.

Ethan came back into the room a short while later to find Cydney in the bathroom applying makeup. He had a bagel in a Styrofoam container and set it on the counter beside her. He kissed her on the side of the head as he set it down.

"I thought you might be hungry," he said. "I need to head out of here soon."

She ran a lip gloss wand across her lower lip. "Thanks for the food," she said, glancing at him in the mirror. "What's going to happen now?"

He leaned back against the counter, watching her as she applied her makeup. "To Rome Police headquarters," he replied. "J.D. is having a briefing in a half hour."

Her expression grew serious and she stopped putting powder on. "Then what?"

"Then we go get Olivia."

"Do you know where she is?"

He thought about his answer and what he had to do to get that vital bit of information. "Yes."

He didn't say anything more and she lifted her eyebrows expectantly. "Are you going to tell me?"

"Does it matter?"

"I guess not," she set the makeup down and wrapped her arms around his waist, embracing him tightly. Ethan swallowed her up in his big arms.

"Please," she begged. "Please tell me this is going to be all right. Please tell me that no one is going to get hurt and you'll be back, safe, with my daughter in a few hours."

"It will be all right," he murmured, his cheek on the top of her head. "Olivia and I will be back in a little bit."

"Is this going to get crazy?"

"Possibly."

She sighed heavily. "Please watch out for my baby," she whispered. "And please watch out for yourself. Stay away from flying bullets."

"I have so far."

She looked up at him, studying his exquisite face. "Thank you," she murmured after a moment. "For everything you've done for me and Olivia, thank you."

He smiled and kissed her on the forehead. "I would do anything for my future wife and stepdaughter," he paused a moment as he brushed some hair from her eyes. "I was thinking something the other day but I don't want you to be offended by it."

"What?"

"I was thinking... well, what would you say if I wanted to adopt Olivia?"

Cydney blinked with surprise. "*Adopt* her?" She thought about it briefly. "I don't know. It never even occurred to me."

"It's not like she would lose the Hetherington name," he

said. "We could hyphenate her name to Hetherington-Serreaux. I told you I'd love her as if she were my own flesh and blood. I meant it."

Cydney smiled faintly. "That's very sweet," she said, touching his cheek. "I suppose I don't have any problem with it. But let's let Olivia make that decision, okay?"

"Sure."

He leaned down and kissed her deeply, completely wiping off her lip gloss. Tyler chose that moment to enter the bedroom and he slapped a hand over his eyes at the sight of his father and Cydney lip-locked.

"Geez, you guys," he said, walking blindly into the bed and tripping over it. "Get a room."

Ethan cocked a dark eyebrow as Cydney tried not to let Tyler see her laugh. "What do you know about getting a room?" Ethan wanted to know.

"Nothing," Tyler said innocently as he sprawled out over the bed. "Dad, can Cydney and I go walk around while you're out?"

"I'd prefer you didn't," Ethan said quietly. "I'd like you both here where I can get a hold of you if I need to."

Cydney looked up at him. "I'll take him out for a little while after you leave. Then we'll head back here and stay here until you call."

He shrugged. "All right," he said. "But don't be out too long. Just an hour or so, okay?"

"Okay," Cydney pulled herself from his arms and turned to Tyler, now with his head hanging off the bed and looking at them upside down. "Where do you want to go, young man?"

He was suddenly right-side up. "Really?" he was excited. "Can we go to the Vatican?"

"No," Ethan said flatly. "Just walk around here. I'm sure there are things to see. Go buy something for your mom."

"Cool!" Tyler leapt off the bed and held his hand out to his father, who begrudgingly gave him a few Euros.

"You're expensive, dude," Ethan grumbled. "When are you going to get a job?"

"When my band starts getting gigs. Then I'll be rich."

"Good," Ethan snorted. "You can support me in my old age."

"No way. You'll be my roadie and I'll pay you minimum wage."

Ethan rolled his eyes to let his son know what he thought of that idea and collected his suit coat off the other bed. His gaze moved between Cydney and Tyler as he pulled on the jacket. He was glad that Tyler wasn't lingering on the potentially violent job his father was about to undertake but he could tell that Cydney was very apprehensive. He didn't blame her. Fixing his tie, he bent down and kissed her again.

"I'll see you for dinner, I hope," he said. "Do you have your cell phone with you?"

She nodded. "I do."

"Good," he moved to the door as he finished fidgeting with his tie. "By the way, what did your ex-Marine security chief have to say?"

Cydney looked at him, wondering if she should tell him the real reason for Stu's call. She opted not to; she didn't want anything to distract him right now. Later, she would tell him, but not now.

"He's fine," she said. "He was bored. Just released from the hospital."

"Oh," Ethan was successfully satisfied with her explanation and looked pointedly at his son. "I'm out of here. But you listen to Cydney, okay? Don't stay out too long."

"I won't," Tyler assured him.

Ethan paused by the door leading to the hall as his gaze

moved to Cydney once more. They exchanged heady, mean-ingful glances; there was emotion in the air, thick, the fear and anticipation of what was to come. For Cydney, it was a double-whammy. Not only was her daughter's life at stake, but so was Ethan's. Ethan doubted she had the strength to lose another husband.

He went back over to her and took her in his arms one last time. Cydney squeezed him tightly.

"Good luck," she whispered.

"Thanks," he kissed her again, looking her in the eye. "I'll get her back, Cyd. I promise."

"I know you will," she murmured, kissing him one last time. "Take care of yourself. I love you."

He stroked her cheek before letting go. "I love you, too, baby. More than you know."

Tyler was standing by the bedroom door impatiently, rolling his eyes at the sentiment going on.

"Geez, you guys," he snorted. "Get a room!"

Cydney snickered as Ethan turned to his son. He passed the kid as he headed out the door.

"You and I are going to have a talk about what getting a room really means when I get back," he said as he walked by.

Tyler made a face at his father as Ethan went out into the hall and closed the door. "I already know what it really means," he muttered bravely once his father was gone.

He didn't realize Cydney was standing right behind him, zipping up her purse. When he heard the noise of the zipper and turned and saw her, he just smiled sheepishly. Cydney shook her head, not doubting him for a minute. Kids grew up so quickly these days.

"Come on, Ty," she went back into the bathroom to grab half of the bagel Ethan had brought her and eat it on the run. "Let's go find your mom something nice."

Tyler didn't have to be told twice. It was a beautiful day outside as they walked the charming Italian streets but Cydney didn't really notice. Her thoughts, heart and mind were with Ethan and Olivia, wherever they may be.

Her daughter's salvation was at hand.

NINETEEN

THE HOSPITAL SAN PIETRO FATEBENEFRATELLI was founded in 1848 by a healing Catholic Order. It was an older hospital with gorgeous architecture that sat on the heavily-foliaged Isola Tiberina a couple of miles down the Tiber River from the Vatican.

It had been the place that Coral had named and J.D. had asked Ethan what he had done in order to secure that particular bit of information. Ethan wouldn't respond, something that both irritated and concerned J.D., but he couldn't imagine Ethan doing anything truly unethical or immoral. Risky, yes; but not unethical or immoral. Still, Ethan was so desperately in love with Cydney that there was no knowing the lengths the man would go to for her. J.D. suspected Ethan would tell him in his own time. But until then, J.D. was both seriously curious and seriously concerned.

It was early afternoon by the time J.D., Ethan, Christophe, Penryn and Daniels, plus six U.S. Marines and a S.W.A.T. team from the Rome Police arrived at the hospital. The compound sat on a little island in the middle of the Tiber and parking was limited. So was the ability to arrive unannounced.

The police parked their white S.W.A.T. van around the corner from the front entrance beneath the shelter of some lovely old trees while J.D., Ethan, Christophe and several agents from the U.S. Embassy parked along the east side of the structure. They got out of the black unmarked sedans, popped open the trunks, and began putting on flak vests.

Ethan removed his coat and put on the heavy dark Kevlar vest over his dress shirt and tie. With his dark aviator sunglasses and stunning good looks, he looked like a movie star getting ready to shoot a scene. J.D. was next to him, also wearing his Kevlar vest and handing him a Glock 22, a police issue forty caliber weapon.

Ethan took the gun, plus a Springfield XD 9mm that he personally owned, and strapped the holsters on; one to his belt and the other over his shoulder. He was focused yet anxious, preparing for the battle to come. He'd never faced anything more serious.

Christophe came around the side of the car, a cigarette hanging out of his mouth, a vest on, two handheld weapons holstered to his body and both hands holding shotguns. Rounds of extra ammunition bulged from his pockets and he looked like he was about to invade a small country single-handedly. J.D. and Ethan gazed at him with some amusement.

"Are you sure you've got enough firepower?" J.D. asked with mock seriousness.

Christophe pumped a shell into the chamber of the shotgun in his right hand. "Perhaps," he shot J.D. a pointed look. "Perhaps not."

"I can give you more if you feel you need it," J.D. pressed, obviously making fun of him. "I don't want you to go in there under-manned."

As Ethan snorted, Christophe blew smoke in J.D.'s face. "I've got plenty. Worry about yourself, hotshot."

Ethan laughed out loud as J.D. coughed away the smoke. He finished securing the holster around his shoulder. "We're going into a hospital, Christophe," Ethan said. "I'm not sure you can pick and choose your targets carefully with four guns blazing."

Christophe puffed heavily on the cigarette. "Cela est la façon il va."

Ethan cocked an eyebrow. "Faire attention vous ne tirez pas la mauvaise personne."

Christophe flashed a toothy grin and Ethan snickered, shaking his head in resignation. Christophe was going to enjoy this just a little too much. J.D. made a face.

"Quit babbling in a foreign tongue, both of you," he snapped at them. "Are we ready?"

Ethan slammed the trunk of the car. "I was just telling him not to shoot the wrong person," he said, facing J.D. and removing his sunglasses. "I'm ready."

J.D. eyed him. This was the professional agent he had known for so many years. Flawless in judgment and execution, someone he trusted his life to. Ethan was a model agent. But he knew what was at stake and knew that Ethan, in spite of his calm façade, was edgy. He found the need to be clear, just between the two of them.

"Your objective is to get Olivia," he lowered his voice. "Don't try to be a hero and take anyone into custody. Just get her out of there."

"If we meet resistance?"

"That's why we brought half of the Rome police force and six Marines."

Ethan drew in a long, deep breath. "I'm worried that they might kill her when they realize we're on to them," he muttered. "That's been haunting me for a while."

"We can only hope the element of surprise is on our side,"

he slapped Ethan on a big shoulder. "Focus on your task and we'll get through this."

Ethan simply nodded, his worries clouding his focus at the moment. By this time, several other agents had joined them at the back of the car, all dressed for action. More police cars pulled up and Ethan waved them over to park on the side streets. With more back up showing up, J.D. got down to business.

"This hospital isn't particularly large so it's not like we have a tremendous amount of ground to cover," he said, unrolling a schematic that they had managed to get from the Rome police. It showed the floor plan of an older building with straight halls and square rooms. J.D. laid the plan on the trunk of the sedan and thumped a finger on it. "We've been able to discover that Dr. Gioia works on the second floor of the west wing and, according to a call placed to the hospital an hour ago, he was scheduled to work for the rest of the afternoon. We are simultaneously serving a warrant on him and searching for the captive young woman. You have your teams and you've already been given your assignment; you'll search by two's, room-to-room, until the entire second floor is covered and the American captive is located. Any questions so far?"

Everyone seemed to be clear. J.D. nodded with satisfaction. "Good," he went on. "Break up into your pre-designated teams for entry; Group One goes in through the front entrance, Group Two has the east entry and the east stairwell and Group Three has the west entry and the West stairwell. The S.W.A.T. boys go with Group One and the Marines are split between Groups Two and Three. We have units covering every entry and exit, so the entire structure is covered. If there are no questions, then let's get going. Keep the radios on and in constant contact. Let me know when your rooms have been cleared and, subsequently, when the girl is located. If you run into any trouble, holler."

Everyone scattered. J.D. had command of Group One, Ethan had command of Group Two and Christophe had command of Group Three. The air was heavy with anticipation and excitement, especially for Ethan, as they ran to take position.

With their earpiece radios all on the same frequency, they all gathered into position. J.D. spoke into the radio, his gaze on the big glass doors before him. He could see a few people in the lobby beyond as they stood there, gathered against the exterior of the building. People walked in and out of the facility. A few noticed the group of cops and hurried away as fast as they could.

"Try not to scare people to death," J.D. said. "We have a purpose. We're not here to roust the place so everyone stay focused."

The agents around him nodded, including Agent Penryn. Daniels was with Ethan. With a sharp bob of his head, J.D. gave the signal and the teams began to move.

———

The room was dark. Olivia struggled to open her eyes, feeling the effects from the powerful anesthetic they had used to put her under. She had been fighting so much that they had ended up giving her too much anesthesia to knock her out and now she was both groggy and nauseous.

Still, she struggled to open her eyes, trying to figure out where she was. A cold and sterile room met with her foggy gaze. Moving slightly, she was aware that she couldn't lift her arms or legs. It took her a moment to realize that she was wrapped in restraints.

With a groan, her head slammed back on the pillow and she

stared up at the asbestos-tiled ceiling. She had an itch on her chin and she couldn't even scratch it. The angry tears came and ran down her temples onto the pillow.

Gazing up at the ceiling, her mind was gradually clearing and she began to count the holes in the tile just to keep from screaming. Anything to keep from going crazy. She was so far beyond fear now that all she was feeling was fury; deep-seated fury that grew by the hour. She hated these people more than she could put into words. She just wanted to go home.

At some point, the door opened softly and, startled, she closed her eyes quickly. She wanted to convey the illusion that she was still asleep, just for the moment until she could figure out what was going on. She heard soft footsteps on the cool linoleum, moving towards her from the open door. The gentle pit-pat drew close. Olivia could hear someone breathing. Slowly, she opened her eyes.

Joseph stood there, gazing down at her. He looked particularly pale. When he saw that she was awake, he smiled wanly.

"Hey," he said. "How are you feeling?"

Olivia was in no mood for his pleasantries. "Why am I tied down?"

Joseph immediately moved to the ties on her wrists. "Sorry," he murmured, releasing her arm and going to work on the other. "We didn't want you to wake up and go crazy."

Olivia rubbed her wrists as soon as he released her second hand. She watched him as he moved to her feet. "I'm not going to go crazy," she muttered. "I don't even know where I am. Where am I going to run that someone, somewhere, doesn't have ties with you guys and will turn me in? I thought I was safe with the Paris Police but I was wrong. Even if I do run away, you guys will just find me again."

Joseph released her feet, listening to her rant in relative

silence. When all four limbs were unrestrained, Olivia sat up and rubbed at her ankle.

"Can I have some water, please?" she asked with an attitude.

Joseph went into the adjoining bathroom and she could hear water running. He returned with a plastic cup and handed it to her. Olivia drained it.

"So," she said, licking her lips, feeling her stomach settle. "What happened to me? What did they do?"

Joseph didn't seem his normal jovial self. He had just come from a very disturbing conversation and had been pondering what to do about it for the better part of the morning.

They were at the end of a very long journey and, more than ever, he was having difficulty justifying what was happening. He'd never been keen on his role in all of this but as the days and hours passed, and as Olivia Hetherington's role became larger than his, he was beginning to question everything. The tides were beginning to turn.

"I need to talk to you," he said quietly.

"What about?"

He sighed, moving up on the side of the bed. "I think there's a problem," he said after a moment. "Look, Olivia, I know you don't trust me and I know this whole adventure has been like a nightmare for you, but I think we've reached a crossroads and I need your cooperation. If you want to live, you're going to have to trust me."

She looked at him curiously. "What are you talking about?"

Joseph chewed his lip as he thought on how to tell her what he must. "There's something wrong with your eggs," he lowered his voice. "When they knocked you out and went in to harvest whatever eggs they could from your ovaries, they discovered that something was wrong with them. I'm not a doctor but from what I can gather, the fertility specialist said they're underdeveloped or something like that. Anyway, this means that you're not a viable subject for their DNA plot. Right now, they're talking to the doctor about what they should do with you."

Olivia's fear returned. "*Do* with me?" she repeated. "What do you mean?"

Joseph looked rather fearful himself. "I don't know," he said. "But I don't like it. They're talking about hormone therapy and other crazy stuff. But if that doesn't work, I'm afraid they'll just get rid of you and find somebody else for their experiment."

Her eyes widened. "They're going to kill me?"

"Maybe," he said honestly. He suddenly reached out and cupped her sweet little face, forcing her to look at him. "You need to trust me, Olivia."

Her big eyes gazed back at him apprehensively. "What are you going to do?"

He hesitated before speaking; what he was about to say went against everything he was brought up to believe and fulfill. "I'm going to get you out of here," he finally spit it out. "This whole scheme with you was never what was originally intended. I was never too hot on the idea of kidnapping you, anyway, and now it's just getting worse. The plans we've had for decades have suddenly turned into something convoluted and scary. There's no knowing when or how it will stop, or what will be the result. This is more than just creating a new Holy Roman Empire. This has turned into creating God in Man's image and I don't like it. I don't want to be a part of it."

Olivia was staring at him with more terror and hope than she could process. "Seriously?" she hissed. "We're going to leave?"

"Yes," Joseph went back into the bathroom, looking for and finally tracking down the clothes she had worn when they had arrived at the hospital. He scooted out of the bathroom. "Your clothes are in there. Hurry and get dressed."

Olivia didn't need to be told twice. She tossed the sheet off her and walked quickly, and a little unsteadily, across the cold floor, shutting the bathroom door as Joseph lingered nervously outside. When she finally emerged in the bright pink t-shirt, white Capri pants and pink, white and green sneakers, Joseph grabbed her by the hand and pulled her towards the door.

He paused suddenly before opening it, his edgy gaze falling on her. He seemed to be grasping for words.

"I'm really sorry about all of this, Olivia," he said. "You were never supposed to be so deeply involved. I'm sorry you got sucked into something that went so out of control."

She gazed steadily at him. "I'm not going to tell you that it's okay," she said. "I'm not going to forgive you for anything if that's what you're looking for."

He smiled, shaking his head. "I'm not looking for absolution, at least not from you," he cracked the door and peered outside. "Maybe I'm just righting a wrong in my own mind. I think this has more to do with me forgiving myself for being a part of all this."

Olivia didn't have an answer for that but it oddly made her feel sorry for him. Joseph held her hand tightly as he emerged into the cool, dimly lit corridor that smelled strongly of antiseptic. The floors were old green linoleum and the walls a sickly white. There was a nursing station about twenty feet away and he could see a couple of women moving about. One was on the phone and one was on the computer, neither of them paying any attention to him. He pulled Olivia out after him and took her, very quickly and quietly, in the opposite direction.

The stairwell was out of a small set of doors and to the right. He took Olivia through the set of doors and shoved open the stairwell panel. The steps beyond were concrete and poorly lit.

Joseph raced down the stairs with Olivia right behind him, turning the corner on the landing and taking the first two steps when he suddenly came to a halt. Olivia plowed into the back of him and almost sent them both tumbling over.

"What the...?" she began, righting herself to see what had Joseph stopped. And what she saw turned her blood to ice.

Nat was standing on the landing below them. At the sight of Joseph and Olivia, he suddenly smiled quite jovially. For a man that was perpetually surly, the sudden joy on his face was frightening. Olivia knew it couldn't be a good sign.

"I *knew* it," he said it happily, slapping his thigh and slowly moving towards the pair. "I had this feeling... don't ask me why, but I just did. As we were sitting with Dr. Gioia discussing Olivia's future and you suddenly got up and left, I just had this feeling where you were going. I see my instincts were right."

Joseph made sure to keep Olivia behind him. "Let us go, Nat," he said steadily. "Olivia no longer serves a purpose for us. There's no reason to keep her any longer."

Nat was still smiling although his brow furrowed. "Are you crazy?" he said. "She knows too much about us now. She knows everything. We can't let her go."

Nat was getting closer and Joseph backed up a step. "For God's Sake, what's the point of hanging on to her?" he argued. "She's just a kid. Let her go home and resume her life like a normal, everyday teenager. She doesn't need to be a part of this madness."

Nat pursed his lips as if the suggestion were ridiculous. "She stopped being a normal teenager the moment we took her," he replied. "She's part of us now."

"No, I'm not!" Olivia said hotly from behind Joseph. "I just want to go home. You don't need me anymore."

Nat's gaze moved between Joseph and Olivia. "She'd make a great empress, Joe," he said. "Pretty and smart. Keep her for yourself; marry her."

Joseph shook his head. "She's a little too young for me," he replied steadily. "Come on, Nat; just let us pass. We can find someone else to supply eggs and carry a child to term."

"You always were an idiot, Joe."

"Maybe so. But at least I have a conscience."

Joseph began to descend the stairs again, yanking Olivia along, but suddenly stopped. Olivia smacked into him once more. Irritated, frightened, she peered around him to see why he had come to a halt this time and was not surprised to see Nat with a gun pointed at them.

That was when all hell broke loose.

———

Ethan took the east entry, having to pry the door open with a small pry-bar type tool that one of the agents had brought. The door wasn't highly secure and popped open after a couple of tries. It opened up into a small lobby area that was both cold and deserted.

The door directly in front of them led to a main corridor while the door to the left opened into the stairwell. Ethan silently directed two of the officers with him to cover the door into the main corridor while he took the door to the stairs. The second floor was their objective.

Quickly opening the fire-proof panel, Ethan ran headlong into a man standing on the landing. The man's back was to them and Ethan was only aware of an average-sized male in a white shirt but little else. It was when he heard a shriek and looked up the stairs that events suddenly seemed to roll in slow motion; it was odd and painful and drawn out, like a movie scene that seemingly had no end.

Ethan turned to see Olivia about midway up the steps, standing behind a man who appeared to be protecting her. The man who stood with his back to him suddenly whirled on Ethan with a gun in his hand and Ethan felt the impact of the bullet as it plowed into his Kevlar vest. It felt like he'd been hit by a battering ram, literally knocking him off his feet and throwing him into the wall near the door.

Seeing Agent Serreaux hit, the Marines behind him opened up and fired several rounds into Nat before the man could get off another shot. Nat was dead before he hit the ground. Olivia started screaming as Joseph threw her down onto the stairs to protect her, covering her with his own body as the bullets flew. But a ricochet caught him in the back, plowing through a kidney, his liver and through a major artery before exiting his belly. That same bullet ripped through Olivia's right calf.

Dazed, Ethan began yelling for his group to cease fire. He was terrified that Olivia was going to be mowed down. A couple of men were kneeling next to him asking if he was all right. One of them was Agent Daniels; he was mortified that Ethan had been struck. He had started screaming into his headset for a medic the moment Serreaux had gone down, but other than having the wind knocked out of him, Ethan wasn't injured. The Kevlar vest had done its job and deflected the bullet. With Daniel's help, Ethan struggled to his feet.

As the dust and smoke settled, the first thing he saw was Olivia lying on the stairs with a man on top of her. There was blood pooling beneath her and horror such as he had never known seized him. Struggling with his diminished physical state at the moment, Ethan labored up the stairs with the Marines in tow. It was the longest run of his life.

Already, he was calling for J.D. to send a medical team to the east entrance. He could hear too much shouting and air traffic in his earpiece and he ripped it out of his ear about the time he reached Olivia. Yanking the body on top of her off and casting it aside, he knelt over the weeping young girl.

"Olivia," he breathed, trying to see where she was wounded. There was blood everywhere. "Where are you hurt, honey?"

Olivia abruptly sat up and nearly smacked him in the head. She grabbed at her lower right leg. "My... my leg," she gasped. "Something hit me."

Ethan's hands were shaking as he ran his fingers over her head, neck and arms, just to make sure there wasn't something else going on. His focus quickly moved to her leg and he could see the puckered, bleeding wound. Swiftly, he examined the leg and found the exit wound on the other side of her calf. A bullet had hit her but it had passed through. He cupped her face with his big hands, forcing her to look at him.

"Are you hurt anywhere else?" he demanded.

Olivia was a weeping, quivering mess. She shook her head and threw her arms around Ethan's neck. He picked her up and held her, cradling her like a baby. The relief he felt at that moment was indescribable.

"Are there any more people involved in this, Olivia?" he asked, trying to determine if more gunmen were going to pop from the walls. "Are there others?"

She shook her head. "I... I don't think so," she dared to lift her head from the crook of his neck and look around at the carnage. Her gaze fell on Joseph, lying dead a few feet away, and her tears returned with a vengeance. "He was trying to get me out of here."

Ethan turned to see who she was looking at. "Who?"

"Joe," she sobbed. "He... he was going to be the next Holy Roman Emperor."

Ethan took a deep breath to steady his nerves as he gazed down at the still form on the stairs. "That's the d'Orleans heir?"

Olivia nodded, wiping at her eyes. "He didn't like what they were doing and he was trying to get me out of here. But Nat stopped him."

"Nat?"

Olivia nodded, straining to catch a glimpse of the body at the base of the stairs, riddled with bullets. The tears turned angry.

"Him," she pointed at Nat's bloodied corpse. "He was so mean and scary, Ethan. He's the really bad guy, not Joe. He's the one who kidnapped me from my house."

Ethan gazed down at the crumpled figure. "So that's the guy," he muttered. "And he was trying to stop Joe from taking you out of here?"

"Yes."

"Where was Joe taking you?"

Olivia sniffled. "Back to my mom. He said that he didn't want anything to do with the Cardinal's plans anymore and we were escaping."

Ethan sighed heavily, noticing that one of the Marines had found a roll of gauze in his field pack and began wrapping Olivia's leg with it. He watched the man put pressure on the wound to stop the bleeding before returning his focus to Olivia. At that moment, and only at that moment, did he began to feel as if they were safe. He began to hear from the other agents around him that they had Dr. Gioia in custody, but Ethan wasn't particularly interested in that. He found that nothing else, at the moment, mattered to him. He had what he came for.

With Olivia safe in his arms, he descended the stairs and exited the building into the bright Italian sunshine. J.D. was crossing the parking lot, heading towards them with medics in tow. Ethan and Olivia, with two Marines flanking them, met J.D. halfway across the lot. J.D.'s gaze was intense on Ethan.

"Someone said you'd been hit," he gasped. "What idiot told me such lies?"

Ethan smiled weakly. "It wasn't a lie," he assured him. "Thank God for Kevlar."

"You're all right, then?"

"I'm fine." Ethan looked down at Olivia, cradled in his arms with her head against his shoulder. "Olivia's going to be fine, too."

Olivia lifted her head at J.D. and smiled faintly. "Hi again."

"Hi to you, too," J.D.'s black eyes glittered at the pale young girl. "Glad to finally see you again, Miss Olivia."

"I think she's had enough for one day," Ethan sounded suspiciously like her father. "I'd like to get her leg looked at and get her back to her mother."

J.D. nodded, indicating the medics. "These people can take care of her. Let her go with them. I need to talk to you for a minute."

Ethan went to set Olivia down but she clung to him. Gently, he whispered a few words to her and she eventually loosened her grip to the point where the medics could take her back over to the ambulance. But she looked panicked that she was being separated from Ethan.

"I'll be there in a minute, I promise," he assured her.

Reluctantly, she let the man and woman take her over to the waiting rescue vehicle. Ethan watched her until they sat her down inside the vehicle before turning to J.D.

"The east stairwell has two dead bodies in it," he said. "According to Olivia, both men are her kidnappers. I didn't push her for the entire story but from what she said, one of them was trying to help her escape and the other one was trying to stop them. It's only by sheer coincidence that we entered that stairwell when we did. We walked right into it."

J.D. nodded. "Are there any more suspects we need to locate?"

"Olivia said that was it."

J.D. digested that information. "I've got a crime scene unit on its way over right now. We'll interview your team and find out how it went down," he eyed Ethan. "I need to interview Olivia. I need to do it while it's fresh in her mind."

Ethan sighed heavily. "It can wait until tomorrow," he told him. "Let her get back to her mother and get a good night's sleep before you question her."

J.D. didn't look pleased but he knew it would do no good to argue. "First thing in the morning."

"Sure."

Ethan's attention was again drawn over to the ambulance where Olivia was sitting on the gurney having her leg tended to. Christophe had joined her and Ethan smiled faintly as the man climbed into the ambulance, with all four guns, and gave Olivia a gentle hug. He sat next to her with his arm around her shoulders while the medics worked on her leg, glad to see his young friend again. J.D. followed Ethan's gaze, quite casually, before speaking.

"There's something else," he muttered, rubbing his chin. "I was informed that Cardinal Bishop Wildegrav was stabbed to death in his offices about a half hour ago."

"Really?" Ethan looked at him with mild surprise. "By whom?"

"That's what I was going to ask you."

Ethan cocked his head. "How in the hell would I know?"

J.D. scratched his chin and shifted on his big legs, looking as if he wanted to say much more of what he was apparently thinking.

"Because no one can seem to locate Coral Chastity Aames," he said flatly, watching Ethan's stone-like expression. "Ethan, earlier today you had a private conversation with that woman, the contents of which you would not disclose. She was released when you were finished because she had supplied us with everything she knew, including Olivia's location. Three hours later, the Cardinal is murdered. He was a man she insisted was, in fact, going to kill her and now no one can seem to find her. Does that sound strange to you?"

Ethan's lips twitched with a smile. "And you think I had something to do with it?"

"I didn't say you did. But I want to know what happened with that woman in the interrogation room."

Ethan crossed his powerful arms, averting his gaze as he thought of what to tell J.D. "I didn't tell her to murder the Cardinal," he said. "You've known me a long time. I would hope you would know me better than that."

J.D. nodded after a moment. "I do," he said. "But I still want to know what went on after I left."

Ethan looked at him a moment before leaning over and whispering something in his ear. J.D. closed his eyes tightly as Ethan straightened up and walked away, heading towards the ambulance where Christophe and Olivia were now laughing. J.D. opened his eyes and watched the man as he moved towards the rescue vehicle.

"Oh, Jesus," J.D. muttered. "Ethan, please tell me you didn't."

I took it all off....

TWENTY

THEIR FLIGHT out of Rome was delayed by two hours due to bad weather. Seated in the AirFrance terminal on a stormy afternoon, J.D. was already snoring in one of the seats while Christophe, Olivia and Tyler played gin rummy a few seats down from him. Christophe was betting his chocolate candies against Tyler's red hot jelly beans and Tyler seemed to be winning. Olivia was wise enough not to bet, but she wasn't beyond eating Christophe's chocolate candies when he wasn't looking.

Ethan and Cydney sat together opposite the kids and Christophe; she was reading a book, her feet draped over the arm rest and into Ethan's lap while he gently rubbed her feet. He was watching Olivia and Tyler as they stole all of Christophe's candy.

"They're going to be wired up on sugar for the flight," he commented.

Cydney looked up from her romance novel. "Huh?" she noticed where he was looking. "Oh, right. But I think Olivia might actually sleep; she hasn't slept very well the past couple of nights. I think she just needs to get out of Rome and away from everything that's happened here. Then she can relax."

He looked at her. "How does she seem to you?"

Cydney closed the book. "All right," she shrugged. "Tough, like it doesn't really matter when we all know it does. But you know what I think bothers her the most? The death of Joe. That really seems to upset her."

Ethan nodded, his gaze moving back to the young lady seated with his son. She was dressed in new clothes her mom had bought her and brand new shoes from Ethan. Her hair was in a ponytail high on top of her head and she acted and laughed just like any other normal American teenager, not like a girl who had spent the past week in fear of her life. Tyler seemed particularly attentive to her which had Cydney's motherly intuition in overdrive. Ethan convinced her that it was just natural brotherly instincts; Mr. Fun Bags had been a complete gentleman.

"From what Olivia said, Joe was more of an ally than a kidnapper," he commented. "She related to him and a bond was forged. So to her, it's like losing a friend. It's all very psychologically explainable."

"Maybe," Cydney said. Then her attention shifted to Ethan. "And you? How are you feeling about all of this?"

He looked down at her pretty feet as his hands rubbed at the flesh. "I've got a bruise the size of a softball on my gut from that hit I took to the Kevlar."

"I know; I saw it. But that's not what I meant."

"I know what you meant." He looked at her. "I feel okay, I guess. We got Olivia back and that's the main thing. But the robe is still missing and I don't think we'll ever get it back. It's weird, but I feel a strange sense of personal loss. I can't begin to describe it."

Cydney sighed faintly. "It wasn't in the Cardinal's offices

when they were searched after his murder. It's like it just vanished."

Ethan nodded with resignation. "We're going to have to go back to square one and start from scratch. We've got agents in the Vatican interviewing some people that we've been allowed access to. But, being the Vatican, we've got to go through their security for everything. I just don't know how far we're going to get. We may never find the thing."

He seemed genuinely distressed and Cydney reached out, grasping his hand. He lifted her fingers to his lips and kissed them.

"You'll figure it out," she said. "Meanwhile, we go home. I go back to work, you go back to work, and...."

"And we get married," he reminded her.

She smiled. "I hope you don't mind that I don't want anything big. I'd be happy going to the County Clerk's office. To me, it's more about who I'm marrying, not how I marry him. I don't need a big splashy wedding. I just need you."

He smiled at her and kissed her fingers again. "You've got me forever."

She returned his smile, distracted from their warm moment when Christophe figured out that the kids were cheating. He threatened Tyler, who leapt over the seat back and went to hide behind the snoring J.D., using him for cover. Olivia just sat there and laughed. Cydney grinned at the antics while Ethan just shook his head.

"I'm raising a card sharp," he said, lifting her feet off his lap and standing up. "I'll be right back."

"Where are you going?" she asked.

"Les toilettes," he told her.

She blew him a kiss and he was off, making his way out of the seating area and into the main hallway crowded with people. The restrooms were about halfway down the terminal, across from a couple of gift shops and a coffee house. Just as he was nearing them, a figure suddenly bumped into him and he turned, irritably, to find himself gazing into gaudy raccoon-made up eyes.

Shocked, Ethan realized he was looking at Coral. He instinctively reached out and grabbed her.

"What in the hell are you doing here?" He couldn't think of anything else to say.

Coral smiled at him. "I've been waiting for you."

"Waiting for...?" he shook his head, perplexed. "What are you talking about? How did you know I was here?"

Coral was dressed in a white pant suit with a bright yellow shirt. With her big white hat and bug-eyed sunglasses, she looked like another tourist just passing through. She suddenly thrust a backpack at him and Ethan scrambled to catch it.

"This is for you," she said simply.

Ethan was deeply confused. He looked at the backpack warily and tried to hand it back to her. "Coral, I can't accept...."

She was already walking away from him. "Take it," she commanded. "It's what you've been looking for. Now you have it. And I ... I am truly free."

His confusion didn't ease. "What?"

She paused and turned to him. "You did me a favor," she said. "When you rescued Olivia, you really did me a huge favor."

"I don't get it."

She lowered her glasses, peering at him from over the top of the rims. "You got rid of Nat and Joe. So I did something for you. And now you have your robe. Good day, Special Agent Serreaux."

He watched her disappear into the crowds of travelers, a slight woman in a brilliant white suit. Stunned by her abrupt appearance and disappearance, Ethan gazed down at the black backpack. After a moment, curiosity demanded he open it. Shifting his grip, he unzipped the bag.

The faded, brittle material of The Lucius Robe came into view. Shocked, Ethan zipped the bag up and stood there a moment, his heart racing. Although he'd risked his integrity to persuade her to return to Wildegrav and find the robe, he never actually believed she would do it. But here it was, something of such religious and historical significance that he could hardly believe he actually had it. But the proof was in his hands.

"Enfin, c'est arrière où il appartient," he murmured.

Odd; he didn't know why he uttered those words, only that they seemed appropriate. They were accompanied by a weird sense of déjà vu, something he had a hell of a time shaking off. But something deep inside him demanded he utter those few words. Like the closure of a book or the end of a great quest, those words signified the end of something. Like a curtain closing, he felt it. It was finally over.

Ethan's thoughts shifted from the robe and back to Coral. He thought he'd seen the last of her and, consequently, the robe. But she had done as he'd asked; she'd retrieved the robe. As Ethan had told her during his private interrogation, she was the only person in the world that could have gotten into Wildegrav's offices without suspicion. Who would have suspected the scatter-brained televangelist to be capable of such cunning and deceit? And, as he suspected, of murder.

Whatever she did to Wildegrav had been on her own. Even if she was guilty of the murder of the Cardinal, Ethan wouldn't turn her in. From what Olivia had told him about Wildegrav, the man was evil to the bone. Perhaps what Coral dispensed was justice. Perhaps she had done the world a favor. Ethan considered the score even.

Cydney nearly had a heart attack when he handed her the backpack with the robe in it. Ethan told her the truth about how he had gotten it back, although J.D. had suspicions that it wasn't the entire story. Still, he never voiced his reserve. The return of The Lucius Robe was something he would have to chalk up to one of life's great mysteries even though it was evident that Ethan knew more than he was telling. J.D. would let the man have his secrets, at least for now.

Later on as the flight from Paris to Los Angeles glided over the dark north Atlantic and everyone was fast asleep, Ethan found himself gazing out of the window and into the moonlit sky. Cydney's head was on his chest as he held her, glancing down at her every so often just to watch her sleep. She was so beautiful when she slept. Next to Cydney, Olivia lay on her mother's torso, sleeping the sleep of the dead. She was snoring louder than J.D. was in his seat. Ethan smiled, reaching out to gently touch Olivia's blond head, grateful that she was finally able to sleep. He was grateful that she finally felt safe enough to.

But it was impossible for Ethan to sleep at the moment with his thoughts in turmoil. The robe, Cydney, Olivia, Coral... all of it was swirling through his mind. He was relieved that there was closure on so many issues. But there was still one thing that bothered him, an ominous feeling that he couldn't seem to shake.

The tooth wasn't returned with the robe. It was still out there, somewhere. Either the person who had it didn't know what, exactly, they had, or there was the more chilling thought that they knew *exactly* what they had. As long as the tooth was still out there, fate unknown, there was always the possibility that someone else might try to finish what Cardinal Wildegrav started. He wondered if Coral had kept it. Perhaps they would never know.

Eventually, sleep claimed Ethan. When he dreamt, it was of beautiful museum directors and rock stars.

EPILOGUE
FIVE YEARS LATER

"MOM!" the front door flew open and a young lady with a good deal of luggage stepped through. "Mom? I'm home!"

Ethan tried to grab the door before it slammed back on its hinges again but he was only semi-successful; he, too, had his hands full of baggage. He couldn't grab the handle fast enough. Picking Olivia up from college for the summer had meant that his car was stuffed to the roof with her possessions. The six hour drive down from Northern California had been crowded. He set the gigantic laundry bags down just inside the door and scratched his head.

"I swear you didn't have this much stuff when we took you to school in the fall," he pointed out. "This stuff must be breeding."

Olivia grinned at him, calling for her mom again. "Mom!" she bellowed, then she turned to Ethan. "Is Tyler here yet?"

Ethan grunted as he set a plastic tub down against the wall. "His flight comes in at eight tonight."

From down the hall came the patter of little feet. Olivia's baby sisters, four-year-old Justine and two-year-old Ruby, came squealing down the hall. Olivia's cries had roused them from their nap. Olivia fell to her knees and embraced the babies, laughing and squealing with them.

"Oh my God," she gasped. "They've gotten so big. Ruby, you're huge!"

Little Ruby was jumping up and down happily at the sight of her big sister; a brown-haired, brown-eyed child in the image of her father, she was a gorgeous little doll. Justine, resembling her beauteous older sister and mother to a fault, put her little hands on Olivia's face so her older sister would look at her.

"She doesn't wear a diaper anymore," she informed her. "Mommy potty trained her."

As Olivia pretended to be very impressed with Ruby's accomplishment, Cydney emerged from the master bedroom, waddling down the hall. She was moving very slowly, her enormous belly evident.

"That's because I don't want two children in diapers," she said frankly. "One is enough."

Olivia stood up and embraced her mother as the woman came near. She put her hands on her mother's very pregnant stomach, bending down to kiss it.

"Hi, John David," she talked to the belly. "Hurry up and come. We can't wait to see you."

"It's not John David," Ethan said as he shoved Olivia's smaller suitcase against the wall. "One J.D. is plenty."

Olivia looked up from her mother's stomach. "J.D. was pretty adamant that you name this child after him," she looked at her mom. "So if it's not John David, what is it?"

Cydney rubbed her back, sighing heavily. "Ethan wants to name him Alec Scott," she said. "I don't want my son to have the initials A.S.S."

"I like Jackson, too. We can call him Jack."

"That's better than A.S.S."

Olivia burst out laughing as Ethan pursed his lips irritably and went back outside to the get the rest of Olivia's junk from his car. Ruby was jumping up and down at Olivia's feet until her big sister picked her up and squeezed her.

"I love you, Rubes," she kissed the little cheek. "I've missed you."

Cydney reached out and put her hand on Olivia's shoulder, steering the girl into the kitchen.

"We've missed you, too," she said softly. "I can hardly believe you just finished your junior year of college."

"Me, either," Olivia sat at the kitchen table with Ruby and Justine battling to sit on her lap. She pulled both girls up. "I just can't believe how big these monkeys are getting. It seems like Justine was just born yesterday."

Cydney put the tea kettle on; Olivia's roommate at school was from England and had gotten her hooked on tea. As Olivia played with the babies, Cydney glanced at the clock and thought she might as well start dinner. Being on maternity leave from the museum, she found herself very bored during the day even though she was running around after two toddlers. Preparing dinner made her feel useful.

Ethan came into the front door and closed it behind him, taking a load of Olivia's possessions to her bedroom. The two bedroom bungalow had seen major expansion in the past few years, especially with the births of Justine and Ruby. Now the bungalow was a craftsman-style two story with two additional bedrooms, another bathroom, and a family room built off the back of the house that nearly swallowed up the back yard. But it was a beautiful home with four kids and another one imminent. Ethan almost couldn't remember that little bungalow he had moved into after he and Cydney had married. That lonely, bitter man didn't exist any longer. Now his life was something he was totally in love with. He dropped off Olivia's stuff and emerged back into the kitchen.

"Liv," he said. "Take the rest of your stuff to your room, please. We don't need your mother tripping over your junk."

Olivia was in the process of tickling Justine but nodded. "Okay."

She set the babies down but they didn't take kindly to it. Justine began to whine and followed Olivia into the entry hall but Ethan managed to grab Ruby before she could pursue. Unhappy, she began to whimper and Ethan spent his time kissing her nose and trying to tickle her. As Ruby perked up, he glanced at Cydney as she reached into the refrigerator.

"Honey, let me make dinner," he offered. "You don't need to be up moving around."

Cydney put a head of cauliflower on the counter. "I don't want to sit," she said flatly. "I need to feed the girls and Tyler will be hungry when he comes in."

"I'll feed Tyler on the way home from the airport. Don't worry about him." He tried to steer her towards a chair. "Sit down and I'll make dinner."

She shrugged him off. "I don't want to. I've been having contractions all afternoon and it's more comfortable to move around."

Ethan's expression grew concerned. He went to stand next to her as Ruby put her arms around his neck and squeezed him enthusiastically.

"Why didn't you call me?" he demanded softly.

She turned to look at him. "Because you were driving Olivia home from college," she insisted. "You had a six hour drive and I wasn't going to call you and freak you out so you would speed home. I didn't need you getting a speeding ticket or worse."

He exhaled sharply, not agreeing with her but understanding her reasons. Ruby squirmed and he set her town, putting an arm around his wife's shoulders and a hand on her rock-hard belly. He laid his forehead against her blond head.

"How far apart are the contractions?" he asked gently, kissing her temple.

She paused in dinner preparation, allowing herself the comfort of her husband's big arms. Even though this was her fourth child, she was feeling some apprehension and his strength eased her mind considerably. Ethan's lips drifted over her temple again and across her forehead. Cydney sank against him, giving into his power and comfort.

"They're irregular," she replied. "Anywhere between seven and twelve minutes apart."

"Have they been getting stronger?"

She grunted softly as a contraction hit. Ethan had his hand on her stomach, feeling it tighten. He counted the contraction out softly and she let her breath out heavily when it was over. He'd been through this drill three times before and was becoming quite an expert as a childbirth coach. But it never got any easier; every time scared him to death.

"That one was pretty strong," she admitted. "It was only five minutes after the last one."

"Then maybe we better call the doctor."

"I already did. He said to get over to the hospital when they're less than ten minutes apart."

Ethan looked stricken. "Then we'd better get our asses over to the hospital," he said. "Olivia can watch the girls."

She lifted an eyebrow at him. "Why do you think I waited until you got back?" she said. "I couldn't just leave Justine and Ruby alone."

"Did you call your mom and dad?" he persisted.

She nodded, waddling to the hallway. "They should be here any minute. They wanted to see Olivia and Tyler when they got home, anyway."

"They're going to have to go get Tyler from the airport."

"My brother will get him. He lives closer to the airport."

"Fine, fine," Ethan said quickly; he didn't want to waste any more time and directed her towards the bedroom. "Get your shoes on and let's go."

They passed by Olivia's room as they headed to the master bedroom, noticing that all three girls were on the floor of the bedroom playing with something. Ethan stuck his head into the purple-painted room as Cydney continued into their bedroom.

"I'm taking your mom to the hospital," he told Olivia. "Your grandparents are on the way. Can you please watch the girls until they get here?"

Olivia's eyes widened. "Mom's going to have the baby?"

Ethan nodded, eyeing Justine and Ruby, who were now gazing up at him. He smiled at the younger girls.

"Mommy's okay," he assured them. "She's going to go to the hospital so they can take the baby out of her tummy."

Justine jumped up, followed by Ruby. They raced past Ethan, almost tripping him, and into the bedroom where Cydney was struggling to put her shoes on. Ethan came into the bedroom after the little girls and took pity on his wife, pulling her flats on. Justine climbed onto the bed and tried to sit in Cydney's non-existent lap.

"Mommy?" She was a very verbal, very bright child. She put her hand on Cydney's hard belly. "Can we come with you?"

Cydney smiled. "No, baby," she said. "Daddy and I are going by ourselves so the doctor can take the baby out."

Justine produced the pouty lip. "I want to go."

Cydney shook her head. "You and Ruby need to stay with Olivia so she won't be all alone. She'll make cookies for you and pretty soon, Daddy and I will be back with Baby Brother."

Because Justine was starting to cry, Ruby was starting, too. Ethan picked up Justine, calling softly for Olivia who came into collect Ruby. Cydney struggled to stand up from the bed, softly reassuring her younger daughters that she wouldn't be away too long. She kissed pouty little faces and wiped wet noses. Olivia was very good with the girls and did a good job of distracting them as Ethan and Cydney finally slipped out. It was an exciting time for all of them, far away from the horror that had originally brought them all together. Finally, life had come full circle for them all and the latest addition to their family only deepened the bonds. There was no greater love than the love of family and the love that Ethan and Cydney felt for one another.

Cydney's parents arrived shortly after Ethan and Cydney left for the hospital. Kyle picked up Tyler from the airport and the two of them rushed to the hospital just in time for the main event. Exactly four hours after leaving for the hospital, Lily Victoria Serreaux was brought into the world weighing nine pounds eight ounces, twenty inches long, and had a full crown of luscious auburn hair. Ethan cut the cord, took her from the doctor, and wouldn't let her go.

But he eventually relinquished the child so she could be bathed and fed, and then held her long into the night, just as he had with Justine and Ruby when they had been born. He told her the story of how her parents met. Although Cydney was supposed to be asleep, she heard every word. When Ethan finally looked up from his new daughter, he caught his wife watching him in the darkness. He smiled at her, a gesture of joy and adoration.

I love you, he mouthed.

Cydney smiled wearily and closed her eyes. Although she didn't know it at the time, they would repeat this process again two years later when twins Connor and Cole Serreaux, weighing a solid seven pounds each, came into the world. Each time, it just got sweeter.

Life was good. From the ashes of despair, a resurrection of

sorts had taken place for both Ethan and Cydney. No more bitterness, no more loneliness. Both of them had been reborn, more alive and joyful than they could have ever dreamed.

Cydney fell asleep to her husband's gentle declaration burrowing deep into her heart.

THE END

ABOUT THE AUTHOR

ABOUT KAT LE VEQUE

KATHRYN LE VEQUE is a critically acclaimed, USA TODAY Bestselling author (having hit the list over 30 times), an Indie Reader bestseller, a charter Amazon All-Star author, and a #1 bestselling, award-winning, multi-published author in Medieval Historical Romance with over 150 published novels. Kathryn also writes Romantic Suspense as Kat Le Veque.

Kathryn has received praise for her writing and has won several awards for her work, including two nominations for the Holt Medallion. Her books have topped bestseller lists, and she has gained a loyal fan base that eagerly anticipates each new release.

Kathryn is a talented author who has made a significant impact on the world of historical romance fiction. Through her captivating storytelling and meticulous research, she has enchanted readers with her tales of love, adventure, and the enduring power of the human spirit.

Kathryn loves to hear from her readers. Please find Kathryn on Facebook at Kathryn Le Veque, Author, or join her on Twitter @kathrynleveque, and don't forget to visit her website at www.kathrynleveque.com.

ALSO BY KAT LE VEQUE

The Unholy Angels

Hour of Surrender

Trent Chronicles

Valley of Shadow

The Eden Factor

Canyon of the Sphinx

The Eagle Brotherhood

The Sunset Hour

The Killing Hour

The Secret Hour

The Unholy Hour

The Burning Hour

The Ancient Hour

The Devils Hour